Midnight in
Manhattan

Midnight in Manhattan

Francesca Delbanco

ORION

She thought she need not worry about her youth; it wasted itself spontaneously, like sunshine elsewhere or firelight in an empty room.

—Elizabeth Bowen, *The Last September*

Midnight in Manhattan

Prologue

In my job as the relationship advice columnist for *GirlTalk* magazine, I receive thirty letters a day. Teenage girls, as many keen academics and social scientists have observed, have a lot of insecurities: how to kiss, when to kiss, whom to kiss, how to flirt, how to steal your best friend's boyfriend, how to admit you're not a virgin when you've pretended to be one. Because I'm twenty-six years old, I'm not so far away from any of these crises to have trouble sympathizing with them, yet I'm also supposedly old enough to have accrued the wisdom and experience readers are looking for when they send their most pressing questions to "Annie Answers." Sometimes I worry about these kids, actually. What does it say about our culture that ten thousand teenagers a year solicit counsel on the most intimate matters of their personal lives from a total stranger without a graduate degree? Possible research topic for the above-mentioned keen academics and social scientists.

To backtrack: my name isn't Annie. Anne Chang-Hirosaki, my predecessor in this job, quit magazines for business school, and has now launched a line of press-on tattoos sold in the makeup sections of high-end department stores. People can make lives out of ventures like that. Anyway, when Anne quit, I happened to be answering phones for the editor-in-chief of *GirlTalk*—temping, really, and adjusting to the daily humiliations of post-college life in Manhattan. My boss liked me, or at least liked the way I collated and stapled large copy jobs, and before she hired a replacement for Annie Answers, I asked for a shot at the column. For some reason (probably the prospect of saving $40,000 a year in staff salary) she gave it to me. The column's name stayed the same, which is fine with me. First of all, who needs a fifteen-year-old stalker who's pissed that her boyfriend dumped her after you told her to admit that she'd cheated on him? Second of all, my name is Rosalie Preston, which, at least when paired with *Answers,* lacks something in alliterative pizzazz.

The twist here, or the "hook," as the pack of *GirlTalk* editors who wish they worked for real news magazines are fond of saying, is that I don't want to be an advice columnist. It's a perfectly good day job, and it makes for easy dinner-party conversation with strangers ("Yes it's true, the letters *are* real!"), and it calms my art-phobic parents to think that I have a real, life-sustaining spot on a corporate payroll. But what I really want to be is an actress. That's why I moved to New York in the first place. That and the fact that when you graduate from an Ivy League college and your chances of a career in politics have already been dashed by drug experimentation and unpaid parking tickets, New York is the only place people really move to. Except for the vegetarians, who go to San Francisco.

So I arrived here four years ago, after a miserably lonely post-college year abroad in Ireland, and joined up with my five closest friends. Together we set out to start our own acting company. Turns out a lot of young people have that idea, but we had a few advantages in our corner: we're not as experimental as most—no staged pubic-hair shaving, no animal puppets, nothing designed explicitly to alienate the few paying audience members we're lucky enough to attract. (Here my pride compels me to add that while I'm an aspiring actor, you might not know it at first glance: I don't sing loudly in elevators, I speak with the standard slurred intonation of my generation, rather than the painfully enunciated English promoted by voice coaches, and I've never had any part of my body surgically altered for a film role.) Back to the group: we also make a good ensemble. I get the feeling that in most fledgling acting troupes, 98% of the members secretly think they're the stars. We're decent sports about rotating out of the limelight—I've played Grocery Checkout Clerk #2 for every time I've played Ophelia, and never held a grudge.

Finally, and I'd be lying if I didn't admit this was our most important asset, our producer is rich. Staggeringly rich, New York rich, as in her dad's name is carved on the marble donor columns of museums and libraries and hospitals all over the city. And since Bella herself—that's my friend the producer—doesn't have a day job, she can spend all of her non-spa time hustling donations out of her parents' friends, most of whom love to think of themselves as patrons of the downtown art scene.

A word about money, which I now know is the prerequisite to understanding any New York story: most of my friends have a lot of it. I don't know how that happened, exactly, except that I went to Harvard, where the admissions officers were clearly lying about 78% of students being on financial aid. I myself am the only child of a dentist and a piano teacher, Tom and Joan Preston, of Hanson, Massachusetts, a workaday town on the South Shore.

While I grew up wanting little, mine was a one-house, two-car family operation, where I did chores for my allowance and took one vacation a year, usually to visit my grandparents in their *Golden Girls*-esque Sarasota retirement community. I'm not a have-not, by any stretch of the imagination, and wouldn't claim to be one. But I somehow fell in with a crowd that was more upper than middle in the broad belt of the upper middle class, and these distinctions have daily manifestations in New York life. It's easy to tell how much money a girl in this city has, even though we all wear black and carry small purses crammed with portable electronic devices. I rely solely on the subway, for example; my friend Bella takes cabs.

Since I'm a theater person, it seems fitting to close out these program notes with a brief dramatis personae for the events you're about to see, events which began just about a year ago. The members of the First Born Company, which is the name of our troupe, are Grace Lerner, Jacob Braverman, Camden Post, Bella Starker, Evan Weiner, and Rosalie Preston: me. Grace, Jake, Cam, and I are the actors; Bella's the producer; and Evan is our exacting director. I could say, and will say, a great deal more about each of them, but to start with what you need to know is this: we were friends in college, are surprisingly optimistic for non-union actors heading into year five of total professional anonymity, and are all convinced that we will succeed and flourish in the little pack we've always been. It goes without saying that stories like this one end in a different place than they begin, and since I earn my keep as an advice columnist, I have, at least, to play at being sage and jaded in the ways of the world. But I'll tell you the truth, which is a new habit I'm trying to get into: last summer, I felt confident that I understood some of the intricacies of ambition, talent, money, sex, and friendship that characterize adult life in this frenetic city. If I'd only paid more attention to that horrid *Education of Henry Adams* book I was forced to read twice in college, I would have known that mine was the self-assurance of someone whose education had yet to begin.

Dear Annie,

I'm thirteen, but I have the hormones of a fifteen-year-old. My problem is that my mom thinks I am too young to date, which is a joke since I am taller than she is and way more mature than my older sister, who has had the same stink-punk boyfriend for the past three years. How can I convince my mom to let me go out with guys? All of my friends are allowed to, and I'm really losing good chances right and left.

—Locked Up in Maryland

Dear Locked Up,

If only you could take a skin patch test, or pass a multiple choice exam, to prove to your mom that you've got the common sense to earn your dating license. But until Congress passes a federal Romance Law with a minimum age requirement, you're pretty much stuck following your parent's rules, whether or not you like them or think they're fair.

I say your best bet for a more boy-friendly arrangement is to talk to your mom, using your calmest, most grown-up conversational skills (i.e., no cracks about her height). Ask her for some clear, specific instructions about how you can *earn her trust* (moms love that one) and prove to her that you are, in fact, mature enough to hang out in public non-school locations with members of the opposite sex. Would going out in a group reassure her? Would it help if you promised to get grown-up rides to and from the movies, say, or the mall? Would meeting the boy-predator in question beforehand put her heart at ease? Would she like to consult with any of your friends' moms about how they reached their decisions?

Hopefully, once your mom understands your willingness to compromise and meet her halfway, you'll be on the path to a more satisfying social life. Because here's the thing: maturity and savvy don't really get measured in *years*. If they did, none of the boys in your class would still be into action figures. No, behavior and experience are far more accurate ways to judge maturity. And those, fortunately, are under your control.

Trust me. I've lived through it.

Annie

Chapter One

In the northeastern reaches of the Adirondacks, halfway between Tupper Lake and Saranac, lies a large private property called the Fort Sassquam Association. Several stuffed black bears frozen in menacing poses flank a "No Public Admittance" sign just outside its iron gates. On either side of the road, which remains rough enough to justify the use of sport utility vehicles for those who travel it regularly, stand two wooden posts bearing the names of Fort Sassquam's members. The posts are old; the names are older. Bella Starker's family has owned property on Fort Sassquam Lake since the nineteenth century, when the Adirondacks became the country's hotspot for tuberculosis rest cures. New York Society has always clung together, in sickness and in health.

The camps themselves (that's what the residents call them, in the spirit that might prompt Queen Elizabeth to call Buckingham Palace a studio) form a loose ring around the large mountain lake. They are grand homes, built in the time of Teddy Roosevelt and with his spirit of aristocratic ruggedness. Modern renovations have tried to preserve this aesthetic, resulting in such rustic touches as exposed-log saunas and antler-shaded light fixtures. On the Starker property the eco-landscapers allow no non-native flora, which accounts for the woodsy, flowerless look of the place, a haven for mosquitoes, ticks, blackflies, and all manner of biting thing. Indoors, the mounted animal carcasses are trophies from the surrounding Adirondack National Forest. When I first saw the gallery of stuffed deer heads lining the dining room walls, I remarked that hunting is the pastime of the very rich and the very poor. My friend Camden, who grew up in the gun-happy state of South Carolina, took offense, so I have amended my observation to include the very rich, the very poor, and Southerners.

Since becoming friends with Bella, I've been an occasional guest at Starker estates throughout the continental U.S., mooching wine from her dad's cellars, learning how to ski downhill and sail boats without motors, generally playing the supporting role of Unathletic Friend With Rough Edges. I may as well come right out and admit that Bella's family fascinates me, with its many branches and demesnes and soap opera divorces that inevitably make the gossip columns in and around New York City. The Starkers are what my own parents persist in calling "high society" people, though I have tried to talk my parents out of such (antiquated) one-dimensional categorizations. In any case, last summer's weekend itinerary was no different from any other. So it was that I found myself stretched out on Bella's dock on the breezy Saturday morning of the Fourth of July, staring at the glittering surface of Fort Sassquam Lake, and scribbling down possible leads for this month's Annie question, which was due almost immediately upon my return to work: *"I've been going out with my boyfriend for two and a half months, and he still won't tell me he loves me. How long do you think I should I put up with this crap?"* People my age like to snicker at the questions I'm paid to answer; it makes them feel mature and adult to pooh-pooh the dramas that kept them up tossing and turning a few years back. But Sick of It in Wisconsin, though she's on a problematically accelerated schedule, is trying in her own teenage way to navigate some of the deeper waters of relationships: commitment, trust, balance, patience. Who among us can pretend to have solved all that?

I was halfway through a vamp on letting romance evolve at its own pace when footsteps rocked the dock where I lay. I sat up and turned around, surprised, since I'm usually the first member of my vacation cohort awake by hours. It was Camden, wearing boxer shorts and a faded T-shirt, carrying a Frisbee with several strips of bacon on it.

"Did you cook that?" I asked, impressed by this step up in his culinary repertoire. I had to shield my eyes from the sun, which was rising directly behind him.

He nodded, and handed me a piece. Cam has a remarkably blithe, handsome face, so that on the rare occasions when he looks downcast, as he did that morning, you suspect the world may be minutes away from nuclear devastation. "Something wrong?" The bacon was overcooked, halfway to pork jerky.

"Evan. I called 'line' so many times yesterday he almost asked Vicki to play my part."

Evan, as I mentioned, is our director, and Vicki is the Starkers' local housekeeper, and calling "line" means you don't have your role memorized well enough to rehearse it. Which was what we'd come up to Fort Sassquam that weekend to do—rehearse our entry in the Footlights Festival, a week-long showcase of young acting companies, all performing material on a single pre-determined theme. This year's theme was Disease, a challenge for a troupe as consummately healthy as ours, and also a summer-long buzz kill, since it meant spending night after night in grungy practice halls, trolling the imaginative depths of wheelchairs and iron lungs. We'd settled on performing a series of scenes and sketches rather than a single piece; I was doing a Mary Tyrone monologue from *Long Day's Journey into Night*, for which I was about thirty years too young and way, way too sober. Evan had us on a tight rotation up at the Fort, and since Bella's father and his fourth (third? fifth?) wife were off trout fishing in Montana, we had the place to ourselves and nothing to do but rehearse in it. I'd watched a bit of Cam and Jake's run-through yesterday—they were doing Genet, from *The Balcony*, and it was true: Cam knew his lines about as well as I know the Lord's Prayer, which is to say he could have mumbled them convincingly if there'd been a large crowd around to blend into.

"Do you want to do me a huge favor and run my scene with me?" Cam asked, holding his script in my direction.

"I can't. I have to work on my column." Juggling my full-time magazine job with my acting career has turned me into an efficient time manager, and I have the unattractive habit of lording that skill over other, less organized people. Cam has a freelance job doing something computer-related for a medical advertising firm, which allows him to work from home and at odd hours of the night, whenever *SportsCenter* isn't on. Time management isn't his forte.

He stretched and scratched the back of his head, shaking off sleep. "How about I write your column for you and you memorize my lines for me?"

I shook my head and turned back to my notebook. "It's illegal for minors to sell nude pictures of themselves to *Penthouse*. Beyond that, I can't think of what you'd advise."

He smacked my shoulder with his script and sat down. The dock dipped an inch in his direction; I grabbed my pen before it rolled.

"I thought of getting Jake up to run lines," Cam said, looking out at the water. "He could use the practice, too, you know."

"And?"

"His room was empty. He must be with Grace."

The summer's headline social development was a new inbred romance, one of the only unexploited mathematical possibilities left to us: Jake, Cam's roommate and scene partner, and Grace, my closest friend. While I love them both, I must say they made a frighteningly unlikely couple—not the way sitcom odd couples do, not like perfectly calibrated opposites whose strengths and weaknesses balance out to the letter. No, they were more on the order of Genghis Khan and Heidi, characters from such opposing genres they could only share the stage for something like Ice Capades. Jake comes from Berkeley; he talks very quickly and mostly about himself, and has more notches on his proverbial bedpost than I'd care to count. Grace grew up in Providence, on one of those beautiful old streets called Hope or Faith or Charity, and she's never quite sloughed off the Emily Dickinson complex that comes from having attended an all-girls school. Even their looks are ill matched: Jake is thin and dark, always one too many days from his last shave and slightly greasy, as if he just emerged from a bed whose sheets need to be changed. Grace has the fair-haired, doe-eyed thing down so well she actually gets carded in New York bars. I knew they'd come to terms with their incompatibility on their own soon enough, so I was biding my time, curbing my natural instinct to contribute my opinion, smiling patiently whenever the mood struck Grace to share some new absurd detail from the annals of their courtship. And I was not taking gossip bait from Cam, or anybody else who strung it up.

"You know how to learn lines on your own. Work for a while and then I'll test you."

That quieted Cam down, and I went back to thinking about the impatient Wisconsin kid, though I wasn't as focused as I had been because of Cam's habit of moving his lips while he silently recited his part. He has a lot of tics like that, that could be indicative of either a chronic need for attention or a slight intellectual deficit; I go back and forth on assigning cause. Anyway we were quiet, and the fish occasionally jumped and the breeze occasionally ruffled the pages of my steno pad, and I felt peaceful and nature-y, which I wouldn't describe as characteristic. After some length of time I had another piece of bacon, and the sun felt hot enough to signal noon, which was when rehearsal was scheduled to start. Cam hoisted me up by the elbows, with an obnoxious little grunt that made me feel self-conscious about my weight (which is totally average, by normal human standards, and irritatingly above average, by emaciated actor standards). And off we went, up the flagstone path to the Big House, to see who else was awake.

. . .

Rehearsals, for the First Born Company, are a finely tuned blend of casualness and formality. We're welcome to show up in pajamas, unshowered and wolfing down bagels, but if we arrive more than two minutes late, or without the necessary prop/CD/bit of memorized text, the whole day could be shot. Evan sets these rules in his unspoken authoritative way, and the rest of us obey in subservient, lemming-like fashion that sometimes makes me question the staunchness of my political convictions (at what point would I refuse to follow orders?). By and large, I believe groups need captains. The whole commune thing you hear Gary Sinise talk about when he's raising money for Steppenwolf just seems so implausible. Evan determines our agenda, our work style, our unwritten company policies. The rest of us follow his lead.

Two complexities of the group dynamic: Bella's dad, Berglan Starker, pretty much cuts all the checks for our studio rentals, performance halls, etc. This is why you rarely see Evan giving Bella attitude when *she* strolls into rehearsal half an hour late talking on her cell phone, an offense that would consign any of the rest of us to auditioning for dinner theater on the Jersey Shore. Also important, Evan earns his salary working as the assistant to Manny Flax, a Broadway director whose credits include dozens of multimillion-dollar musicals that cater to tourists and elementary-schoolers. This gives Evan a kind of quasi-professional status that he wields like an axe. Personally speaking, I'd rather plunge headlong into the void of teenage magazines than take a role in *Tap Attack* (Manny's most recent blockbuster), but the allure of Broadway, and the power granted Evan by his proximity to it, is undeniable.

Out of town, rehearsals can get weird and unpredictable. Groups, in addition to needing captains, thrive on routine. So when Evan called us to order at 12:01, in the middle of the three-story Starker living room, I knew it would be a challenge to get into character. I hadn't yet done much work filling out the background of my Mary Tyrone, but I was already certain she had no business with overstuffed leather armchairs, interior rope swings, or carved birchwood family crests. I volunteered to do my monologue last.

After a cursory warm-up (voice, body, face), Grace and I sat down next to each other on the straight-backed couch facing the woodstove, and Cam and Jake started their scene. Though I'd just refused to help Cam with his lines (Cam gets a lot of *help*, in general, one of the perks of his being a *nice guy*), I was pulling for him now. I was also trying to block out Grace's monomaniacal concentration on Jake, who, up until three months ago, had been only one of her friends, and who had belonged equally to all of us. But their scene was going to be good, I could tell already, and the guys were getting through it off book, and the vibe in the room was happy and productive, which is us at our best. Then a door slammed on the second floor, which is us at our best plus Bella, and a stream of curses followed. Evan made a silent Time-Out with his hands and down she came, enveloped in a white terrycloth bathrobe that made her look like a guest at the Ritz, carrying a Dustbuster in one hand and something small and angular concealed in the other.

"This," she said, maintaining the dramatic pitch of the scene she'd just interrupted, "is an insult to me." She held up a miniature porcelain figurine of Abraham Lincoln, and pointed it at each corner of the room, presumably so we could all get a good look. "It is an insult to my mother. It is an insult to my brother. It is an insult to Stiles and Mugsy, who have behaved like perfect feline angels all weekend but who I am now going to set loose to pee all over this horrible fucking Camp David furniture."

Bella often takes inflammatory political stances, but objecting to the Thirteenth Amendment was too perverse even for her. I assumed her outrage was based on aesthetic/symbolic grounds: her new stepmother was a big-time Washington lobbyist and the daughter of a former Vice President, and since the wedding last summer, the entire house had been subject to a spasm of patriotic interior design. Bella laid the Lilliputian savior of our Union on the floor and paused, then smashed him into clean pieces with the butt of the Dustbuster. A shard of stovepipe hat rolled across the floor towards my foot. Nobody moved. The best way to handle Bella's temper is to ride it out; after a few minutes she always wants a cigarette, and then things settle down to normal again.

"It's like living on Air Force fucking One. I can't even find my hiking boots," she said, vacuuming up the mess with the appliance that had made it. "My *hiking boots*! What kind of woman would clean out somebody else's closet?"

It seemed a rhetorical question. She sat down on an ottoman and dropped her forehead into her hand. Bella has an angular, almost asymmetrical face. With her mane of curly black hair she looks like a Picasso model, or an Almodóvar leading lady. New

Yorkers find her challengingly beautiful; people from my home-town would probably find her weird-looking, even scary. That's actually one of the ways I've learned to distinguish transplanted men from city natives: the natives hit on Bella; the transplants go for me and Grace. Edginess is a pheromone; it has physical manifestations.

Comforting Bella was a thorny proposition, since none of the rest of our statistically aberrant group has divorced parents, and she mistrusts any kind of empathy not based on shared experi-ence. People take marginalization wherever they can find it, I guess. Sometimes, when I read the Annie letters from fourteen-year-olds coping better with divorce than Bella does, I think she should get over it and move on with her life. She has pots of money, a good education, parents who are estranged from each other but who love and support her. Enough bitterness is enough. But then again, I can't say I'd enjoy having a new mom on a semiannual basis, or an unrecognizable cast of steprelations around the Thanksgiving table. That's the dilemma of being twenty-six, or at least one of them: you're old enough to know your parents aren't the perfect role models for adult life, but young enough to still be pissed at them about it.

After a bit more pouting and vacuuming, Bella consented to settle into an armchair and watch Cam and Jake finish their scene. Poor Cam, who is so unused to conflict as to be quite unhinged by it, was addled out of remembering his lines, so Evan decided we might as well break for lunch. That's not the sort of thing he would ever do in New York, but we were on vacation, and even our tireless director is susceptible to the relaxing properties of the Great Outdoors. I wasn't particularly hungry, but I was in the mood to get back outside, so I synchronized my watch with Evan's, sprayed a toxic layer of insect repellent on my arms, and left for a walk.

The shady depths of the Adirondack woods have a hint of the supernatural about them, as if you might bump into a bridge-keeping troll or centaur somewhere along your pine-needled route. As a child of the South Shore, I'm more at ease with the wilderness in its sandy, expansive incarnation, so I always stick close to the hiking trails right around Bella's house, rather than bushwhacking off on my own. Often I listen to my Discman, too, which may seem antithetical to the gestalt of the forest, but it prevents me from getting paranoid that every snapping twig or blowing leaf is a rabid bear on the hunt for girl meat.

My mind, as I set out from the house, flipped through its usual Rolodex of topics, beginning with my lines, and the fact that I ought to run them, then moving almost immediately to the daunting list of other things I ought to do (finish my column, start going to the gym again, find an affordable voice teacher, cook at home more and eat out less). I can work myself into a state of stress remarkably easily, even alone on a mossy path in the remote countryside, with sun dappling the ground and birds chirping overhead and a warm breeze keeping the temperature perfect. I know this to be a sign of some essential discomfort, a nagging suspicion that I don't belong on private country paths with the perfect sun, birds, breeze, etc., that I might not be frolicking in such idyllic paradises for long if I don't accomplish all the tasks on the above list. Over the years

I've developed a special skill for dealing with these episodes of doubt and anxiety. I call it Mind Control. What it is is a method of willing your concentration elsewhere, skipping over the stress-inducing topics like so many slippery stones until you land, for good, on a manageable one. An example: an audition goes poorly and I don't get called back. This leads me to question my talent as an actor, which leads me in turn to wonder how I will ever support myself financially, which leads me to feel guilty about my parents and all the sacrifices they've made on my account, which leads of course to my Dad's angina, and the diminishing intervals of time between his attacks, and suddenly I realize that my heart is pounding at marathon speed, so I invoke Mind Control, and instantly I'm thinking about Grace's birthday, and whether I should get her a Patsy Cline CD or a Kiehl's Rare Earth facial masque. Presto. Simple as that. After years of practice I'm good at it, and if this seems questionable on psychological grounds, like the mental equivalent of the buy now, pay later plan, so be it. Economic debt is different than emotional debt, anyway. You can set your own interest rates on the latter.

After twenty minutes I slowed down, heeding the damp tingle on my arms and legs that's a precursor to sweat. My body has recently started to interpret brisk walking as exercise, as inevitable a sign of aging as sagging breasts and cellulite. I'm not exactly vain about these changes, just surprised by how early they set in, and a little annoyed that no one (i.e. my mother) warned me. Even three years ago I could eat and drink with an abandon that would leave me hospitalized now. This may have something to do with why people used to get married so much younger: in purely physical terms, we're not built for going club-bing or wearing bikinis much past twenty-one. Our bodies and our culture haven't kept good pace with each other, evolutionar-ily speaking.

I realize now that I've dropped enough references to weight and appearance to indict myself either as an anorexic or a 400-pound eating machine. I am neither, but the combination of working at a magazine and as an actress leads me to think about these topics more than I otherwise might. What I am is average in height (5'5"), average in weight (size eight), average in hair color (brown), eye color (brown), and skin color (fair but not albino). My non-average marks of distinction include a small chicken pox scar on the bridge of my nose, the slightest gap between my two front teeth, a good set of dimples, a better set of breasts, a broad smile, and an unusually loud and spirited laugh (which I know isn't a physical trait, strictly speaking, but it's part of the general effect). I don't audition for roles described in *Back-stage* as classic, elegant, beautiful, graceful, or refined. Instead I trot out the headshots for charming, sexy, winsome, gamine, or minxy. Not that anyone in *Backstage* ever uses that last adjective, which doesn't actually exist in the dictionary, but it's still a favorite of mine. Rosalie, you little minx!

By the time I headed back for the house, an Orion's Belt of mosquito bites trailed up my right thigh, their pinkness camou-flaged against my sunburned skin. Towards the bottom of the path a group of benches signify the beginning of the Starker property line; I thought of pausing once I reached them to apply some anti-itch medicine and cool down. When I turned the cor-ner into the clearing, I saw Evan's red hair through the slatted back of an Adirondack chair. He was sleeping or reading, I couldn't tell which.

"Hey," I called. "What's doing?"

He craned his neck around and squinted at me. "My, my, don't we look rugged."

"What are you reading?" I sat down next to him and examined the bound xerox in his lap. *This Carnival Life*, it was called.

"Scripts. For Manny." Part of Evan's job was evaluating the new musicals sent to the Flax office in Times Square. Dozens of them arrived each day, with hopeful cover letters and amateur soundtrack recordings, sometimes even gift baskets. Writing musicals is as grim a business as trying to get cast in them, apparently.

"Does a carny sing the torch song?"

"This isn't a musical. It's a play."

"A play? What does Manny want with a straight play?" As far as I could remember, Manny Flax had never directed anything with less than a hundred-person chorus and a half hour of special effects set to synthesizer music.

"He's getting old, starting to think about his legacy. I think he's beginning to grasp how phenomenally trivial it is. He wants to do a serious production."

"So what's wrong with a serious musical? Maybe something about hate crimes or the Middle East peace process?"

"He wants to do a play." Evan shrugged. "I'm not complaining."

"Which one?"

"He doesn't know. That's why I'm reading scripts."

I looked back down at the plastic-laminated cover of *This Car-*

nival Life, written by one J. C. Bryce Penderhoffer. "A contemporary play, then?"

He nodded. "I'm supposed to discover a new talent." Evan's voice gets flatter and flatter, the more serious his subject. Just then he was speaking like a computer. "I haven't told everybody about this yet, because it's not official until Manny picks his show. Don't say anything, okay?"

I raised my eyebrows.

"Just for a little while."

I'd only ever met Manny Flax once, after a First Born showcase on the Lower East Side. I'd been standing outside the theater wearing a negligee covered in fake blood from a suicide scene, sharing a cigarette with Jake. Suddenly an old man in a bespoke suit had emerged from the stage door with the furtive look of someone used to fleeing the paparazzi. "You kids were fantastic tonight," he'd said, squeezing my bare arm. "Fantastic! Next time, how about a happier ending!" Then he'd handed each of us a throat lozenge and darted into the back of a Lincoln Town Car idling across the street.

"Do you think Manny will have any idea what to do with a serious play?"

"We'll see," he said. "I hope not."

I looked at Evan. The gist of his news was that Manny would soon be putting his considerable clout and even more considerable resources behind a production he couldn't possibly direct. Musicals and plays require a different set of abilities; it's the same principle that keeps action-movie directors from attempting nineteenth-century novel adaptations. Enter Evan, young, brilliant, ambitious Evan, to save the show and make a name for himself. Exit Evan, frustrated, bored, ambitious Evan, from the dim, depressing rehearsal rooms of an unknown acting company with no immediate prospects and no promising leads. Evan's professional success had always been a foregone conclusion in my mind; the only mystery had ever been how his big break would come about. And now here it was, in the form of Manny Flax's septuagenarian reincarnation as a serious artist. It only required a few filled-in blanks before Evan would be standing in front of a real rehearsal hall, directing real actors, staking his claim on a real career. And where did that leave the rest of us? First Born was a fragile pyramid, and Evan was our entire bottom row. Without him, who knew what we were capable of? I was getting ahead of myself and I knew it, but as I said, that's my weakness. Or one of them.

"What's the timetable?" I asked, wondering how fresh a plan this was.

"We need a play in a hurry. We're looking at spaces for next spring."

So he had known about this project for months at least. I looked towards the house. Suddenly I wanted water and a jug of painkillers; I was itchy with heat. "You're really not telling anyone yet?"

He shook his head. "It's still a long way off."

Next spring didn't sound that long off to me, especially since Evan would have to start casting almost immediately. But I didn't argue. Evan has a particular way of withholding information, a way that makes other people look foolish and out of the loop. He himself has often felt out of the loop in a social sense, since he's gay and therefore aloof from all of the puerile romantic dabbling the rest of us did with each other during college. Not that Evan would ever admit to such whiny motivations, but I do think the lingering sting of sexual isolation is somewhere behind his incredible drive to prove himself, the nerd in the basement with his chemistry set, etc. Anyway I was freaked out, and must have looked it.

"It's not that big a deal, Rosalie," he said, which of course meant the exact opposite. "I'm just assisting him, like usual."

"Right. Take a few lunch orders, pick a new show to open on Broadway. The standard day at the office." My voice sounded peevish; I tried to cover with an unconvincing combination of laughter and awe. "Seriously, this is great news, Evan. An original play is a big deal."

"I'm just assisting," he repeated. "Now let's go inside and run your piece."

One of the chief reasons for unknown actors to form companies is the sense of comfort and security a group can provide. Often wholes are greater than the sum of their parts, witness all sixties folk bands. But ensembles are worth even more than that. I do a lot of traipsing around New York with my headshots under my arm, reciting audition monologues for heavily pierced film school types who may or may not contract my gratis services for their senior theses. On good days, I go to open calls and wait in cramped unfinished hallways with 700 other young women who look frighteningly like me, all of us just waiting for the thirty-second chance to knock the socks off Mark Brokaw's assistant's assistant. It's not a deeply fulfilling existence, and it's not for the thin-skinned. Which is why First Born is crucial to my emotional as well as my artistic well-being: I have colleagues—talented, serious colleagues—and I don't have to prove myself from scratch every time I sit down to read a scene with one of them. The privilege of regular collaboration is the occasional off day, or failed experiment, or bad artistic choice. It's the safety net that allows creativity to flourish, if you'll forgive my sounding like a drama school brochure.

That's why it was so alarming to find myself standing in front of Evan with a nervous stomach and a case of pre-performance dry mouth, while the rest of my friends sat on the couches finishing their lunchtime Fritos and Cokes. It was just Evan, I reminded myself, grouchy old Evan, who wore T-shirts from his parents' bakery in Wichita, who refused to eat spicy food in Chinese restaurants, who let his pixie boyfriend Constantine boss him around. But hard as I tried to knock him down, I couldn't stop imagining him sitting behind a casting table making notes on famous people's résumés in red ink. Power is a delicate thing always, but especially in ensembles, and I think I'm not making too much of the memory of that moment to say that I knew, right then, that something permanent and irrevocable had just shifted for all of us.

Or maybe what I'm looking for is an excuse, because my monologue went terribly. I dropped lines, I overcompensated for my nervousness by spastically throwing myself around the room, I spit so much the floor looked like it had just been mopped, and the whole performance culminated with me flailing my arms over my head and breaking a piece of crystal on the mantelpiece. For the second time that day, the sound of something delicate splitting into pieces silenced the room. Only this time the object apparently had some value, because Bella shot up from her chair and stared at me the way Abigail stares at Mary Warren in *The Crucible,* just before getting her hanged.

"That's Steuben," Bella said.

I was on my knees, picking up the jagged chunks of glass. "I know," I said, though I had no idea whether Steuben was a person, place, or thing. "I'm so sorry."

"We've had that frog since before I was born."

"I'll replace it," I said, gathering the fragments of what I could now see had once been a creature with webbed feet.

Bella paused, then shrugged with a resignation that suggested so much had already been ruined I might as well go ahead and break the Steuben, too. "There's a lot of valuable stuff around here," she said, sighing.

"I'll replace it," I mumbled again, though I feared I would never be able to; any decorative glass in her father's house would have to be either art or heirloom, and not replaceable via mail order or the Internet. In my eagerness to whisk away the evidence I cut myself on a sharp corner of bulging cheek, adding incompetence to my growing list of clownish traits, along with clumsiness and insecurity. A few drops of blood beaded on the tip of my index finger; I sucked them off and tried to be discreet.

"I'll get you a Band-Aid," Evan said.

"Don't worry about it," I called after him, but he was already on his way upstairs. And that was how I ended my first conscious attempt to impress Evan with my professionalism: on my knees, holding my sliced finger over my head to speed the clotting, while my friends scattered in every direction for ice, bandages, brooms.

I don't follow horoscopes, I've never had my palm read, I don't even bother opening fortune cookies. But there are some forms of prophecy a girl simply can't ignore.

Dear Annie,

I've been going out with my boyfriend for two and a half months, and he still won't tell me he loves me. I can tell he's really into me: I have six different CDs he's burned for me and he has pictures of me all over his locker and everything. But when I tell him I love him, he gets all squirrelly and mute and robotic. What's his problem? Is he just playing me? How long do you think I should put up with this crap?

—Sick of It in Wisconsin

Dear Sick of It,

I can see how it might be frustrating to declare your undying love and get a nice, friendly pat on the head in return. But here's my take: I think the Boy Universe divides into two categories, the talkers and the doers. The talkers take you out for one slice of pizza and call you the next day to say they've never met anyone half as beautiful, smart, talented, funny, and exciting as you are. Sounds great, at first. But can you really trust a guy who claims to be able to tell that much about you from the way you chew your food?

Then there are the doers. The doers burn CDs for you, and bother paying attention when you mention your favorite songs and bands. They post every snapshot of your gorgeous face they can get their hands on, so that all the poor suckers who walk down the hall can see how fine their girlfriend is. They remember to ask how your geometry test went at the end of the day, remember to bring your favorite candy bar to your soccer game, remember to wear the shirt you once said looked cute. And sometimes, when you ask them how they feel about you, they clam up. But that's usually because it's so, so real.

I say, be patient. It's usually a good sign when it takes a guy (or anybody, for that matter) a while to pour his heart out. As long as his actions are saying love, love, love, try to relax and let yourself enjoy them. And when you get to feeling nervous or insecure, just remember how much time and thought it takes to burn a good CD. Time and thought count for a lot, in my book. Maybe that's because they're finite and hard to come by. And if we measure love by what's hard, instead of by what's easy, you're one lucky girl.

Trust me. I've lived through it.

Annie

Chapter Two

Though I am part of a generation known for its technological wizardry, I have no gift for computers and am in fact
rather phobic about them, have seen too many futuristic movies
in which whole societies are obliterated by the impetuous click of
a mouse. Most of my peers seem to have emerged from the
womb with Internet cables for umbilical cords, but in the Massachusetts backwater where I grew up, children played with retro
toys such as blocks and coloring books, and I have never quite
caught on to the craze for the World Wide Web, which seems
mostly to be a dehumanizing way to go shopping. But every so
often even the most pigheaded Luddite must resort to these
research tools, or she must sweet-talk a friend into helping her,
and it was on the Internet that Grace located a purveyor of
Steuben on the Upper East Side.

"There's one on Fifty-sixth and Fifth, and the flagship looks
like it's on Sixty-first and Madison. But maybe you'd rather go to
a boutique that sells other brands, just in case," she said over the
phone from work on Monday morning, after our return from the
Adirondacks. "Here's one. I bet this is one of those places where
you have to ring a doorbell to get let in. It's called La Maison,

Seventy-fourth and Madison. I'm thinking the French is a bad sign."

I swiveled my office desk chair away from the hall, where a group of editorial assistants were hanging up an Ortho-Cyclen poster. "How much do you think that frog could have cost? Does it say?"

"The website doesn't have a price list. But some of these things seem to have gemstones for eyes. If the diamond barons in Sierra Leone could only see what their soldiers are dying for."

"I can just buy something cheap and say they were out of frogs, don't you think?"

"The place doesn't look very sale-rack-y, Rose. But you already know what I think—I think you should take Bella's advice and just send her dad a note and forget about buying anything. The guy's not going to notice one fewer reptile on his mantelpiece."

"Frogs are amphibians. I looked it up."

"Whatever, Bella said to send a note."

Grace had a point—Bella's proposed solution let me off the hook, in an economic sense. But on the drive home from the Adirondacks her retroactive attachment to the Steuben toad had grown exponentially, so that by the time we hit the West Side Highway her mood was so reproachful an outsider would have guessed I'd shot her brother. I didn't like the idea of something so replaceable (and, frankly, so ugly) being held over my head. Anyway my mother raised me to be a good houseguest, and though she probably never imagined I would be weekending in places where a small accident could result in thousands of dollars of credit card debt, I could not so easily undo years of her training. I took down the name and address of the shop.

"Sometimes you can try to bargain at these boutique-y places," Grace said, in the whisper she used whenever her boss was nearby. "But don't go crazy and offer them an organ or anything. Call me when you get back."

Because the idea of becoming a permanent fixture at *GirlTalk* gives me the creeps, I keep my office spare and impersonal: easy in, easy out. A company phone list, a guide to performing the Heimlich maneuver that was tacked to the bulletin board when I moved in, some generic props from the supply closet to fill up my desk drawers and convey industriousness—nothing I'd miss, if I walked out the door and never came back. I enjoy hanging out with the girls while we're all in the office ("girls" being a holdover from the *Mademoiselle* days of Mary Cantwell, connoting flair, not subjugation). But I usually skip the daily pilgrimage to the salad bar across the street, am not well enough versed in the nutritional content of roughage to run with the lunch crowd. So no one noticed when noon rolled around and I grabbed my umbrella and headed for La Maison, clutching my billfold with the nostalgia one feels before long goodbyes.

Outside it was raining, that sticky summer rain that steams the cockroaches out of their holes and onto the pavement, so I walked over to Madison Avenue and rode the bus uptown past bridal boutiques, day spas, baby couture stores. La Maison was on a block of antique shops and galleries. On display in its velvet-lined window were a decanter and a group of cut-crystal glasses that looked heavy and old, like chalices, though I doubt chalices are sold in sets of six. A couple of men with Secret Service–type wires in their ears opened the doors for me, and I shook off my umbrella and left it in the brass stand.

Somewhere I've read that the first rule of the great auction houses is to treat everyone who walks in off the street like an heir to the throne of Saudi Arabia, since one never knows, in this era of the ubiquitous jean jacket, who might have the funds to buy an Old Master drawing. But when a saleswoman approached me to offer her services, looking trim and efficient in her black pantsuit, her smile was cool and supercilious.

"Can I help you find something?" she asked, taking in my wrinkled linen dress and my straw-heeled sandals, which were squishy with water.

"I'm looking for a present, actually a replacement present, from your Steuben line. Something on the order of a frog is what I had in mind, though any kind of animal would do, really."

"Mm, the hand cooler collection," she said, leading me to a display of carved figurines, not unlike the glass trolls my grand-parents keep on the shelves of their powder room. "In the eigh-teenth century young women used these to chill their hands before being led onto the dance floor. The American eagle is the traditional design, but we also carry a limited edition Forest Floor series."

I picked up an eagle from the bottom row. It had the same heft as the thing I had broken, and a kind of stuffy Federalist look that would fit nicely in the newly appointed Fort. The price tag read one hundred and ninety-five dollars.

"A classic," the salesgirl said, pursing her lips. "Of course, we usually sell them in pairs, but one is a charming little way to say 'thank you.'"

"I'd like it in a box, if you have one."

"Wrapped and mailed?"

"Wrapped, please." I had legs, and could therefore do the dropping off myself. We struggling actresses must take our small economies wherever we can find them.

Bella's father, Berglan Starker, had compounded his prodigious family wealth by starting up a venture capital firm called Starker Futures. Venture capital has never exactly been explained to me, but Mr. Starker's business enterprises seem to have been wildly successful, judging from the number of boards he chairs and causes he funds. He invests mostly in industrial development, but you wouldn't guess it from meeting him, he's not a thuggish anti-union type. In fact he's one of those highbrow businessmen, a rare books collector and a big-time financial contributor to the city's cultural life, which I know from seeing pictures of him in *New York Magazine* at all the black-tie galas. In these pictures he's often captured chatting up attractive, lithe young women, but I suppose this is just what one does at such parties, the way one is often lectured on obscure Coltrane recordings at grad school parties. All social gatherings have their circumscribed rituals.

I'd been introduced to Mr. Starker on a number of occasions, had each time felt the sort of embarrassingly undemocratic servant girl's thrill at meeting the King, but to say he and I had any kind of personal relationship would be overstating the case. He'd been underwriting First Born since our founding, had always been cordial and polite to Evan and the rest of us after our shows, the way I imagine heads of state are cordial and polite—shaking hands, conspicuously avoiding the use of proper names, distributing conversation evenly around the room so that no one could feel neglected or snubbed. He had the CEO's gift for making a person feel remembered, and though he probably didn't know me as anyone more specific than one of Bella's artsy friends, it was still a kick to imagine him untying the ribbon on an elegant charcoal-and-cream-colored gift box that had been left in the care of his secretary, and trying, for a tenth of a second, to conjure up the face (mine) to match the name on the card. At least it was a stylish way to throw away half a week's pay, and I took some care composing my note in a bakery next door to La Maison, where I laid out another half week's pay on a cup of Viennese coffee and three almond tuiles. My first couple of drafts were weirdly formal, "it is with regret that I must confess to having broken your blah blah blah," but I eventually settled on a simple please-accept-my-apologies line and sealed up the envelope. The Park Avenue address Bella had given me for Starker Futures was on my route back to work; I could walk there and drop off the package on my way.

It seems odd, in retrospect, that I would have taken such pains with a three-line note and then not even stopped in front of a mirror to pull my damp hair out of my face, but the truth is it never occurred to me that Mr. Starker would be back from his fishing expedition, much less back in the office. Most of my notions about business come from Hollywood, where the tycoons never do anything so mundane as go to work, or if they do it's only late at night to shred documents or steal files. So when the elevator doors opened on the twenty-sixth floor, I was shocked to see Mr. Starker himself standing in the reception area, talking to an assistant-ish-looking person holding a stack of manila folders. In a play, my character's stumble into the scene would have been heralded by some palpable signal like a light change or a sound cue. But real life deprives us of such reflective pauses, and Mr. Starker and his assistant and the front desk receptionist were all staring at the wet, shopping-bag-laden specimen in front of their elevator bank as if Starker Futures didn't get a lot of that kind of traffic. The room was so quiet I could hear the elevator I'd arrived in whir back down its shaft.

After a moment, Mr. Starker said: "You look as if you could use a towel."

I looked down at my dress, which was indeed soaked. "I'm a friend of your daughter's," I said, as if that explained anything. "I was one of her guests at Fort Sassquam this weekend, at your house there. My name is Rosalie Preston."

"Certainly, Rosalie. We've met before, I think. In your dryer incarnation you're one of the actresses, aren't you?"

"Right, from First Born, I am," I said, that easily flattered into stuttering.

"And here I've just been invited to watch some of your troupe's rehearsals. Evan Weiner tells me you've got *The Balcony* on the docket for an upcoming festival. I'm a great devotee of Genet, he's one of the major dramatic geniuses of our century, as far as I'm concerned. Though he'd probably roll over in his pit grave in Marseilles if he heard someone like me say such a thing. Tell me, are you involved in this scene?"

I shook my head, surprised that Mr. Starker had ever had time to read Genet, much less time to keep up with the First Born rehearsal schedule. "I'm doing Eugene O'Neill. A Mary Tyrone monologue from *Long Day's Journey into Night.*"

"Oh what a shame. Catholicism is much less fun in the New World. O'Neill can be awfully dreary when he gets going on one of those endless tirades of his."

"Tell me about it. It's woe, woe, and for the last act, some more woe." I took the Steuben box out of its shopping bag. "Speaking of woe, I've come by today because I accidentally broke that nice frog on your mantelpiece at Fort Sassquam."

"Frog?" Mr. Starker asked, examining the package as if it might contain something that belonged in a terrarium.

"The crystal hand cooler right over the fireplace. I knocked it over during a rehearsal and one of its feet chipped off. It was a real low point for me, in terms of motor control."

He unwrapped the box and stared at the eagle nestled in its folds of tissue. It didn't appear to ring any bells. "This is very thoughtful of you, Rosalie, running about in the rain on my account. But I can't possibly accept it."

"Please, it's the least I can do."

"That house is groaning with clutter; you've done me a favor by breaking some of it. Really." He closed the lid on the box and held it out towards me.

"Well I can't be responsible for it. I'm terrible with housepets."

Mr. Starker smiled, the kind of smile you might give a foreign person who's just cooked a lovely meal for you and then set to work on eating it by dropping her face into the plate. He put the box into the shopping bag and handed it back to me so that I couldn't refuse it, then he looked at his watch. "I tell you what. I'm just off to an installation downtown at the Hoyt-Purvis

Gallery, a Canadian woman whose work is absolutely spectacular. Why don't you come along and have a look?"

Technically speaking, my lunch hour was almost up. But the good thing about working for a magazine is that you can always play hooky on the pretext of covering a story. In that way, it occurs to me, reporters have to stay on their toes the same way actors do: you never know what's coming at you, you can only be prepared to swing back.

When Mr. Starker and I got out of our cab it was raining so hard he took a book from his briefcase to hold over his head. And when he opened the door of the Hoyt-Purvis Gallery, heads turned. This may sound unlikely, a piece of campy exaggeration on my part, but it is simply a fact. Berglan Starker is the sort of person New Yorkers are always on the lookout for—not crassly famous, like the movie stars tourists gather to ogle outside the *Today* show, but subtly powerful, like a major bank president or a judge whose name they would recognize, if only they could attach it to the face. For my part, I felt foolishly thrilled that this person, this distinguished head-turner, was holding the door for me, though I tried not to cop that self-important expression you see on the faces of interns who fetch coffee for consequential people.

"Dunja Overstjokrach," Mr. Starker said, in the sort of proprietary tone most people reserve for their own living rooms. "I met her two winters ago in Banff, and I've been following her work ever since."

He clapped his hand on my shoulder, as if we two were in the habit of spending many a friendly afternoon in each other's company, and ushered me towards the information desk, where he flashed a card and asked the girl behind the counter to hold on to his book and my shopping bag for us. "If you're an admirer of Woodrow Wilson, this is a tremendous biography," he said, sliding the wet volume across the desk.

Dunja Overstjokrach, according to the brief biography stenciled on the wall in what looked like chocolate icing, was renowned for her work in perishable mediums such as baking potatoes, exotic foliage, and reconstituted human sweat. In the first room of the exhibit, we found ourselves staring at a large armchair built entirely out of flank steak. I read the title card: *Germs and Feelings are Communicated by the same Mechanism, Study III.*

"That's our Dunja, flouting the collectors," Mr. Starker said, pacing around the chair like a customer in an automobile showroom. "What do you make of this?" He pointed to a small pool of blood on the floor next to the ottoman, just too bright to be convincing.

"It's certainly an argument against decorating your living room in raw beef. Who would want to mop up all those drippings?"

"Her work is never tranquil," he said, sliding his glasses down the bridge of his nose. "But then that's not what one turns to young artists for, is it? Speaking of which, why don't you tell me about this festival you're involved in."

"We're submitting three different scenes: mine is O'Neill, then there's the Genet and one by a German playwright named Jergen Becker."

"I love Becker. I once heard a stunning reading of that radio play of his, *Houses,* while I was in Berlin. Didn't he write mostly for radio?"

"Yes, but more and more people are trying to mount full-scale productions of his work these days. Evan says it's liberating not to have to follow any stage directions."

On the floor of the next gallery, a windup toy duck jumped back and forth over a live salamander. A cheap contribution to the technology vs. nature dialogue, in my opinion, but Mr. Starker appeared engrossed. He asked some more cursory questions about First Born: where we'd been rehearsing, what undertaking was next on our schedule, how the plans for our fundraiser were coming along. The whole conversation had the feel of an extremely polite charade, as if Mr. Starker didn't give a French fuck what we actually did with his money, as long as we kept Bella happy and occupied. Without being too direct about it, I assured him of both.

"You know I used to dabble in the theater," he said. "I directed an appallingly pretentious production of *Blood Wedding* when I was a senior in college. Luckily videotape wasn't readily available, back in those days. Your friend Bella would be mortified."

As he said this we stepped into the next room of the exhibit, which was dark except for a set of glowing red wires wound around a costume dummy. There was no one else there, aside from a fat guard slumped on a stool next to a sign that read "Caution: art is hot." The room's movie-theater ambiance and the unavoidable emphasis on the female form shut down all conversation, and we stood in silence, cocking our heads at various angles meant to convey contemplation. But darkness, however public, has a way of suggesting the clandestine, and suddenly there was no getting around the fact that Mr. Starker and I were standing extremely close to one another in a pitch-black empty room in the middle of a weekday afternoon and none of our mutual acquaintances had any idea of our whereabouts, including my friend his daughter.

If I could just freeze this scene for a moment and interject some background information: I come, as I've said, from a small New England town, the sort of place that in earlier times might have served as Hawthorne's model for *The Scarlet Letter,* the sort of place where the pharmacist keeps the condoms behind the counter, to shame the unmarried folks out of asking for them. My mother is the organist at the Methodist church; my parents were high-school sweethearts; my grandparents sleep not just in separate beds, but in separate rooms. Add to this biographical mix the fact that I'm an advice columnist and an actress, and voilà, you have our two great paradoxical strands of American sexual temperament rolled into one twenty-six-year-old: Puritan and libertine; virgin and strumpet. All of which is to say I have a past, but a tame and predictable one, and my sense of adventure is less conventional than my carnal résumé might suggest.

So I was hardly oblivious to the implications of standing in a deserted dark room with a handsome man more than twice my age. All I could think was that it felt slightly awkward and inappropriate, like watching *The Unbearable Lightness of Being* with an uncle, or wearing a halter top to thesis tutorial. And yet I was also strangely happy to linger, breathing in Mr. Starker's rugged, woodsy scent, guessing at his exact height (> 6'), imagining how all this looked from the vantage point of the fat security guard. It wasn't until a group of art students tramped into the room talking about hegemony of the body that we finally left.

A series of bright white corridors led us back to the central atrium where we'd begun. "That's it?" I asked, disappointed. "It's over?"

"She's not very prolific." Mr. Starker shrugged apologetically. "She's Canadian." He looked at his watch, excused himself, and returned a second later with a bag from the gift shop. "Here," he said, handing me a tiny windup duck like the one we'd seen in the exhibit. "A souvenir for your mantel, to keep the eagle company."

The duck's flippers rotated in my hand, emitting a little electronic wheeze that made me smile foolishly. "This is hardly right. I don't have a fireplace in my apartment. I don't even have a gas stove."

"Well now you have quite a menagerie, so you'll have to find a home for them. Thank you for keeping me company on what would otherwise have been a tedious afternoon. I'm afraid I've got to get uptown for a meeting. Can I put you in a cab?"

Outside the glass doors the rain had stopped. "I'm not going that far. I'm fine to walk."

"All right, then," he said, "have an excellent night." He leaned down and planted a kiss on my cheek: a quick, formal, leave-taking kiss, in the paternalistic/continental style I expected. But there was a shadow of something more to it, some extra tenth of a second or extra lip on the follow-through, that made me feel woozy and embarrassed and a little silly, all at once.

"Thanks for joining me. We'll do this again soon." That was

all he said. Then he strode out of the gallery without turning to look back.

It was either Hume, Locke, Kant, or Nietzsche who observed that we come to understand the world by reducing it into categories, making meaning through organization and division. I, for example, have broken my own unwieldy species into two distinct groups: parents and non-parents. Fathers, such as my own, whom I mentioned earlier is a dentist, tend to have certain skills (diaper-changing, hot-dog boiling), drive certain cars (minivans, station wagons), look a certain way (good-natured, exhausted). Non-fathers are characterized by a wholly separate set of traits, physical attributes, cars. If a psychologist were to bark "Father" at you and ask for your instinctive response, chances are you wouldn't answer "Elegantly tousled hair, impeccably groomed skin, stylishly cut three-button suit, tall, dark, and not unlike a mannequin in the Bergdorf men's department." Perhaps this is why, when Berglan Starker disappeared into the back of a cab across the street, perfectly fitting the above description, it was easy for me to momentarily forget that he was a father at all, much less the father of one of my best friends. I've always known that one day I would wake from my lingering adolescence as from a trance, and begin to find gray hair and reading glasses sexy.

But there is a dark side to the business of blending categories, of allowing oneself to see the gray in absolutes, and I'm sure my jitters on leaving the gallery had to do with just this. Mr. Starker was the father of one of my best friends, yet he was also extremely handsome, the first seriously older man I'd ever been attracted to (aside from Peter Jennings and Paul Newman, who don't count, I've never seen either of them in person). Mr. Starker was married, yet he had been married something like three or four times, and thus could not be described as fully invested in the sanctity of the institution. Mr. Starker was wealthy and powerful, yet sufficiently down to earth to slouch around a museum with one of his daughter's chums. (Though I must say that his shoes, those pointy black loafer-ish things, were way too dainty and effeminate to qualify as down to earth.) So—he was simultaneously paternal and desirable, married and available, larger than life and Regular Joe, and where are the absolutes in that? When I ran this question by Grace later, keeping the scenario abstract and hypothetical, she reminded me of my specially perspicacious talent for reckoning with such complexities, i.e., the time I slept with our People's Republic section leader right before the midterm, and a few similar examples from my ancient history so old as to be irrelevant.

What I am trying to say is that I think I knew, right then and there in the lobby of the Hoyt-Purvis Gallery, that a crush on Mr. Starker would have been a cinch to develop, given the merest encouragement. In retrospect I understand that men like Mr. Starker are addicted, as if by genetic compulsion, to engendering such crushes, but since I'm trying to tell this story in the way that it happened, and not in a way that makes me look as wise as I wish I'd been, I'll save the retrospect for later. My mother, who is on a doomed crusade to turn me into a passable cook, always reminds me that the order in which you do things actually does matter. You can't just dump all the ingredients into a pan and stir.

I did have the presence of mind to collect Mr. Starker's book from the information counter, after he'd strode off in such a hurry without it. *League of Heroes,* it was called, or something equally bestseller-ish. No juicy inscriptions or marginal notes, but a decent reason to get in touch sometime, if I ever wanted one. And so I left the Hoyt-Purvis Gallery, mildly nervous about what to tell Bella, mildly guilty for entertaining PG-13 thoughts about her father, and lugging a 422-page excuse to see him again.

Outside the sky had turned that polluted pink glow I used to love until I took Astronomy and the Atmosphere, and I wandered back to my office at an ambling pace. The middle of the workday is a strange time to be set loose in New York City; you realize how many people, mostly women, are out on the streets, picking up dry-cleaning, returning videos, walking dogs and toddlers. Of course some of these women might have night-shift jobs at hospitals and restaurants, but my impression is that most of them don't work at all. (Or they "freelance," as Bella calls it, since she once wrote a movie review for the *Village Voice.*) Is my disapproval based on anything more substantial than envy? Will I someday be a stroller pusher, a weekday marketer, myself? Do former "theater dabblers" (as Mr. Starker put it) always find their past pursuits appallingly pretentious, and is life's natural trajectory a shrugging off of such frivolous goals? (Yes! I can hear my parents shriek. Yes, yes! A master's in social work! Praise God!)

After work, faced with the prospect of an empty refrigerator, I walked four blocks out of the way of my Second Avenue apartment over to Cam and Jake's. They live a few streets away from me in an East Village tenement I call Stanislavsky Hall, for the peaceful cohabitation of old Russian ladies and young actors from the Strasberg Institute. I buzzed up to them on the off chance they were home and hungry. Cam answered.

"It's Rosalie. I have to pee."

"I didn't order no Rosalie." The buzzer sounded and I let myself in through the doors, then up in the rickety old elevator, which must violate at least fifteen city safety codes, to the fourth floor, where I followed the smell of burning food to their apartment. Cam stood over the stove, taming a pan of smoking ground beef. "Tacos," he said, without looking up. "Blackened. Cajun tacos."

In the bathroom, one of the shelves had been cleared of trial-sized aftershaves and empty toothpaste tubes to accommodate makeup remover and body lotion: Grace. A permanent store of toiletries is a landmark step in any relationship's development; when I shared this observation with Cam he shrugged and handed me a block of orange cheese to grate.

"I told you, they're with each other all the time. It's like I have two roommates now. They just left to go look at new glasses frames for Grace."

This news irritated me on a few different counts, since I've always been the one to help Grace pick out her glasses frames, and since the notion of Jake in any retail establishment that requires shirt and shoes was ridiculous. "I thought Grace had rehearsal tonight. What's she doing going shopping?"

"Evan canceled it. He had to go to some meeting with Manny."

So it had happened that quickly, the beginning of the end. Evan never canceled rehearsals, not for sickness, not for inclement weather, not for bomb threats. I looked at Cam, who continued to chop onions with the concentration of a child playing pick-up sticks.

"Don't you think that's a little weird?"

"Weird?" He put down his knife. "Why weird? Something must have come up, I guess."

I had an unfair advantage, knowing what I did about Evan's plans to storm Broadway and leave the rest of us eating his dust. But Cam still displayed a degree of trusting optimism I both envied and scorned. Envy and scorn seem to be the emotions most often provoked in me by good-looking, cheerful people like Cam, people who are sure the world will serve them up some piece of wonderful fortune if they're just nice and easygoing about stuff. He rubbed his onion-y, beef-y hands on his pants.

"You look freaked out, Rose. What's up?"

"Nothing. Nothing. It just strikes me as unusual that Evan would give us a night off, considering how soon the festival is and how badly we suck right now."

Cam looked wounded. "We don't suck. You think we suck?"

I shook my head. "I've probably just had a long day. Forget it."

He went back to chopping. "So what's in the bag?"

I looked at the shopping bag from La Maison, which I'd dropped by the door when I walked in, along with my things from work. "Twelve silver place settings and an extra-large soup tureen. Just getting a leg up on your birthday shopping, sweetheart."

This reference to the bag would have been the perfect opportunity to mention Berglan Starker, if I were going to mention him at all. But Cam had begun to massage my temples in a lulling, therapeutic way that made me not want to talk about anything, period. Instead I sank down to the kitchen floor, dust bunnies and onion skins and sticky patches of unknown origin and all, while Cam stood above me and kept up with the scalp-temple-acupressure treatment. Sin of omission #1. Watch carefully for these; they pile up fast.

What followed next is a theater-world cliché, and while I'm slightly ashamed to prove anything so predictable true, sometimes the best way to handle stereotypes is to own them whole hog, no apologies. Mob bosses carry guns; gay men have nice apartments; actors fuck their costars, their directors, their stage managers, and whoever in the audience admires them enough. So, Cam and I have a bit of a sexual history. We've been lovers on a casual and infrequent basis, when neither of us is dating anyone else and assorted intangibles stack up just right. Things had ended with the last guy I'd dated a few months ago, a sports reporter named Charles Buffernaut, when he'd decided to quit the sports reporting business and move to Chicago for medical school. Cam's most recent girlfriend, a blond Shetland sweater type named Blaine, had recently dumped him for her father's college roommate. So there Cam and I were, together again, a couple of old pals with conveniently complementary body parts. Conventional wisdom has it that sleeping with friends is a bad idea, but I've found that if you regulate them carefully, the isolated incidents don't add up to much. Or so I chose to believe, as I kicked off my sandals, unzipped my dress, and let Cam shimmy my underwear down my legs.

It had been many months since our last clothing-free encounter, and rustiness and sheepishness combined to produce the kind of sex that was more like wrestling with an attractive cousin than like making love. Cam, as I've mentioned, is incredibly handsome, but he isn't particularly imaginative in bed, and our sex life has always amounted to a sort of acrobatic extension of hand-holding and snuggling. That's another thing about making it with your friends: even when you get sweaty and roll around on the linoleum, there's a lethal air of amicability about the whole endeavor.

But familiarity was what I was after that night, whether I knew it then or not. Change isn't my strong suit, big or small, and sweet old Cam, panting his milky breath on my neck, making his familiar warbly exhalation as he came—that was anti-change, or my attempt at it. Of course it's a big mistake to use sex as a way to preserve anything, but that's one of those home truths that make plenty of sense on paper and less sense when a guy has his head between your legs. When we'd finished, we turned off the stove and ordered Chinese food from the restaurant around the corner. I borrowed pajama bottoms and a T-shirt, and we perched on the couch eating dinner straight out of the boxes. I hoped Jake and Grace wouldn't come back to the apartment that night; the idea of seeing them together in their full-blown domestic bliss made me feel foolish and immature. Deserved or undeserved, a friend's disapproval is hard to brook. I was glad when they didn't come home.

In Cam's room, after the twenty seconds it took for him to fall asleep, I kicked off the flannel covers and lay on my back, looking around for things that might have moved or been replaced since my last overnight, almost a year ago. But all was more or less as I'd left it: the piles of unfolded clothes on every available surface; the parched, drooping ivy craning towards the barred window; the formal antiques shipped up from the Post homestead in South Carolina, proportioned for a bedroom three times as large and ten times as grand. No big changes. No big changes, I told myself, looking at Cam, whose limby sprawl colonized the entire bed. First Born was still First Born, the same tight little knot it had always been, and nothing on the horizon seemed likely to undo it. A tiny feather from one of the down pillows had settled into a corner of Cam's open mouth; it shifted up and down rhythmically with his breath. Business as usual.

Except for two developments. Evan was canceling our rehearsals for meetings about this new Broadway play of his, and Berglan Starker, the man who'd bankrolled every scene we'd ever read out loud, had invited me to be his date for an afternoon of mediocre Canadian art. Often you can sense that two things are related before you have any specific idea of how; think of the romance languages, or Banana Republic and the Gap. This was one of those conundrums. Success, prestige, money, influence, crystal eagles, plastic ducks, naked friends. Such were the dim notions swirling around in my head as I fell, finally, to sleep.

Dear Annie,

I have a mad crush on this guy in my class, and I swear it is taking over my life. I think about him all the time!!! Like when I am walking to school, I imagine he's with me, or when I watch TV, I pretend he's sitting next to me on the couch. I've had crushes before, but they were always normal and under control. Why am I so obsessed with this guy? And what can I do to get my brain back?

—Freaked Out in Nevada

Dear Freaked Out,

First of all, take a few deep breaths. It's totally acceptable to get a little loopy when you really like somebody: crushes are called crushes because they can knock the wind right out of you and leave you all flattened out. And as for pretending the boy is sitting next to you on the couch, don't panic about that, either. Our minds try out all sorts of imaginary scenarios, and it's perfectly fine to linger in the pleasant ones for a while.

Now, the important question of getting your brain back. Maybe you've heard your mom or dad talk about "diversifying the portfolio." That's a fancy way of saying never put all of your eggs in one basket. What else did you used to like to do, pre-crush? Were you a tennis fanatic? Did you spend hours every day reading mysteries? I ask because the key to staying sane, when you've got your eye on someone, is to stay busy. The more activities you cram into your day, the less time you'll have to worry about what your crush will think of your haircut, or your sneakers. And P.S. What's more intriguing than a busy, in-demand girl?

One more thought to file away, in case this crush blossoms into something bigger. Try to keep the portfolio diversified, or the eggs in different baskets, or the day super-booked even if you *do* start dating this guy. No boy deserves 100% of your brainpower, no matter how amazing he is. You'll be happier and more satisfied if you hold on to the other parts of your life that matter to you, too.

Trust me. I've lived through it.

Annie

Chapter Three

As a rule, Eugene O'Neill's leading female characters are either whores, addicts, or freaks. Apparently he and Carlotta had a nice long-lasting marriage, but I, for one, would have taken a cold hard look at that guy's body of work before consenting to a second date. Contemporary directors trot him out for ballast, to prove their chops are meaty and they're not afraid to put moral parables on stage. But the question remains, does anyone actually *enjoy* Eugene O'Neill? Does anyone thrill to the prospect of an evening of drinks at 44, dinner at Café Un, Deux, Trois, and eighth-row tickets to *The Hairy Ape*? I know he's good for us, like doing sit-ups or eating kale. His politics are as relevant now as ever, remember what the *Iceman* revival did for Democratic Party fundraising. But he certainly wouldn't be my first choice for a complimentary house seat.

This innate "resistance" (Evan's term) was what I was trying to overcome in my Mary Tyrone monologue. It's a tall order to deliver any show's last speech in isolation; this one in particular depends on a four-hour windup to give it depth. It's a beautiful scene, really: Mama Tyrone, all withered and strung out on morphine, remembering her Catholic schoolgirl years when she planned on becoming a nun, before James Tyrone waltzed into her life and saddled her with two good-for-nothing tubercular sons. The moving part is that she's so drugged out by the end of the play she truly believes she's a kid again: the stage directions have her "staring dreamily with youthful innocence," and "tossing her head with girlish pique." Of course, that chilling effect would be lost in my rendition, since I'm a lot closer to schoolgirl age than the sixty-five-year-old actress who's supposed to play this part. But this is Evan's inspired twist. Something about time and age and the ironic poignancy of regret.

We were rehearsing for the festival in our usual Tuesday night space on Orchard Street, me and Evan and the rest of First Born. Last week another company had loaded in their set for *Struwwel Peter,* so I was sitting cross-legged on a thick carpet of Astroturf in front of a cardboard chalet and a mural of the Jungfrau. Background scenery like this seeps into your consciousness no matter how hard you try to block it out, and a certain Swiss milkmaid aspect had crept into my monologue over the course of the night. Sensing a dead end for character development, Evan had stopped my run-through to sit onstage and give me a crash course in Catholic iconography (the Blessed Virgin vs. Our Lady of Lourdes; why some nuns are called Mother and some Sister—talk about juicy parts for women), while I penciled notes on my script. People in the industry call this phase "table work," meaning you're not on your feet reciting your lines and moving around the stage. I like it. It reminds me of being in school.

At the beginning of the night, before vocal warm-ups and the evening's schedule breakdown, Evan had casually mentioned— oh so casually, hiya folks, hope the heat lets up by the time we're through, go Yankees, love that Jeter action in the bottom of the fifth—that a few people might be stopping by to watch our rehearsal. Jake: A few people? Evan: Some work associates, nobody to worry about, just proceed as usual and pretend they're not here. Me: We're already doing plenty of *pretending*; maybe you'd like us to concentrate our imaginative energy on the scenes themselves, rather than on *pretending* we can't see the strangers sitting in the audience. Fair enough, Evan conceded, and he gave us the guest list: a couple of Manny's producing partners, who wanted to see what a non-musical piece looked like in early development. And Bella's dad was maybe going to come by, too, if he could find the time. It would be nice if one Starker made it, Jake said under his breath, since Bella herself had called to say she wouldn't be showing up. Evan pretended not to hear.

Onstage, I kept my eyes on my script and tried not to look up every one of the twelve million times Cam pushed open the theater door to go to the bathroom. I'm an actress; by definition I like to perform, I like it when people watch me, and a few extra faces staring at me from the folding chairs would only grease my wheels. So: eyes on script, pencil in hand, brain not concentrating on the fact that Mr. Starker was about to walk into the theater. Why had I worn the sweatpants with elastic at the ankles? Why hadn't I washed my hair? Even at the time, I was conscious that my major source of distraction ought to have been Manny's scouts, and that something was grossly out of whack in my worrying about my hair when professional producers were about to arrive. But that's the dark convenience of acting: you can write off vanity as part of the job.

Though I'd thought about my afternoon with Mr. Starker a

fair amount in the week since we'd gone to the gallery, I hadn't specifically mentioned our outing to anyone. Grace knew about the Steuben mission but she hadn't followed up on it, which was characteristic of her new Jake-centric universe, nothing but his comings and goings registered on her radar for more than a few seconds at a time. I could have reminded her, but I'm actually getting sick of reminding her of the outside world, I'm not her personal assistant, and one really prefers to be asked about one's life than to have to constantly volunteer such information. The contract of best-friendship allows for periods of self-absorption, sure, but part of me was looking forward to the time when I could spring something big on Grace after the fact, my birthday maybe, just to let her twist for an hour or two. Yesterday? Oh, no biggie, I just went to work and the girls had ordered me a birthday cake, it was awfully thoughtful of them, then I came home and watched TV and opened a few cards from home. So what did you do? Like that.

Telling Bella about my Hoyt-Purvis outing was a stickier wicket, of course. She didn't take her father's business lightly, had spent years in therapy complaining about him (this, I believe, is what's meant by the phrase "poor little rich girl"). Therefore the most sensible approach would have been just to tell her, straight out, that I'd run into her dad at his office while dropping off the eagle, etc. She probably wouldn't have given the whole thing a second thought. Only I didn't tell her. Because it had been a busy week, with rehearsals, and column deadlines, and besides it's not like the guy had called me again or anything.

The truth is that all important facts out themselves eventually, and sometimes it is better to hang back and let them unfold in the course of due time, this is what gives life its mystery, its edge of unpredictability. Think of plays: one sees the mounted rifle in the first act, one knows it will be used, but when? And how? And by whom—the lovable humpbacked boy, or the all-knowing butler, or the suspiciously cosmopolitan priest?

The other truth is that I'm a little afraid of Bella.

Anyway, I'd privately burned off my residual nerves by plowing through the first section of the Wilson biography. Mr. Starker and President Wilson had thus become conjoined in my mind, and when Mr. Starker walked into the theater that night, I half expected to see him in a wide-brimmed straw hat and a bow tie. Instead he looked quite the well-coifed CEO, dark suit, dark shirt, dark tie, and when he held up his hand to wave to me, my heart sped up. He took a seat in the back of the house, a few rows behind Cam and Jake and Grace, and as soon as I made it to the end of a beat Evan gave me the high sign, climbed down the steps, and went to greet our distinguished guest. I followed him off the stage and joined my friends.

"Is it just me," Jake asked, staring into the alpine distance, "or does anyone else feel pimped out?"

"The guy just wants to sit and watch for a while," Cam said. "It'll be good practice for us."

"Maybe we could pass a tin cup around the rehearsal room and ask people to contribute according to how good they think we are."

"Oh, relax," Cam said. "The whole point of entering this festival is to get our name out there and have people come see us. This is like a preview."

"No, it isn't," Jake said, fussing with his pants leg. "This is a rehearsal, which is why it bugs me when Evan invites an audience."

"Jake," Grace said, "these are just some of Evan's friends from work, and they're obviously here to watch him, not us. Don't worry about it."

"Maybe tomorrow night I'll invite some of my friends from work." Jake did tech support for secretaries on Wall Street, and the job got under his skin in a way the rest of ours didn't; it made him antsy, even a little desperate, for something better to put his energy into. He could be touchy about First Born, touchy about work, and then touchy about his inability to be breezy, like Cam. "Shouldn't we get to vote on stuff like this?"

"Sure," Cam said. "But that's probably not going to happen tonight."

When Evan rejoined our huddle, he told me that my shift had ended and summoned the guys for their turn onstage. I said my goodnights and headed up the aisle to change out of my sweats, unsure of how to proceed. Going home immediately would mean missing Manny's producers, if they actually bothered to show up. It would also mean forfeiting all interaction with Mr. Starker. But then again, sticking around for no reason had a slightly pathetic, stalker-ish edge. Worse, it implied active voli-tion on my part: no coincidence here, just me, lingering around the theater in hopes of catching a word or a glance from my friend's hot dad. So I took my time walking up the aisle, praying that something would make my decision for me. Sure enough, Mr. Starker motioned to me as I passed his row. I sidestepped folding chairs to get to where he sat.

"I'm sorry I missed your scene." He tapped the chair next to him.

"I can cough on you. You'll get the idea." I put my backpack down and sat. "What brings you to the Lower East Side?"

"I've been promised Genet," he whispered. "And it's a pleasure for me to watch a little behind-the-scenes action. The smell of fresh paint and sawdust is good for the aging soul."

Honestly, someone could make a mint off the idea of extracurricular clubs for corporate executives. Onstage Cam and Jake hammered through a line-check with all the enthusiasm of kids reciting the pledge of allegiance. "Don't worry," I said to Mr. Starker, "this is just the warm-up."

He nodded and kept watching. I thought of Dunja Overstjokrach, the rolls of half-used cellophane scattered around her steak armchair. These days, it can be a challenge to separate the warm-up from the actual show. Steak armchair; steak; food. I'd had a yogurt and two packs of peanut-butter sandwiches from the *GirlTalk* vending machine for lunch. Unlike the rest of my coworkers, who seem able to survive on this kind of squirrel food for weeks at a time, my stomach was expressing an audible desire for a square meal. Mr. Starker looked at me.

"You need to be fed."

I unearthed half a chocolate bar from the outer pocket of my backpack. The cap of a ballpoint pen was stuck to one end, and the lettering on the wrapper had partially rubbed off. He took the mangled candy out of my hand.

"Properly. Why don't you go get yourself dressed."

Under normal circumstances, I can't say I relish being ordered around. But for a free meal, I can be persuaded to follow instructions.

I joined up with Mr. Starker on the stoop outside the studio. The night was heavy with humidity and the hot air smelled ripe, as if the city had been trapped under a circus big top. Mr. Starker claimed to be game for dinner in the neighborhood, but when I led him around the corner to Katz's Deli, the line backed out the door and a sign in the window said the air-conditioning was broken. We conferred on the sidewalk, got bumped and jostled by legions of the tattooed and pierced, and after a shirtless kid with a snake around his shoulders asked to bum a cigarette, we were in the next cab heading up First Avenue.

New York at night can look like almost anything from the backseat of a cab. If you're in a doleful mood, it's all toxic smoke rising from manholes and people sleeping in doorways and primordial rats bigger than your foot stalking the pavement; if you're tipsy or stoned or just home from vacation, it's the miracle of those fifty-story buildings and how anyone thought to build them so tall. That night with Mr. Starker, turning onto Madison Avenue, what I saw out the car window was money: block-long storefronts displaying a single high-heeled shoe; block-long limousines idling outside pre-war hotels; block-long churches with grounds so manicured they looked bucolic. And all this wealth a mere three miles from my apartment.

We pulled up to a building on the corner of Fifth and some

street in the high sixties, not a restaurant awning in sight. I read once that during World War II the British rearranged their road signs, so that in the event of an Axis land invasion the Germans would be hopelessly lost. The residents of the Upper East Side have clearly turned to the history books for strategies to keep out the rabble.

"This is my club," Mr. Starker said, handing a bill to the driver. "There won't be any line, and the air-conditioning always works." He reached his arm all the way across me to open my door.

I've always imagined clubs to be repositories of calcified old men sitting in wingback chairs playing pinochle, getting their jollies by reciting membership rules and dress code regulations. Not so with Millennium, the name I read off the brass plaque on the gated townhouse we approached. True, inside the drawing rooms looked like nineteenth-century American interiors at Epcot Center. But there were women all over the place, and no one looked askance at me for wearing a tank top, which meant they either mistook me for Bella or they were less averse to exposed bra straps than I'd assumed.

"I hope you don't find this too ridiculous," Mr. Starker said, as we wound our way up the spiral staircase to the dining room. "I know it's old-fashioned, but I do like to have a place to duck in without reservations."

"I'm happy to be here," I said, surveying the leather-and-mahogany ecosystem before me. "I've always wanted to see the inside of one of these places."

We were led to our table by a white-haired gentleman with a slight limp whom Mr. Starker addressed as Mr. Thorne-Thomas. The old man handed us paper menus with the evening's entrées listed in calligraphy. When a woman wearing a white lab coat came to take our order, I chose my dinner by process of elimination: fennel knocked out the duck, ginger knocked out the skate, calf's liver knocked out the calf's liver. I settled on quail, hoping it might taste like rock Cornish game hen, which I've heard tastes like chicken.

"Tell me, Rosalie," Mr. Starker began. "When did you first fall in love with acting?"

"Hmm." I sipped my fizzy water. "It must have been when I played a hairbrush in my fourth-grade class's production of *Charlotte's Web*."

"One of my favorite books, though I can't say I've ever seen the stage version."

"My costume was amazing. Full head of bristles."

"And so you were hooked."

"Nipped by the personal grooming bug. I've since played hair-styling implements in four of the major Shakespeare tragedies."

"When I was an undergraduate in Lowell House we did a production of *Anthony and Cleopatra* and cast the housemaster's son as the asp. The poor boy wiggled terribly in his basket."

"I think they have rules against that kind of thing now, minors biting bare breasts onstage."

Being an actor, I sometimes think, is simply practicing the artifice of living as a full-time career. There I was with Mr. Starker, playing the smart aleck, plain-talking American girl (I throw in nationality because there was something so tweedy and

Lambert Strether–ish about the club). That's a role, isn't it? A series of choices, conscious or unconscious, to pitch oneself a certain way, highlight certain traits of one's character? Job interviews, first dates, dinners with new acquaintances—those are all non-union acting gigs. We professionals are only more aware of the aspect of performance since it's what we do every day.

So that night, faced with four separate forks and a wine list in a language I couldn't understand (my parents, bless their practical souls, made me take Spanish in high school), I took the only route available to me: to make not knowing into a merit. I was unapologetic about not knowing how to cut my bird when it arrived in front of me, legs sticking tragically into the air. But I hacked away at it according to Mr. Starker's instructions, unapologetic about my appetite, too. Our conversation started off as the generic get-to-know-me stripe, but it was easy and familiar from the word go. He asked me all about *GirlTalk*; I treated him to some of the more memorable questions I'd received in my days as an advice columnist. ("Why is it called a blow job? Is there something we're doing wrong?") Whenever we came back to the topic of acting he got genuinely worked up about it, the way only a former drama club geek can. The guy obviously had more than box-seat interest in the theater. Suddenly I could picture him, minus the suit and plus some hair, giving his all to a soliloquy from, say, *Julius Caesar*. It was kind of adorable, actually.

As our plates were being cleared, the lights in the dining room dimmed. "Vincent Steeplecroft must be on his way up," Mr. Starker said.

I glanced at the door. "Is he a vampire?"

"He's the president of the public library, and he's extremely light-sensitive."

Sure enough, an old man wearing Jackie O–style sunglasses and a beret was making his way slowly into the room. Behind him a crowd of people had assembled, waiting to be seated.

"The theater probably just let out." Mr. Starker said. Mr. Thorne-Thomas limped past our table again, seating two men to our left. The older one looked familiar, in an impeccably tailored suit with matching ascot and handkerchief. Possibly he was a celebrity, or someone I'd seen on the cover of the *New York Times Magazine*.

"How was your food?" Mr. Starker asked.

I felt woozy with butter and wine. "I haven't eaten this well in months."

"I'm glad."

"Glad that I haven't eaten this well in months? What kind of thing is that to say?"

"Glad that you're eating well now. Here. With me."

So there it was, the end of the line for the feed-a-starving-artist charade. Berglan Starker was flirting with me, and I was not exactly pushing back from the table. Sometimes I feel that it's my duty, as an advice columnist, to experience as many permutations of the complex world of romantic relationships as possible. Who wants their love advice from a novice? This logic has gotten me into plenty of small-time scrapes, sleeping with friends, sleeping with boyfriends' friends, sleeping with friends' boyfriends, etc. Friends' parents are another story, though. Even on the dregs of a second bottle of wine, I knew that much.

But I also knew that Mr. Starker was extremely attractive and intriguing, and if I took Bella out of the equation, it seemed like an exciting new possibility. There was the fact that he was married, and to a woman who spent her days courting favors from all three branches of the federal government. What would it be like to sneak around on someone with so much clout? What would it be like to be an actual mistress? Wouldn't it be different than sleeping with some profligate guy whose girlfriend was out of town? Curiosity in children is such an admirable, promising quality. It's tolerable in teenagers, as long as it doesn't involve growth-stunting drugs or lice-y facial hair. But once you reach a certain age, curiosity takes on a dangerous, destructive, cat-killing, Pandora's-Box-like power. My yoga teacher always talks about the positive and negative energies to every human emotion. This kind of pseudo-Zen baloney can be annoying when you're trying to bend your leg around your neck, but it does make an impression.

A hearty laugh burst from the old man at the next table, and suddenly I knew who he was: Manny Flax. I looked at him again, surprised at myself for taking so long to place his face. He was pouring carbonated liquid from a silver flask into his wine glass.

"That's Evan's boss," I whispered. Mr. Starker nodded in confirmation. "Do you know him?"

"Not particularly well," he whispered back. "This place is less like a fraternity house than you might fear."

Certain that Manny would never recognize me, I turned back for another look. He was leaning halfway across the table and talking to his dinner companion about kissing the Blarney Stone. Seated across from him was a young man, the only person my age I'd seen since I'd walked in, dressed in faded jeans, a jean shirt, and a stringy tie. He looked bored and hostile, and like he hadn't washed his hands before dinner.

"Do you know the guy he's with?" I asked Mr. Starker.

"Never seen him before in my life. He's rather intense-looking, don't you think?"

I nodded. "He looks too young to be a son but too old to be a grandson." In fact, he looked as unrelated to Manny Flax as it was possible for any two humans of the same sex and race to look. He was twice as large, and his features bulbed in all the places where Manny's pointed. His elbows rested on the table, as did his napkin, and he was holding a piece of bread up to his nose and smelling it.

"I wonder if Evan knows him," I said. Flax was married, and even if he was in the habit of entertaining boys from time to time, the one he was talking to now seemed an unlikely candidate. Suddenly the young man turned towards me and glared, as if he'd felt my eyes on him for too long and didn't enjoy the attention. I looked away quickly, and felt my cheeks heat up. Pushing at the bread crumbs on the tablecloth, I imagined what I must have looked like to him, or to anyone my age, downing expensive wine with an older married man. Trashy. Or climbing. Or like I was being bought. None of the possibilities sat well with me, and I excused myself from the table to use the ladies' room. Mr. Starker said he'd meet me downstairs.

Sex, in my experience, has always borne the athletic stamp of youth. I'm blessed with the ability to be satisfied easily, usually multiply, and always demonstrably. Boys like going to bed with me. I'm not a physically intimidating conquest, not liable to make them feel nervous about their bodily shortcomings, so to speak, but I give pleasure with the kind of convincing generosity that inspires relief, and I receive it with the kind of gratifying enthusiasm that boosts the ego. I say this without vanity—Lord knows there are plenty of things I'm terrible at, such as sustaining meaningful long-term relationships, which trumps sex in a heartbeat as far as desirable skills go. But we take our romantic talents where we can get them, and I've always felt capable when the lights go off (or stay on) and the sheets get pulled back (or don't).

This is relevant because a long time had passed since my sexual confidence had been challenged, and standing in the bathroom of the Millennium Club, gripping the basin of the porcelain sink, I suddenly felt out of my league. What even *happened* to men's bodies, as they got older? I tried to remember from movies (Donald Sutherland's ass in *Animal House*), from anatomical diagrams in biology textbooks, but I drew a blank. Liver spots? Gray pubic hair? Prostate problems? And what exactly *is* a prostate, anyway? What about birth control—would he have condoms in his wallet? Would a man his age even consent to swath himself in latex and Nonoxynol-9? Well, he would have to if we were going to go to bed together, since I wasn't about to mother Bella's half-sister or catch some tony STD. I reached for a bottle of perfume to spray on the back of my neck, the only dignified thing I could think to do. Most of the opened bottles on the counter seemed portentous: Obsession, Poison, Envy, Gold. I picked Flirt, sprayed twice for luck, and left, smelling like a gallon of pressed grapefruit juice.

"Do you and your millennial brethren know what that Latin

means?" I asked Mr. Starker, looking over my shoulder at the words carved above the front door of the club.

"Yes, but not because I know any Latin." He smiled down at me, stepped in close. "Refuge In Our City; Companionship In Our Time."

"I can't wait to see the secret handshake."

He guided my chin up to his mouth. The kiss this time was gentle but definitive, in the same genus of first kisses I'd known, but of a less grasping, aggressive species. He hailed a taxi and ordered the driver to the Pierre.

As our cab sped down Fifth Avenue, unencumbered by daytime traffic, I stared out the window at the park. Mr. Starker sat beside me, unconcerned with making small talk or foreplay. This approach struck me as distinctly Old World, though I had no clear idea of what I meant by that term, aside from its obvious literal connotations of age and worldliness. I was used to one of two pre-hookup taxicab scenarios: either bumpy, uncomfortable makeout sessions that entailed tooth-knocking and lip-biting at sudden red lights, or jittery, zealous conversations, babbled at top speed to smooth over the awkward transition from bar to bed. Neither model applied.

Inside the enormous suite on the hotel's top floor, Mr. Starker strode around the sitting room switching on a selection of table lamps to their lowest settings. He took off his jacket and hung it in the hallway closet, a move that seemed practical rather than seductive, so I remained fully clothed and took a seat in a large white armchair. Mr. Starker sat on the chair's arm and leaned down in an amiably predatory way. "So, Miss Preston," he said, brushing a strand of hair out of my face. "Can I get you anything?"

Probably old-person code for something I didn't understand. Was there some liqueur I was supposed to be in the mood for? Some private feminine ritual I was supposed to excuse myself to perform in the bathroom? With the exception of guys who've had too much therapy, people my age are pretty blasé about sex; I could sense a bit of a black-tie buildup coming on, and I worried I would lose my nerve if we didn't hurry up and dive in. So I leaned up and kissed him. His mouth, with my eyes closed, tasted like other mouths; when I spread my hands over his chest I felt a solidness through his button-down shirt. I moved my hand down to his pants and sure enough, there was the outline of an erection jerking around in there. He pulled me up and slid my tank top over my head, fumbling gently when my hair got caught in one of the straps, then he unzipped my skirt and it fell to the floor. Pink cotton bra and white cotton panties, bikini cut. Not the ideal lingerie for the Presidential Suite at the Pierre, but possibly sexy, in a sort of prep school way. He looked at me, pleased, fingered my breast through my bra, watched my nipple get hard.

"I'd like to make love to you, Rosalie."

His formality was so embarrassing! What did he think I was there for, the pay-per-view movies? I unclasped my bra and stepped out of my underwear, in case my previous signals hadn't been strong enough, and we kissed for a while longer, me fully naked and him fully clothed. Eventually Mr. Starker loosened his tie and took off his shirt, revealing a film of gray hair covering his chest. I averted my eyes when he stood before me in briefs and black socks, those unappealing accessories that separate grown men from the boxer-clad, gym-sock-wearing guys my own age.

When he was naked, he turned out the light behind me and led me to the bedroom, pausing to pull back the tightly tucked sheets.

And now, a brief timeline of the first night after you've had sex with the father of one of your best friends:

3:12 a.m. Wake up with start. Study striped curtains, chintz armchairs, floral carpet, and king-sized bed of unfamiliar hotel room. In disoriented haze, confuse sleeping gray-haired man next to you with college comparative religion professor; regret having skipped New Testament lectures before final exam. Go back to sleep.

3:18 a.m. Wake up with start. Sleeping gray-haired man next to you is not college comparative religion professor, but rather unclothed father of dear friend. Spend next half hour propped up on elbows recalling events which led you to king-sized bed in unfamiliar hotel room. Have difficulty recollecting mind-altering drugs that must certainly have been involved.

3:56 a.m. Crouch on marble floor over hotel toilet. Try to vomit. Curse parental genes for stalwart metabolism, which has already converted rich four-course meal into army of new fat cells. Put on underwear and tank top, return to bed.

4:10 a.m. Fall into fitful non-REM sleep. Dream of sailing with aforementioned dear friend in large lake, possibly ocean. Waves, storm, symbolic peril.

7:47 a.m. Wake up alone in king-sized bed. Overhear gray-haired man's voice in bathroom. Remember phone mounted above sink. Fly out of bed, get dressed at top speed, settle on white couch behind shield of morning's newspaper.

If this description of my night sounds casual, I invoke the analogy of a criminal who's just knocked off her first bank. What she feels initially is a kind of hyper panic, disbelief that she's had the moxie to go through with the heist, giddiness that she hasn't gotten nabbed for it. It takes a while for the real significance of her act to sink in, to think of all those senior citizens whose IRAs she's depleted, all those teenagers who've worked three summers at McDonald's to save up for a used car. That was how I felt, at least, the morning after: jumpy, freaked out, shocked at myself, scared of being caught. But not exactly remorseful, in the true Christian sense. Fear of consequences and regret are two completely different animals, as any former teenager knows. And once Mr. Starker came out of the bathroom, all meticulously dressed and groomed and full of ideas about room service, I was right back in the Bella-Free Zone where I'd been the night before. We ate omelets; he checked his work messages while I read about the mayor's plan to sanitize hot-dog carts; he knotted his tie and asked if I might like to join him for a non-club dinner sometime. And I said yes. Now tell me, before you judge too harshly: what single, roommate-less, ramen-noodle-eating heterosexual girl would have said otherwise?

Dear Guilty,

As you know, it is my professional obligation to slap the back of your hand with a ruler. Repeat after me: cheating is wrong, because it betrays the trust of someone I care about. Fifty times, please. Now, on to damage control.

Obviously, there are transgressions you have to admit to, in order to clear your conscience and make things right again. If you think there's so much as a 0.00001% chance of this ever happening again with your boyfriend's best friend, or with any other guy who happens to be in town next time your boyfriend takes off with his six-string, then you've got to confess. That's because what you're realizing is that you're not entirely sure about your relationship, and you might want to date around. In that case, let your boyfriend know about the slipup, explain how much you regret it and how much you care for him, and start negotiating a more realistic policy that might include seeing other people.

But. If you can swear on a stack of *GirlTalks* that your lips will never, ever touch anyone else's while you're dating your boyfriend, I say forget this whole thing ever happened, make sure Side Dish forgets it happened, too, and bury the hatchet before your boyfriend gets hold of it and uses it to scalp the both of you. In a one-time-only situation, what your boyfriend doesn't know is less likely to hurt your relationship than what he could find out. If you're sure you're still in love with him, why torture him with graphic details of your big mess-up? Some secrets—the ones you regret ever having happened, the ones you learn *not* to repeat—are better kept to yourself. Not because you'll save yourself the punishment, but because you'll save the person you love the pain.

Trust me. I've lived through it.

Annie

Chapter Four

On Saturday mornings, every other weekend, Bella, Grace, and I have a standing date for manicures at Nails Plus Wax, a Korean operation in Murray Hill. This sounds more froufrou than it is, there are no terrycloth robes or slippers involved, no complimentary baskets of organic fruit. Actually, at twelve bucks it's cheaper to get a manicure in New York than it is to see a movie or have brunch, and while I've always been uncomfortable in proper spas (Bella has given me a few gift certificates, over the years), there's something relaxing about having your hands groomed by a business-like non-English speaker, no pressure to make conversation or feign interest in advice on top-coat brands. Usually these meetings are a high point of my week; they have the comforting patina of ritual about them. Grace brings coffee, I bring a sack of Swedish fish from the penny-candy shop on my block, Bella brings her own supply of steril-ized emory boards and cuticle sticks from home. Then we spend an hour playing *Steel Magnolias* beauty shop, giving ourselves brief license to be the kinds of people who care about nail polish colors and fashion magazines, those covert pleasures of Ivy League girls.

Of course this week there was something creepy and grotesque in the air, an understatement in some ways, not in others. No one had died, for example, or been attacked or stolen from; nothing truly tragic on the Euripidean scale had gone down. But is there anything worse to do to a friend than to sleep with her father? I tried to think about this, walking the blocks to Murray Hill slowly and breathing in the soft July air, but mine was such a gigantic betrayal that its scope somehow defied my powers of concentration, the way you can try to force yourself to imagine death but your mind, in its kindly self-protective way, will always come back to something less existentially terrifying. Though invoking the existentialists is not quite accurate here, since they were the ones all hopped up on taking responsibility for your actions, precisely what I could not yet manage to do.

What it came down to was that I arrived early outside of Nails Plus Wax with no real strategy fleshed out, just a weak-minded hope that I could preserve my secret from Bella and that whatever words I needed would come to me on the spot. No part of me was afraid of being caught out or accused, since she would have no reason to suspect anything untoward had happened: in the first place she hardly ever saw her dad, and in the second place all those years of therapy had convinced her that his unreliability was grounded in something more complicated than truth. Still, I hoped Grace would hurry up and show before Bella did, so that I could unburden myself of the story and get some advice. Grace is good for advice. She has a clear-eyed, forgiving sense of right and wrong, and she can guide you out of a bad spot without ever making you feel judged. And sure enough, she came around the block just when I was praying for her, only she came around the block with Jake, and with bedhead, and with four cups of coffee instead of three. There is nothing like love to rob you of a best friend. And in that instant I decided I would never tell Grace what had happened between me and Mr. Starker—not that morning, not ever.

"Fancy meeting you here," I said to Jake, who was swinging Grace's hand back and forth like they were in a Gene Kelly movie. "Will you be wanting a manicure or a pedicure this morning?"

"Just dropping the little lady off," Jake said, checking out the storefront, which was considerably scruffier than we'd made it out to be when reporting on our salon dates to the guys. "'Nails Plus ax.' Are you two sure they pass routine hygiene inspections in there?"

"It's less of a health risk than your apartment," I said, taking the cup of coffee marked "R" (milk, no sugar) off of Grace's tray.

"I was just telling Jake about my new billion-dollar idea. It came to me this morning. We're going to retire early off this one, Rose. Ready? Beauty spas, in *hospitals*. Think of all the pregnant women who go into labor needing a bikini wax. And it's not like someone who's nine months pregnant could paint her own toenails, even if she wanted to. We're talking about a target audience of people with nothing but time on their hands, time and a genuine need to be cleaned up."

"Sounds European," I said. "Like how the pharmacists in France are trained to do makeup consultations and prescribe medication for yeast infections."

"This is a put-on," Jake said. "As soon as I leave you guys are going to start talking about recycling or Flemish landscape painting or something, right?"

"Aromatherapy." I took a sip of my coffee. "Single-process highlights. To trim, or not to trim, the cuticles."

"What language did she just start speaking?"

"This stuff is supposed to make you puke, Chairman Mao. You have a very strong record on hating the consumerist trappings of contemporary urban life. You can date my best friend but don't go soft on the rest of us."

Jake smiled down at Grace. He looked like he might be in danger of cooing. "Don't worry, I'm going home. Cam and I have a soccer game at noon."

Which was lucky for him, because at that moment Bella was rounding the corner and propping her sunglasses on top of her head, and scowling. "Ew gross, what are you doing here? This is invitation only."

"I'm not here, don't worry." He kissed Grace on the cheek and took his cup of coffee from the tray. "I'm gone."

Inside we picked colors and waited for three adjacent stations to open up. Bella had news; she'd met a good-looking fashion assistant named Jean-Marie who in spite of all odds wasn't gay, just French. Bella has a long history of dating foreign guys with names of indeterminate gender. She seemed happy—excited, even—as she described the date they'd gone on the night before, at a wine tasting downtown.

"He was a snob about the California vineyards, but you expect that from someone who's French. It's really the only thing they have to feel good about these days, after that monster with the eye patch got so many votes. Anyway, I wouldn't say Jean-Marie's brilliant, not book-brilliant at least. But I saw some of his designs and I think he could do costume work, he's really got an eye. That's its own kind of intelligence, a feeling for the visual world."

"You saw his designs?" Grace asked. "Like, come up to my place and I'll show you my designs?"

"I'm going to introduce him to Evan. It's a problem, how Evan never thinks about sets or costumes until the last day of tech. A play is more than a bunch of words, it's a picture, a tableau, there has to be a reason to *watch* it otherwise we would just listen to it, it would be a book on tape. We need a designer. It seems to me that if you're going to enter a festival with one hundred different acting companies, and if the whole purpose of entering said festival is to get your company seen by the producers and reviewers who are there scouting for fresh ideas, you need to get noticed any way you can, including visually. What's the point of doing all this work on the script and then going into the festival six weeks from now wearing surgical scrubs? Who's going to remember that?"

Bella was right: Evan worked fiendishly hard, so hard he must not sleep at night, and always with a kind of sweaty immigrant vengeance. But he favored the cerebral part of directing over the aesthetic part of it, another way of saying he trusted his brain more than his taste. I understand; it's an insecurity you're born with when you come from the places he and I come from. You can read every book in the public library but that doesn't mean you'll ever have an innate understanding of the difference between wall-to-wall carpeting and area rugs, or pure cotton bedding and polyester fill. Evan and I are alike in this way, not that we ever talk about it.

"I know he thinks it's trivial, worrying about the way the stage looks. We've disagreed about it for six years now. The only time he's ever pretended to listen to my point of view was when Constantine agreed with me, and that lasted until Constantine left the room."

Constantine was Evan's sometimes-boyfriend, a contract lawyer at one of the big firms in the city, Shaddock-and-somebody-or-other. He was imperious and fussy, the kind of guy who pronounced foreign words with an extravagant accent, *Rome-aah* and *fa-hii-ta* and *ccchhhroissant*. None of us liked him very much, but it was so amazing to see Evan cowed by anybody that sometimes Constantine was worth having around, just to prick a hole in the Evan-cum-World's-Leading-Expert show. Not that Constantine bothered spending a lot of his non-billable hours hanging out with us.

"Anyway," Bella went on, "I'm starting to think I might go ahead and hire someone. Costumes aren't just gift-wrapping. Or maybe they are. But gift-wrap is important, damn it. You guys are actors; you should understand that better than anyone else." She eyed the bottle of nail polish sitting in my lap; it was dark and vampy. "Jesus, Rose, that looks like dried blood. It's seventy-five degrees out there. Lighten up."

Here, then, was a microscopic index of the ways things were changing, had already changed, between Bella and me. Last week her scolding would have made me want to drag her out onto the sidewalk and kick her. This week it rolled right off my back.

It goes without saying that New York apartments are small, that New York rents are exorbitant, and that New Yorkers are extremely pleased with themselves for being tough enough to survive these adverse conditions. My apartment is the approximate size of a Winnebago, or, as I prefer to think of it, a rich woman's walk-in closet. All one room, windows (three) facing south onto Eleventh Street and west onto a brick wall, hardwood floors, fire-hazard wiring, functional kitchen. Or functional for my purposes, i.e., room for the toaster oven and microwave. My favorite detail is the dumbwaiter in the coat closet, a relic of the building's single-family days. Sometimes I imagine lowering my back issues of *Vanity Fair* to the nice Pakistani couple living downstairs.

I keep the place neat, since I don't mind cleaning and since dust bunnies start to feel like roommates in a space this small. My design scheme, insofar as I can pretend to have one, is sort of nest-in-the-treetops meets American Superstore, meaning I've crammed a lot of possessions into one tiny apartment with the well-concealed help of stackable plastic storage units. I inherited most of my furniture from my grandparents, who cast off their red velvet living room set in favor of rattan when they retired to central Florida. The couch and armchairs alone take up more than half the room, which feels cozy in winter, if Dickensian, and unbearably hot in summer, when my pre-industrial air conditioning unit pipes in soot from the service alley. I was reading *Ah! Wilderness* in one of these armchairs on Sunday morning, trying to keep my exposed flesh as far as possible from the sun-broiled upholstery, when the phone rang. It was Evan, calling to tell me his news.

"Hi, Rose. News. Hold on a second."

An instrumental medley of hits from the Manny Flax directorial oeuvre pumped into my right ear. Evan was calling from the office. On Sunday morning. His work ethic exhausted me.

"Okay, I'm back. I've got my playwright."

It took me a second to figure out what he was talking about. He hadn't mentioned Manny's project since Fort Sassquam.

"He's this young up-and-coming Irish guy named Declan Pearse. Wait until you read the play. It's brilliant. Manny's in love. He's ready to emigrate, or convert or something. He's building a goddamn float for the Saint Patrick's Day Parade."

"How young is young?" I asked, thinking of that pit bull in a jean tuxedo from the Millennium Club.

"Our age, maybe few years older. You've got to read this script and tell me what you think, Rosalie. It's going to knock your socks off. I want you to meet him. We're having drinks next week. I think you should come."

Talking to Evan was like taking orders from your mother. Wear the pink dress. Pull your hair back. Tie your shoelaces. Don't chew gum. "Tell me what night," I said, suddenly way too tired for someone who'd waked up at eleven a.m. "I'll be there if I can."

I mentioned earlier that I spent a difficult year living on my own in Ireland, and now might be a good time to say a few more words about my bitter experience there, and my subsequent feelings towards that country. I had written my college thesis on the role of the outsider in the plays of John Millington Synge; having received some flattering attention for it, and having no idea what else to do with myself after graduation, I applied for a fellowship to move to Dublin for a year to continue my research at the Synge collection in Trinity College. All I knew of Dublin came from U2 videos and movies like *The Commitments,* in which the city seemed to combine small-town charm with a young urban scene more happening than the well-trodden circuits of Paris and London. Not that I'd ever been to Paris or London.

Disaster ensued. Almost as soon as I unpacked my bags into the grimy apartment I'd rented near the college gates, I realized my mistake: I hated spending lonely, isolating days in the third-rate stacks of Trinity Library; I hated the formulaic, folksy plays of J. M. Synge; I hated the weather, the bone-chilling rain that fell simultaneously from so many directions it made carrying an umbrella futile; I hated the food, that every meal had to contain pastry dough, butter, and discolored meat; I hated the pubs, how you had to bring your own supply of toilet paper and a night out wasn't a night out until one of your "mates" threw up on the street. I could go on with the list, but I won't. Categorical antipathy makes people uncomfortable, especially when it's directed against a historically oppressed nation.

What I will say is this: my misery that year might have had as much to do with me as with the town where I lived. I was homesick, I was lonely, and I wasn't cut out for the scholarly life. I might have been equally depressed in Madrid, say, or Prague. (Although I doubt it, since I've heard most residents of those cities have full sets of teeth in their heads and don't consider fiddle-and-flute jam sessions their ideal Saturday night out.) Anyway, the bottom line is that I was unhappy, unhappier than I'd ever been, and since emotions have a way of binding themselves to places, I've never overcome my aversion to Celtic jewelry, to Enya, to *Riverdance.* Even now, I avoid all bars with shamrocks on their signs and stick to earthy neutrals on March 17. The mere smell of a pint of Guinness can send me fleeing in search of Prozac. So when Evan gave me a copy of Declan Pearse's play, *Last Winter in Dame Street,* I stuck it in my in-box at work, somewhere beneath the press passes to Andrew Dice Clay's come-back vehicle. Dame Street is a few blocks from where I lived in Dublin. I needed to read about it almost as badly as I needed to go on a diet of black pudding.

On the appointed night for drinks, Wednesday (still no follow-up call from BS, for those keeping score at home), I dressed nicely, made an effort with my clothes and my hair to compensate for my lack of effort on dramaturgical fronts, and slipped the play into my pink patent-leather bag. On the train downtown, crammed between a pregnant woman and a yo-yo peddler on break, I glanced at the opening pages of the script. The terse bits of dialogue were promising, in the clipped style of Harold Pinter but with remarkable poetry, too. I'll admit that part of me, the ugly, selfish, childish part, was hoping for some-thing mediocre or dismissible, so that Evan's directorial debut wouldn't be a guaranteed home run out of the starting gate, if I may mix my sports metaphors. But I could tell immediately that he had something serious on his hands. This script he'd found seemed like the real deal.

At the bar I took a seat in the back and kept reading. The plot, from what I could tell, hinged on a self-exiled Irishman's return to Dublin, with his young American lover in tow. The main char-acter, Paul, had walked out on his wife and left his staid middle-class life in Dublin for Boston, where he'd reinvented himself and taken up with a twenty-something American kid named Gregory, whom he was bringing home to Ireland for the first time. There were some great parts to be had, Paul and Gregory, of course, and also Paul's aging mother and his chilly ex-wife, whose forgiveness he spends much of the play trying to earn. This guy, this Declan Pearse, was a poet in playwright's clothing. By the end of the first act he'd actually written scenes about love, about the pull of home and the claustrophobia of home, things people my age only dare to speak of ironically or academically or under their breath. I don't think I'll ruin the story I'm telling if I say right now that this play changed a lot for all of us. It changed us professionally; it changed us as a group; it changed me, personally. It's hard to scrape away all of what I know now to remember what I felt then, looking at those pages for the first time in that noisy, dimly lit, overpriced bar. I think it was a dead heat between awe and fear. Awe, that someone of my tender young age was taking his work so seriously, with such mature results. Fear, I imagine, for much the same reason, and for whatever it said about me.

I looked up from the script and saw Evan standing over the table holding two drinks. "Amazing, right?" He set a glass down in front of me and pulled up a chair. "The guy didn't even have an American agent until now. He's been produced in Dublin, but only in tiny, nowhere spaces. This time last year he was working as a bus driver. Can you believe that? A fucking bus driver?"

I could tell this detail impressed Evan a great deal. People like their artistic geniuses to spring forth from unlikely places, such as the Bonanza Terminal at Port Authority. "So where is he?"

Evan signaled with his head towards the men's room. "The jacks."

Before I could punch him for using Irish slang, the bathroom door opened and out came the hulking, balding specimen who'd shot me ten straight minutes of evil eye at the Millennium Club last week: Declan Pearse. He wore the same all-denim ensemble he'd been wearing then, never mind that it was still eighty degrees outside. To describe the way he looked, making his unsmiling way towards our table, I could invoke the standard physical details of height (substantial), build (stocky), coloring (take a wild guess). But truthfully, none of those qualities made as immediate an impression on me as did his expression, that sour disdain I'd been treated to a few days back. At first I took his punishing look to mean he remembered me, but to my relief he sat down and introduced himself without any show of recognition. His voice was low, his accent was thick, and his shirt was sweaty. Shaking his hand was like being swiped by a bear. "Good to meet you, Rosalie," he said, pulling a smashed pack of cigarettes out of his shirt pocket and lighting up.

"It's nice to meet you, too. Welcome to New York."

He nodded and wiped his forehead with a handkerchief.

"Have you been enjoying yourself so far?"

Another mute nod.

"Excellent. That's great."

"Great?"

"That you've been enjoying yourself. So far."

He gave me a hostile look. "I suppose you could call it that."

At the risk of damning myself as a racial essentialist, I'll confess I'd been expecting someone a little friendlier, a little more eager to talk and joke and slap my shoulder with unwarranted familiarity. Misapprehensions, all. After a long silence, long enough to, say, recite pi to the twenty-thousandth place, we three reached for our drinks. Mine looked impossibly pink and syrupy, and I saw Declan Pearse make a note of it. Suddenly I was mad at

Evan for ordering such a sugary drink for me, even though I often drink syrupy pink cocktails.

"Rosalie used to live in Dublin," Evan announced. I glared at him. Glares all around.

"Did you, now?" Declan was still looking at my drink. Maybe he'd never seen an orange slice before, Ireland suffering from a dearth of fresh fruit and vegetables. "Dublin's a grand city for the American kids these days. A McDonald's on every corner."

"That's certainly why I moved there," I said, smiling icily. The Mc-Fish-and-Chips. The McShepherd's Pie. Who was this asshole?

"And what do you do here in New York, do you mind me asking?"

"Do?"

"For work, like. What's your job? Or do you not have one?"

For some reason I didn't want to talk about acting. Not with Evan beaming across the table at his Artiste, not with the Artiste smirking at me and trying to guess my favorite Extra Value Meal; not in that bar, where every third twenty-something was an unemployed actress trying to make her latest ad audition sound impressive. It was such a losing battle, being an aspiring actor. So much scrambling, so much selling, so much self-serving exaggeration. I didn't need to get on the hamster wheel just then. "I write an advice column for teenage girls."

"In a newspaper?" He smiled for the first time. It made him look less menacing, as smiles are wont to do. "Dear Friend, my knickers itch, that kind of thing?"

"More or less."

"Brilliant. You'll have to tell me where it runs, so I can keep a lookout for it." He lit a second cigarette and stamped out his first one on the floor, the whole "ashtray" concept never having gained momentum on the Emerald Isle. "We didn't have those kinds of write-ins, where I grew up. It's God's wonder any of us survived."

I was too polite, or too concerned with behaving well for Evan's sake, to do anything but smile, even though I knew I was being mocked. Being confrontational doesn't come naturally to me; I'm better at stewing silently and holding lifelong grudges. So I sat back in my chair, listened while Evan and Declan stroked each other's egos (so many admirers of the script! so many people interested in the project!), and begged off as soon as I could drain my glass. Neither of them seemed particularly crestfallen when I said I had to leave, but Declan stood up and made an awkwardly formal point of manhandling my arm again, as if someone had once told him that was how to treat a lady, and he was proud of himself for having remembered.

"I want to tell you how much I loved your play," I said, not because I owed him any compliments, but because it was true.

"Did you?" He smiled again. "Well then I should tell you how much I love your purse."

Evan laughed loudly, as if he'd never heard anything remotely so witty. I said goodnight and walked out of the bar.

I have always believed the "artist as social misfit" paradigm to be a foolish one. Artists aren't artists when they're getting potty trained, or learning to dress themselves, or figuring out sandbox etiquette. They're children, just like the rest of us. But if they grow up to compose a symphony or choreograph a ballet, then we suddenly don't mind if they sleep in the bathtub, or carry their pets to dinner. It's eccentric and exotic, often a sign of brilliance, not to be able to function normally in society. Artists can be—*should* be—mean, loud, drunken, unwashed, egomaniacal, abusive, and, ideally, shabbily dressed. In fact, if you admit that you can brew a pot of coffee and match your shirt to your pants, your chances of accomplishing an artistic endeavor of any significant merit decrease by a factor of ten. This is the kind of sophism that excuses someone like Declan Pearse for being so patronizing and rude to a total stranger. Condescending behavior has become a kind of shorthand for profundity, in our culture. The guy wrote a good play. Big fucking deal. He still smelled like an armpit and looked like an egg.

Such were my thoughts as I walked to the subway station, nursing a chocolate milkshake. Bella, as I've mentioned, has been in analysis since she could talk, and she insists that anger has more to do with you than with the ostensible target of your anger. Sounds like a piece of wisdom she could have saved forty thousand dollars on by buying a self-help book, but still worth contemplating. A troubling dichotomy had sprouted in my mind, where "they" (Evan, Declan) were the artists and "we" were the people who could speak in complete sentences at parties. But wasn't I an artist, too? Or didn't I at least want to be one? In Declan Pearse's opinion, I had probably forfeited my membership in the club by committing some inexcusable sin like wearing lipstick, or asking how he liked New York. But why did I give a shit what some stranger thought of me, just because he'd written something decent? And who, exactly, was I mad at?

Like most industries, theater has a kind of internal hierarchy to it, and while actors are the ones who make the magazine covers, playwrights are the true celebrities of the trade, as a good play is rarer than a good performer, and anyway it lasts longer on a library shelf. Too, there is the Utilitarian question of intrinsic worth, for a play is a play whether or not anyone's performing it, and an actor without a play is a like a sailor without a ship, or a dot-commer without a DSL line. So Declan Pearse had written a play, probably based on his journal entries about fleeing the motherland, and now we were all supposed to bow and genuflect before him.

At my apartment door, fumbling with my keys, I heard Evan's voice talking into my answering machine. I wasn't fast enough to catch his call, but as soon as I got inside I played his message back. I turned on the kitchen light and pitched my milkshake cup into the trash can while he rambled on about how grateful he was that I'd joined him, how relieved he was I liked the play, blah blah blah, clearly worried that I felt ill-used. On my way to the bathroom I thought I heard him mention something about Cam; I came back down the hall and pressed rewind. ". . . for Cam, don't you think?" he was saying. I hadn't cued back far enough. "That American-boy part, Gregory, could be perfect for Cam, don't you think?" That was the whole sentence. I stood still for just a moment, then I played the message again.

It's probably some bizarre form of transference that makes me process the major events in my life by way of analogy. But here was how I felt, listening to that message: like an orphan in an orphanage, watching from the infirmary window as my only friend (Cam) got scooped up and belted into the backseat of a friendly, well-dressed young couple's car. Rain streaming down the window pane, kids with whooping cough fading in and out of the background, the whole sappy tableau.

It's always the same order. First I get sad, then I get angry.

Let it never be said that I don't love Cam. Let it never be said that I have anything less than total admiration for his handsome face, his beautiful body, his easy charm, his natural grace. He appeals to audiences, he follows instructions, he looks gorgeous onstage. But he is not the most talented actor among us. Choosing Cam is like choosing cheese pizza, or a black umbrella, or Sonnet #18. Not that Cam had read a lot of Shakespeare lately. Or ever.

See? See what competition does?

Dear Annie,

There is a guy at my school who I'm super into and who likes me back in the same way. So I know what you're thinking is what's the problem and here it is: he has a bad image, like my friends say he dates girls just to get with them and that's it. Personally I really don't get that feeling from him, but there are a lot of stories floating around our school, if you know what I mean. Who am I supposed to trust, my friends or this guy? I think my friends want the best for me, but they also believe A LOT of what they hear.

—Second-Guessing in New Mexico

Dear Second-Guessing,

I'm having a psychic moment here, and I'm feeling very strongly that your friends don't have boyfriends, themselves. In fact, I'm feeling that they are a little bit jealous that you might be on the brink of kissing one of your school's Romance MVPs. Oftentimes, the most delicate boy envy comes wrapped in a big old blanket of concern, caution, and we-just-want-what's-best-for-you. What do you think, am I channeling well today?

Now of course that doesn't mean you should ignore everything you hear. Lots of grapes on the gossip grapevine have a seed of truth to them, so it's a good idea to proceed into this relationship with caution. You might want to go especially easy on the steamy stuff in the beginning, just so you can get a good strong read on this boy's intentions before you get in too deep. If he's just after you for your kissibility, he'll only stick around for so long. But if he puts in the hard time during study groups, family dinners, and important home field hockey matches, I say he deserves a kiss or three.

The important thing to remember in all this is one of our fundamental tenets of American jurisprudence: the accused is innocent until proven guilty. Giving this guy a shot is only respecting his rights. And honestly, if everyone I knew believed every tiny little thing they'd heard about me over the years, I'd be spending my Saturday nights at home alone, rearranging my miniature teapot collection. If you trust yourself to keep your eyes open and take it slow, why not give a guy chance?

Trust me. I've lived through it.

Annie

Chapter Five

While I stewed silently over the developments with *Last Winter in Dame Street*, the rest of the troops fared well. Cam was around, the way Cam is forever around, diddling away whole days on his computer, watching baseball, killing time in that mysterious guy way that probably has more to do with masturbation than any of us want to know. Either Evan hadn't approached him yet about auditioning for *Dame Street*, or Cam was keeping quiet, which was not usually his way. So far, at least, nothing seemed to be different: when I called him he was happy to go to a movie, or meet up for a burger and a beer. When I didn't call him that was fine, too. Cam is rather dog-like, in some respects, and I don't mean that as derogatorily as it sounds, dogs being renowned for their loyalty, companionship, etc. What I mean is that he comes when you call him, but he's equally happy to lie around and watch the world go by. A nap here, a bowl of kibble there, maybe some digging. The essential things in life.

Bella, mercifully, was caught in the grips of her new romance with Jean-Marie. At first I had assumed that I was the one avoiding one-on-one encounters with her, and that our recent lack of contact had to do with my guilt over sleeping with her father. But after a while I realized Bella wasn't exactly tying up my phone line twenty-four hours a day, either. She, like Grace, was busy falling in love, or at least busy having sex and getting taken out to dinner. She had commitments, distractions, people with accents in their names to meet.

Which brings us back to me, and a chicken-and-egg question for the psychologists: did I get involved with Berglan Starker because my friends were so busy and wrapped up in their own lives that I felt abandoned/cut loose/left out? Or, alternatively, did I use my friends' absence as a convenient excuse for starting an affair beneath their noses, knowing full well they were too preoccupied to catch on? Either way, or both ways, Grace had her Jake, Jake had his Grace, Evan had his playwright, Bella had her Frenchman, Cam had his audition and his ESPN, and I (as of Friday afternoon) had a huge bouquet of orange Gerbera daisies from Berglan Starker, with a note attached thanking me for the lovely night and informing me of his West Coast whereabouts since I'd seen him last.

Flowers. I never buy them for my apartment. They're twelve dollars per week I might be able to afford for sheer functionless beauty if I lived in some other city, or had some other job. But let me say this: my living room sure looks good with something blooming in it. I put them in a vase on the windowsill, right next to the American eagle hand cooler. The orange of the daisies even complimented the red velvet furniture, in a loud, Moulin Rouge kind of way.

Sometimes I wonder what would have happened if Mr. Starker had sent a mindless batch of roses, or something obnoxiously lavish like a diamond tennis bracelet. Might it have been easier to wake up to what he and I had done together and walk away from the whole affair? As it stood, the daisies had just enough quirky originality for me to believe he actually chose them with me in mind. Of course now I know that men like Berglan Starker don't specify flower preferences. They don't even tell their secretaries which florists to call. But then, I felt flattered beyond reason, so that when Mr. Starker left me a message saying he'd be staying at the Pierre on Saturday night, and in the mood to buy an attractive young advice columnist a drink, I knew I would go to meet him. I even entertained the idea of wearing a garter belt, or no underwear at all. If you're going to have an illicit affair, you might as well do it right. *GirlTalk* doesn't pay me the big bucks for nothing.

I had suggested meeting Mr. Starker at a bar around the corner from the hotel, mainly because I liked the brazen, Girl Friday forwardness of knowing just the right little smoky spot, even though I had to look through Zagat to find one. When I arrived he was already seated in a banquette, sipping something predictably single-maltish; I ordered a vodka martini.

"So," Mr. Starker said once my drink arrived, "cheers."

This was another one of these weird ceremonial moments of his that made me squirm in my seat; me thinking yeah, obviously, cheers, but do we have to be so stiff about it? "What were you up to in San Francisco, or is it classified?"

"My company has some business in Oakland; we've committed to doing neighborhood revitalization in parts of downtown and I was there looking into sites and zoning regulations. It was a very productive trip, I think."

"I've never been to California. Do they, I mean, are their neighborhoods in trouble?" This sounded idiotic, of course, but I had always understood the Bay Area to be a prosperous place, full of Gortex-clad computer types who spent their weekends volunteering for the Parks Department, and so it surprised me to learn there were any slums left there at all.

"Oakland is an interesting case: it has a few remaining swatches of economic depression, and the idea is to make these parts of the city more habitable without gentrifying them completely, so that they become unaffordable to the people who live there now. You might think of it as the opposite of white flight: there's a great demand for real estate within the city proper, but we don't want to squeeze out all the original occupants. We've done work like this in other places, New Orleans, for example, Savannah. It can be a real boon for everyone involved, from the developers right on down."

My understanding of such matters is that what's a boon for the developers is often not such a boon for the people whose houses are being razed, but I hadn't come uptown to rabble-rouse. "I guess that means you're on the road a lot?"

He nodded. "But a bit of jet lag is hardly a sacrifice if you enjoy the work you're doing. And there's something to be said for wandering, too. I'm not really one for the office, growing roots underneath the institutional carpeting and that sort of thing. Luckily that's not a risk you'll ever run, as an actor."

"Oh, I have an institutional carpet, too. Mine just happens to be pink."

"Which reminds me that I saw your column in the airport the

other day. I got quite a look from the girl behind the counter for reading it, but it was terrific stuff, somebody wanting to win her old love back, or get rid of him, and you were right on the spot about it. Must be a hell of a thing, to have all those kids depending on you."

"Yes and no. They wouldn't depend on me if I were perfect, I take comfort in that. Also they don't know my name or street address."

"But still, that it should be only your sideline is what strikes me. You must be a busy young woman, having so many strings to your bow."

"Things fall by the wayside. I can't cook. I'm horribly unathletic and disastrous at all crafts."

He gave me the foreigner-eating-without-hands look again, the same one he'd given me that first day in his office. "Crafts? Such as?"

"Such as, I don't know, Home Economics. Embroidery. Stenciling. That stuff is really popular in my hometown."

"How Moorish." He shook the ice cubes in his otherwise empty glass and looked at mine, which was still half full. "Look, do you anticipate finishing that? Because I'd very much like to take you around the corner, whenever you're through."

Strange to say, but what I thought of in that moment was Cam, and Jake, and my ex-boyfriend Charles Buffernaut, none of whom would ever even think of trying out a line like that one. Might they grow into such weird courtliness, thirty years from now? Or was I, like Margaret Mead before me, trolling around in a dying culture, in this case one of chivalrous fat-wallet philandering? Only time will tell, I suppose. I ate my olives and took a last wincey gulp of my drink, and then we were off like bats into the still-hot night.

About our second night together, there is the truism of all times being better than the first. For starters I was less nervous, not only about my body but about his, and whatever liver-spotted deficiencies of age I might have to contend with (none). Also I had worn the right underwear, had in fact *bought* the right underwear for the occasion, a filmy little nude-colored one-piece thing, with snaps. BS retained some of his strange formal flourishes, undressing me slowly and looking me in the eye the whole time, asking how I liked whatever he was doing even as he did it. But this time I caught on and understood that he wasn't looking for an answer like "more pressure, a little to the left," so much as a nice affirming moan, with some corroborative biting of the bottom lip. Actually, his appetites were rather racier than I would have guessed from seeing his picture in, say, a *Forbes* profile, but then I guess a married man doesn't pick up a twenty-six-year-old for a cozy night of spooning under the flannels. And anyway, it wasn't so much the positions that surprised me; I had been taken from behind before, and also pressed up against a wall before (though never at the same time, and never with such a God's-eye view of Central Park, those windows are incredible!). No, what surprised me was how bracing a full night of lovemaking can be, how much more satisfying it is to feel invigorated and charged by sex, rather than spent and noodle-sleepy at the end of it. Maybe it's only experience that can teach a man that. Younger guys, the

Charles Buffernauts of the world, are so afraid of making passes they waste hours in bars drinking beer after beer to work up their courage, so that by the time you finally get back to their apartments they're bloated and snoozy and ready to pass out. Not so with BS. He was alert and focused on my raptures into the small hours of morning, and even if part of that had to do with jet lag, it still impressed the hell out of me.

I am thinking now of Venus in Furs, the shiny, shiny, shiny boots of leather Lou Reed sings about on the Velvet Underground album with the banana on the cover. Everyone knows that sex and theater are related: even our tamest encounters of the flesh deal on some level in props, costumes, roles. But the stripping away of clothing is not the same thing as the true stripping away of masks, however tempting that metaphor may be. As an actor, as a professional advice-giver, you'd think I'd have an easy time remembering this. But here is what I learned from my second stay in the climate-controlled splendor of the Pierre penthouse suite: unless you're vigilant, nakedness and intimacy can be damn hard to separate. And once someone has turned your body into hot molasses, look out.

Festival rehearsals that week were individual: Evan had scheduled us for one-on-one scene work, a final luxury of the home stretch before tech, when all of his attention would shift to light cues and glow tape and interlude music for the transitions between scenes. My particular assignment for those last substantive days was supposed to be "inhabiting stillness," one of the more elusive challenges of my scene. Frankly I would have preferred fencing practice or jitterbug lessons—in my opinion the implied promise of theater is a bit of spectacle, and watching someone sit and stew in a rocking chair isn't the kind of fare people show up to see. But Evan has other ideas about plays, loftier and more meta-theatrical than mine, and ultimately the director's interpretation is the one the actor submits to, the way a model submits to being dressed in whatever piece of frippery a designer wants her to wear. There is the sense in which actors are vessels for other people's words and other people's visions. I can imagine that getting tiresome someday, but for now it's a relief not to have to have a vision of my own.

"You need to commit here, Rose." This from Evan, after I'd spent forty-five silent minutes in a folding chair staring at the wall, his idea. "You still haven't really imagined what it would mean to spend month after month confined to the house. It's not a glamorous situation we're in. This woman never sees anyone except for her two sons, she hasn't even gotten dressed or gone outside in how long?"

"I don't know," I said, trying to remember from the script, also trying to wake up my right leg, which had been asleep for half an hour. "A year, maybe?"

Evan looked at me as if I'd spit at him. "What do you mean, *maybe*? Haven't we been working on this scene for a month and a half? This is information you need to know about your character; make it up if you have to, I don't care. There's a pretty big difference between someone who left the house yesterday and someone who hasn't gone out in five years, wouldn't you say? Can we pin this down, please?"

"A year," I said, this time without the question mark. "I haven't gone out in a year."

"Well you sure look bouncy, for someone who's been indoors that long." This with a kind of suspicious, jealous sneer to it, as if he could tell I had a secret reason to be happy, and I wasn't going to give it up.

A weird event in the drugstore, Sunday afternoon, where I am picking up refills of my prescription astringent, horrible still to get zits at my age. Walking towards the pharmacy counter I see the back of a big, balding giant of a man in jeans and a jean jacket, talking to the pharmacist. And I duck into the deodorant aisle to avoid him! Then I put on my sunglasses and hotfoot it out of the drugstore altogether, to wait by a news kiosk across the street. Three minutes later the guy emerges: he is older, wearing glasses, carrying a little girl in a turquoise bathing suit on his hip. How odd, that I could have mistaken him for Declan Pearse. How much odder, that I took off in the first place without even pausing to think about it. There is that spooky, animal moment when your body sends a signal before your brain catches up to it, think of pulling back from a boiling pot before you've even felt heat on your fingertips. Why did I bolt?

I didn't bother going back to the drugstore. I picked out a pack of Junior Mints from the kiosk to thank the guy for letting me hang out there, and when I handed him a dollar he waved it away. He gave them to me for free.

. . .

A couple of days later Bella called. She and Grace were going out for sushi, the only food Bella consented to eat between the months of June and September, and they wanted to know if I would join them for dinner. We'd all been so insanely busy with rehearsals, Bella said, it was like we'd forgotten to be friends, too. A line like that could pierce a stake through even an innocent heart. I had to go.

At the restaurant, waiting in line for a garden table, we covered our requisite pre-show topics: Grace's despotic boss at her temp job; the course of Bella's electrolysis; my plans, perennially on hold, to get a pet of some kind. (I don't really want a pet. I don't even like animals that much. But I like the pretend-feeling of chewing over a long-term decision like that, thinking in terms of years and decades rather than days and weeks.) As soon as we got seated and placed our orders, the subject shifted to men, as it always does. Jean-Marie's Svengali-like interest in Bella's wardrobe; Jake's principled frugality that bordered on stinginess. I try not to get on my Girls vs. Boys high horse too often, but I must say that I doubt men spend even a fraction of the air time obsessing over us that we spend obsessing over them. There we were, three intelligent, well-educated, newspaper-reading women, out for an evening of conversation, stuck on the medieval topic of male possessiveness, how much of it is healthy for a relation-ship(!!). Could we not grant two minutes of our attention to the human rights crisis in Colombia, or the economic repercussions of sanctions against Cuba?

"So here's something," Bella said, pouring me a full glass of sake, which I hate. "A couple days ago at dinner I met this PR guy who Jean-Marie works with. I noticed him at first because he had that crooked smile you always go for, Rosalie, the whole nerdy-sloppy-Jewishy look. His name is J.P. He had us laughing so hard about echinacea and all that homeopathic crap you're always ranting about, I almost called you out of bed to come meet him."

Nerdy-sloppy-Jewishy may be Bella's distillation of my type, but it is certainly not mine, never mind the implausibility of someone named J.P. turning out to be Jewish. "Sounds like a fun night," I said, unwrapping my chopsticks.

"I think you guys might really like each other."

Current circumstances aside, I've never been one for getting set up: even in my loneliest, most celibate months, blind dates smack of a singles desperation I'm not willing to concede. Anyway my plan for dinner was to deflect all topics having to do with me and the opposite sex, so as to avoid telling any out-and-out lies. "Maybe we'll meet sometime."

"I think I could arrange that."

Case closed, painlessly enough. Except that Bella and Grace were smiling at me with their best charity-workers-on-a-home-visit smiles. And suddenly I understood that they had *talked* about me, about why I'd been boyfriendless for the past few months and what they could do to rectify that tragedy. I'd become their cause, the lucky recipient of their compassionate aid. Only I didn't want their help, for reasons I could never explain. And even if Berglan Starker hadn't been in the picture, I still wouldn't have wanted it, not from them, not from anybody.

I know pride is one of the seven deadly sins. But unlike gluttony or, say, sloth, pride has some redeeming qualities that get short shrift in the black-and-white schema of Christian morals. For example, I take *pride* in my acting, and in my pursuit of a theatrical career. I take *pride* in my ability to support myself without financial help from my parents (except for my renter's insurance, which is on their policy). I take *pride* in being a fundamentally sane person, able to control and manage my own friendships, work relationships, and romantic involvements. Must all of these things necessarily goeth before a fall?

"You know, I'm not sure I'm in the market for getting set up at this specific second. We've all got so much on our plates, with the festival coming up and everything. I can barely bring myself to brush my teeth before bed, I'm so tired after rehearsals."

"God, you're a bad liar," Bella said.

Liar? My stomach froze. I looked at Grace. She looked at her dish of soy sauce.

Bella went on: "Cam told Jake you guys made it on the kitchen floor right after we got home from the Fort, and Jake told us. You've got to find a better way to rebound, Rosalie. We know you miss the Buffernaut, but there are a plenty of people out there you might even like, if you started paying attention and letting us help you."

"I don't miss him, actually. I hardly find myself thinking about him at all."

"Well that's even more alarming. Please say you're not saving yourself for Cam, or something insane like that. You two are going to stunt your emotional development if you keep carrying on like a couple of eighteen-year-olds."

"Don't worry about me, Bella. That night was nothing, it was stupid."

"Then why didn't you tell us? Keeping it a secret just makes it a bigger deal."

Grace looked up from her plate. "We aren't exactly her confessors, Bella. She's not required to bring every blow job before the grand council. If she doesn't want to tell us something, she doesn't have to tell us."

Bella measured this assessment and shrugged, moved on to the subject of her brother's new girlfriend. I tried to catch Grace's eye to mouth the words thank you, but she wouldn't look at me for the rest of the meal.

On the walk home, after we put Bella in a cab, Grace filled up the silence with nothing stuff, a Spanish class she was thinking of taking at City College if she could find the time. I knew she was upset with me for not telling her about Cam, and I could tell from the cool tenor of her small talk that she was embarrassed, herself, about being upset. Grace and I have always told each other everything; that's the way our friendship began freshman year, and the rules and habits established by our eighteen-year-old selves have cemented over time, making omissions into betrayals, or worse, rejections. There is a way in which all relationships lock into place at whatever age they're formed, which is why people who marry their high-school sweethearts are such a mystery to me, braces and asymmetrical haircuts being a phase of my own life best forgotten. Anyway this was our struggle, Grace and mine: trying to carve out the thumbnail's worth of privacy and distance appropriate for two people who no longer shared a bunk bed in a college dorm. We were working on it, and not always getting it right.

"Grace," I said, as we walked in and out of the pools of neon glowing from the bars on Fourteenth Street, "I'm sorry I didn't tell you about the Cam thing. I wanted to, but I haven't seen you for a while just us, and calling seemed dumb. It wasn't ever a big deal."

"You don't have to apologize." Grace's cheerfulness can be frigid. "Your and Cam's business doesn't have anything to do with me."

"Okay, but I mean I'd also like to hear more about how you are. Not just Spanish class or work, but you know, you, you and Jake."

She laughed, a cold little laugh that went right through me and made me feel stupid for having asked. "Me and Jake? Oh, we're still campaigning for that Least Likely Couple of the Century Award, I guess."

Had I said that? Surely not to her face, but that's the problem with groups, your whole life becomes a giant game of Operator, you can't hold on to anything for longer than it takes to whisper it in someone else's ear. "That was dumb of me, I'm sorry. I hope you know I don't really believe that."

"Don't worry about it. I can take a joke."

I wanted to tell Grace about Berglan Starker, I wanted her to sort out the mess I'd made and put everything back together for me, but it was impossible to start. She seemed so aloof already, catching me in a lie about Cam, catching me in a stupid bit of nastiness about her relationship with Jake. I was the one who looked like the eighteen-year-old. I couldn't bring myself to give her any more reasons not to like me.

"Do you want to have lunch this week?"

"Maybe," Grace said. "I have a project at work they need me

to finish, and since I can't stay late because of rehearsals I may have to work through lunch. But let's try for it."

"Well aside from work and rehearsal I have nothing planned," I said, which felt true in every sense of the phrase. "So give a call if you have the time. If you want."

The next time I met Berglan Starker at the Pierre was a week later, and though it was only our third assignation, it had the definite feel of a habit falling into place. He called; we met for a drink; we made love; I ordered room service, a hamburger platter with a side of turnip fries. I had, I suppose, the morally convenient feeling of being pulled along by forces I wasn't exactly in control of; I simply got the call and showed up where I was supposed to show up. Not that BS was bossy, he was just used to making plans and having people accommodate them. For example the time he'd carted me off to the Hoyt-Purvis Gallery in the middle of my workday, which I eventually asked him about, the ritual rehashing of the first encounter:

"Well you were wet, and I couldn't be expected to let you stand around dripping on my floor all afternoon. Anyhow I don't recall your mounting much of a protest."

"I'm asking about you, buster," I said, my mouth full of fries. "I didn't have much copy to work on that day, or else I wouldn't have gone along. But I bet it never even occurred to you that I had a job."

"Of course it did. Who doesn't have a job? I only thought you might like to see an exhibit before you went back to the office, because you seemed like the sort of girl who could appreciate fine art. If I'd known then I'd wind up answering to the name of buster, I might have thought twice."

"I do appreciate fine art, but I'm not convinced that Canadian friend of yours is so fine."

"You have an awful lot of opinions for a girl your age, don't you?"

"I'm generally known as a one-woman op-ed page. Though to call me a girl is very outmoded, as I suspect you know."

"It's one o'clock in the morning. Wouldn't you like to get into bed, now that you've polished off that platter of fried root vegetables?"

"Turnips are loaded with vitamins. I won't hear anything said against them."

"Come to bed, Miss Preston, girl, woman, whatever you are. Come to bed."

Spending nights with Berglan Starker, I began to see that what we crave in the way of human companionship is whatever we've been deprived of for most of our lives, be it good or bad. Berglan Starker had only known a world that said yes to him, and he appreciated me, I think, for giving him a mildly difficult time. Even princes and kings like to be stood up to by their girlfriends (Scheherazade), for what is being challenged if not a sign that attention has been paid?

For my part, aside from the obvious perks of my association with Berglan Starker (complimentary toiletries, etc.), I can say that our time together gave me a sense of myself as an independent person, in some ways fundamentally different from the private-schoolers in whose pack I ran, and though I had of course lived and breathed this fact all my life, I had always thought of it as something to stamp out of myself and apologize for, as opposed to something that could make me attractive, even compelling, in another person's eyes. I know it sounds retrograde, coming to terms with your inherent worth because a man has chosen you, but I do think that catching Berglan Starker's attention represented something important to me, something I had yearned for since I went off to college and got my first taste of how much bigger and richer the world was than the *Hanson Town Crier* had led me to believe. Is it too much to say that I craved his approval? I suppose that's what's most often said of the girls of the world who get mixed up with presidents, big shots, CEOs. Who am I to claim to be different?

As for the question of human companionship, I myself have not been deprived of much in that way, and grew up with two adoring parents for whose attentions I never had to compete. But how I used to envy the chaotic, massive families of my hometown, whose kitchen doors were forever slamming and whose dinner tables looked like camp messes and whose upstairs hallways were obstacle courses of sneakers and racquets and backpacks. It was always just the three of us Prestons, and three is such a quiet, worrying number. It's not elemental, not like the mother-daughter duos who have only each other and who become entwined in unhealthy, codependent ways, nor is it enough for a gang or a gaggle or a brood or a pack. First Born was the closest thing I'd ever had to a pack of my own. Maybe that's why I had so much invested in its survival, and why I felt so dismal about the things threatening it right then. If you're part of a pack you get a niche: punctual Rosalie; team-sports-hating Rosalie; D-cup Rosalie; Rosalie the early-morning riser. Your identity is perfectly defined in relation to the rest of the group. Take away the rest of the group, and poof, there goes everything you thought you knew about yourself.

On a somewhat different note, tangentially related to my earlier reference to Christian morals, I had been thinking for some time of volunteering my services at the Adele Goldberg Senior Center, a shabby little nursing home in the East Village, halfway between Cam and Jake's apartment and my own. The idea probably got into my head because I walk past the brick building and its neglected dirt courtyard every day, sometimes more than once, and it often strikes me as I pass how confined the lives of the residents must be. On mornings with decent weather, a band of old men in golf caps and jogging suits sit on the peeling benches out front; usually at least one of them will raise his cane and wave to me, or call me by some inoffensive diminutive name, and I always wave or smile back. It's a boost to have even glancing contact with people of experience and perspective so much broader than my own. My job at *GirlTalk* gives me sustained exposure to teenagers; my daily life gives me sustained exposure to young-ish adults; but little, aside from my annual Thanksgiving trip to Sarasota, gives me sustained exposure to retirees, or seniors, or whatever we're calling old people these days. I remember my mother, who is not a woman given to macabre thoughts or fear of the abyss, once saying that aging frightened her chiefly for its power to isolate, to render a person invisible to the rest of the world. She was right, in that people my age don't really tend to *see* old people, we just assume they dislike our body pierces and have done with them. Perhaps it is because I am an actress, someone who wants so badly to be seen, that this invisibility strikes me as a cruelty. Anyway the thought got into my head that I could help.

The question of what exactly I should *do* at/for Adele Goldberg Senior Center was one I hadn't figured out yet, being a mediocre singer and a bad cook and a disaster at cards. But it occurred to me, one day when I passed by on my way to the subway, that I could simply read aloud, an activity the visually impaired residents might appreciate. They could vote on a novel or a biography or a book about history, for example, and I could show up one evening a week and read a chapter out loud. I pictured a loose circle of La-Z-Boys and wheelchairs, me sitting at one end with a well-worn copy of something short and uncontroversial, maybe *Silas Marner,* on my lap, striped shafts of evening light seeping in through the louvered windows. That was a person, that kindly and tender volunteer reader, whom I wanted to be. I mean, I know most nursing homes are dingy, depressing places, but what is literature, if not transportive?

My previous experiences of volunteering had been organized for me by college groups and community service agencies and the like, so I had no idea how to go about making an independent contribution, other than to stride right into Adele Goldberg and pitch the idea myself. It seemed a little iffy—even charity is mass-marketed nowadays—but I worked up the nerve to walk over, one evening on my way home from work. The old ladies take over the benches at that time of night (interesting how social groups revert to gender division, in old age), and they clammed right up when I opened the metal gate and walked into their courtyard. I smiled and hastened towards the door, aware of all the eyes fixed on my back.

Inside, the lobby was as charmlessly utilitarian as I'd imagined it: cinderblock walls, linoleum floors, a Spanish-language game show blaring from a TV in another room. An orderly at the front desk told me the manager's office was closed for the night; she took my contact information and wrote "Regarding: Reading Club" in the subject line of the message. I thanked her, gave her my improbably pink *GirlTalk* business card, and left.

The courtyard was chattier on my way out, and I had just reached the gate when I heard a gravelly voice behind me croak a word that sounded distinctly like "Pierre." I paused with my hand on the latch and waited for the rest of the sentence, but when nothing else followed I turned around to see who had spoken, and whether she had in fact spoken to me. There sat a little black woman in a wheelchair, with a knitted yellow blanket over her knees and a matching yellow scarf wound around her head. I looked at her inquiringly and she looked dead ahead at the street, tapping her foot against the pedal of her wheelchair. Was she blind? Was she listening to a Walkman underneath her turban? I lingered for a second, waiting for her to speak to me, but she didn't. On my way down the block, I swore I heard her say it again.

Pierre: a man's name, French, possibly a reference to a husband, a brother, a son. Also first name of a clothing designer favored in the seventies. Also rhymes with, and therefore might be easily mistaken for, where, pear, hair, etc. Not exactly a common word, but not an obscure one, either.

Tiresias, the Sibyl, Yoda: our cultural references instruct us to see something wizened and prophetic in the aged. Maybe it was that, or maybe it was superstition, or maybe it was my plain old guilty heart, but something inside me made me take off running down that street. Backless mules, pencil skirt, jam-packed shoulder bag. And I didn't stop once until I got home.

Dear Annie,

I just found out that my boyfriend is moving. His dad got a new job far away, and now we'll only see each other on vacations and maybe during summer, if we can even save up for the airfare. We're both heartbroken (plus who wants to live in Arkansas). Do long-distance relationships ever work? College is still three years away, so we won't have a chance to be in the same place forever.

—All Alone in Florida

Dear All Alone,

Weep not. Okay, weep a little, but only if it makes you feel like Catherine in *Wuthering Heights*. The important thing to remember is that you have a wonderful boyfriend, he loves you, you love him, and pretty soon he's going to have one of those adorable Southern accents and say stuff like "How're youu, suugar?"

What I'm saying is that long-distance romance can work. It has its downsides, to be sure, and it can be frustrating at times. But there are lots of secret perks to long distance, too. For example: How many of your friends have a stack of love letters underneath their beds? How many of your friends get to plan big reunion dinners and weekends? And don't forget all the crappy girlfriend duties you get out of, when your boyfriend lives somewhere else: no more babysitting his little sibs, no more pretending to like his mom's tuna casserole, no more nights watching his friends battle over PlayStation. Long distance boils love down to its purest, finest elements: you and your boy. No outside distractions, no taking each other for granted. You might even start to like having your own space.

I'm not trying to say his move is ideal—it's probably safe to assume you'll get a fair bout of the lonelies every now and then, and insecurity can be part of the game, too. That's why it'll be extra important to keep the communication lines up and running: check out good calling plans, sign up for an affordable Internet deal, and never underestimate the power of the care package. It's possible to be in someone else's thoughts all the time, even from far away.

Trust me. I've lived through it.

Annie

Chapter Six

Fact: according to the U.S. Department of Labor, Americans spend roughly one-third of their waking hours on the job. Unlike Europeans, with their cushy lunch breaks and maternity leaves, we can expect to pass a full hour of our adult lives working for every two we get off the clock. Add to the mix the mundane chores of cleaning, grocery shopping, laundry, and the like, and the equation tilts alarmingly towards half and half. One hour for work; one hour for eating, reading the paper, returning phone calls, working out, showering, having sex, catching up with the family, walking the dog. It's enough to make a person emigrate to Norway. Even taking into account those itchy patterned cardigans with the metal buttons.

Luckily for me, I have one of those jobs where it's possible to accomplish a fair amount of non-work-related business at the office. That's because as a whole, the teen magazine industry suffers from a giant insecurity complex, and one of the happy by-products of that condition is an overstuffed masthead, as if bankrolling an enormous staff might convince the snobs at *Newsweek* and the *Economist* that ours is a legitimate, time-consuming, intellectually demanding enterprise. Hence such job titles as "Beauty Consultant, Indoor Sittings" and "Vintage Market Assistant, Accessories."

Any barely competent human could do four of those jobs at once and still have time for Pilates during lunch. But around *GirlTalk,* you won't catch any of us complaining.

Our editor-in-chief, Ginger Kaplan, is a piece of Connecticut work, whose job qualifications, as far as I can tell, are limited to her two nightmarish daughters and their treasure trove of adolescent experiences at private school. The mystery of how Ginger got installed at her post is a favorite subject of speculation among the junior *GirlTalk* staffers; my theory is that it must have had something to do with her bottomless collection of pastel suits, which probably seemed teen-friendly to the incompetent CEO of our parent company. In any case, Ginger has peopled the *GirlTalk* corner offices with her Greenwich Garden Club cronies, which gives our editorial content a certain touch of noblesse oblige. 20 tips for a charming tea party! The best straw hats of the season!

Just beneath Ginger and her lunch partners on the senior staff are a band of resentful, embittered handling editors, all of whom meant to have serious journalistic careers and somehow got waylaid in the fluffiest media niche on earth. I sometimes feel sorry for these women, pitching their hard-edged features on girl sex slaves in Thailand and exploited child laborers in China, while Ginger gets misty-eyed with compassion and then picks an all-prom-dress lineup. It must be frustrating, to be so utterly thwarted at every turn. But then, you have to ask yourself about people who stay in low-paying jobs they loathe. Are they still here because they couldn't get hired at *Ms.*? And if that's the case, why not just throw in the towel and roll with it?

We workhorses of the junior staff understand this principle. To us, *GirlTalk* equals free beauty products, free movie passes, reasonable hours, and the chance to exorcise the trauma of our own high-school years by giving readers the advice we wish we'd had, back then. Of course, this mission is often compromised by a handling editor's need to turn every 400-word piece into an exposé, or by a top editor's mandate to "focus on the positives," since "a pout is never pretty!" Small wonder it's so confusing to be a teenage girl. Even the professionals bicker over how to get through it.

As a monthly, our production schedule is sufficiently accelerated so that we couldn't possibly cover anything newsworthy, even if Ginger got a big enough brain transplant to suddenly give a rat's ass about current events. So it was that I found myself in a Monday morning editorial meeting in early August, drinking iced tea and tossing around ideas for the December issue. Santa's elves cover shoot? Holiday party punches? Expanded wish list and where-to-buy directory? As usual, a bumper crop of possibilities. The great virtue of Annie Answers is that I can distance myself from the inanity of the feature well and do my job with a clear conscience. That's probably what the ad executives at Philip Morris say. We don't make the product, we just draw pictures!

This particular meeting promised something more than the standard Monday fare because the Kaplan daughters were in attendance, a treat that happens on a semiannual basis. Ginger likes to bring her two kids in as consultants every so often, lest we writers and editors forget what the face of teenage America looks like. If we are to take Jenna and Veronique Kaplan as representative samples, the face of teenage America is anorexic, petulant, and partial to expensive black clothing.

"Girls," Ginger said, once we'd finished our scheduled agenda, "why don't you go ahead and explain your idea?"

A general stiffening of shoulders swept the conference table. The unsolicited contributions of the Kaplan daughters are never popular with the staff.

"Okay," said Jenna, the elder one, sitting up straight for the first time since the beginning of the meeting. "So Veronique and I think you guys should start an arts page. You know, where you cover stuff like independent films and jazz musicians and poetry slams and stuff. I mean, isn't it kind of weird that you guys only write about mainstream Hollywood movies and sellout bands, when so many talented young artists are, like, starving in agnomany?"

One of them must have been reading *On the Road* for summer school. The staff nodded with phony enthusiasm.

"I think this is a wonderful idea," Ginger said, beaming. "Very now. I want to start by profiling one new artist every month. We can call the page 'The Next Hot Thing.'"

Jenna rolled her eyes and shook her head tragically. Veronique sucked her bottom lip. "That's so wrong, Mom. It defeats the entire purpose."

For 0.2 seconds I actually felt sorry for Ginger, and swore never to raise my children within a hundred miles of a major urban center.

"Okay, girls, the slug isn't important now. What I need from each of you writers is a list of candidates on my desk by five o'clock this afternoon. I want to get this page under way as quickly as possible. Meeting adjourned."

All around the room, hands gathered diet soda cans and steno pads. Investigative reporting at its finest.

Back in my office, I closed the door and slumped into the purple beanbag across from my desk. The company furnishings at *GirlTalk* suffer from a degrading Romper Room aesthetic, as if dressing up the corporate landscape with the occasional Easter egg-colored accessory might propel us deeper into the hearts and minds of our readers. I doodled stick figures on my notebook with thought bubbles saying "Very *now*" attached to their faceless heads. One pushed a lawnmower. Very now! One swung a golf club. Very, very now. Trying not to think too hard about the intellectual fiber of the place where I work can make me a little wonky.

But really what I was doing was stalling, praying that some name other than Camden Post's would come to me for the Next Hot Thing. In all of my rounds, at all of the B-list star parties I'd been dragged to by Bella, surely I'd met someone who was clean-cut and vaguely artistic enough to nominate for this column. Cam would have been perfect, of course: I could just imagine his heartthrob mug smiling out of our feature well, with some insipid pull quote about following your dreams and believing in yourself. It was too much. He'd already been handed his big break on a silver platter; I didn't need to rush his conversion into an overnight star.

Which is how I wound up submitting Declan Pearse.

And wouldn't you know that Ginger Kaplan, who has summarily disregarded every opinion I've ever voiced on the subject of fashion, of beauty, of trends, of exercise, of where to put the damn page numbers on the damn magazine, chose this particular column to defer to me. If I'd been thinking, I would have seen it coming: I'm the resident bohemian on staff, the weirdo who spends her free time at rehearsals instead of sample sales, and as such, it would make sense to trust my take on which up-and-comer was about to "pop." Unfortunately, what my boss didn't know was that the brilliant young Irish playwright she was so thrilled about profiling was a balding, sour-tempered behemoth who would look about as appropriate in a *GirlTalk* spread as, say, Kim Jong Il. I tried to explain this to her when she summoned me into her office to announce her choice, but she looked insulted, as if I were questioning her commitment to the arts. "He's foreign," she said with finality. "They'll understand if he has bad teeth."

So cut to me, backing out of Ginger's floral showroom of an office, smiling and yessing and promising to "hook my fish," dizzied by an intense tingling in my brain and limbs. How to proceed? I didn't know Declan Pearse's phone number. I didn't even know his agent's name. All I knew was that the guy got a natural high off of making cutting remarks at my expense, and I was about to give him the pithy-comeback opportunity of a lifetime.

Consider, for a moment, the experience of breaking a plate. Scenario one: you have just been promoted at your job, so you come home to share the momentous news of your five-figure raise with your boyfriend, who celebrates your success by whipping up a three-course meal and breaking out his secret reserve case of Veuve Cliquot; at the end of the night, clearing a few things from the table before adjourning to the bedroom for wild sex, you drop a plate on the kitchen floor. Who cares?

Scenario two: it's 94 degrees out and you've spent your whole afternoon on the side of the road under the beating sun, filing a police report against the jerk who bashed the rear passenger-side door of your car and then bolted without giving you any insurance information; you come home starving, but your air conditioner has blown a fuse in your apartment so your refrigerator isn't working and the only non-spoiled thing to eat in the entire house is a can of tuna fish, which you are spooning onto your plate when said plate falls to the ground and smashes into 4,000 pieces and you start to sob harder than you have at any funeral in your life.

It's never about the plate.

Likewise, calling Declan Pearse and asking him if he wanted to be interviewed by *GirlTalk* was not about calling Declan Pearse and asking him if he wanted to be interviewed by *GirlTalk*. It was about our careers, and the fact that he had an adult, creative one and I had a hack, juvenile one; it was about *Last Winter in Dame Street*, and the fact that Evan and Cam were about to abandon First Born because of it; it was about Jake and Grace, who had already abandoned First Born for each other; it was about Berglan Starker, the married father of one of my best friends who was leading me down the garden path to eternal damnation. The bashed-in car, the blown fuse, the tuna fish. I got Declan's phone number from Evan.

"Wha?" a voice said, after I'd waited through five rings and a series of electronic beeps.

"Is this Declan?"

What came next sounded like a bowling ball striking a row of pins. "Who's this?"

"Rosalie." Again, a crash. "Rosalie Preston. Evan's friend. With the purse."

"That's a desperate way to introduce yourself."

Another crash, this time accompanied by the sound of running water.

"Are you . . . building something?" I asked, nearly shrieking to be heard.

"No."

"Listen, I have a strange proposal for you. I'm calling because I wonder if you'd like to be in my magazine."

"*Knickers Are Us?*"

"Right." I closed my eyes and rested my head against the wall next to my desk. Sometimes, rarely, things are exactly as bad as you expect them to be.

"Ehm, do you know where I can get a proper cannoli in this town?"

"Viniero's," I said. "Eleventh and First. I'll take that as a 'no.'"

"Would I take the orange train from Amsterdam Avenue?"

"Take the D to Fourteenth Street and switch to the L, going east."

"I'll walk out the door now, then. Meet me there and I'll buy you a sweet."

If this sounds eerily familiar, my being summoned from my office to meet a virtual stranger for a late-afternoon rendezvous at a random place, don't worry. This one doesn't end up at the Pierre.

. . .

When I walked into the bakery, Declan Pearse was bent over the counter clouding the display glass with his breath. He straightened up and regarded me warily, as if he hadn't just invited me to join him at this exact location twenty minutes ago. Then he bent down again.

"Four of those ones," he said to the girl behind the counter, pointing at the cannoli tray. The contents of the paper plate she handed him could have killed off a small village. "Do you want a coffee?"

When I figured out that he was talking to me, I thanked him and said no.

"I met that friend of yours," he said, sliding into a booth. "The one with the Southern accent and the Prince Valiant hairdo."

"So I heard." Evan had introduced Cam to Declan last week. All parties reported getting along famously. Men always get along famously right off the bat; they're born with a benefit-of-the-doubt chromosome built into their genetic code.

"He's a great actor," I said. "But I'm probably predisposed to like his work, since he's one of my dearest friends."

Declan looked unimpressed by my endorsement. "Glad to know you've got some dear friends your own age."

When a man insults your clothing, your job, and your country the very first time he meets you, you stop searching for the reasons behind his abuse and start chalking it up to a social personality disorder. That was how I missed the significance of this particular barb, and responded with some prissy line about having plenty of friends my own age, thank you very much.

"Such as your man from the club? What was it called, now, Apocalypse? Eternity? Overpriced House of Wank? He didn't look your age to me."

All of a sudden I understood: Declan had recognized me from that night with Berglan Starker, after all. Not only had he recognized me, but he'd recognized that there was something going on between me and BS, otherwise he would have mentioned it the first time we were introduced, in front of Evan. I'd been seen. But this is where being an actor comes in handy, because I've studied enough primetime to know my way around an interrogation scene, and the cardinal rule of getting caught is never giving up anything of which you haven't been accused. "Millennium," I said, sticking to the specific question at hand. "The club was called Millennium."

"Ah, yes, Millennium. The most expensive crap food of the Millennium. A meal that lasts a millennium. Your man was older than the millennium."

"That was a work meeting."

"Ah, go on." He took a bite of his pastry and cream spooged out the opposite end. "You're not putting old ones like that on your magazine cover so far as I've seen. Who was he?"

I couldn't very well lie about Berglan Starker's identity; he and Declan were bound to meet each other eventually, at a First Born event or a theater opening. But I couldn't very well tell the truth, either, since Declan had just proven himself less discreet than any human being or animal I'd ever met. "He's the father of a friend."

"You shagging him because he's rich?"

"I'm not going to dignify that with a response."

"I suppose that's meant to be an insult? You can only understand so much in this world if you're polite all the time, Rosalie. Or did they not teach you that at cocktail party training school?"

"The fact that I chew my food with my mouth closed does not mean that I went to finishing school."

"That' a girl. You do have something to you, after all."

"I didn't know that was up for a vote. I should try writing a play sometime. It certainly gives one broad license to judge."

"You take the license first, you write the play second, gorgeous."

Suddenly the room seemed very quiet. The old man in the booth behind us shuffled a deck of cards, snapping them down on the Formica table one by one. No one in the bakery was talking besides us.

"Look," I said, lowering my voice. "I called you this afternoon to see if you wanted to be profiled in my magazine. If you'd like to hear more about the story, I'd be happy to tell you more about the story. Otherwise a simple yes or no answer will suffice, and we can both get on with our days. Much as I'd love to sit here and defend my personal life, my very existence to you, I'm afraid I have a rehearsal to get to."

"Ah, cop on. I'm only messin'. I'm not after telling anyone, if that's what you're so wound up about. " Another blob of cream dropped out of the pastry in his fist. The tabletop looked like a Jackson Pollock. "So when am I going to be in your magazine?"

"If you'd like to do the article, I'll have the art director set up an appointment for next week."

"Your people call my people, one of those?"

I picked up my bag and slid out of the booth. Standing over him, I had the height advantage for the first time. "Sure, whatever."

"Right, then." He wiped a trail of powdered sugar from his cheek. "I didn't know you were an actress, Rosalie."

I nodded.

"So why do you work for that magazine, then?"

"Because I'm an actress who pays rent."

He stared up at me, and I could practically see the jigsaw pieces rotating in his mind. The penetrating writer, discovering that things are not what they first seemed to be, blah blah blah. If the revelation that I paid my own rent was all it took to throw his character sketch off course, maybe he wasn't the next hot thing, after all.

Once I was out on the street, and the rope of bells tied to the door had stopped jangling behind me, I turned around and looked back in the bakery windows. Declan had opened a newspaper and he was sipping coffee from his paper cup. When I lived in Dublin, I'd go for days at a time speaking only to people who worked behind counters: the postman, the grocery clerk, the girl who sold magazines at the stand on my block. Most afternoons, asking for directions on the street was my big social event. The loneliness of living in a foreign country is a loneliness like no other I've known. Even the things that usually offer comfort— the foods, the walks, the familiar routines of a day—are strange. The chicken soup has bones in it. The park closes for lunch. I thought of Paul, the main character in Declan's play, someone who says goodbye to everyone and everything he knows because of how badly he needs to escape the smallness of his life. What a risk it is, to go somewhere with nothing but yourself. For a second, looking over my shoulder, I almost felt sorry for the guy, sitting by himself with his newspaper and his cannoli and no one in this city of eight million people to talk to until the *GirlTalk* art director gave him a call. And then I remembered everything he had just said to me, and I turned around and crossed the street.

Living, as we do, in an age of hodgepodge commercialized Eastern mysticism, it's easy to buy into a watered-down notion of karma. To be honest, I'm not even sure if karma is a Zen concept or Hindi, or if it's accurate to refer to it as a "concept" in the first place. But the contemporary colloquial definition has a suggestive power all its own. Example: The O'Neill scene was going badly. *GirlTalk* grated on my nerves even more than usual. My skin was sprouting acne at an adolescent rate. My air conditioner had broken just in time for the worst heat wave of the summer. How easy, and therefore how tempting, to connect all this bad news back to the very bad thing I was doing on a now-weekly basis at the Pierre, Room 1801. I have said before that I'm not superstitious. But it's one thing to renounce superstition when your conscience is clear and your mind is at peace. Try breaking a mirror sometime when you're secretly sleeping with your friend's father, and see if it doesn't keep you up nights.

Guilt and third-party complexities aside, Berglan Starker was the one thing in my life that could be described as going well. He called me once a week or so, and on those nights I would go to meet him at the Pierre after rehearsal let out. I assumed his wife was in Washington on these occasions; they kept an apartment there, and her work apparently took her to our nation's capital for at least a few days of every week. This was information I had gleaned from Bella; BS never mentioned Mrs. Starker the Fourth in my presence. Part of me was dying of curiosity about her (obviously), but I also liked the fact that I hadn't been drafted into service as a toll-free marital complaint line, the way I suspect some mistresses are. It was almost decorous, how BS never spoke of his home life to me, and I did my part by tarting it up in the sort of lingerie women his age can't get away with—thongs and demi-bras and see-through stuff without straps. Turns out there's a whole industry out there, capitalizing on affairs. Entire luxury stores devoted to fabrics so delicate you have to wash them with a toothbrush. My credit card bills racked up fast.

In truth, I didn't have a clear idea of what Berglan Starker was after me for, since we never spent any time talking about the hard facts of our case. Being liked can be strangely unsettling, if you don't exactly know what you're liked for. I assumed it had something to do with youth, that being the only thing money can't buy for people like him. But youth is a big umbrella, one that covers more than firm thighs and smooth skin. There's innocence. There's naïveté. There's energy and passion and idealism, though I've never been particularly long on that last one. There's the whole carefree thing. Which of these qualities did he see in me? And more to the point, which of these qualities did he like? I worked up the courage to ask him that one morning, while he shaved and I sat in the bathtub, molding a cone of bubbles into a horn on the top of my head.

"Good God, Pink," he said, Pink being his affectionate translation of Rose from the French. "You're beautiful and funny, and I've never spent time with anyone like you before."

Like me as in poor? Like me as in unconnected? "Like me how?"

Something in my voice must have made him put his razor down. He leaned over and scooped the bubbles off my breasts, getting his shirtsleeves wet. "You're undauntable."

Of course I wasn't. I was daunted by everything in my immediate line of vision at that very instant: the size of the bathtub, the proximity of my friend's father to my naked body, the wedding ring on his hand, the time on the clock that meant that I was going to be late for work again, the telephone which reminded me that if something went wrong no one in the world would have the first clue how to find me. "I believe the word is dauntless," I said, standing up and making a mini-tidal wave against the side of the tub.

He handed me a thick white towel. "See?"

"No. Or at least I was hoping for something more specific."

"Such as a character dossier?"

"As you know, I have a job to get to. Are you going to answer me or not?"

"Please sit down on this ledge and let me speak. You are a dear, brave girl, and I admire you for it, even if you're hell in the morning. You are choosing to become an actress—in fact you are an actress right now, and that takes a great deal of gumption and stubbornness, both of which I prize in you. In fact I think you are a small miracle, and I'm very grateful that you're such a klutz, otherwise we might never have gotten to know each other so well."

"You can stop with the lecturing now. I'm late for work."

"Did you once have a very traumatic life experience before ten in the morning? And does the memory of it haunt you and account for your vile manners?"

"Come on. I don't go in for that suppressed memory junk."

We said a breezy goodbye in the hotel lobby, BS hailing a taxi and me walking towards the train. But as soon as I got through the turnstile I burst into tears, tears so thick I had to bury my head in my shawl. I am not a crier by nature, so I had no choice but to recognize this opening of the floodgates for exactly what it was: a sign that I was falling for Berglan Starker, falling hard indeed, and that I would therefore be vulnerable to whatever decisions he made about me, and that someday, ultimately, this would bring me to grief. All professions have their statistics. Doctors track heart disease, DJs chart record sales, bankers study stock trends. One hundred percent of affairs with married people end unhappily for at least one party involved. Any advice columnist worth her salt can recite that number in her sleep.

In an unprecedented turn of events, Manny Flax had graced our last two First Born rehearsals with his presence. He spent most of his time sitting in the back row reading Nelson DeMille novels with a penlight. But whenever Cam took the stage, Manny and his handlers snapped to attention, as if their horse had just come out of the stable for course exercises. Cam knew he was being scouted and he rose to the challenge, bellowing his lines with performance-level intensity, offering spontaneous flourishes here and there to prove he could improvise and keep scenes fresh. There's an old saying among actors that nothing helps a play like an audience, and Cam got better and better the more people watched.

The opposite could be said of the rest of us. Manny's eyelids went heavy as soon as Cam left the stage, and there are few things more dispiriting than simulating a nervous breakdown while the people sitting in the house fill in crossword puzzles and whisper into their cell phones. I knew better than to take their disinterest personally, but it made me self-conscious, and Evan's coaching—more variety here, even grief has a range—couldn't penetrate my sense of embarrassment. A different sort of actress would have risen to the occasion, hypnotizing the Flax entourage through sheer force of will, or at least she would have gone down swinging. But not me. When Cam gets famous and fans start rushing our stage door, I'll probably lie down so as not to block their paths.

On the Saturday a few mornings after Manny's last visit, I was lying in bed listening to the tinny noise of rain driving onto my air conditioner when my buzzer rang. It was Cam, wanting to know if I was game for a walk. "The weather's not so bad anymore," he said, when I tried to beg off. "Put on a baseball cap and you'll be fine."

Whole weeks had passed since Cam and I had spent time together out of rehearsal, so I pulled on sweatpants and flip-flops, brushed my teeth, and went downstairs. I didn't want to see Cam, exactly. He had gone to his official audition for Manny and Evan the day before, and I wasn't ready to hear about it just yet. My pom-poms needed a day off. In all of Cam's excitement, he hadn't spent much time considering how the rest of us might feel about his big success. But out on my stoop, seeing him there holding a paper sack full of my favorite donuts, my heart softened. It was no use, trying to make Cam into a villain. He was too loyal and sweet.

The rain had slowed to a tolerable drizzle, so we decided to walk down to Tompkins Square Park. The benches were wet, but Cam fanned out the slack fabric of his umbrella and dried off a space for me to sit down. We picked seats facing the dog run, and ate our breakfast watching an unlikely alliance of dogs catch Frisbees and dig in the mud. A slight breeze shook drops of water from the tree above us, and I flinched each time one landed on my bare skin. Cam shifted his arms and legs on the narrow bench, too limby for the spare slats of wood.

"So Manny called last night."

"Last night? Wasn't last night Friday?"

"I guess so, yeah. I guess I got that part."

I stopped chewing. A lump of custard lodged in my cheek. "That's . . ." A list of superlatives fell out before I could string them together. "That's *amazing*, Cam. I'm so *proud*, you're . . ." I wiped my hand on my knee. "They decided yesterday? The same day you auditioned?"

"Uh-huh."

"That must have been one hell of a reading."

Cam wound a strip of paper napkin around his index finger. We both watched in silence as the tip turned red. I raised my arm and patted him on the shoulder but the gesture felt forced, lame. Imagining this development, I'd worried that jealousy would cloud my happiness for him. But now, sitting on this soggy bench, jealousy slipped away and became something looser, something internal and invisible and harder to name. It was fear, really, fear that an irrevocable change had just been set in motion, that new people and new events would start to matter to Cam more than I did, and that I would go on sitting on this bench forever, holding him in the same esteem I always had, missing him, adoring him, watching myself get replaced. I blinked slowly, simultaneously aware of the moment's weight and of being trapped inside it, as if watching from above while a concrete wall dropped between us. The park looked colorless, bald.

"I wanted . . ." The tip of Cam's finger looked like it might explode. "I came so I could tell you first, Rosalie."

I winced at the sound of my full name. The formality of it saddened me; I hated the air of apology beneath his subdued tone, his calculated goodwill that robbed me of my right to feel upset. "I'm thrilled for you," I said, trying again for a convincing shoulder squeeze, clamping him in his place.

"It's good stuff, right?"

I nodded, and moved my hand absently up into his hair. A series of barks and yowls came from the dog run; we both turned to look. "You should get a dog, Rose," Cam said. "That could be *your* new project for fall."

My hand froze in his hair. I knew he meant no insult, but I was tired of excusing his unintended rudeness. "Don't get smug too quickly. I'm not in the market for new projects just yet."

Cam watched, surprised, as I stood up. "I'm only kidding. You don't need a dog. I know you don't need one; I was just kidding."

Something in his bewilderment locked steel shutters inside me. "I'll give you a hint." I pulled off my baseball cap. "The problem with what you just said has nothing to do with dogs."

"Will you please sit back down, Rosalie?"

He stared at me with such confusion that I reached down and cupped his face firmly in my hands. His skin was pliant and smooth, like a boy's. His getting this part meant that things were different between us; if he hadn't figured that out yet, he would soon enough. I didn't need to wait for him to turn away—it was inevitable, and I could only spare myself by doing it first. "I'm going home."

"Can I come with you?"

I shook my head, dropped my hands to my sides. "I'll call you tomorrow."

"Why not?"

I wanted him to come home, to beat me up the stairs and make fun of my trouble with the sticky lock, to track his muddy sneakers onto my beige rug on the way to bed, to complain about my futon and how his feet hung off the end. "Because I'm afraid of getting left behind." He opened his mouth to respond but I cut him off: "Don't say it, Cam. Don't promise it's not going to happen, because it is."

He leaned his head against my stomach and I backed away. "I'll call you tomorrow."

Walking out of the park, I tilted my head back towards the gray sky to keep the tears from forming in my eyes. Here they were again, another round of them. I thought of the first time I'd ever seen Cam, eight years ago. I'd watched him star as John Proctor in a production of *The Crucible*; feet and hands manacled with heavy chains, he'd conveyed a curiously upbeat response to imminent hanging. Afterwards, in the makeshift dressing room where weepy parents handed bouquets to kids in Puritan costumes, someone had introduced me to Cam. He was sitting on a folding chair in his boxer shorts, drinking water from a plastic bottle whose label had been peeled off. I always remember the way he placed the bottle on the counter and stood up, grinning, to meet me, his hand outstretched for a proper gentlemanly shake. Nothing ever deflated Cam: not the death sentence, not bad reviews, not rainy Saturday mornings or lonely Saturday nights. When I reached the park exit I turned around: to my surprise he was still sitting on the bench, frozen where I'd left him, his shoulders sagging and his gaze lost in midair. He looked wilted, stoned. It broke my heart.

Part of me suspected, maybe even that afternoon and for a little while afterwards, that Cam and I would keep circling back to each other as friends and lovers and who knows what else, the same way we always had. But it didn't happen that way. Fear of abandonment unleashes some weird impulses in me, and if I'm not of a mind to check them, look out. In *Respect for Acting*, Uta Hagen writes that "the actions of human beings are governed, more than anything else, by what they *want,* consciously or subconsciously." Forty years at HB Studio. Starring roles on Broadway in Chekhov, Albee, Williams. Uta Hagen should know.

Dear Annie,

I've had sex before with two different guys and I'm not ashamed of that or anything since it's pretty normal for a girl my age (16). The problem is that I told the boy I'm going out with now that I'm a virgin because it seemed like he might be jealous, you know how that goes. Now he wants us to have sex and I do too, but what about this whole virgin story? Like, will he definitely be able to tell? He's never had sex before and might not know the difference. (!!)

—Wigging in California

Dear Wigging,

The only physical difference between a virgin and a woman of experience is an unbroken hymen, and since hymens can get broken by all sorts of vigorous activities, the physical facts of virginity are easy enough to fudge, especially if you start to spend a lot of time biking or horseback riding in high-visibility places. Not all virgins bleed during their first time having intercourse, so sure, if you act really nervous and pretend like you're not having much fun, you might successfully pull the wool over your boyfriend's eyes.

But before you start outfitting yourself in white veils and dresses, ask yourself this: do you really want your first full-scale body-to-body encounter with your boyfriend to be clouded by a lie? Sex is supposed to bring people closer together, it's supposed to be an expression of trust and intimacy. What better way to express your trust and intimacy than to lay a little truth on your boyfriend, before the big event? It's not like there's anything wrong with the fact that you slept with other people before you started dating him, and if he feels a jealous sting for a minute, it's okay, he'll get over it.

I'm playing it conservative here for two good reasons: first of all, dissembling sets a bad precedent in relationships, and if your most passionate feelings and experiences with your boyfriend are plagued by lies, or even half-truths, you'll be building a very sticky web for yourself, Spidergirl. Second of all, there's nothing more awkward and clumsy than virgin-on-virgin sex. Tell him the truth and you'll both have more fun.

Trust me. I've lived through it.

Annie

Chapter Seven

If there is a God, or a Supreme Being of any kind, and if She keeps track of our comings and goings in some sort of record book, I was earning a weekly check-plus next to my name on Wednesday nights at eight. That's when I went to the Adele Goldberg Senior Center to host my reading circle. I realize that morality isn't a zero-sum game; you can't just go around canceling out your bad acts with your good ones. But in some roundabout way, hanging out with the oldies was making me feel better about myself, or at least better about the crap that was going down in the other, less exemplary arenas of my life. (Had skipped celebratory drinks for Cam in favor of dinner at Chanterelle with BS, that kind of thing. Five stars for the braised beef tenderloin.) It's amazing what a dose of perspective can do, in the way of making a person grateful for what she *does* have, i.e., bladder control and a full set of teeth. Plus I liked most of the residents I met there, liked their old-fashioned nicknames for me, Doll and Rosie, and the poodle-skirt imagery such endearments called to mind.

Our group's first book, *Cicciarelli's Secret,* was a hard-hitting Cosa Nostra novelization set in Sicily and Brooklyn, and though by all appearances it went over well enough, someone lodged an anonymous complaint with the Adele Goldberg brass about the amount of profanity in the dialogue, so I was forced to restructure our nomination process and screen proposals in advance. Democracy languishes wherever small-time administrators hold sway. Our second venture, *Who Will Teach the Charleston?*, was less controversial but not sufficiently compelling to keep the majority of members awake much past 8:15. As the group's de facto president, I made an executive decision to change horses midstream and read *Huck Finn*—funny, plot-driven, and thematically in line with the audience's nostalgia for America of yore. It was a popular choice. Mrs. Lybynchek, whose attention to detail was perhaps the sharpest in the group, took to wearing overalls and a bandanna to meetings. Attendance swelled.

Pearl Coleman, the shrunken old woman who had unnerved me on my first visit to AGSC, had been coming to meetings sporadically since the reading circle got started. She never took her headphones off, though she nodded knowingly during the passages where a person listening to *Huck Finn* might be tempted to nod. She never spoke, either. For a while I worried that she found the Huck/Jim relationship racially problematic, which it is, though I'd been hoping to gloss over that critical debate for the purposes of the nursing home book club. In the first weeks I made a special effort to draw her out during our discussion period, but she was not an enthusiastic participant. All of the other group members had shown me snapshots of their grandkids and dearly departed spouses, and I was beginning to take Ms. Coleman's total indifference personally. I had come to Adele Goldberg as a reader, sure, but I also considered general good-moodsmanship part of my overarching purpose, and she was holding out on me. Every disenfranchised population has its skeptics, as we know from watching movies about inner city public schools, and among the oldies Pearl Coleman was my obligatory tough nut to crack. Even the orderlies seemed aware of her off-putting reticence, and would urge her to thank me and say goodbye when they came to wheel her back to her room at the end of the night.

Once, during a Sanka break, I made my way over to Ms. Coleman's wheelchair and tried to strike up a conversation. She stared straight ahead and made no acknowledgment of my presence. I sat down next to her on a folding chair.

"Good evening, Ms. Coleman," I said loudly, in case she had her Walkman cranked up. "Are you enjoying the novel tonight?"

She gave me one of her dour nods, and fished around in the fanny pack underneath her lap blanket for a pack of tissues.

"I hope you're thinking of some other books you might like us to read in the future?"

"I am thinking of a few."

"Great!" I said, elated at having gotten her to speak. "You just give me your list anytime, alright? I'd love to see it."

She nodded again. For a moment we sat side by side in silence while I tried to think of some further way to engage her. It was weird, how intent I'd become on winning over some old lady with an ambivalent attitude towards nineteenth-century American literature, but as I sat there I realized that I did, in fact, want her to like me. There is a selfishness to every act of charity, and just as the Puritans performed good works to prove their membership in the quorum of the elect, so I depended on my Wednesday nights for proof that I was essentially a decent kid, maybe a little mixed up in the ways of sexual honesty, but decent all the same. In this way Pearl Coleman was raining on my parade. My eyes followed her gaze up to the activities bulletin board. A big orange poster winking with silver glitter and exclamation points advertised "FATHER–DAUGHTER DAY" at the senior center. "Attention Dads!" read the fine print. "In the mood to share memories, trade secrets, and spend an afternoon with the little girl you love?"

I looked at Pearl Coleman. She looked back at me. The phony candy striper color drained from my cheeks. Here I was, masquerading as a pious National Honor Society do-gooder with a heart of gold, when really I'd been eyeing my watch for the past half hour to be sure I got out in time for my 9:30 table at Le Bernardin with BS. I was like one of those Playboy bunnies who comes out in a crisp white nurse's uniform for the beginning of her routine, only to unsnap it and strip down to caduceus pasties. And from Ms. Coleman's unwavering stare, it almost seemed, in some cracked, Faulknerian way, like the old lady had my number.

"Ms. Coleman," I said, making an effort to lower my voice from its usual suck-ass nursing home range, "If you ever have any thoughts or suggestions about the reading club, I would be honored to hear them."

"Well." She looked around confidentially. "I do enjoy Atlantic City." Next to the orange poster, a flier announced a chartered bus trip to the casinos, all meals included. "I have won over three thousand dollars at blackjack, in my day."

I had no idea what this information had to do with the book club. But insofar as it signaled my release from Pearl Coleman's sphinxy gaze, I was relieved. Two more minutes with her and I might have succumbed to the temptation to confess myself. It's a rough business, keeping a major life secret from all your friends. You start to look for absolution in some pretty desperate places.

The *GirlTalk* art director had rented out the top floor of the Irish Historical Society on Fifth Avenue. "It's fabulous," she said, dropping the Next Hot Thing folder on my desk Monday morning. "Antique portraits of Joyce and Eliot everywhere. We're shooting in black and white, so let Market know if you have any ideas."

I picked up the folder and flipped through the Polaroids. "I've never seen Declan Pearse in anything but denim, top to bottom."

"Denim." The art director squinted, made a camera lens with her fingers. "Denim is good."

On the day of the shoot, I packed up my notebook and climbed into the van with a crew of six plus Jenna and Veronique Kaplan, whom Ginger had sent along to write behind-the-scenes coverage of the column's launch. The girls were dressed in head-to-toe black, and they carried their Dictaphones with perfect indifference, as if they'd just come back from covering a G-8 summit in Stockholm and this afternoon's assignment was child's play. Traffic heading uptown was in a snarl, and before we'd even reached the Park the makeup artist was preaching the merits of a new holistic treatment called vortex therapy.

"Our chakras get so depleted in this industry," she said. "If you don't reenergize, you can numb your healing base."

When our van pulled up to the corner of Eightieth Street,

Declan was sitting on the stoop of the Historical Society eating a hot dog, which the crew found outrageously quaint and foreign. I introduced him around; he made a point of shaking hands and calling all the women "Miss," which raised the quaint-and-foreign quotient exponentially.

"I hope you can make me look like Brad Pitt," he said while the assistants unloaded box after box of camera equipment. "I've been told there's a resemblance, though my cheekbones are much better than his. Now what can I carry for you?"

Upstairs, in a room crammed with mahogany tables and busts of Irish luminaries, the photographer set up his gear. Declan moved patiently from station to station, stripping out of his T-shirt and jeans into a more expensive version of the same outfit, submitting to the hairstylist's comb and apologizing for such scant raw materials, asking which of the makeup artist's potions were edible. I have always believed that first impressions don't lie, that we are each born with a fixed opening gambit that does us either harm or good in the eyes of others. But that afternoon, watching Declan charm the designer pants off of every last member of the *GirlTalk* crew, I learned that first impressions are as easily manipulated as anything else.

Our subject was remarkably at ease in front of the camera. Potbellied and unkempt as he was in real life, the Polaroids made Declan look like a rock star or an actor, maybe the loose-cannon lead of an IRA action film. He joked with the crew while the photographer snapped away, like an old hand on a publicity junket, and after five or six painless rolls the shoot was over. No smashed furniture, no tirades on the intellectual bankruptcy of girls' magazines, no burping or farting out loud. In fact Declan behaved well and cooperated from start to finish, even when I vetoed his proposal to adjourn to the Madison Pub for interviews. The Kaplan girls, who swooned and heaved every time he came within a yard of them, pleaded his case for the pub, explaining the importance of an intimate, relaxed setting for a successful interview. Unfortunately for them, I knew how old they were and I worked for their mother. We went to the pizza place a block away.

"That's all right by me," Declan said, winking at Veronique. "As long as you've got the neck for pineapple on your pizza."

My commitment to truth in journalism compels me to report that Declan continued on his charming roll throughout lunch. He fielded all inane questions about Dublin with a forbearance one had to admire, and he asked the crew members about themselves and their jobs in a way that seemed more than perfunctory. The girls in particular were riveted, which just goes to show that attractiveness has as much to do with magnetism of personality as with anything else, since the river of orange grease running down Declan's forearm couldn't have been winning him the big points. He was funny, haplessly trying to sort out the *Girl-Talk* target audience, and he was plenty irreverent about the magazine, too. But somehow none of his jokes seemed as rude or patronizing as they had on our previous meetings. Why was that? Had he been ruder and more patronizing then, or had I been more inclined to take offense? I am not, in general, one to doubt my initial assessments of people. But watching Declan convince the waitress to try a bite of his mayonnaise-dipped pizza crust, the thought occurred to me that I might, perhaps, have gotten this one slightly wrong. I'm not saying that I liked the guy—just that I was open to reconsideration. Which, intransigence being an emotional trait characteristic of only children, was a start.

"Do you know that your friend Rosalie lived in Ireland for a time?" he asked the table at large, as he dug to the bottom of a butterscotch sundae.

The Kaplan girls looked at me for confirmation. I nodded.

"She loved it," Declan said. "She thought it was brilliant. She made loads of friends and she thought the weather was gorgeous and the pubs were rapid. She can't wait to get back there. She's saving up money for her fare. Go on, ask her."

"You know," the art director said, "I've always thought you looked Irish, Rosalie. It's the whole fair skin/rosy cheek thing. It's all falling into place. My grandmother on my father's side was Irish. God, could that woman tell a story."

"There's a statistic about how half of all Americans can trace some degree of Irish ancestry," I said. "I can't, but living there for a year has to count for something."

Declan was smirking at me from across the table. "Honorary citizenship, I believe."

"I'm going abroad for the summer," Veronique said to Declan. "Paris. I want to work in fashion after college. I love the cappuccino in Paris. It's just not the same here, no matter where you go."

On the street, while the office-bound team did their Barnum and Bailey pile back into the company van, I thanked Declan for being such a good sport all afternoon. He thanked me for inviting him to be in the magazine.

"Someday you're going to have to tell me why you had such a bad time in Dublin. I won't take it personally. You'll notice I'm not living there myself."

"I didn't have a bad time there. Living overseas was a great learning experience."

"And the rents in New York are affordable."

"You'll have to remind me, did I ever say anything bad about Dublin in your presence?"

"No, but am I not correct anyhow?"

I cocked my head at him. He had the same blithe expression he'd had on his face since we'd left the restaurant. "Okay, you're right. I hated it."

He shrugged. "So there's no use in lying to me. Anyway you're woeful at it. Why is it that actors make the worst liars?"

"Because we don't like to work when we're off the clock. Anyway I was just trying to spare your feelings. But the truth is you come from a vile, dreary, vomit-splashed place."

"Vomit-splashed?"

"On Sunday mornings I couldn't even go around the corner for a newspaper without endangering my sneakers. The pub next door to my apartment was a real hotbed."

"Well there's the problem, then. There are some lovely old folks' homes on the far side of town in Killester, you should have looked into one of those." He reached out his hand to shake. "Your mates are about to leave without you. Thanks again for the afternoon, Rosalie. I enjoyed myself."

"I can send you the proofs once they come in, if you want to see them."

"I'd like that. Cheers, then."

We stood there for a second, thanking each other, shaking hands. International diplomacy at work.

The film, when the photographer sent it in, was decidedly more sophisticated than the standard *GirlTalk* fare. We all held our breath while Ginger inspected the contact sheets.

"He's gorgeous," she said, hunched over the loop. "Look at the size of him! Look at that bald spot!"

"That's *exactly* what I loved," the art director said. "*Exactly.*"

I messengered a set of proofs over to Evan at the Flax office, with a little note saying Declan was about to revolutionize the face of heartthrob America. At the end of the day, when I still hadn't heard from Evan, I called him at work. The secretary put me on hold for five minutes, and he finally picked up for long enough to tell me he'd have to call back later. "And before I forget," he said, "don't go making my playwright into some teen magazine pinup, okay?"

"No need to get jealous," I said, tidying my desk and getting ready to leave. "You'll have your day in the glossy magazine sun."

"No, Rosalie, I'm serious. You really, really don't want to do that."

My arm was halfway through my jacket sleeve. Was he threatening me? "What do you mean, *I* don't want to do that? Do you mean you don't want me to?"

"You, me, we, whatever. I'll call you when my meeting's done."

I did not stick around my office to wait for that call. Instead, I left in a hurry without pausing to figure out where I should go. I had no dinner plans, no rehearsal, not even any mindless errands to do, so I went to the bookstore across the street and milled around the drama section, leafing through books of audition pieces. I had no idea whether Evan was joking, or just being his usual bossy self, or if he was actually trying to lay down the law about who owned the rights to Declan Pearse. For all I could guess, Evan was working up some demented crush on the guy; he always fell for the burliest straight men around. All I knew was that "we" had a false kind of ring to it, when he'd said it on the phone. There was no "we" anymore. There hadn't been for a while.

Grace was planning a dinner. I knew this not because she'd called to tell me, not because she'd mentioned it on any one of the recent occasions when we'd seen each other at rehearsal, but because I'd received an actual handwritten invitation, stamped and delivered by the United States Postal Service to my home address. I suppose some people, the kind of people who dip their own candles and keep mulled cider on the stove, might be in the habit of sending out handwritten invitations. I found it alarming. "Come Celebrate the Autumn Equinox," the gold-bordered card read. "177 Second Street #45, 8:00." When had she learned to use a calligraphy pen?

The air on the night of the party was nippy, coat-button air. The liquor store where I stopped for a bottle of wine had gourds on display in the window. It was only a matter of days before supermarkets would be selling Halloween candy and summer would be gone, a distant, sleeveless gingham memory. New York hunkers down in the fall. The grown-ups come home from their beach houses, the interns head back to their college towns, and the median age of the city shoots up by decades. Junior staff members do their own photocopying. Friends stop ringing buzzers unannounced. It's a sober, nut-gathering, pre-hibernation time.

Jake greeted me at the door of Grace's apartment with a man-of-the-house élan I was unaccustomed to, taking my jacket and pouring me a glass of red wine from the makeshift bar on top of the television set. The place smelled cozy, as if things had been stewing and baking in it for days. All the living room furniture had been drafted into dinner party service: trivets balanced on the telephone stand, stacks of plates and mismatched silverware were piled on the steamer trunk. From the kitchen I could make out Bella's voice, and Evan's and Cam's. It suddenly seemed like a long, long time had passed since we'd all been together socially in one place. Busyness was part of it, but not the routine busyness of doctor's appointments and work deadlines and trips to the Laundromat. It was the busyness of Cam's audition, and Grace and Jake's courtship, and Evan's play, and my affair, and each of those pursuits annulled us as a group, by very definition. I felt strangely shy, imagining the scene in the kitchen. My affair with Berglan Starker meant I had to watch everything I said, and what could be lonelier than guarding your tongue in the company of your best friends, your family? I sat down on the futon and Jake sat down next to me.

"It smells delicious in here," I said. "What did you guys make?"

"Grace made everything. I sliced the bread." He stretched out a little and I retreated, dwarfed, into a corner of the couch. Grace could bake brioche and chocolate bread pudding; she could quarter a chicken and take out the bones. If I'd been set down in the wilderness with a mess of vegetables, a soup pot, and a sharp knife, I would have managed to starve to death.

"Tell me what you've been up to, Rosalie. I haven't seen enough of you lately." As he spoke he fiddled with the corkscrew on the coffee table, a mechanical contraption that looked more complicated than my dad's power drill. Even Jake was succumbing to the gadgetry of the upper middle class. He had always been our voice of youthful minimalism, of only-buy-it-if-it-fits-in-your-trunk. How unsettling, to see him lovingly twirl a bar tool.

"Let's see, what have I been up to. Work. Rehearsal. Nada."

"How's life among the lovelorn?"

"It creeps in its petty pace from day to day. You know. It's a job."

"A slave, as Malcolm X would say. I'm thinking I may have to quit mine sometime this year and find something else to do for a while. It's toxic, going into that office every day, doing the same meaningless thing for eight hours, watching the second hand move around the clock. And toxic can't be fun to date."

Evan, Cam, and Bella came out of the kitchen carrying drinks.

"*Mi amore,*" Cam said, squeezing onto the couch between me and Jake, giving me enough of an air kiss so that I could feel the pouch of food in his cheek. "What's this about toxic? Did Jake take an STD test?"

"Look at this." Bella picked up a glass bowl with flowers floating in it and held it out to Jake. "You've turned Grace into Martha fucking Stewart. I'll be using this as an ashtray between courses, for your information."

As if on cue, Grace brought out a tray of cocktail-napkin food, canapés and stuffed puff pastry cut into little diamond-shaped bites. Jazz was playing on the stereo, in rotation with a world music album of Latin extraction. You add up these symbols, the wine, the hors d'oeuvres that aren't prepackaged, the CDs you'd give your parents for Christmas, and the conclusion is irrefutable: you're getting old.

"This is fabulous, Grace," Evan said, refilling glasses. "You should open a restaurant. Jake can be the headwaiter."

"The only business more capricious than acting," Grace said.

"What's my job?" I asked Evan. "I want a job there, too. Or a slave, as Jake tells me Malcolm X would say."

"You can be the expediter. Bella can be sommelier. Cam can be the hostess."

"Table for one, Mr. Weiner?" Cam asked. "Your usual solitary booth?"

"Speaking of which, where's teeny Constanteeny tonight?" Jake asked. "I thought he was coming with you."

"Rescuing some insurance company from an apocalyptic breach of contract. He had to work late. He said he'd swing by later if he could."

"I can wrap up some food to send home with you," Grace offered.

"Or Evan can just cab uptown to Constantine's favorite sandwich place, special order him the most expensive thing on the menu, cab back down to Constantine's, and leave dinner outside his apartment door so it's waiting for him when he comes home."

Evan gave Cam the finger. "You'll understand the pleasures of generosity someday, too, if you ever get a girlfriend."

Moods, softened by alcohol and defanged by the presence of salad plates, were good. Once I submitted to the evening's smothering domesticity the gathering felt warm and familiar, like a big, heavy, moth-eaten sweater. Grace passed rack of lamb on a wooden carving board; the rest of us devoured every last grain of couscous and stalk of asparagus she set in front of us. Bella propped her feet up on the trunk/dinner table and told us about Jean-Marie's costume designs for the festival; Cam tossed olives into the air and caught them in his mouth. For the first two courses, at least, no one veered far from the script.

And then came dessert, the most dangerous part of any meal not sponsored by Alcoholics Anonymous. I was halfway through my plate of pumpkin pie when I realized no one had made a toast yet, so like a proper dinner guest I raised my champagne flute and offered one up. "To the chef," I said, smiling at Grace in a way that felt good and uncomplicated, the way happy friends with full stomachs are supposed to feel. "An inspiration and example to those of us who subsist on frozen food."

Everyone cheered and clapped. Cam bleated like a lamb.

"Hear, hear," Jake said. "And since we're drinking champagne anyway, Grace and I figured we might as well come up with something to celebrate."

Engrossed as I was in the distribution of vanilla ice cream, it took me a second to register that something significant was about to be announced. When I did look up all heads were turned towards Grace, who was beaming. I looked back at Jake: he was beaming, too. And then simply, instantly, it was clear as water in my mind's eye. They were engaged. I could see it all before they said it: the party in Providence at the Lerners' house, the futon I'd be offered as a hand-me-down, the change-of-address cards in Grace's maddeningly perfect hand. I could even picture the block they'd end up on: tree-lined, with brownstones, and flowers protected by those little wire cages. Brooklyn. They were in love. Not passing, flaky, here-today-destroyed-by-intrigue-and-selfishness-tomorrow love, but real love, move-in-together love, move-to-Brooklyn-for-the-rest-of-our-lives love. I swallowed champagne, I clinked glasses, I tried to listen to Jake's canned explanation of how it had all come about (Cam could afford his own place now that he was a big man on Broadway, so the orphaned and the poor were teaming up), but the inside of my lip was going raw from biting. How could I have been so utterly blindsided by the biggest life decision of my best friend? How could Grace not even have pretended to want my advice? How could I be hearing this news for the first time in a room full of other people? Had I somehow fallen down on the job of being a good friend to her, or was good friendship moot, now that she had her life partner all lined up? I thought of the infinite ways in which we'd all have to realign our friendships over the years, as marriages and betrayals and success mucked with the status quo. It was so exhausting to imagine those inevitable changes, and so sad. But when I looked around the room for an ally, everyone else seemed elated. What was my problem? Why couldn't I just be happy for my friends?

When my turn came to hug Grace in the impromptu receiving line, the embrace I gave her was limp and chilly. "Jacob Braverman," I whispered, hating the sarcasm in my voice. "Big points for courage, Gracie. Courage and optimism. Thumbs up."

My coat was on in seconds. I could see Grace staring at me like I'd just slapped her across the face, but it didn't matter. Neither did the looks that must have gone around the room after my exit. No: all that mattered was that I made it safely to the elevator before I burst into tears.

One winter in college, when I'd been hard up for spending money, I signed on to take a battery of personality tests for a psych student who was doing dissertation research. I didn't much like the guy—he was one of those smarmy lab jocks who doesn't change his clothes often enough—but he paid seven bucks an hour and he taught me an important lesson about the diagnostic value of the hypothetical scenario. Example: Imagine you find yourself in a spare white room with five locked doors and an open one. You are either the kind of person who sits contented in the spare white room, or the kind of person who strides on through the open door. Bella: locked. Cam: locked. Evan: locked. Jake: locked. Grace: locked.

Berglan Starker: open. Or at least ajar.

I started returning his phone calls. Before, when he'd left me messages, I'd waited for him to try again instead of calling back, partly to be on the extra-safe side—the man has more assistants than I have shoes—and partly to cement him in the role of Pursuer and me in the role of Pursued. The morning after the autumn equinox, however, his direct work voicemail could be found on my memory speed dial, entry number nine, under BS. Another change: I started inviting him places. Dark places, like the movies and anonymous high-end bistros in my neighborhood. Once I even had the maniac idea of inviting him to my apartment for dinner. I must have conceived of it as a kind of test of his affections, as in, did he like me enough to spend a night in my jail-cell-sized studio? But as soon as he accepted my invitation I was seized by a horror and panic only the truly culinarily hand- icapped can know. If he'd been a normal guy, a nice young law student, say, I could have had Grace help me whip up a meal and then scram, leaving behind a convincing heap of dirty pots in my sink. But Berglan Starker wasn't a normal guy. And Grace didn't owe me any favors.

Pop feminism had fooled me into believing that cooking was simple and demeaning work, that the girl who learns to fold egg whites when she might otherwise be declining Latin verb forms is deliberately letting her brain go to mush. But a quick browse through *The Joy of Cooking* reveals thermonuclear physics to be a cinch compared to baking a fruit soufflé. On Sunday morning I bought the ingredients for three recipes I could follow without the use of a dictionary: herb pasta, field green salad, and baked pears. I spent the afternoon soaking my apartment in cleaning chemicals, and when the sky began to darken I faced the inevitable: it was time to set about making dinner. I sliced toma- toes. I poured spices from a jar into a bowl. Venetian glass blow- ers never worked with such precision. When Berglan rang my buzzer, I chugged down the cup and a half of Madeira I'd mea- sured out for the pears and greeted him at the door.

"What a lovely room you have, Pink," he said, handing me a batch of flowers fit for an equestrian champion. "And I feel so braced from all of those stairs! My doctor has suggested I buy an artificial stair-climbing machine like that, but I think it might be more pleasurable to build an oubliette and spend weekends in it."

"Have a seat. I couldn't remember which kind of scotch you

drank so I bought all the ones that start with Glen. What would you like?"

"Don't fuss. Whatever's easiest. Can I have the grand tour, Miss P?"

I put the flowers in water while Berglan nosed around, then I showed him my vintage advice book collection, my signed copy of *Death of a Salesman,* the framed reproduction of the Book of Kells that was my only souvenir from Dublin. Having a person in your home is terribly intimate; it's like stepping out of your tortoise shell and inviting your dinner partner to try it on. Everything I owned looked cheap and impermanent when I saw it through Berglan Starker's eyes. In the Pierre, I could costume up in some extravagant lingerie and leave the rest of my story to BS's imagination; on Eleventh Street the jig was up. No family heirlooms, no remarkable finds carried home in a duffel bag from the bazaars of Rajistan. My possessions were as ordinary as they come. I could see Berglan Starker sizing this up and it stung me, as if my imagination or my innate worth could be judged by the pillar candles on my bedside table. I suddenly wished I hadn't invited him over.

"This is the solarium," I said grimly, pointing at the windowsill.

"Look, you can almost see trees at eye-level. There are some people's heads. The lower floors have their advantages."

"So did the Russian Revolution."

"You're not allowed to be unpleasant to your guests, my darling. It's part of the contract of inviting someone to dinner. To feed and to be civil."

"I can only do one thing at a time."

"Well put me to work, would you? What needs doing?"

I took a dubious look around the kitchen but I couldn't think of any suitable task to ask him to do. It didn't matter: the next second he was rolling up the sleeves of his button-down shirt and rummaging through my cabinets.

"Hey, what are you looking for?" I asked, regretting the inedible collection of vitamins and painkillers he was discovering in the spice cabinet. "Don't you want to sit down? I have this thing under control, I promise."

"Don't be silly, Pink, cooking isn't meant to be a spectator sport. Anyway I make a crackerjack salad dressing with which I'm hoping to impress you and lure you into bed."

"That would be original."

His voice went high and wavery, as if he were imitating somebody I was supposed to recognize. "First a little olive oil, then a dash of salt and freshly ground pepper, and just a pinch of Tylenol PM."

I stared at him blankly.

"Come on, Pink. You look awfully unhappy for someone whose idea this dinner was."

"I'm not unhappy. I'm just, I don't know, considering the sight of you in my kitchen. It's not something I was prepared for, after all. You're handling my things."

"Well I don't see how I can avoid that if I'm going to make us a salad dressing."

"I'm adjusting, that's all."

"While you're adjusting, why don't you take this old-person music off the stereo. Do you have any sour cream?"

"You can probably find some spoiled milk in the back of the

refrigerator if you look hard enough." I walked over to my CD player and exchanged the Schubert I'd put on for a Serge Gainsbourg album. When I turned back to the kitchen Berglan had his nose in a container of yogurt, which he then shot into the trash can, layup style.

"I see you are a gastronomic minimalist, Pinklington. I wouldn't have guessed."

"I've warned you. I've warned you on several separate occasions; now you can see for yourself."

I sat down in one of the chairs at the table, which I'd set earlier in the afternoon. Berglan put down the jug of olive oil he'd been holding and pulled out the chair across from me. He moved the enormous vase of flowers so that we could see each other's faces.

"Will you tell me what's the matter, my darling?"

He looked so easy, slouched on his metal folding chair. Now I saw that I had invited him to my apartment to prove how ridiculous it was to be falling for him, to confront the implausibility of having a married man in my life by socking him on a folding chair and watching him squirm. Only he wasn't squirming, he was playing along. He was making salad dressing. My heart surged in my chest.

"I loathe civilized dinners. If I had my way I would eat all of my meals standing up at the kitchen counter, with a fork and a salt shaker and no plate."

He reached for my hand across the table. "Look, we have the makings of a lovely dinner in there, and my idea is that we can do it together. Believe it or not I have made a sandwich or two in my lifetime, and I would be happy to throw on a T-shirt and do some quick chopping. Then we can eat in the kitchen, or at the table, or on the couch, or in bed. Lady's choice."

I gave him a reproachful look. How could he be so tolerant? There was nothing for it: if I lent him a T-shirt, and if he did some chopping, I would fall that much more in love with him because he would be that much more real, a real person in my kitchen, in his real stocking feet, assembling a real dinner from the things I'd bought. All of a sudden I understood how the anonymity of the Pierre had protected me, by keeping the details of our actual lives separate. That's the reason why careful lovers meet in hotels: hotels are generic, they blot out the paraphernalia of everyday life. As soon as you renounce the generic in love, you are in true-blue dangerous waters, for sure. The T-shirt was a bad idea, I knew it, even as I scrounged up a Buffernaut cast-off, a baseball crewneck from the Texas Rangers that had "Rodriguez" written on the back. Berglan pulled it on without missing a beat, and then he led me into the kitchen and showed me how to make salad dressing, and he fixed us another round of drinks, and he rid my refrigerator of all expired food products. Somehow he had an intuitive domesticity; every drawer he opened had just the knife he needed, every task he set about doing was just the one that needed to be done. And what I thought, as I watched him move about my kitchen, was how sweet it was to have him there, and how now, forever, every time I opened one of those drawers or used one of those knives, I would remember the time he'd done it, and how happy it had made me. For that is the curse of a heart like mine: no moment, however happy, can exist without the shadowy knowledge of the time that happiness will be gone.

. . .

When we eventually sat down to dinner, the pasta I'd produced was terrible, a dry, bitter tangle of noodles coated in oregano leaves that tasted more like tobacco than like food.

"These tomatoes are sensational, Pink."

"It looks like I cut up a joint and sprinkled it all over our dinner."

"A dash more oil will make it perfect. If not, you can smoke it later with your friends."

After the meal we sat on the couch and watched late-night news. At the Pierre this was our 11 o'clock ritual, but in my own apartment our familiar habits seemed more domestic than usual, and I got scared. There I was, lying on my couch, stroking the chest of a man whose wife's name I'd never once said, whose daughter's name I'd never said in front of him. What a ludicrous, elaborate charade it all was—did he think I'd forget he was married if he just didn't mention it around me? So I said their names. Julia. Bella. Like that. The same way I might pronounce any old words out loud. Invertebrate. Soup tureen. Barbados. Really, I didn't have more of a plan than that. There they were, a couple of proper nouns, waiting to be addressed or excused or wept over or tossed around irreverently. Gentleman's choice.

Berglan shifted his gaze from the television screen and looked down at me. I was splayed across him in a tranquil, frog-like way that did not suggest confrontation. His eyes narrowed a little, enough to let me know he'd heard me, then he turned back to CNN. Protests against the WTO were apparently severe. Maybe he was a WTO board member? During the next ad break he muted the sound.

"Pink, you are a dear, dear, beautiful girl."

I stopped breathing. Those words were definitely the preface to something I didn't want to hear the rest of. If he would only stop right there I would never, ever say their names again; I would never provoke him or make naive demands or mindless bids for attention. I would learn to talk about the stock market; I would move to a more convenient neighborhood; I would wear lacy underwear even during my period. Our relationship was *fine.* It was better than fine—it was practically perfect. Perfect!

"I suppose in beastly reality what we're doing here is more complicated than it feels."

"No," I practically shrieked. "It's not complicated, really. We could make it complicated, but we don't have to. There's no point. Let's not. Let's watch MTV instead and I'll tell you who all the bands are."

"But you seem to want to have a conversation, my darling. You must know that I have no objection to talking about Julia or Bella with you, though I can't say they were much on my mind until you mentioned them."

I winced at the sound of their names. They were different, realer, in his voice than in mine. "I don't want to have a conversation. For three-thousandths of a second I might have thought I did, but I was wrong; I don't."

He raised his eyebrows, offering me the chance to change my mind. His willingness only made me feel foolish, which was probably what it was intended to do.

"It has occurred to me more than once that you and I come from different generations, and the concerns on our horizons are bound to be different. You know I'm smitten with you, but I would absolutely hate to stand in the way of the forward motion of your life. It wouldn't be right."

"I don't want to talk about this." He *was* the forward motion in my life, but I didn't dare say it out loud. Any future we had would have to be won by stealth. "I want to watch MTV. I'm serious. I don't think you listen to enough rock and roll."

"I resent that assumption. I bought the last Sting album."

I wrestled him for the remote control, and won. If youth was my number one asset, I could be plenty young.

For someone who receives a biweekly paycheck in exchange for her professional expertise on love, I can be remarkably dim about it. It's as if all my conviction gets gobbled up between ten and six, and I have none left over for myself. To be perfectly honest, I'm not even sure if I've ever *been* in love. I've had lots of boyfriends—in college I was almost never without one—and I've gone through all the requisite stages, inadvertently speaking baby talk in public, winning over prickly parents, lying in bed broken-hearted popping St. John's wort. But I'm an actress, and some-times I think I can't distinguish the rehearsal from the real thing. I mean, yes, for fourteen months during my junior/senior year I claimed to be in love with a Social Studies concentrator named Philip Winglaar. I also claimed to enjoy Hermann Hesse novels and baked goods made from carob. Does anything from that era truly belong on my emotional résumé?

The kids I write for in Annie Answers are thirteen, fourteen, fifteen max. They're learning how to ride with love training wheels on, and I'm steering them around the playground. I know that material like I know my multiplication tables. But then I put on my coat, step out of the office, and my friends are engaged, and my boyfriend is married and nearing retirement, and all that so-called experience I racked up in the past seems to be floating hundreds of miles away, on the sandy shores of another life. Did I love Berglan Starker? How could I ever know for sure? How could I separate his millions of dollars and his picture in *Time* and his knowledge of food and wine and high-ranking elected officials from the man himself? And what did it matter? Is love ever purer than that?

But now I sound as if I'm sure that I loved Berglan Starker, and simply unsure of whether I loved him for good enough reasons. If only. If only I knew my own heart well enough to recognize its pangs: jealousy, insecurity, loneliness, the residual fear that I'll be unmasked and revealed as no more than a pleasant orthodontist's daughter from Hanson, Massachusetts. People like me, looking rationally and objectively at a situation like mine, would probably come to the conclusion that I wanted approval, the approval of the president whose club I wanted to join. Maybe I did. But isn't that a kind of love, too?

Confused as I was, at least one hard fact became clear to me the night BS stayed at my house. I could no longer pretend to be tortured with guilt and self-loathing for sleeping with my friend's dad. Speaking Bella's name out loud had stripped away that pretense once and for all, because even her real live specter hadn't changed anything. I wanted to be with Berglan Starker, and I wasn't about to give him up for anybody else's sake. People do worse things than that; they do them all the time. I wasn't a murderer or a thief or a thug; I was a mistress. For all I knew, Bella had been one herself. Going to bed with a married man distills what's best about sex—the danger, the urgency, the forbidden act. Of course in the back of my head, some part of me knew what would happen next with Berglan Starker. He was married. He was my friend's dad. What would happen next was nothing.

But then, knowing a fact and really, truly believing it are two different things. And the flickering flame of optimism—naive, pathetic, whatever you want to call it—is the aspiring actress's lot. When the time came for the two of us to adjourn from the couch to the futon, I handed Berglan the hangers I'd freed up for his work clothes and pointed out the guest towel I'd hung on the back of the bathroom door. You can't *really* know the future, none of us can. But you can clear a space and hope.

Dear Annie,

This summer I went to Lake Tuckaho with my family and I met the boy of my dreams, initials D.T. Jr. We really hit it off and we hung out basically every night on the lake, and now that I'm back at home I am totally MISERABLE. I hate all the guys in my class, they are so immature and busted, and I think D.T. Jr. and I had something very special that I may never find with anyone else. But the problem is that I will never see him again since my parents say it was just a summer thing. Like they know.

—Can't Let Go in Missouri

Dear Can't Let Go,

I sincerely hope that someday you and D.T. Jr. wind up at the same college, fall in love all over again, get married, and buy yourselves a summer home on Lake Tuckaho, just so you can have the pleasure of telling your parents "Told you so!" about 15,000 times. You're disappointed, your heart is aching, and you're stuck back home with the same losers you've known since kindergarten. Do what you have to do. Seethe.

But once you've seethed for a good long time, I hope you'll come to feel, as I do, that all relationships have their time and place, and at least for this chapter of your life, D.T. Jr. was the perfect summer lake boy. I bet he looked great in jean cutoffs. I bet he could roast a marshmallow like nobody's business. But who knows how he'd fare in a snowstorm, or during exam period, or over Thanksgiving dinner? What you need is a little spiritual trust that you and D.T. Jr. were meant to be for the summer, and you were meant to end there, too. For the time being, at least.

I know this is a bitter pill to swallow, but it's good practice, too. Most romances have natural endpoints, and if you get into the habit of kicking and screaming and dragging dead horses along for miles, you're in danger of souring memories that might otherwise be sweet.

Trust me. I've lived through it.

Annie

Chapter Eight

The abruptness of my departure from Grace's party must have raised a few eyebrows, but whatever speculation or analysis it engendered went on behind my back. I'd half expected to be treated to an intervention, or at least a couple of angry phone calls, but for the next few days I didn't hear from anybody, which in its own way was worse. One night at the Pierre I let myself tell Berglan Starker about the whole event, that's how eager I was to have someone forgive me and see my side, that it was suicide for a couple of kids who'd been dating for six months to up and get married to each other. I tried to keep the details general—Grace and Jake's news wasn't mine to spread—and this formality amused BS.

"But didn't you say these two young people—let's call them X and Y, for argument's sake—didn't you say X and Y had been friends for nearly a decade? Surely that alleviates some of your anxieties about their hasty courtship?"

"Yeah, sure, they've been friends forever. But ultimately that's just another reason to be concerned. I mean, if they were really meant for each other, why did it take them eight years to figure it out?"

Berglan smiled indulgently, which I didn't exactly like. "Pink, you know people change and grow up over eight years. You mustn't buy into this immediate gratification syndrome that's strangling your generation; not all love blooms at first sight. X and Y may have just the right foundation, having known and cared about each other for such a long time."

He was lecturing me! This man, who had hopped into bed with his girlfriend before his wife's plane left New York airspace, was lecturing me about marriage! "Maybe," I said. "I guess I lack perspective, since I've known them both for so long. And I definitely lack experience. That's why I wanted to ask you about it."

"Ah," he said. "Here come the arrows. I'd been wondering what all this moodiness was about."

"I have a legitimate topic here. You don't have to call it a mood. If you want to see a mood, I can arrange that."

BS pulled me on top of him. He liked me best whenever I was cranky. How thrilling it must be for the aristocrats of the world to get a glimpse of what we plebs honestly believe, when we're not just being polite. "You're acting awfully forward, for someone who's known me for less than eight years. I'm not sure we have the right foundation for heavy petting just yet."

"Oh, Pink dearest." He put his fingers over my mouth. "Do shut up."

However badly disagreements with lovers may sting, we expect them to crop up every now and again, know how to smooth them over with the time-tested simulacra of contrition, flowers and kisses and extra help with household chores. Platonic disagreements are trickier; you can't lash out at your best friend and then make things right with a peppermint-oil backrub. I knew I had to call Grace and apologize for the way I'd behaved at her engagement party, but I dreaded it, couldn't imagine how to explain my reaction without sounding like a sniveling, jealous, insecure rat. What I wanted from Grace was our old intimacy back, but I couldn't demand that while secretly sleeping with Bella's father. What I wanted, in essence, was something neither of us could give.

On Saturday, a week after the party, Grace and I met for a walk around the farmer's market in Union Square. Few things make Grace happier than fresh produce, and I dragged along behind her while she squeezed eggplants and chatted up the food vendors, waiting for an opportunity to talk. We bought a sack of cake donuts and sat down on a bench.

"These would be better if they were dipped in chocolate," I said.

"Pink sugar roses would be nice, too, and some swags. Basically we're after cupcakes. This scene is too no-frills for a couple of girls like us."

I pulled a stack of wedding magazines out of my backpack. "Look, this is a peace offering. I was a brat at your party and I'm sorry about it. I just couldn't understand how you wouldn't have told me first, and I guess it stung me to find out about your impending marriage at a press conference. But that's my problem."

"Is that supposed to be an apology?"

"Yes. I mean, I came and fished you out of Space, Time, and Motion the morning after I lost my virginity. You do remember that?"

"You losing your virginity eight years ago was not group information. This is different. Jake wanted to tell everybody all
together. He thought it would be more festive to make one big
announcement instead of a lot of little phone calls. And we
wanted to get to tell all of you, instead of you telling each other
first."

That was just it: all of Grace's decisions were now Grace and
Jake's decisions. They were a *we*; everything that happened to
them went into a joint file. The unconscious shift to first-person
plural, that ultimate grammatical rite of passage. "I'm not talking
about a lot of little phone calls. Anyway I could have faked it, if
the surprise were so monumentally important."

"Jake has these ideas. He wanted to make a big announcement
and pop a champagne cork off the ceiling. The secret truth about
men is that they like ceremony, even though they pretend to go
along with it reluctantly. It's the only way their life decisions seem
real to them. I could get married tomorrow in City Hall, but Jake
needs a few months of planning to get used to the idea."

A shiver went down my back. The end of summer was upon
us; the squirrels in the park were fat as lapdogs. "You can't get
married in City Hall. Your mother would die of grief if she didn't
get her full year of cake tastings and floral consultations."

"Please stop looking so stricken, Rose. This is normally viewed
as a cause for celebration."

"You're getting married. It's the end of life as we know it."

"Oh, for God's sake, stop being dramatic. Here's all that's
going to happen: I'm going to dress up in some queer family
gown that makes me look like I'm in a Gainsborough portrait,
and I'm going to be given lots of nasty little picture frames and

cordial glasses, and then it will be over. And you'll come over to my apartment on Saturday afternoons and drink crème de menthe, or whatever you're supposed to drink from cordial glasses, and tell me about all the exotic men you're sleeping with, and I'll put on my apron and listen enviously while I bake an apple spice cake to send home with you."

"Please say twenty-six is too young to qualify for Baked Goods Welfare."

"I'd like it if you could be a little happy for me, Rose. Even an imitation would be nice at this point."

"I *am* happy for you, Grace. I'm completely full of awe and wonder. I can only imagine what it feels like to have such a strong conviction about the future. I don't know if I even *have* a future, once this stupid festival is over. My only conviction is that I loathe apple spice cake, and would rather face a firing squad than watch you bake it. It's not fair of you to be so flip about this wedding stuff—I'm trying to learn by example, here."

"Oh, convictions. Every time I look around Jake's room at his electric guitar and his Soviet propaganda posters, I have heart failure. I think to myself: I'm going to have to live with that electric guitar in my bedroom. I'm going to have to stare at those Cyrillic letters for the rest of my life. I feel totally uncertain about this whole thing. But I don't know that I'd ever feel any other way. That's about normal, isn't it?"

"You're asking me? I know as much about it as I know about the Human Genome Project. Sure, it's about normal. You love Jake. Jake loves you. Who cares if he practices Pink Floyd when he's alone in the house? You're getting married. Happy, happy."

Grace looked as if like she might cry. So did I. And then at the same exact instant tears spilled down both of our cheeks.

"This is foolish," I said. "I keep botching this up. Here, let's look at one of these magazines. Gosh, what a clever way to preserve a bridal bouquet! This stuff makes *GirlTalk* look like the *NewsHour with Jim Lehrer*. Why are we crying?"

"I don't know." Grace took a sniffly bite of her donut. "I feel like an imposter. I want a known future. I love Jake. But I don't want to be the first one to leave our little band of nomads, either. I'm not ready to be a complete grown-up yet."

"Well ain't the grass always greener," I said, wiping my nose with my sleeve. "You can still be a nomad, Grace. Now you're just a nomad who's getting married. You're the nomad bride."

"Sounds like an Athol Fugard play."

"Everything sounds like a play to me. That's the problem." I wrapped the scarf I was wearing, a gray wool number Grace had knit for me, around my neck. The future was a maze of doors and boxes lined with tall, dark trees. "This one, this play, has your name in lights."

You know what they say in my business: the show must go on. The Footlights Festival, ugly and dim-witted stepcousin of *Last Winter in Dame Street,* was only ten days away, and however much Evan might have liked to forget this denouement of amateurs, First Born's name was already printed on the schedule of events.

Ironically, what had once been the great challenge of my scene was now my entry point for it, that is, Mary Tyrone's stubborn

and willful insistence on living in the past. At its core my monologue was about a woman whose very survival depended on taking refuge in the nostalgia of years gone by, before everything in
her life soured and went to shit. *Only the past when you were
happy is real.* Earlier in the summer, this emotional terrain had
baffled me; now I could have read aloud portions of my diary
and the homage to innocence-manqué would have been pretty
damn similar. Of course in O'Neill's version, Mary Tyrone gets
committed to a state insane asylum by her own two sons, a cau-
tionary tale of the limits of imagination whose poignancy was not
lost on me.

On an emotional level my scene was going well, but the con-
textual trappings of the monologue—the morphine, the old age,
the faint trace of that wretched Irish accent—were still giving me
trouble. By tech week, the week when we moved from our
rehearsal space into the theater, Evan turned his attention to the
business of sound cues and light cues and props and sets, and I
began experimenting with every last dysfunctional-old-lady
crutch I could think of: bifocals, dialect tapes, extra caffeine
before rehearsal. But they only made the whole performance feel
more Halloweenish.

One night, after everyone else had been dismissed, Evan kept
me around late and had me sit down onstage and do my monologue straight, just to him. No drugs, no accent, no shaky senior
citizen shtick. He shut off the overheads so the theater's only
light came from a single bulb on the prop table backstage. Suddenly goose bumps popped up on my arms and my scalp went
tight.

"What's the matter?" Evan asked.

"I don't know." My head tingled. "It's awfully dark in here, isn't it?"

"Boo. Monsters. Go ahead and get started, Rose. Don't ruin it by thinking too hard."

So I began reciting my lines, lines I'd said dozens of times, maybe a hundred, over the course of the summer. Too much repetition can drain the meaning out of anything, but I tried to hear the words for the first time again as I said them: *I had a talk with Mother Elizabeth. She is so sweet and good. A saint on earth. I love her dearly. It may be sinful of me but I love her better than my own mother. Because she always understands, even before you say a word. Her kind blue eyes look right into your heart. You can't keep any secrets from her. You couldn't deceive her, even if you were mean enough to want to.*

"Okay, hold it." Evan said. "Do you remember what David Mamet says about acting?"

I shook my head.

"He says there's no such thing as a *character* onstage. It's you onstage. Everything you are. Nothing can be hidden."

I waited to be struck by a great bolt of insight, but none came. "You mean I should drop the accent?"

"Yes, but I'm not talking about the accent. You're such a literalist, Rosalie. I'm talking about you, onstage. I need *you* up there, not some crazy imitation of a strung-out grandma. Stop hiding. *Nothing can be hidden.* You think acting is a dodge, a chance to be somebody instead of yourself. But the truth is it's the exact opposite. Acting is you, yourself, giving yourself up completely in front of whoever happens to be sitting in the audience. You can't just speak the words and fake around, pretending to be someone you have no idea about. This scene would be a whole lot simpler and a whole lot better if you forgot Mary Tyrone, whoever she is, and put yourself up there instead."

"And what if I don't have a Mother Elizabeth?"

"Literalist." Evan said it like a scold. "Literalist, literalist, literalist. This piece is about a woman who's so terribly frightened of revealing her true self, even to her own family, that she's driving herself nuts. It's awful to watch. Mother Elizabeth is beside the point."

I stood up and paced around in a circle. My chest was closing up around my throat.

"The tragedy of your character is how hard she works to be someone she isn't. Mary Tyrone believes that if she stops pretending to be completely together, completely happy and under control, her own family will cast her out. She never lets herself crack. Why do you think I gave this piece to you? Where do you and I come from?"

My body felt heavy, like I'd been pulled out of the wash and slung over a clothesline. "My family didn't cast me out of southern Massachusetts, if that's what you're suggesting."

"I'm suggesting that you have some firsthand experience of compartmentalization, if you will, and that thinking hard about this experience might help you do a less shitty job in your scene. I'm being serious, Rose. If you want a dodge, go be an advice columnist."

"Alright, I'm being serious now, too. Because you're wrong about one thing: you think Mary Tyrone is a con artist, that she's out peddling some virginal picture of herself she knows is a lie. But I think she believes in this act she's doing, and the person she's out to convince isn't her husband, or either one of her shitheel kids. The one whose life truly depends on believing the act is Mary herself."

"You're the one who's going to be up there," Evan said, folding his arms across his chest. "You tell me."

When I did the monologue again I felt angry at Evan, maybe even angry at Eugene O'Neill himself, for twisting nostalgia into the stuff of tragedy. Mary Tyrone's last lines are about love and happiness—*I fell in love with James Tyrone and was so happy for a time.* I wanted to stand up for her, for her entitlement to that happiness, no matter how imaginary or far-gone it was.

On my way out of the theater I found Declan Pearse leaning against a radiator in the foyer. He wore a pair of thinning corduroys and a lightweight V-neck sweater that looked soft and worn, like something you might want to launder and use as a pillowcase. He straightened up when he saw me and stepped on his jean jacket, which was sitting in a heap on the ground.

"Oh, hello," he said. "I'm here for Evan. We're going across the street for a jar."

I was tired enough to be glad Declan didn't go in for pleasantries. "He'll be out in a minute. He's closing up shop."

"Would you ever think of joining us?"

"A beer would put me straight to sleep. And then you two would have to haul me home and get me into bed, and my apartment is in a state of disarray unfit for human observation."

"First your trainers, now your flat. Are you quite obsessed by hygiene in all aspects of your life?"

"Disinfectant separates civilized man from his Cro-Magnon predecessors. Plus I especially like to clean when I feel my inner life going to seed, so to speak."

"And what's the matter with you?"

"Evan called me an escapist. He thinks my acting is a puffed-up version of playing dress-up. Then he explained why I'm perfectly well suited to playing a junkie whose entire life is a tragic charade."

"And? What do you think about it?"

"What is this, an interview? Why don't *you* tell me something about *your*self?"

Declan gave me the look of a cow being swarmed by biting gnats. "I've got nothing to tell. All I do is sit locked in my flat working on revisions. This is the first time I've been out of the house all day."

"Huh," I said grimly. "Well I guess *you* won't be getting any reproachful lectures on the importance of committing to your art."

"Would you like me to tell you a joke? I got a new one off the radio while I was eating supper. Have you heard about the pirate movie that's coming out Saturday week?"

Declan Pearse was truly an enormous man. He looked like the kind of person you might hire for protection if you were the ruler of a large country or the sole heir of a diamond fortune. I shrugged up at him. "Nope. Can't say I've heard a word about it."

"It's rated Aaaaarrrggghhhhhh."

The swinging door pushed open from the theater: Evan. "That's a good one," I said. "Here comes your date."

I walked home up Second Avenue. For the millionth time that

week I thought blackly about how all my friends had gotten their acts together and turned into wretched little Responsible Citizens, with careers and relationships and ardent dreams of matching flatware. Traitors. Suckers. I slunk along the street and scowled at all the well-turned-out youths, eating dinner on the sidewalk, discussing politics, rushing home with bakery boxes tied up in string. If you are not marked for domestic tranquillity, such ease in the world is a personal affront.

On Wednesday nights, Book Club nights, Evan organized our rehearsal schedule so that I could be free in time to get to Adele Goldberg by eight. The reading circle had become my feel-good activity of the week; I felt about it the way healthful people feel about going to the gym, that is I got an actual boost (endorphins?) from just doing it, as the slogan says. Pearl Coleman had begun to participate more actively in our discussions, and the Wednesday night orderlies, Ramon and Tyrell, made a point of complimenting me on my way of drawing her out. (This before and after they took their two-hour smoke breaks while I read *Our Man in Havana* in the game room; those guys were nobody's fools.) Anyway I loved it, and loved that my weekly reward after AGSC was a standing dinner date with Berglan Starker, virtue and sin being flip sides of the same coin, in the vaulted treasury of human emotions.

On the Wednesday night of tech week I was especially tired, having left my apartment for work at 9 a.m. and gone straight to rehearsal, then straight to Adele Goldberg, but when the reading circle broke up I hopped in a cab and went uptown, to Café des

Artistes. There are plenty of ways to drop a lot of money on dinner in New York, and I admired Berglan for being so resolutely stodgy in his choice of venues. Other men probably tried to impress their young consorts by keeping pace with the latest celebrity-packed Vongerichten offering, but not my Berglan. Strictly jackets and white table linens for him.

A detour on Madison Avenue, something about security for heads of state in town for a UN conference, caused me to arrive at the restaurant a few minutes late, and when the maître d' led me over to the table, Berglan was engrossed in a stack of white documents. He looked up when I took my seat, and for a flicker of an instant he seemed disoriented, as if he hadn't remembered I was joining him. This is not the most reassuring expression to see playing across your lover's face, but I consoled myself by thinking of his schedule, how many appointments he had in an average day, how many meetings and briefings and conference calls with business associates whose names he had to remember. I would have liked to kiss him out of it, but public displays of affection are not for the unmarried, in restaurants like Café des Artistes. So I asked him what he was reading, and settled into my chair.

"Something you surely know more about than I do." He lifted up a page from the top of the stack: Pearse/Dame Street/32. It was Declan's script. I was not pleased to see it. I was never pleased to see any artifacts from Real Life at the dinner table with Berglan Starker, and this one threatened to be particularly intrusive.

"I don't know much about it at all, actually. Except that Cam's turning into a minor celebrity for his part, and the thing hasn't even gone into rehearsals yet. They ran a profile of him on some Broadway website last week."

BS slid the breadbasket towards me. My sensitivity levels must have already been high by this point, for it seemed a hostile gesture, an unspoken commentary on my lack of self-restraint.

"Evan's asked me to put up some money for it. He thinks it's a good gamble."

"Evan's a regular Don King these days."

"You think he's wrong?"

"I'm not saying that. I'm just not in the habit of reading plays for their investment potential. What do you think of the script?"

"It's not bad. I find it a bit melodramatic in patches, but that's just a matter of taste. And the current numbers on Broadway do suggest that melodrama sells tickets."

If I could have sealed the man's bank accounts and frozen all of his assets, I would have. I wanted him as far away from that play as possible. But even more unsettling than the prospect of his getting on board the *Dame Street* caravan was his assessment of Declan's script. True, I wouldn't have minded watching the entire production sink like a stone, but melodramatic it was not. It was bitter, and raw, and full of the anguish of love and the pain of having no home to return to. It was about someone who'd made actual choices to escape the unhappiness of his life, and who'd then been brave enough to go home and answer to the people he'd abandoned. Woe to the man who mistook those genuine emotions for melodrama. And double-woe to the girl who had fallen for him.

After dinner we went to the Pierre and had a nightcap, then got into bed. My stomach hurt from a long day of coffee, vending machine candy, and boeuf à la Bourguignonne, but I peeled down to my stretch lace skivvies and went to work just the same. It was easy, in bed, to see that I pleased Berglan Starker, that he appreciated my stamina and my youthful enthusiasm. He liked to watch me do whatever I was doing to him, which was quite a change from the self-absorbed pleasure of guys my own age, who rolled their eyes back in their heads, squeezed pillows over their faces, and no doubt tried to pretend that the body straddling theirs belonged to Nicole Kidman. In the beginning of our affair all that naked eye contact had creeped me out, especially since Berglan's expression was so clinical and appraising, not unlike a doctor's expression mid-physical. But I'd come around to liking the attention, and even liking the faint client/laborer dynamic it gave our lovemaking. They don't call it "performing" oral sex for nothing. In the infomercials I've seen on the Playboy Channel at Cam's apartment, experts always say the key to good sex is getting out of your brain and into your body, as if human beings can actually separate the two. Maybe that makes for good sex if you're a virgin, or a repressed Westinghouse finalist, but the rest of us need our brains to tell our bodies what to do. That night, my brain commands came straight from dinner, from that dead-cold look of non-recognition I'd gotten when I first walked into the restaurant. Make this old man remember you, my brain said. Make him need something from you that he can't get anywhere else.

When we finished making love, Berglan propped a pillow up in bed and read from a bound report he pulled out of his briefcase. I could see how some women might find this offensive, getting cheated out of the post-coital cuddle in favor of a government briefing on commercial real estate tax codes, but I found it sweetly domestic, and I nestled up next to him and closed my eyes. Endless sex and pillow talk are the provenance of short-lived affairs; our kind of comfort and routine was different. In my cozy sleepiness I murmured something to this effect out loud, that I slept best when he was working in bed next to me, that I sometimes kept the bedside lamp on in my apartment just to re-create the effect. He patted my head when I said this, and when he didn't say anything back I figured he was engrossed in his reading, some scintillating numbers from the state budget report. But I didn't hear any pages turn for a while. And then he snapped off the light and whispered that it was time to go to sleep.

I passed the workdays during tech week like a zombie, staring at my computer screen and signing off on proofs without even having read them. The Annie questions piled up in my in-box by the dozen, teenage angst metastasizing before my very eyes. Each morning I lifted the stack onto my lap and tried to sift through it, but I couldn't face the rainbow stationery or the bubble handwriting for more than ten-minute intervals without getting up for a drink or a pace. Think of doctors, I told myself. Think of social workers. People devote their entire working lives to managing other people's pain; they come up with ways not to let it overwhelm them. All I had to sort through were a few hundred letters from girls with minor heartache. But it seemed impossible that heartache should accrue at such a relentless rate. Every day the letters came, dropped onto my desk by one perky Reader Mail intern after another, and every day I made it through fewer and fewer of them, slipped fewer form letters into SASEs. What good can a xerox do someone who's truly heartbroken? What good can a column of magazine print do, for that matter? I had my doubts about whether any of it could make any dent in any girl's sliver of pain, but my doubts didn't stop the mail from coming.

What had started bothering me about the letters, beyond the sheer quantities I received, was their general tone of confusion and shock, for example, "I am normally so popular and boss and then homeboy busts outta nowhere and dumps my a–s so why I still hung up on him?????" Suppose I had developed a filing system according to topic; here's what it would have looked like: Surprised and Outraged by Boyfriend's Behavior (40%); Shocked and Pining after Breakup (30%); Perplexed and Stymied by Unrequited Love (25%); Misc. Complaints About Parents, Long Distance, Exes, etc. (5%). Bewilderment was the common denominator, the unifying theme to the panoply of romantic quandaries large and small. *How could this happen to me? How could I have gotten myself into this?* I had always understood my role in this exchange to be the Voice from the Other Side, the experienced spokeswoman from post-high-school reality, where the patterns and rules governing love were predictable, even logical. That was why *GirlTalk* gave me salary, benefits, and an ergonomically correct desk chair: to spell out the hows, whys, and what-to-do-nexts. But what if the patterns and rules governing love were just as incomprehensible and random to me as they were to my readers? There it was, the brick wall I slammed into every time I slit an envelope. *I don't know,* I wanted to write back. *I'm just as mystified by the whole business as you are. Do your home-*

work, take your vitamins, and don't get pregnant. The rest is any-body's guess.

I started dropping the letters into a cardboard box in the bottom drawer of my file cabinet, as if sequestering them might make their contents less contagious. No such luck.

My time-honored companion for gloom and malaise was Bella, whose flair for depression was as natural as some people's flair for gardening or table tennis. Bella loved to nurse a good foul mood, to suss out its most obscure roots and pore over it as one might pore over a blood-bloated tick, with gruesome reverence. Bella was my girl in a snit. I called her from the office and found her at home.

"I hate all of our friends. Let's go have you buy me a tattoo of a dagger."

"Tattoos are for the unbeautiful. Let's go have me buy you a really excellent pair of calfskin gloves."

"I can't afford calfskin, B. Anyway I was kidding about the you-buy-me-something part. Let's just go hang out somewhere."

"I insist. Fall is upon us, and I can't bear to see you wear those Von Trapp family mittens of yours ever again. It's lunchtime, isn't it? I'll meet you outside Saks in twenty minutes."

I walked from my office over to Rockefeller Plaza and waited for Bella on a bench that faced Fifth Avenue. She got out of her cab and took me by the arm. "Get away from all of these Japanese tourists. Too much exposure to flashbulbs causes epilepsy."

Inside the heavy doors of Saks, Bella led me to the glove

counter and explained the difference between silk linings, cashmere linings, and fleece linings. Bella knows from accessories. I tried on ten different pairs she approved of, and wound up with a dark brown pair of gloves so soft I wished they were slippers. Bella slapped down her credit card and asked for a box.

"Merry-almost-Christmas, Rose. Now give us the interpersonal grievance list," she said, as we wound our way around the labyrinth of perfume counters. "Would I be correct in guessing that this skunked humor is about the curse of holy matrimony that's about to befall our friends Grace and Jake?"

"Sort of," I said. Of course I couldn't tell Bella the whole story, that half my bleak mood had to do with my dead-end pursuit of her father. But just being around her felt weirdly satisfying, like the root cause of my gloom was good and tangible, something I could sink my teeth into. Concrete unhappiness is an autumn hayride, compared with generally unfocused misery.

"I suspected as much, when you dashed out of that O. Henry party without so much as an air-kiss."

Bella stopped to spritz something fecund on her neck. "You realize that Grace has been gunning for marriage since the day we met her, right? The girl's been collecting her trousseau since her sixteenth birthday. I bet she secretly keeps a layette in the back of her closet."

"What about Jake? He's supposed to have the libido of a platoon of soldiers on recreational leave from Saudi Arabia. Why do you think he's suddenly so excited about getting married?"

"Who knows? It probably turns him on to play at despoiling a virgin, night after night. The erotic imagination is nice and rangy. You just can't sweat it. We weren't all cut out for the breezy nuptials of our forbears."

"But doesn't it make you feel slightly developmentally retarded?"

"Not a speck. But then I suppose you're at a disadvantage, being the progeny of such sweet responsible folks as Mr. and Mrs. Preston. Those of us born of sharks and neurasthenics don't put any stock in the institution of marriage to begin with."

"That's not true, Belle. If you hadn't put any stock in the institution of marriage, you wouldn't have been so upset when your parents' crashed and burned."

Bella looked at me, her eyes slightly narrowed. I couldn't read what was in her face but it was darker, less set than it had been a second ago. "So I was born innocent and then I wised up. It happens to everybody sooner or later; it's in the Bible. I suppose we can thank my father for kicking me out of the garden nice and young."

I ran my hand along a rack of silk shawls; they fluttered against each other, their hangers jangling. I avoided Bella's eye. "You think everybody can do that? Point to the one thing that spoiled their innocence?"

She shrugged. "Sure, probably. But not everyone wants to look that hard. Once you start to plot it out all the other nice charades fall away, too, and there you are, revealed, the supposedly brash girl flashing her family's gold card to ward off her own insecurities, the sweet little church mouse toting around her free pair of gloves. People don't like to see themselves that lucidly, when it comes down to it."

"No one can be boiled down so easily, Belle. You know that—

people are full of surprises, none of us could have possibly pre-dicted Jake and Grace on their way to the altar, five years ago."

"You're talking about divining the future. I'm talking about knowing the present." She smiled at me and for a second I felt spooked, as if the box of gloves in my hand might slip out of my grip onto the floor. But then she looked away and her voice got hard and Bella-like again. "Anyway I think marriage is perfect for Jake and Grace, you should cheer up about it. The track is just going to get more and more uneven for the lot of us. As soon as you get used to that idea it's remarkably liberating."

I thought about this while she examined evening clutches. Everything she picked up looked expensive and handsome in her hands—all she had to do was touch her finger to a sequin to spin it into gold.

"It's not that I wish *I* were getting married. You understand that, right?"

She slid a tiny beadworked purse over her wrist and inspected it in the mirror. "Of course I understand that. If you wanted to get married you'd have taken me up on one of the ten dates I've tried to arrange for you in the past month. You just hate change. I hate it, too, but I'm a realist. And here's my best realist advice—I know, I know, from a dilettante to a professional. Make like Cinderella, Rose. Don't stay too late at the ball."

Props, of course, count for something, in real life as on stage. The Chekhovian rifle. Or in my case, the brown calfskin gloves. BS noticed them right away when I showed up wearing them for drinks at the Carlyle.

"My, my," he said, summoning the waiter. "Aren't those handsome. They look like just the sort of thing that should be given to a lovely girl by an admirer."

From time to time BS made this sort of quasi-jealous remark, though he was far too correct to ever pry any further. "In fact they were given to me by your daughter," I said. "Yesterday afternoon, at Saks Fifth Avenue. Pretty nice, aren't they?"

For a second Berglan looked horrified, but he recovered quickly: "Well she has very good taste, doesn't she. Did you have a birthday you didn't tell me about?"

"Nope. You just have an incredibly generous kid. My birthday isn't until June, so we have plenty of time to plan for it. I wouldn't mind going somewhere far away, don't you usually do that in June?"

BS was silent. Of course.

"Europe, for example." I looked around the bar, at the piano player, at the illustrations on the wall next to us, drawings of New York in Ludwig Bemelmans's hand, all the girls looking like Madeline. "I've never been to Europe, except for Ireland, which doesn't really count. How pathetic is that? What could my parents have been thinking, spending every vacation in Florida, year after year?"

"It's not pathetic."

"Yes it is. I'm twenty-six years old and I've never even seen the Eiffel Tower. We should do something about it, don't you think?"

The waiter appeared before BS could answer. "I'll have what he's having, please."

"This is your awful scotch, Pink. Wouldn't you like some soda in it, at least?" And then, before I could answer, he flashed the waiter an imaginary inch. "Give her a smidge."

"Actually, don't." My face was suddenly hot at being spoken for. "Just the scotch, please. But you can bring the gentleman a tumbler of soda on the side, since he seems to want one."

The waiter retreated and BS cut me a look, almost fatherly, that said he was in no mood to deal with a petulant kid. I knew I wouldn't be kept around for much longer, no matter how well I behaved. I knew it in my heart, the way you know the sound of a telephone ringing when bad news is on the other end of the line, the way you know you're going to lose the raffle even as you shell out for the ticket book. Berglan Starker had liked me and my charming dreams of becoming an actress, he'd liked my home-spun little studio apartment, and best of all, he'd liked himself for keeping company with someone so far off the map. But he wasn't about to go to bat for any of it. The pat on the head a few days ago had been my answer. Which meant the thornier I could be to him, the better. That way, when he left me, at least I wouldn't have to think I'd given him my best shot.

BS's dismissal of me happened, like all efficient business transactions, early on a weekday morning. I remember this detail because we'd been rushing to get dressed and off to our respective offices, and as soon as he suggested we pop into the coffee bar next door I knew something was up. On mornings when we had the time for it, we ordered breakfast in bed. On mornings when we were running late, we skipped breakfast altogether. We never popped into coffee bars. The man is congenitally opposed to drinking beverages out of cardboard cups.

"We would like to have two large mugs of your coffee," he told the girl behind the counter, who looked at him as if he were speaking a foreign language. "One black, the other with a dash of hot milk in it. Thank you. We'll be sitting at that corner table next to the newspaper selections."

Taking my seat across from him, I felt as if I'd been summoned to see the school principal. I was about to get a talking to, and my heart rebelled.

"You look as if you're about to throw your scone at me, Pink. It's making me very edgy."

I gave him a dark look. "The meter is running. I'm going to be late for work and Ginger has me on tardiness probation. Perhaps that's the tension you're sensing."

"Pink, dearest, listen to me," he said gently, and I knew I was in for it. "I'm beginning to fear that the complexities between us make it impossible for me to give you what you deserve."

"Complexities?" My voice came out so meekly I almost didn't recognize it as my own. Somehow, when I'd pictured this scene unfolding, I'd imagined a conclusion dramatic enough to suit the harlequin circumstances of our affair: threats of blackmail, sobbing fits, maybe a slap or two across the face. But of course there wasn't going to be any of that stuff. There was just me, sad, literalist, incorrigibly realistic me, sitting at a wobbly table in a Starbucks, forfeiting the good fight before it had even begun.

"Maybe it would be the better part of valor for us to spend some time apart from each other, my dear. You know I admire you far too much to be able to stand doing you any harm. When we first took up with each other I promised myself that as soon as things took a gloomy turn, we'd do better to go our separate ways. What do you think about that?"

"I think it's not up to me, is it, and so you shouldn't try pretending that it is."

"Alright." Berglan sighed the sigh of a man facing the inevitable, a man facing something tiresome and perfunctory he'd faced a thousand times before. It was mortifying. "Alright. I am the one with the obligations, it's true. But you're the one who's young and on the verge of a whole rich life, and I'm not a speck worried about you, if that's what you're thinking. Not a speck. I'm only sorry for me."

The guy was perceptive, I had to give him that, because that's exactly what I *had* been thinking: that he was going to try to piece together some delicate, chivalrous way to save me, or to buy me out. Part of me wanted to tell him to shove it, that he didn't need to worry about anything beyond his fleet of ex-wives and his daughter's analysis bills. The other part wanted to suction myself to his pants leg and hold on for dear life.

"Will I see you again?" I asked, which was a dumb question, since I knew I would see him in less than 48 hours at the Footlights Festival.

"Of course you'll see me again. You'll see me the day after tomorrow, for starters, at your grand performance, which I'm very much looking forward to. You mustn't cry, my darling. I'll be sitting right in the front row cheering you on."

"But will I see you after that?"

"I have no doubt of it. I believe we're quite fond of each other, and that shouldn't have to come to an end."

Well, I had gotten what I expected. Just exactly that. And the tiny, infinitesimally small part of me that had dared to wonder if life might not have some rare capacity to surprise, to deal the long-odds outcome in spite of all the accumulated wisdom to the contrary, to beat, as it were, the house, had learned its repeating lesson. Life doesn't surprise you. Not in that way, at least. It's a rare twenty-six-year-old who's innocent enough to still believe that it might. By 9 o'clock that morning, I'd wiped my name off the list.

BS stood up and kissed me goodbye, a soft kiss on the cheek that I had to close my eyes for so as not to cry. I stayed in the Starbucks and watched through the window as he got into a cab. I knew he wouldn't turn around to wave to me, and I was right. The Berglan Starkers of the world don't turn around after they've said goodbye. They do things neatly, and they do them once. I sat in the coffee shop, just sat there and stared at the corner the cab had turned around, for a long, long time. Call it my actor's instinct for dramatic conclusions. *Exit, Berglan Starker. Slow fade to black.*

Dear Annie,

I'm going out with the most excellent guy. He's a poet and a photographer and a feminist, and one huge breath of fresh air from most of the jock toads who populate my nightmare high school. He's like Jean-Paul Sartre only better. Here's the problem: my parents hate him. They think he's not goal-oriented enough. They prefer guys who play rugby and tennis, and they're always trying to set me up with my dad's partner's heinous son. How do I make them understand that I'm serious about my boyfriend?

—Oppressed by Closed-Mindedness in Connecticut

Dear Oppressed,

Hmmm. It sounds like you need to get your parents a wall calendar, since they clearly haven't replaced theirs since 1952. Do they try to choose your outfits and your girlfriends, too? Or do they save the FBI background checks for your gentleman callers?

Practical advice: while it may be tempting to start wearing Ralph Nader T-shirts and calling your dad's partner by his first name, declaring war against your mom and dad will only make your life harder. The more subversive solution is for you and your boyfriend to play as nice as you need to in order to get your parents off your back. What are some safe conversational topics the three of them have in common? School? Travel? Books? (Sounds like your poet is pretty smart; that always impresses even the most avid rugby fans.) Whatever you do, do not, under any circumstances, allow the following subjects to come up: golf, SUV gas mileage, vegetarianism, Robert Mapplethorpe. Remember, you want to find common ground here. You want to create the illusion that your boyfriend is nice and normal, even though you love him because he's not.

It's definitely a bummer that your parents are trying to force you into a mold you're obviously not cut out for. But try to be patient with them—instead of thinking of yourself as a victim, think of yourself as a teacher, a guide, someone who's opening their eyes to the world beyond the country club gates. Make your love for your boyfriend contagious, if you know what I mean. Before you know it your folks will be reading Adrienne Rich out loud to each other every night before bed.

Trust me. I've lived through it.

Annie

Chapter Nine

On Thursday, the day of our Footlights performance, I woke up with a sore throat and called in sick at *GirlTalk*. I boiled a pot of tea and drank four mugs of it, with lemon and honey and a few shakes of salt, which helped my voice but made me have to pee constantly. Between trips to the bathroom I sat at my kitchen counter with a scarf around my neck and dreamt of crawling back into bed. There is no weariness like the weariness of performance anxiety. My eyelids were made of lead.

When I got to the theater for our 6 o'clock call, Grace had strung a strand of white lights around our dressing room, which was really a large storage closet with two clothes racks and a full-length mirror. The theater, in fact, was not much bigger than a storage closet, but it had risers and a small lighting booth and black velvet curtains separating the backstage from the playing space. First Born was sandwiched on the program between two other companies, one called The Dink Department and one called Guerrilla Thespia. From the dressing room next to ours came a series of primal chants and whoops that would have made history's bravest explorers tremble for their lives.

"Oh, I get it," said Jake, who was swathing himself in priestly raiment, custom sewn by Bella's boyfriend Jean-Marie.

"They're, like, guerrilla guerrillas. They're going to attack the audience."

"What does that have to do with the theme?" Cam asked, as he penciled on loads of black eyeliner. "This festival is supposed to be about disease. Anybody can attack the audience. They better be doing it from wheelchairs."

In general, our company was too square for the downtown festival scene; we stuck to scripts that had been published by Samuel French, which made us real throwbacks in a world of inflatable penis costumes and plays without speech. At the drinking fountain, where I went to refill my water bottle, one of the inflatable penises from the first ensemble sized me up and patted me on the shoulder. "Break a leg, Harvard." I supposed he meant that as a farm-team version of trash talk, but I thanked him anyway.

Bella came back to our dressing room half an hour before the house opened, carrying a plate of shortbread cookies in the shape of crutches and stethoscopes. She'd special ordered them for us from her neighborhood bakery. "This place is like the trunk of a bumper car," she said, moving all of our props and scripts and makeup cases off the room's single chair so she could sit down. "The house is filling up nicely, you guys. We've got someone here from *Time Out* and *Thrust,* and at least one casting associate from MTC. Now listen, here's the schedule. Evan wants you warmed up and in your places by eight. The dinks are slated to go until eight-twenty, but they're all improv, so if things go well and one of them gets struck by lightning, they could be done early and you guys should be ready to go on. Remember that there's no break between sets. I have cards from Evan for each of you, he says to read them when you have some down time, ha ha. He also says that the guys should set the rocking chair for the O'Neill scene, there's glow tape downstage marked out for it. Nice peignoir, Rosie," she said, fingering the muslin of my white nightgown. "It looks like one of those Mormon undergarments. Very kinky, all of you."

We went over the schedule together: warm-ups; Dinks; Genet; O'Neill; Becker; then insurrectionary warfare from the company next door. "I think we're going to have a sold-out house," Bella said. "Flax and his Irish Nancy boy are front and center. There's a party afterwards at the sound op's apartment in Fort Green, but we can also go back to my place, if that would be more congenial. I stocked the bar."

When Bella left, Cam, Jake, Grace, and I did a few vocal exercises together; my voice was in decent shape in spite of the itch in my throat. Through the curtains we could hear the audience filing in. It would have been helpful to go off somewhere and have a private look at my note from Evan, but there was no inch of unclaimed space in the entire theater, so I opened the envelope in the dressing room and the others did, too. *R—* mine read, in Evan's sloppy hand. *You have reserves of strength inside you that you have to trust out there, my sweet little drug addict. Nothing can be hidden. And remember O'Neill's own words about MT: "her most appealing quality is her innate unworldly innocence." Dare to be an innocent, R. I can't wait to see—*

The cover of the card was a reproduction of a John Singer Sargent painting: a girl in a field of poppies, holding a golden parasol to shade her from the sun.

· · ·

As soon as the house lights dimmed for the opening act, Cam and Jake left the dressing room and set themselves for their entrance. Grace put her hand on my forehead; it felt cold to the touch.

"Clammy," she whispered, putting her cardigan around my shoulders. "You're white as a sheet. What's up?"

"*Folie à deux*," I whispered back. "I don't think I'm ready to go out there, Grace."

"Of course you're not. We're never ready; that's the fun, remember? Readiness is for the chorus of *Cats*. Now teach me some of that nice yoga breathing you do. The boys are going on any second."

The stage, when I stepped onto it, was blue in a wash of eerie light. The special set on my rocking chair was so bright I couldn't make out a single person sitting in the chairs on the risers. It was the fog in my monologue, Edmund Tyrone's famous fog, blue and concealing as a low-hanging cloud. I tilted my head up at the grid and stared into that light until my eyes burned with its washed-out brilliance, until everything in my vision was scorched and spectral, far away. When I looked at the audience again the faces were blanks, dozens of Edmunds and Jameses and James Juniors. The shuffling programs and shifting legs were the drinks of the Tyrone men clinking on the table, and I waited until they died away. I breathed in the stillness of the room.

My voice had a halting hoarseness to it in the opening beats. But once I got launched into the story of Mother Elizabeth the monologue starting rolling, and I heard the words as if I were hovering above myself, in a kind of fever dream. It is a trance, performing by yourself, a voodoo you submit to without knowing how you're doing it or if it's really happening at all. It is like breathing with your whole body, or watching yourself float on air, or dancing steps you know so well you hardly feel yourself moving through them. And then it's over, very quickly, and you stand up and try to remember where the words went, how they left you so quickly, how they sounded to the people who'd never heard them before. But those minutes onstage before you start analyzing and asking questions are pure nectar, a liquid that runs through your veins like silver light. You can't stop; you can't repeat yourself or undo what you've said; you can't think of going backwards. Ask any actor: the spell of the stage releases you from yourself, for as long as you're out there underneath it. The spell of the stage cuts through anything; it can make a heart as heavy as stone bounce and leap in light.

At the reception everyone seemed giddy. The reporter from *Time Out New York* wanted to interview Cam about outsider theater, and there was talk of a feature piece on him in a future issue. Grace and Jake were hauling off to the party in Brooklyn with a few members of Guerrilla Thespia, but I told them I was too tired to go. The next day after work I was going home to Hanson to visit my parents, and I hadn't even packed.

Evan broke away from a bored-looking Constantine for long enough to tell me that I'd done a good job on my scene. "That was better than you've ever done it," he said, tugging on my sleeve. "I'm beginning to think getting out of the room is the best favor I can do for you. Declan and Manny were knocked out. And Constantine said you looked gorgeous, which you do."

I looked over the sea of heads and spotted Declan talking to Berglan Starker on the far side of the lobby. If I stayed any longer I would have to exchange words or at least a look with BS, and I couldn't do it, not in that room. "There's an odd couple for you," I said, slinging my backpack over my coat.

"I should have hired a professional schmoozer to stand in for Declan," Evan said. "Tens of thousands of producing dollars are hinging on that introduction."

"I wouldn't worry too much, if I were you. The kid is bank."

I kissed Evan's cheek, thanked him, and told him goodnight.

Nothing tamps the smoldering embers of drama quite like five hours on the Amtrak Nor'easter. As Train #401 made its creeping, smoke-spewing way from Penn Station to South Station, the past months of rehearsals, dinners at Le Bernardin, and crotchless teddys receded from my memory, subsumed by the fluorescent reality of unreserved coach seating and frozen pizza from the café car. I'd be exaggerating if I said I'd gotten used to Fifth Avenue life under Berglan Starker's wing, but a fleeting taste of privilege is all one really requires to resent vinyl seat covers and the trappings of workaday life. Fuck it. I'd hated vinyl seat covers since the day I was born.

My parents (have I properly introduced them yet? Joanie and Tom, piano teacher and dentist, respectively) were scheduled to pick me up at the Braintree commuter rail stop on Friday night at 6:37, which meant I had a total of five and a half not entirely welcome hours for reflection. Trains—even our dirty, perpetually late American ones—can be grandly melancholic if you squint hard enough, and I couldn't help feeling, as we wheezed north through the rail yards of Stamford, Hartford, and New Haven, where the fall colors were already beginning to show, as if I were taking some kind of symbolic journey backwards, the proverbial loser's homecoming made by all small-town kids who set their sights too high. My classmates at Hanson Memorial had been more modest in their goals; they'd conquered Massachusetts with middle management jobs at Fleet Boston and First New England, or they'd stayed home and partnered up with the family business. I was the hometown Icarus, thinking myself too good for the South Shore and now slinking back to it, anonymous, jilted, and twelve hundred dollars in debt on my MasterCard, thanks to the exorbitant waxing and lingerie habits I'd developed of late. Not that I planned to advertise the jilted or debt-ridden part.

My parents, punctual and eager as always, met me inside the Braintree station. They looked good, in the bland, competent AARP way parents are supposed to look: my mom had her gray hair cut in a Peter Pan-ish bob, and she wore a lilac cotton cable-knit sweater and a long denim skirt; my dad, whose small amount of hair was combed across his bald spot, wore a short-sleeved button-down tucked into a pair of khakis. It's a New England mania, this L. L. Bean devotion to generic, shapeless clothing that reveals nothing of the wearer's heart or mind. In the back of my brain I couldn't stop thinking about the fact that Berglan Starker was even older than my father, but I made a concerted effort not to dwell on it as we all hugged hello, comparisons being odious and, in this case, just plain gross.

"You look so grown up, Rosie!" my mom said, tucking my hair behind my ears, unable to resist her maternal grooming instincts. "Look at this fascinating necklace!"

I had treated myself to a few new chokers (Berglan Starker had once made an admiring comment about their rough-and-ready saloon-girl quality, and an Indian boutique a block from my apartment sold fake gold ones for almost nothing), but I hardly saw how a piece of costume jewelry could make me look more grown up. Maybe I looked world-weary? Jaded? They'd seen me only six months ago, when I'd come home for Easter. I hated to think the summer's developments had taken a visible toll.

"You look great, too," I said to Mom, even as part of me was assessing the horrifying genetic certainty that I would someday wear a size fourteen. "I'm so happy to see you guys."

"How's my favorite daughter?" Dad asked, pinching my cheeks in his mildly painful way. "Wait till you see what we've done with your room, kiddo. Workout center, tanning bed, kennel, you'll hardly recognize the place." This was Dad's favorite joke. He'd been making it since I went away to college. I'd never before given much thought to the luxury of having parents who behave like parents, repeating themselves, cracking corny jokes, making suspicious remarks about non-Western jewelry. Some people's parents don't play that way at all. I let Dad carry my duffel bag out to the car.

My parents' house, the house I grew up in, looks like a set piece from the original production of *Our Town*. Two stories, three bedrooms, Cape Cod shingles, flagstone path, neighbors nestled with their 2.4 children at respectful distances on either side of evergreen stands. My mother is a strong adherent of the craft-fair school of interior design: baskets of dried wildflowers abound indoors, as do decorative wall hangings and ceramic pots of potpourri. I have always felt like a traitor, aping the snobbish beige minimalism of my city friends. In the home of my girlhood, beds had skirts and wallpaper had borders and candles had scents. Goldilocks might have dropped by at any moment, looking for a bowlful of leftover porridge and a place to crash.

On the night of my homecoming, Dad grilled enough red meat to keep a family of twelve fed until New Year's. I tried my best to play hungry and carnivorous at dinner, even though I had the limited appetite of someone who had just been dumped. I showed them a stack of publicity pictures for the Footlights Festival (one of the techies had loaned me a set of prints, and I looked appropriately ghoulish and pale in each one, an irritating parting image for BS to have had of me, vanity thy name is Rosalie). My parents were impressed. Publicity photos, with their white borders and dramatic lighting effects, could make a prison variety show look professional, so I was especially deliberate in my efforts not to up-sell the festival's prestige. Hyping an event that had come and gone with absolutely no consequence just seemed too desperate, even though it would have been a favor to Mom and Dad, who wanted so badly to be proud of me.

After dinner, Mom informed me that she had volunteered my services to talk—informally, she kept promising, as if I might otherwise have been tempted to hire a speechwriter—at her group music lesson on Saturday morning at the First Presbyterian Church. The girls, she explained cheerily, were awestruck by my magazine job; most of them had been reading Annie Answers for years, as had their sisters, and their fondest hope was to meet me and have me sign their magazines; then they could all live happily ever after, more happily for having met a young female role model (Mom's words) from their very own hometown who would inspire them to work hard and set their goals high, since such achievements had been proven possible by yours truly, etc. I recognized this as a cheap ploy, my own mother trading on my feminist agenda to get me to do her piano class a favor, but what was I going to say? No? That I was sick of *GirlTalk,* that it was the heaviest of all the iron chains dragging my spirit to the bottom of the river, that I'd outgrown it, that if I had any real confidence I'd quit hiding behind a stultifying day job and put my energy into acting, even if it meant moving to Queens and living on canned goods? I was not going to say that. Not to the woman who'd lived in the same three-bedroom house, driven the same Toyota station wagon, taken the same two-week Florida vacation every year of her adult life so that I could go to Harvard loan-free, with as generous a monthly allowance as all of my roommates had. Instead I told her of course, fine, First Presbyterian at ten o'clock. I would take some Nyquil and she could wake me at nine.

It is a weighty responsibility, being an only child. All of your parents' hopes are pinned on you; you alone can validate or indict the job they've done; their many sacrifices are plain as day, funneled straight from their paychecks into your pocket, no greedy or feckless siblings to share the guilt, no one to slough off the attention on, nobody else's failings of sensitivity or achievement to make you feel less bad about your own. Whenever I went home I felt it was my duty to be cheerful and optimistic, to make my parents worry less. I washed dishes; I showed them the festival program and some newspaper clippings from free downtown weeklies; I swallowed my sneezes and stifled my cough. I was as guarded and remote with them on the subject of my inner life as movie stars are with *National Enquirer* reporters. What good could their worrying do?

While I dozed off in Hanson, tucked under my old cottage flower comforter on my old twin four-poster bed, a few important things were going down in New York, 10 p.m. being closer to midday there than to bedtime. (A) Bella was breaking up with our costume designer Jean-Marie, launching what would prove to be a long career of anti-French sentiment, and more; (B) Declan was accepting an offer to visit some friends of his in Boston—I can't remember which ones, Boston is teeming with Irish people; and (C) Berglan Starker's wife was tearing through his closet, looking for a particularly fetching rust-colored tie which she'd apparently given him for a birthday present, though I hadn't known that fact when I'd pinched it from his attaché case on our last morning together, aware, subconsciously at least, that it was more or less time to lay claim to a parting memento and prepare myself for the worst. But I didn't know about any of that stuff yet, obviously. I was 200 miles north, knocked out cold, too cold for dreams. Which I wouldn't bother recounting even if I could remember them. Dreams are the province of the tortured and the tormented, Strindberg says. I'm not quite willing to cast my lot with them, yet.

What happened the next day at the First Presbyterian Church is something of a blur in my memory, as deeply humiliating events often are. Our brains are protective of us that way, though many of my friends suspect their natural defenses, preferring instead to pay $150 an hour to have a stranger force them to remember every tiny horrible thing they've ever suffered through, in paralyzing detail. In any case, the morning started with Dad chirping into my room, snapping the shades up, and announcing that he had it in mind to join Mom and me for piano class.

"Brushing up on the old ragtime, Dad?" I asked, squinting my eyes against the light.

"Nope, just another one of your adoring fans, kiddo. I'm going to set up a refreshment stand in the parking lot and make a mint selling souvenir magazines."

This should have been my first tip that the event was a slightly bigger deal than I'd been led to believe. There were other signs, too—the disapproving look Mom gave me when I came downstairs for breakfast wearing cargo pants, the glut of station wagons and minivans in the church's parking lot, surely more than a single piano class's worth. But I didn't make much of any of it. The great luxury of being at home is that your radar shuts down and you can truly relax, unlike in New York, where the possibility of a run-in with an ex-boyfriend or a casting director looms on every block and makes hair-washing a virtual prerequisite for leaving the house.

At five to ten Mom, Dad, and I stepped into the recital room in the basement of the old stone Presbyterian church. The room overflowed with a sea of giggly, awkward junior high school girls, braces glinting and faces shining like the "Before" shot in a Noxzema ad. The seats in the back were occupied by a fleet of moms and bored little kids who squirmed around on folding chairs, playing with action figures and making heavy artillery sound effects. There must have been sixty or seventy people crowded into that tiny space, maybe more. The chatter was loud and the air was hot, and I thought wistfully of my catatonic circle of friends at Adele Goldberg. Were all these kids here to see me? I gave Mom a look of desperation. The last thing on earth I wanted to do was turn on the juice for an audience of strangers, oily strangers in boy-band T-shirts and banana clips. I hope it's fair to say that publicly, at least, I've always been a good sport whenever my parents have asked me for anything. But good sportsmanship, like Chilean sea bass or crude oil, can get used up.

Mom took my hand and led me up the center aisle to the front of the room, pulled out a piano bench, and gestured for me to sit. Instantly the room quieted down and all eyes were fixed on me, as if I were a rare species of monkey on loan from the county zoo. It was my second performance in as many days.

"Good morning, girls," Mom said, in her churchy piano teacher voice.

"Good morning, Mrs. Preston," they echoed back.

"It's so nice to have all of you here this morning. I see faces from the Tuesday group and the orchestra and jazz band and the Sunday school club. I told our guest of honor this would be a small gathering, but it looks like word got out. Luckily she's used to being onstage."

Mom turned and beamed at me. My spirit of cooperation, which had been slim to begin with, evaporated.

"Let me introduce you to my daughter Rosalie. As most of you know, she grew up right here in Hanson, and she went to Dean Middle School and Hanson Memorial High. Now she lives in New York City, where she writes for *GirlTalk* magazine—that's the one, Carly," Mom said, nodding at a girl who was spastically waving the September issue around. "That's right. Now my guess is you all know about Annie Answers, so I'm going to sit down and let the fun get started. But first I think we should give Rosalie a nice warm welcome for coming to talk to us on her morning off."

Mom put her arms around me, and my body stiffened. I did not have a few words I wanted to say to these girls. The deal had been a Q and A for one class, not an extemporaneous lecture for the entire eighth grade. She stepped back from the makeshift stage and left me sitting on the piano bench in front of the expectant room. When the clapping died down I coughed and cleared my mucusy throat.

"Good morning," I said, trying to sound healthier and nicer than I felt. "It's great to meet all of you. I used to take music lessons in this room myself, so I feel right at home here. Do you guys know Mr. Robertson? Is he still around?"

A few girls in the first row shook their heads.

"He used to be the recorder teacher back in my day, but he

must have retired. He was a real jerk anyway, so count yourselves lucky. Listen, I'd be happy to answer any questions you have about *GirlTalk,* so why don't you tell me what you're interested in?"

The girls looked at their friends, some whispered to each other. I tapped my foot and waited for them to screw up their courage. The first wave of questions were the usual:

"How many famous people do you know?"

None. The entertainment writer does all the celebrity interviews; the rest of us sit in our offices all day and look at our computers.

"Why are all the models in your magazine so skinny?"

Because your reader response surveys indicate you like them that way, and we have no higher journalistic imperative than newsstand sales.

"Do you get free makeup?"

Sure do. See this nail polish color? Free.

"In Annie Answers, do you always write what you really think?"

I liked this question. The girl who asked it wore purple-framed glasses and a sweatshirt with a picture of a lion's head ironed on. I asked her what her name was. Krista, she said.

"Well actually, Krista, the answer is no, I don't usually get to write what I think. My boss, the one who writes that 'Hugs and Kisses, Ginger' letter at the front of every issue, she has very conservative ideas about sex. So if a girl writes to me and asks, 'Should I have sex with my boyfriend?' I might really want to tell her, 'Go for it, that's what people your age are supposed to do, just make sure you use contraception,' but I would probably get fired for saying anything close to that. So instead I have to write about how risky sex is, how having sex is like driving without a seatbelt or smoking crack."

"So you put in stuff you don't really believe?" asked a tall girl in a tennis skirt.

"Well there's a kernel of truth in everything I write. Sex can be dangerous, if you don't use condoms. Drinking can be dangerous, if you have to drive somewhere. But all in all, I'd say the voice of the magazine is a lot more preachy than the people who write it."

The kids were wide-eyed. I could feel my mother's stare burning a hole in my backside, but I couldn't see her, so I kept going. "Any more questions?"

"You know some of the ideas in *GirlTalk* are really dumb. Like that 'how to get your crush to notice you' thing. Like anybody's ever going to put flowers in her hair and go to school looking like a retard. No one wears those kinds of clothes, either."

"I agree. That was lame. You should write to the editor and tell her what you think."

"Can I ask you an advice question?" This from a pretty girl towards the back, dressed in warm-up pants and a white turtleneck.

"Sure you can," I said. "The doctor is in."

"Okay, um, my friend Stacey, she has field hockey practice so she's not here today, but, um, she's got a thing for this guy in our class named Pete who's a total jerk-off." Some of the other girls in the back let out hysterical trills of giggles, then clamped their hands over their mouths. "Some of us think we should tell her about the stuff he's done, but some of us think it's none of our business. Which do you think?"

"Huh," I said, then paused for second. "Huh." A question I'd answered in print about five thousand times. But for some reason I couldn't think of my standard line, or at least I couldn't bring myself to speak it out loud. What was I even doing there? What kind of cosmic scam brought me face to face with the girls of my hometown, to pretend I understood stuff I didn't? "I'm, huh. Let's see." My thoughts were as vague as the stutters coming out of my mouth. "That's a tough one. I guess they're all tough ones, actually. I guess I think she—Stacey?—she probably has to figure this thing out for herself. I mean, she might make a mess. Messes get made whenever people fall in love. They're unavoidable. I don't think you can get in and out of any kind of love very cleanly." For a horrible moment, it seemed possible that I might cry in front of these kids. I remembered Berglan Starker standing across the room at the Footlights reception, the path to him blocked by Cam and Grace and Bella herself. Not that I'd wanted to talk to him anyway. What was there for me to say? Nothing, nothing, nothing. I swallowed hard, thought of my mother sitting three feet behind me. I thought of all the boys these girls had yet to kiss, all the ways their hopes had yet to be been disappointed, all the times their hearts would have to break. This advice thing wasn't a job I wanted anymore. But there was my dad in the back of the room, leaning up against the door and smiling, and I found my *GirlTalk* voice and put it on. "You can tell her why *you're* not wild about Pete, but you can't force her to change her mind or listen to your warnings. She may just have to go ahead and find out for herself."

Other hands shot up. I muddled along for ten more minutes, offered to take a final question. The girl who raised her hand first had a determined look on her face.

"There should be more sex stuff in the magazine."

"I don't think the bosses would go for that. I told you about Ginger. The writer whose office is across the hall from mine thinks Ginger got artificially inseminated so she wouldn't ever have to sleep with her husband."

"But what about sex stuff that's not like in health class, but like real answers? My friend once told me you could get pregnant from giving a blow job. Is that true?"

"Nope. That's like saying you'll give birth to a watermelon if you swallow a watermelon seed. But you can catch an STD from oral sex, so make sure you always use condoms. The polyurethane ones taste better than the latex ones."

"What's polymathane?"

My mother cleared her throat. "Okay, girls, it's time for us to get started with our lessons. You can ask Rosalie to sign your magazines after class. Let's give her a big thanks for visiting us today."

The girls clapped. I waved, got off the piano stool, and made for the door. My parents, all the parents in the room, looked shocked by the graphic turn things had just taken. Understandably. Anyone would say that I wanted to shock them—"acting out" is what the professionals call it, I believe. Well, it's my natural instinct. Put an actor onstage and what do you expect her to do? She acts out.

. . .

Outside in the parking lot, where Dad and I had arranged to wait for Mom until class ended, I peeled off my sweater and leaned against the wall of the church. The sun was shining with more vigor than it had been earlier, and the wind had all but disappeared. I owed Dad an apology, but I was so bewildered by whatever had come over me in the last half hour that I didn't know what would come out of my mouth if I opened it. Dad looked uncomfortable and addled, the way anyone might look whose daughter had just staved off a nervous breakdown by preaching the merits of oral sex to a group of pre-pubescent girls in a church basement. He paced for a few seconds and then sat down on the bench next to me, facing the parking lot. Some benches face the strangest, saddest sights.

"Well the girls sure seemed to have had a lot of fun, didn't they?" There was uncertainty in his voice, but no sarcasm. Sarcasm isn't much in my dad's repertoire. "I have to admit I don't look at *GirlTalk* too often, except for the section you write. I don't know much about what goes on in the magazine in general, but you always do such a nice job, Rosehip. Your mom and I are always impressed by how nice a job you do." He shuffled and rearranged himself, giving me a chance to reply, which I didn't. I couldn't bring myself to talk.

"Do you ever read a magazine like *Newsweek*? Your mother and I really depend on our subscription to it. *Newsweek* and *Time*. They're both published in New York, aren't they?"

I nodded.

"Well I certainly think highly of those two magazines. Not that I know much about how they're run."

I knew what Dad was trying to suggest, of course. He thought what had just happened was about work. He thought that I was sick of my job, that I should put on a nice silk blouse and walk into *Newsweek* and get myself a position there writing My Turn's every week. He thought I could type up a résumé and do absolutely anything I wanted to do, and that a brand-new job at a better magazine would make me into a happier, more fulfilled, smoother-edged person, someone who wouldn't take out her life's frustrations on a roomful of innocent kids. Why is it so painful, to be believed in so much?

I sat down on the bench next to Dad and we waited there together, without talking, staring out at the parking lot and listening to strains of the Moonlight Sonata coming up from the open windows of the recital room. Once upon a time I'd known how to play some of that piece myself, but of course I'd forgotten it by now, forgotten everything about piano except for Chopsticks and Middle C. Piano, Spanish, cartwheels, math—the story of getting older is a story of forgetting. Even this past week's sadness, which made me yearn so badly to close my door and stay in bed for days, would fade and disappear, as surely as the sailor's knot I learned to tie in Girl Scout camp. Knots tied, knots untied. Maybe that's comforting to some people, how fleeting even unhappiness can be. But it seems kind of depressing, to me.

We waited for Mom for forty-five minutes. They weren't bad pianists, those little girls. Even the most halting and apologetic of them made me feel like I might cry. They weren't bad at all.

. . .

Mom and Dad spent the rest of Saturday tiptoeing around me as if I might snap at any moment, or shatter into a thousand tiny angry pieces. I was accustomed to getting wide berth from them whenever a hint of grouchiness flickered across my face, but this wide berth was different. They treated me like a fragile person— not someone whose mood they didn't want to deal with, but someone whose mood they didn't understand. Mom made wary offers of herbal tea and bubble baths, as if whatever was ailing me could be steamed out, but she didn't ask any questions. Even now I am a mess of all those sloppy teenage contradictions, wanting to be left alone, wanting to be fussed over and pried open and understood. We didn't talk about the magazine business any-more, thank God, and we didn't talk about my so-called acting career, either. We talked about chicken breasts and frozen kiel-basas, and who wanted which for dinner. These were the people who taught me everything I know about intimacy, about what to expect from the world in the way of attention and love. I knew they loved me, even if they didn't really understand me; I knew it pained them to see me at such loose ends. But I had no idea how to help them understand. I picked chicken breasts. For once in my life, I couldn't eat much.

It was pouring rain when the commuter rail train pulled into Boston on Sunday afternoon, real Simon and Garfunkel tomato soup weather, and I killed my layover in South Station browsing through the racks of romance novels in the newsstand. When the announcement came to board the New York–bound train, I huddled between gray-suited businessmen on the platform, borrowing the supersized shelter of their golf umbrellas. For all the talk of sexism and glass ceilings in the professional world, the chivalrous conventions of luggage-carrying and door-holding appear to be on their way out. Wet and cold, I lugged my duffel bag on board and found an empty bank of seats. I was fishing through my bag for my book and my ticket when a voice asked if the spot next to me was taken. A loud, Irish voice. It was Declan Pearse.

"What are you doing here?" I asked, too surprised by the sight of him to collect my manners.

"I've been to see some friends in Boston. Just for an overnight."

His backpack was dripping water all over the seat. I moved my things onto the floor in front of me. "Here, sit down."

"I don't mean to disturb you, if you'd like to be left alone."

I put my book away. It was a biography of Margaret Sanger. I'd been on a summer-long jag of reading lengthy and admiring portraits of radical women. "Not at all. I'm glad to see you. I've taken this train a thousand times and never run into anyone before."

"Well how's that for a small world," he said indifferently, as if people he knew were always turning up on interstate transit. He kicked his bag around on the floor until only a portion of it stuck out into the aisle. "Did you have a fine weekend?"

"It was survivable. I went home to visit my parents for a couple of days."

"Survivable is all?"

"Survivable barely. I'm happy to be on the train home, you could say."

"Do you not get on with them, then?"

I was getting accustomed to Declan's directness, which I understood to be a function of cultural mores. In Dublin the guys I'd met in pubs and student travel agencies were direct to the point of coarseness, usually using slang as a nominal mask: "Hey, birdie, fancy a click?" etc. One thinks of America as the land of plainspoken openness, but that's a Tocquevillean myth, really. We probably just seemed plainspoken and open to him because he was French. "I get on with them fine, usually. I'm just not the best company these days, and I guess they could tell."

"What do you mean, not the best company?"

"I mean I've been feeling grouchy and miserable and not unlike the wrath of God. Since you asked."

Declan gave this some thought. "Are we talking about the bank wanker now? Did he drop you?"

There seemed something a touch ungrateful about Declan's referring to Berglan Starker that way, only two days after BS had invested thousands of dollars in *Dame Street*. But I couldn't let myself be Berglan's defender anymore. It was too pathetic, too like those heroines in Simone de Beauvoir novels who are so maddeningly devoid of self-respect. "You could say Mr. Starker has something to do with it."

"Your old man must want to murder him."

"My parents have no idea about that whole thing. It's not the kind of situation they would have much sympathy for."

"Ah, people always have more sympathy than you expect them to."

"I'm sorry, have you met my parents?"

"Which bit would they mind? The older bit?"

"The older bit, the married bit, the dumped-on-my-ass bit. They wouldn't be too pleased about any of it."

He smiled. "You're alright, now. Cool down."

"My parents were high school sweethearts. In their opinion I'm an old maid ten times over. They try so hard to be open-minded about me and my extended adolescence, but an affair with a married man would tax their powers of empathy, I guarantee you."

"Well they've got a point, don't they. You're better off without that old man, I've been saying it to you since the day we met."

As a matter of fact he had said nothing of the kind to me before. He had said that Berglan Starker was too old for me, and too rich for me, but I'd never heard either of those appraisals in a partisan way, oldness and richness not being inherently negative qualities in my mind. This opinion was news to me, the fact that Declan privately thought I'd been compromising myself by settling for an older man.

"Better off and lonelier and poorer. I know." I looked out the window. Our train was passing soaked fields, the outskirts of a subdivision. "So how did you find out about the demise of my so-called affair? Has it been broadcast over the airwaves since I left town?"

"Lucky guess. I suppose it was all the time your man spent with Belgium after the show the other night. He wouldn't have been playing the proud dad if he was going home to shag you. Or at least that's how I saw it."

"Bella. Her name's Bella."

"Apologies. Anyway you're in bits now but you'll be over it, and when you are you'll be wondering why you were torn up in the first place."

The certainty in his voice was exasperating and reassuring at the same time. One never likes to be transparent to others, nor does one like to have her romantic despair dismissed in a single sentence. On the other hand there was something sort of wise about Declan; his disregard for worldly possessions such as a change of clothing was monastic, almost gypsy-like, you could see him owning a pack of Tarot cards. As he spoke he reached into the breast pocket of his button-down shirt and pulled out a cellophane-wrapped sandwich, of which he offered me half, peeling back the flattened wheat bread to display the mustard and salami inside. I pretended to have eaten in the station.

"I never did understand what you liked so much about him, anyway. It's a mystery to me what could be so irresistible about a pompous ass like that. Is he some kind of genius or something? Does he wear lovely red knickers? Was that his secret?"

"Red knickers and a red brassiere to match. He was always very soigné."

"You see, the rest of us poor saps don't stand a chance. The rich ones always have the better underwear."

I appreciated that he was being nice to me, in a George Bernard Shaw down-with-the-ruling-class type of way. Being nice, for Declan, was a manifest gesture of sympathy. So was the can of ginger ale he bought me from the Whistle Stop refreshment cart, which I drank out of symbolic gratitude even though I don't much care for ginger ale.

"Mostly I liked the attention he gave me. And I also liked having a secret, doing something that nobody would ever have thought I'd do. It's not very original, I guess."

"I can't see what originality matters, when you're talking about love. Anyway I'm not going to tell anyone. You can stop worrying about that, like I told you before."

"I know," I said. "I didn't mean it that way." I sipped my ginger ale. Declan bolted the second half of his sandwich. When he finished, a yellow-brick-road of mustard dotted the front of his shirt.

"What about Boston?" I asked. "Did you do anything fun?"

"I went to see those glass flowers in the botanical museum over at Harvard. They were something, the small ones with loads of colored petals and leaves and thorns. There were some butterflies on view there, too, real ones, but dead, pinned up on the wall according to their colors and wing size and the like. I'm more for the flowers, though. I keep thinking about them, about those two men devoting their entire earthly lives to making miniature glass replicas of every species of fern and flower they could find, and then shipping them off across the Atlantic to goddamn Harvard, a place those two poor fools probably couldn't even imagine. It's kind of beautiful, just the idea of that much dedication, you know?"

The glass flower collection at the Harvard Museum of Natural History had been my favorite field trip when I was a kid. My parents had taken me there a few times every year, encouraged no doubt by what must have looked like a fledgling interest in botany, but what was really just a girly fascination with all things blossoming and delicate. When I was a college student I'd often gone by myself on Saturday afternoons, lingered in the dim old halls of geodes and bits of fossilized trees. I pictured Declan, hulking, massive Declan, leaning over the display cases of all those fragile flowers, the same tiny specimens spread across the same white canvas I had to be lifted up to see as a kid. I'm not generally soft on the big-guy-demonstrating-surprising-tenderness genre, and yet I liked the image of Declan with his nose to the glass in that funky old museum, elbow to elbow with the birthday-party crowd. Maybe I was just feeling nostalgic, but it seemed awfully sweet.

"I've been thinking about it since yesterday afternoon, actually," he said. "Why a perfect imitation is so lovely, even when you've got the real thing right outside your door."

I bit my literalist tongue and didn't say anything about the obvious disadvantages of nature compared to glass, bugs and disease and adverse growing conditions. Declan seemed to be speaking metaphorically, anyway. At least he was staring out the window with the abstracted, contemplative look of someone speaking metaphorically.

"How did you ever find your way to that museum?"

"The people I went to see recommended it. One of them works over in Cambridge. He's really more Fiona's friend than mine, but I've know him for years."

"Fiona?"

"Yeah, Fiona. That's my girlfriend." He wiped his mouth. "Have I not mentioned her before?"

I shook my head.

"Right. Well she lives in Dublin, so it's a bit hard to introduce her around."

I flipped through the number of afternoons I'd spent with Declan, at the photo shoot, in the bakery—he'd never once mentioned anyone named Fiona, or any woman at all. "Have you been going out with her for a long time?"

"I've known her since I was six. We were neighbors growing up in Dolphin's Barn. She went to UCD. She does marketing now, for Aer Lingus."

"That sounds serious."

"The marketing or the girlfriend?" He laughed but he looked uncomfortable, like he'd just been made to swallow something that was still alive.

The pages of *Last Winter in Dame Street* shuffled through my mind: a failed marriage, a betrayal, a new life in the New World. Was it possible that Declan was gay? No, that had never seemed true, there was something deeply straight about him, even the way he inhaled his food was heterosexual, crumbs everywhere, all over our seat. How silly and narrow-minded, to think that his play had to be the true story of his life. Still, there were those two sex scenes, both of them hot and unusually graphic for a Broadway show. The one with the ex-wife took place in the kitchen; there was honey involved, some skirmishing on the floor. How weird that I was thinking of these things now! "Well she must be excited about your play and everything. I bet she's really proud."

"Oh, proud enough. She's a good girl, Fiona. We've been together for ages. She's family to me. She'll come visit sometime in the spring and you two can meet."

"You must miss her," I said, without really thinking about it. As it hung in the air I was suddenly struck by all the different ways a person can be heartsick in this life.

Declan shrugged. "It's a bit lonely here," he said, and then he pointed out the window at the rain, which was still driving down in gray sheets that looked almost solid. "But all this sodden misery makes me feel quite at home."

Dear Annie,

Lately I've been having feelings for one of my best guy friends, feelings that I would put in the category of friend + extra. I'm afraid to tell him about this because I don't want to freak him out and make him back away from me. But what if he feels the same way I do? We spend a lot of time together and he doesn't have a girlfriend or anything. But he does tell me about his crushes and girls he thinks are hot. I don't know what to do.

—Torn in Pennsylvania

Dear Torn,

Sooner or later, this is a bridge we all come to at least once in our lives. Actually, scrap that bridge image; it's more like there are two gigantic mountains, one for friendship and one for romance. Right now you're clinging to the face of Friendship Peak, and you're debating a daredevil jump over to Romance Mountain, but the ravine down there between them sure looks rocky and dry.

Speaking as someone who's scaled this terrain extensively, let me promise you that the drop isn't as steep as you think. I say, find a cool, low-key way to tell your friend what you're feeling for him. Don't show up at his doorstep with two dozen roses and a sonnet you've written about your undying love; that'll freak him out even if he does have a crush on you. Instead, pepper your confession with qualifiers like "sometimes" and "kind of" and "maybe." I promise, he'll have had these thoughts himself. Every guy in the world has these thoughts, about every girl who's ever said hello to him. If he's spending a lot of time with you, my guess is that you're crossing his mind pretty often, and there are enough question marks floating in the air for you two to have a talk.

Some friendships blossom into great romances. Others blossom into one-night hookups that get awkward and weird the next day in the halls. Others never go anywhere, because one person dumps water on the other person's flame. But in a way, don't all of these scenarios sound better than spending another afternoon listening to your friend imagine how other girls would look in bikinis? Don't look down. Jump.

Trust me. I've lived through it.

Annie

Chapter Ten

Fall, for those of us raised on the Northrop Frye English Readers, is the season of Tragedy. As such it has never been my favorite time of year, indelibly linked to such literary downers as *The Metamorphosis, Oedipus Rex,* and *King Lear.* I also happen to look terrible in the autumnal palette of burnt golds and oranges, and don't care much for the thickening effects of chenille or tweed. Strangely, winter doesn't bother me nearly as much: winter is dependable, unmitigated freezingness spiked with the occasional surprise of a sunny day or a cab ride past the Christmas trees on Park Avenue. Fall is brutal on optimists. It's the season of dashed meteorological hopes.

October and November passed by with little event, pages of the wall calendar dropping away like so many dead leaves piling up before the incinerator. Work happened. People kept to themselves. Evan stayed buried in the Flax office bunker for days at a time, metabolizing every calorie he ingested into pure crystallized *Dame Street* energy. As a result, a profile on Cam and his co-star, two-time Tony Award winner William Howlitt Smith, made the cover of *Time Out New York,* "Next Winter on Dame Street!" scrolled over their grinning heads. Grace and Jake pilgrimaged back and forth to Providence, listening to swing band demo tapes and sampling basket-weave frostings selected by Grace's mother, who had fallen prey to the wedding mania typical of upper-middle-class women without enough board memberships to keep them busy. Bella I didn't see much of. Every once in a while she would summon me out to dinner to dish about something or other, Jean-Marie's model girlfriend or her stepmother's new Welsh corgi or the upstairs neighbor who'd left flowers outside her door. Needless to say, these encounters were more a source of stress than they were a source of pleasure, and not just because of Bella's high-handed treatment of waiters and busboys. Every piece of information she dropped about her dad's side of the family sent me into a panic (are Welsh corgis the ones that don't bark? what insight on BS and his wife could I gain by factoring in their stumpy little lapdog?). I remained paranoid, really paranoid, that Bella would detect some giveaway blush or bead of sweat on my forehead, not that I actually sweat like that. If she did notice any unusual degree of family interest on my part, she probably just assumed I had a crush on her older brother Brooks. Girls always think their friends are after their older brothers. Narcissism, jealousy, or both?

Without talking too much about it, I'd been going out on a few auditions myself, just *Backstage* stuff and open commercial calls. It seemed like a good idea, given that all First Born projects would be on hiatus for the next nine months at least, and acting is rather athletic in that your voice and whatnot can get out of shape if you don't practice, practice, practice. None of us had said anything official about the fate of First Born, but it was obvious that people's attentions were elsewhere for the time being, and if I didn't get out there and pound the pavement I'd be a full-time advice columnist with lots of headshots on my hands. Out of nine auditions I had netted two callbacks, a pretty good showing—one for a breath mint ad and one to play the sister of a slain Spanish toreador in some no-name no-pay downtown gig. I wasn't quite perky enough for the first or histrionic enough for the second, but I didn't embarrass myself at either, which isn't bad when someone asks you to do a cold reading of a eulogy in a Castilian accent.

I hadn't seen Berglan Starker once since the night of the Footlights Festival. It made sense that we wouldn't run into each other around town—his hangouts were to mine what Gstaad is to Calcutta, and I hadn't exactly been popping in for lunch at the Four Seasons lately. Still, I wouldn't have guessed back in August that he'd have dropped out of sight so entirely, without so much as a single phone call to make sure I hadn't slashed my wrists in extravagant romantic grief. I was accustomed to sloppier breakups, which I now understand to be a luxury of the unattached. A married person can't afford to be sloppy about anything, not even courtesy phone calls. But did this mean my feelings weren't hurt? I wouldn't say so.

Perhaps not coincidentally, I found myself (notice how "found" implies no active volition on my part) spending the occasional weekend afternoon on the Upper East Side. The Met, the Guggenheim, the Frick, the Park, the tearooms and pastry shops of Madison Avenue where a single croissant cost as much as I made at *GirlTalk* in a week—suddenly these attractions seemed the best possible way to pass an October Saturday without plans. Usually I took the subway uptown and wandered around by myself, though once I brought along Pearl Coleman from AGSC, who particularly wanted to see an interior design exhibit at the Cooper Hewitt, which, it turns out, is not a very wheelchair-friendly place. I suppose in some vague way I was trailing the Starkers, who lived on the top floor of a pre-war building on the corner of Fifth Avenue and Eighty-fourth Street. I never did anything brazen like walk into their lobby—it wasn't that I wanted to run into them, or even see them from afar, though I did have the occasional fantasy of catching Berglan's eye as he hurried down Madison Avenue, me sitting in the window of a café sipping espresso and reading something impressive, say a hardcover volume of Rilke in the original. As I try to explain it now it sounds like I might have been coming unhinged, some kind of post-millennial Amy Fisher with a nominal interest in museum-going. But it wasn't like that. I was just curious about what the Starkers' lives were like. Theirs were lives I had gotten so unexpectedly close to, for a time.

Once, on a particularly dreary Sunday afternoon after wandering through a sarcophagi exhibit at the Met, I walked into a diner to order some lunch. I was eating a club sandwich and reading a car industry magazine that had been left in my booth when the door to the place opened and Brooks Starker, Bella's older brother, walked in. My heart froze, as if suddenly we'd been transported back in time to Communist East Germany and I'd been caught by the Stasi without proper papers for the Upper East Side. Brooks was alone; he gave his name to the hostess and waited, crammed into the entryway between the cash register and the mint table, for a booth to open up. Was I staring at him, or did he recognize me? Before I could think of how to pay and slip out the side exit, he walked over to my booth.

"Aren't you a friend of my sister's?"

I put down my milkshake and stood to shake his hand. "Yes. I'm Rosalie Preston. We've met a few times before."

Brooks was tall and attractive, like all of his people, and dressed in overgrown boarding school clothes: Burberry jacket, lamb's-wool crewneck, trousers that needed to be pressed. He gave me the once-over in a distracted, hungover way. "Didn't we have you up for Thanksgiving or something? Are you the one who brought the turkey made out of tofu?"

"I came to a Thanksgiving party at your family's a couple of years ago, me and Evan Weiner, another one of Bella's friends. And I was up at Fort Sassquam when you were there the summer before last." I didn't acknowledge the tofu accusation. There were two pieces of bacon sitting on my plate. "I was also three years behind you at school, but you wouldn't have known me, back then."

"Oh." He looked put out that he hadn't remembered, and also surprised. I happened to be wearing a skirt and knee-high boots with tall heels, which might have made me look more memorable than I did as a college freshman. Brooks sneezed and didn't excuse himself. "Were you in Bitsy Rentmeester's class?"

Bitsy Rentmeester was a department store heiress who'd made herself famous on campus by giving out free merchandise from her dad's chain every year on her birthday. She'd been sought after by all the high-profile upperclassmen, Brooks Starker included.

"Yeah, I was. I once got a free watchband replacement from her. Snakeskin, I think."

"Well I definitely recognize you now. Maybe I met you at one of Bitsy's parties."

"Maybe so. And at the Fort and Thanksgiving and everything." Of course I'd never met Brooks Starker at a college party, though when I was eighteen I'd memorized his social résumé from an admiring distance: member of the Porcellian Club, captain of the sailing team, thrower of intersession parties at his dad's New York apartment. Brooks had been the apotheosis of the desirable senior, and when he and his friends came around to pick up Bella for late-night hamburgers, the rest of us hung about yearning to be asked along, which of course we never were, since all of the seats in the convertible were already occupied by girls with names like Cabot and Virginia. These days Brooks fulfilled his evolutionary destiny by working at an advertising firm and driving his Austin Healey roadster to the country on weekends.

"So are you one of those actor people Bella hangs out with?"

"You don't have to make it sound like a social disease. I can speak in complete sentences."

The diner was small and crowded with lunch-seekers from the Met, mostly tourists willing to pay twenty bucks for a plate of chicken fingers. Waitresses in pastel uniforms shot death looks at Brooks as they pushed past him with their heavy trays; one of them said that he should try sitting down, instead of blocking up the whole damn aisle.

"Would that be alright?" he asked, giving me the sly, slightly insinuating smile I'd seen other members of his family flash before. "I mean, I'd hate to take you away from that study on tire tread safety."

"Have a seat," I said, closing the magazine. "I recommend the chocolate shake."

"I need something greasier than that. I was at this party last night, actually it was a tasting for a new restaurant launching on Reade Street, and I drank so much I still can't see properly out of my right eye. It was quite a scene, let me tell you, this restaurant's going to be big. All they need now is a name. You might know the guys who're opening it, Peter Cook and Osia de la Concorde. They were two years ahead in B-school."

"Can't say it rings a bell. I didn't go to B-school."

"Oh, right." He covered his right eye with his hand. "There you are again. I was losing you. Nice shirt."

"You know," I said, reaching for my wallet, "I'm actually on my way to meet somebody, but you really should try the chocolate milkshake after you have your breakfast. It'll do wonders for your hangover."

"How urgent is your appointment? I'm an amazingly fast eater and I always share my fries, if you'd like to stick around for a minute."

"I'm running late already," I said, lie begetting lie begetting lie. "But will you be at Bella's birthday party? Maybe I'll see you there."

"Oh, I'll be there," he said, with an amiable leer. "Rosalie Preston, snakeskin watchband, chocolate milkshake. Your vital statistics have been filed."

The waitresses were busy so I left Brooks with some money and hustled out of the restaurant. I had the creepy feeling that if I stayed another minute he might start to seriously hit on me or ask me out, which was too weird to make waiting around for my change worthwhile. In some kind of imprecise way this was what I'd been courting, obviously, not a lunch date with Brooks but a Starker-family encounter that might give me a sense of conclusion, or of "closure," as we advice columnists say. And I suppose in one way it did, by reminding me that I'd actually matured some since I was eighteen years old, and had outgrown my fascination with the Tom Buchanans of the world. That was one step. The next was outgrowing my fascination with their fathers.

By mid-November the daylight contracts early in our eastern edge of the time zone, and leaving the office anytime after five means getting home in the dark. One night as I walked out of the subway and onto my block I happened to look up and notice that the lights were on in the windows of my apartment, not just *a* light, which I sometimes do by accident in spite of my best efforts at eco-consciousness, but all the lights. From the street you can actually see a good deal of my living room when it's illuminated like that, the framed posters and the hanging plants and, no doubt, me, when I flit around in my bathrobe without pulling down the shades. For about thirty seconds I stood there on the sidewalk trying to figure out what the hell was going on upstairs, whether to run to the closest pay phone and call 911 or to confront the burglars myself, when I saw a reflection of Cam's head passing by in the gilt-edged mirror from my grandparents' house. I had given Cam a spare key after the second time I'd locked myself out, at my super's (pointed) recommendation. But he'd never just up and let himself in before, and I hoped, for the sake of our friendship, that something worth trespassing for was at stake.

"Honey I'm home," I called from the hallway, unable to open

my apartment door fully because of the chain Cam had secured from inside.

He came to the door carrying a wooden spoon full of spaghetti sauce, and slid it through the open space where I had wedged my nose in. "I think this needs more basil. Better blow on it first."

"Which one's basil? Is that what they put on pizza?"

Cam closed the door, unchained it, and let me in. "Rose. You have three spices in your cupboard, if salt even counts as a spice, and four different brands of single-malt scotch. Either you have a serious drinking problem or something's up."

I threw my bag down onto the chair where Cam had tossed his backpack and two grocery satchels from Key Foods. "Nice to see you, too. Welcome to my apartment."

"Thanks."

We both stood still, me because I was waiting for an explanation and Cam because he was holding a shallow spoon brimming with sauce.

"This is very irregular, Cam."

"Is it? I guess it is."

"Only in the sense that you've known me for long enough to know mine isn't the ideal kitchen for whipping up a pot of spaghetti à la Bolognese, which leads me to guess that you must have something else on your agenda."

"Oh. Right, good guess."

"And?"

"And. Well, I'm here to cook dinner and also to, to kind of perform, like, a one-man intervention."

"Huh." I sat down on the couch and flipped through the stack of mail I'd brought up from my box. "That sounds ambitious."

Cam sat down across from me. "I'm not kidding, Rosalie."

"Well I've already had dinner, I'm afraid. And it sounds like the rest of your business might be an impediment to casual conversation. So maybe you just want to move along to it now?"

Cam looked as if he were the one who'd been taken by surprise, which I assumed meant events had already veered away from the lines he'd rehearsed in his head. "Okay," he said, struggling to improvise. "Here's the thing. I have no idea what's going on with you. I never see you anymore, and when I call you to say that, you tell me it's because I don't have any time, which is clearly not the case since I wouldn't be calling you in the first place if I didn't have any time, and obviously you're the one who doesn't want to see me. Which is fine, I guess, except that you're being so cagey and weird about it. And then you leave all these smarmy 'congratulations' messages on my answering machine when you know I'm not even going to be at home."

"Smarmy. Ouch."

"You can go ahead and read those credit card mailings if you want to, that's fine, I can wait. I wouldn't want you to miss any good offers on a fixed APR."

I laid the mail down on the coffee table and passed Cam a coaster for the spoon he was still holding. "I'm not exactly sure what you're asking me for, Cam. I come home from work to find you in my apartment, and before I've so much as taken off my coat you're haranguing me for not having spent enough time with you lately. Am I supposed to defend my reasons for being absent? Give you a doctor's note or something?"

"You don't have to defend anything. I'm just concerned." He liked the way that sounded. "I'm concerned about you."

"Well I don't have a drinking problem."

"Okay then, you have a sarcasm problem."

"Cam!" I jumped out of my chair. "I know how you resent having things spelled out for you, but has it ever occurred to you that it might not be the easiest position in the world for me to be in, mailing out my own stupid headshots to try to get an *audition* to get into a *class* that might help me with my auditioning skills, while you gad around town chumming it up with your new best buddy William Howlitt Smith, interviewing agents and managers who are literally fighting to represent you? Do you even remember what it feels like not to be able to get into so much as a class?"

Cam looked stung. I must have spoken loudly, because he sounded faint by comparison. "You're so convinced of all the wrongs everyone's done you, Rosalie. I got a part in a stupid play. If you got a part in a stupid play, I'd like to think I could feel happy for you, instead of feeling like the world had served me up some horrible grievous wrong. Isn't that what you'd want me to feel?"

"I wouldn't *want* you to feel anything. I would worry about how I felt, and leave everybody else to themselves."

"That's great. That's really great, Rose. And you're the one getting paid to write the column on friendship."

"It's not on friendship; it's on love. Vive la différence."

At this Cam stood up and stalked off to the kitchen. With his back to me I watched him turn off the gas burners and pour a pot of steaming water down the drain. He made a racket throwing cans into the recycling bin, a racket turning the faucets on and off at full blast, a racket opening and shutting the cabinet doors.

When I stood up and walked into the kitchen he pushed past me through the doorway, clipping me with his shoulder, then he turned and faced me from the middle of the living room. We stood for a minute without talking, and it occurred to me that Cam's face looked less boyish than I thought of it as looking, that there was something sad and dark flickering over all that prettiness that hadn't been there when we'd first met.

"Listen. All I came by to say is that this is your choice, whatever kind of disappearing act you're doing. So just in case you're harboring any fantasies about having been ditched, you better get over them. I'm right here, four blocks away, the same as I always have been. You know the address."

"The same as you always have been." I shook my head at the ground.

"Here's what I wonder, Rosalie. Really. How are you so sure I would have given you up?"

I looked up and met his eyes again. I thought he'd be smiling now, giving me the old insouciant Cam grin, but he wasn't. "What did you say?"

"I'm just thinking that you make an awful lot of decisions on my behalf, and then you go and get angry at me about them. I used to like that, how you did the thinking for both of us. But I feel pretty fucking cheated now." He set his jaw and scratched his hand against his pants leg, as if he wanted to rub something there away. "You don't even listen to me when I come over here to tell you that I miss you. It's like I'm talking to you through a giant glass door, and you could let me in but you're just not going to." He laughed a mirthless laugh. "I let you get away with it for too long, I guess. Thinking you knew me better than I know myself."

I didn't know what to say to that. I'd always wanted some explosion from Cam, some tangible evidence that he would miss me as much as I would miss him as we moved apart into our adult lives. But the truth is that someone else's sadness can't ease your own. I watched mutely as he went over to the hall closet, where he'd hung his coat on an overcrowded hook inside the door. As he reached for it a jumble of things fell onto the floor: my blue down vest, an NPR tote bag I used for the gym, a collapsible umbrella, and on top of it all, like a silver-flecked serpent, fell a rust-colored man's tie. Cam's eyebrow shot up. He looked at me, checking to be sure I'd seen what he had.

"Does this tie belong here, or do you want to put it away with the rest of your tie collection in your tie drawer?"

"I found that in the hallway," I said. "I think it belongs to my upstairs neighbor. I keep forgetting to give it back to him."

"Your upstairs neighbor has pretty swank taste," Cam said, inspecting the label. "This thing cost him a bundle."

"He works at Bloomingdale's," I said, grabbing the tie. "The employees there get discounts."

Cam buttoned his coat and gave me a hard look, then he hoisted up his backpack and slid his arms through the straps. He'd had that same damn book bag since college; it was so familiar I'd never noticed how foolish it looked on him now, a twenty-seven-year-old man walking around New York City with a maroon backpack slung over his shoulder, change dropping out of the back pocket's holes.

"Bloomingdale's." He shook his head. "You're full of shit, Rose. I wish you wouldn't do that, not right to my face." He took his gloves out of his coat pockets. "There's pasta sauce on the stove if you get hungry. I'll see you at Bella's on Saturday night."

I looked at him blankly.

"It's her birthday. Write it down."

"Okay, Cam, here you go." I kept my voice as steady as I could. "I was seeing someone for a while, and it ended, and I felt pretty low. But I'm okay again now. That's all I've got for you. That's all there is."

Cam took his hand off the doorknob but I shook my head. "I don't want to talk any more about it."

"Boy," he sighed. "You don't leave a guy much room, do you?"

"Maybe someday I will. But not tonight."

We faced each other, inches apart. Cam reached out and tugged on the collar of my shirt, gently, as if he could open something up that way. When his hand fell away I looked down at the floor.

"Okay," he said. "Saturday, then. Goodnight."

I stood in the open doorway until his head disappeared down the stairwell, then closed the door and leaned against it. My apartment felt quieter than it ever had before. After a second I hung the little pile of stuff back up in the hall closet, including the tie, which was Prada, and probably not even for sale in a department store, though it's not like Cam would have any idea about that. The trouble with secrets is that they make everything you say—even the truth—sound meaningless and empty. I'd meant what I'd told Cam about auditioning, about how disheartened it made me feel to be stalled in the shadows while he and Evan and Jake and Grace got on with their lives, made their own strides forward without me. I'd meant what I'd told him about being okay again, after BS. I'd meant all the sadness in my silent goodbye—that Cam and I would never be together again, that our paths had split ways for good. But he would be walking home now, angry, knotting his scarf against the cold, thinking only Prada; Oban; Lagavulin; affair.

Bella's birthday, which is a major event every fall, had taken on cosmically significant proportions this year. On November twenty-eighth she would turn twenty-eight, a stellar configuration that combined her golden birthday with her Saturn return, whatever that meant. Gold, unsurprisingly, was to be the party's theme, and our glittering invitations instructed us to let this precious metal "infuse our expectations for the night." Bella is a hard-edged customer, generally speaking, but she puts a lot of faith in astronomy. "It's a science," she once explained to me, after she'd had her palm read by a psychic who'd been featured in *Vanity Fair* for divining the futures of Hollywood's biggest starlets. "They use charts and fractal patterns and calculators and stuff."

Even the least romantic among us are seduced by the idea of destiny, I guess.

I had let gold infuse my expectations for Saturday night by buying Bella a gold-hued tube of body lotion and a glittery eye shadow and lipstick set, nice elegant stuff from a makeup counter at Barney's I knew she liked. I had also thought of gold more metaphorically, in the sense of wondering whether BS would put in an appearance, but Bella's birthday parties have traditionally been loud music/loud liquor affairs, and not conducive to the presence of parents. I dressed in black and tied my hair back with a big gold ribbon, hoping that would be sufficient concession to the night's theme.

Bella lives on Gramercy Park, on the top floor of a nineteenth-century townhouse that her family owns. From the outside, the building has all the charm of old New York, gas lanterns and leaded windows and a brass Historical Society plaque. Inside it's modern and decked out like a James Bond stronghold, with tiny video cameras and voice-recognition codes in the elevator. I rode up to Bella's floor with some disaffected-looking fashion types who preened at their reflections in the video monitor. We stepped out of the elevator into a wall of people, one of whom extended a tray of martini glasses in my direction. The music was loud. I pushed through a crowd of Bella's boarding-school friends, a crowd of her day-school friends, a crowd of her documentary-producer friends, and finally I found Bella herself, taller in stilettos than most of her guests and practically naked beneath a film of gold silk wrapped around her like a see-through sari. Her black hair was braided into tiny cornrows. She smoked from a gold cigarette holder engraved with her name and birth date.

"Rose!" she shouted, turning away from someone to clutch me to her, so that my face landed square against her extremely visible bosom. "I'm so glad you're here, you sweet little thing! Jake and Grace are unspeakably dull and sitting out on the balcony. The smoke is too intense for them, they say. You'd think they'd see enough of each other now that they live in the same room, but the fascination is endless, apparently."

"Happy birthday, Belle. I brought you something teensy."

"Stick it in the bedroom, and make sure you get at least six of these drinks the guys in black suits are passing around. They're absurdly good. I've been trying to pace myself all night and failing, failing, failing. Look, have I told you how much I hate all French people now?"

"Uh-huh. Jean-Marie isn't here, is he?"

"God, no. The funny thing is that it's spreading like a rash, this Europhobia. I'm losing tolerance for the entire continent, at least west of the war-torn bits like Hungary. I couldn't even bring myself to invite Lars and Betsy tonight. Poor Lars! In fact, when Evan showed up with his Irish friend I accidentally said something really outrageously xenophobic, and Declan just laughed at it, so now he's my favorite foreign person of the year. Seriously A-list. He's also kind of hunky, in a potato-fed way, don't you think?"

"Declan's here? Where is he?"

"I don't know. Probably pulling a sword from a stone or building a peat fire in my bedroom. It's so Rob Roy I can hardly stand it. Why don't you go find him and bring him over here, Rose, and then we can all do these awful Goldschlager shots someone brought. Now I'm going to go say hello to that bastard John Sharp, but I'll see you in two secs."

Dismissed, I looked around the living room and didn't see either Evan or Declan, so I carried my gift bag into the bedroom and left it on Bella's desk with all the others. In the hallway I spotted William Howlitt Smith, who was easy to recognize though stouter and more obviously gay in real life than he was onstage. There were film people and theater people draped everywhere, mixing it up nicely with the cashmere-sweater-set crowd, all the branches of Bella's universe assembled in her honor to get plowed off her free-flowing booze. In the kitchen, where I went to look for my friends, I found Brooks Starker, wearing a gold lamé tuxedo shirt with a ruffle down the front and winding a Band-Aid around his index finger.

"Well, well, well, if it isn't Miss Snakeskin herself," he said, wedging himself between me and the dishwasher the caterers were loading. "You've caught me on the tail end of a minor lime-slicing injury, one should always leave that job to the professionals. You know, I had a terribly lonely Reuben sandwich without you the other day. Tell me, Preston, what's your position on sauerkraut?"

"Generally pro. Though I prefer my pastrami with hot mustard and Russian dressing, whenever possible."

"Hot mustard and Russian dressing at the same time? You maniac. If such an item is procurable in this neighborhood after three o'clock in the morning, I may want to watch you eat one. But first let me get you a beverage." He waved his bandaged finger under my nose. "You know it's scientifically possible that I could bleed to death from this cut."

People at this party were drunk, very drunk, and it seemed I could either freeze on the balcony trying to search out Cassiopeia with Jake and Grace, or I could knock back several cocktails in quick succession and attempt to have a good time. I took what Brooks offered, a combination of champagne and red juice that looked like Robitussin, and let him follow me back to the living room, where he sat down very close to me on a couch.

"You actors," he said, stretching out his long Starker legs.

"Aren't you supposed to be a forthcoming set? Where's the drama, Preston? Where's the fire?"

"We're supposed to be enigmatic. This drink you've fixed me is pretty awful."

"Don't be a pussy. I couldn't stand the disappointment."

Evan appeared before us and took a seat on the couch. Brooks seemed to remember him from the summer before last at the Fort, and they shook hands like old finals club brothers, Evan doing his straight-guy best.

"Preston here was just telling me about her bartending expertise," Brooks said, sloshing some of his cocktail onto Bella's leather couch.

Evan, whose capacity to suck up to Starkers knows no bounds, laughed like this was actually funny. "Aren't you in advertising now, Brooks? Working on any accounts I might have seen?"

Brooks complained about business being slow, a tacky thing for rich people to do, in my opinion, but I was only listening with half an ear anyway, giving in to my glassy-eyed 1950s aversion to all topics fiscal and scientific. The party hung around us like a curtain of smoke and noise, and I scanned the room for the friends I hadn't found yet.

"Hey, where's Declan?" I asked Evan, who tore himself away from Brooks for long enough to shrug. I excused myself for the bathroom and went to look around.

There was no sign of Declan among the throngs packed into the kitchen and the dining room. I looked through the sliding glass door that gave out onto the balcony, where Jake and Grace huddled against each other with their backs to the party; no sign of him there, either. Bella's apartment, while enormous by young-person-in-Manhattan standards, was not so enormous that a burly, towering Irishman could get lost in it, so I walked back towards her bedroom, the only place I hadn't yet taken a look. In the hallway, William Howlitt Smith stood inspecting a row of framed David Smith sketches, studies for a piece I knew to be in the Starkers' house in Key West. He glanced at me as I walked towards him, and with a shy knot tangling up in my stomach, I thought that I should introduce myself and say something about how much I admired his work. I'd seen him on Broadway in *The Real Thing*, at the Public in *Buried Child*, and in Shakespeare in the Park two summers in a row. One hates to be sycophantic, but our country's distinguished stage actors are only stars in a certain milieu, it's not like the guy would have been beating off hordes of screaming girls all day. As I got closer he glanced at me over the frames of his glasses, an appraising little smile on his face.

"It's always so odd, isn't it, to find work that belongs in a museum hanging on the walls of people's homes. You feel as if you should carry it off and put it in a place where more eyes could see it. Little children and painting students and such."

His voice was deep and commanding, enunciated to the point of Britishness, in the way you expect a famous actor to sound. I looked at the sketches, tried not to broadcast the awe I felt in standing next to a giant of the New York stage. Did it ever get tiresome, being the object of a young person's reverence? Probably not, as long as you weren't being hounded for an autograph or a personal favor.

"This corner here," Howlitt Smith continued, pointing to a smudge in one of the sketches. "It's so alive, such a mess, look at that scrawl. So much energy contained right in that line. Fabulous." He peered at me again, took off his glasses and chewed on one of the arms, switched into backstage mode. "So who do you know here?"

"I'm a friend of Camden Post's. And Evan and Declan Pearse. My name is Rosalie. I know this sounds corny, but I'm a huge fan of your work."

"How dear of you. So you're part of the *Dame Street* crowd, then. Frightful little group of prodigies, those pals of yours. When I was their age I was checking groceries and sharing an apartment with four boys and an African parrot. Though that was a very different time in New York, I suppose." He looked up at the prints on Bella's wall, drew in a little nasal sniff. "So what do you do, Rosalie?"

"I'm trying to be an actor," I said reluctantly, not wanting to sound obsequious about it. "But I'm sort of more on the African parrot plan than the prodigy plan, you could say."

He looked me over with the kind of assessing glance you get from gay men sometimes. "Yes, now I'm remembering. One of your friends told me about you: you're the one from the South Shore. I'm from New Hampshire, originally. The dreadful town of Concord. You have to train really quite assiduously if you want to get rid of those aspirated A's. Do you have a good voice coach?"

This was amazing, like having Andre Agassi take an interest in your budding tennis game, and I told him I was between teachers, even though I'd never had a private voice coach in my life.

"It's the smartest money you'll ever spend," he said. "Actors must come from nowhere, bringing nothing. That's Brecht, as you know. Funny thing to aspire to, it seems almost outdated,

the willful erasure of the self. But many of us are drawn to it—
too many, frankly, if we had more schoolteachers and fewer
unemployed actors this country would be in less of a mess. Hundreds and hundreds of young people, pouring off the buses from
Topeka, looking to wipe away their lovely farm accents and take
on *Hedda Gabler*. What a strange life we actors seem compelled
to live. Anyway. I'm going to hunt down another glass of
sparkling water, if you'll excuse me. My throat is crackling. I hadn't
understood your generation smoked cigarettes, so incongruous
with the love of fruit smoothies and bottled water. A pleasure,
Rosalie."

The willful erasure of the self—was that what I was aspiring
to? I sort of doubted it, though sure, I'd squelched all traces of
"Paahk the caaahhh in Haaavaad yaaad" out of my accent, but
everybody my age did that, not just the actors. Still, I wonder if
the world of art can be divided in this way, those who seek to be
empty vessels (actors; probably dancers, they don't even eat) and
those for whom the past is the touchstone of all work (writers,
playwrights). There is probably something Freudian to this, but
I was too tipsy then to reason it out, and anyway what I really
had to do was pee. My bladder is cripplingly tiny; when I die
I will donate it to medical science for study and examination,
in hopes that the young women of the future will not be con-
signed to spending a quarter of their waking lives waiting for
a free toilet.

Bella's bedroom has a private bathroom attached to it, one
large and marbled enough to qualify as a day spa, and since I was
right there I slipped out of the hallway into her room. The door

from the bedroom to the bathroom was closed, so I crossed my legs and waited as patiently as I could. Then it occurred to me, in a dim, drunken way, that maybe no one was even *in* the bathroom, so dimly, drunkenly, I put my ear up to the door and had a listen. And heard this:

"What amazes me most is how incredibly sensual I find it, given that their relationship is homoerotic and I'm totally straight. How in the world did you manage to do that?"

Bella's voice purred out of the bathroom. She was obviously in there getting hot and heavy with someone, as people tend to do in bathrooms at parties, the quest for privacy outweighing even the scatological taboo. I had to pee, badly, but a lifetime of road trips will teach even the micro-bladdered to wait.

"I just wanted the scenes to be true between the characters, like. I don't know about the rest. But I'm pleased as piss that you like it."

There are hundreds of thousands of people walking around New York City with that accent on any given night of the week, but only one of them was likely to be in Bella's apartment.

"And then you write about the woman's passion with such sympathy, too. The scene in the kitchen, when she and Paul make love for the first time since he walked out on her, it has an erotic complexity that's very rare in male playwrights. And the honey is a stroke of genius. It's an incredible turn-on for the audience, to watch something so charged unfold between two people."

"Ah, go on. You're too kind. It's only a play."

"Only a play. And the Great Wall of China is only a fence. But really, tell me how you know about passions as ferocious as those.

You must know them intimately to be able to write about them so well."

Intimately! Intimately! My brain swam from a regrettable number of mixed drinks, and it told me to get the hell out of that room, that I had no business standing there with my ear smashed against the door. But my legs, crossed and locked, refused to budge. It's not merely the grotesque that compels us to listen to what we know we should turn away from, it's also the promise that some kind of truth, however shocking or disturbing, might be revealed. By which I mean it took a closed bathroom door and four stiff cocktails for me to realize what I suddenly knew completely, with the absolute fullness of my heart: that I did not want Declan and Bella to make it on the bathroom floor, that I did not want Declan to make it on the bathroom floor with anyone, just yet, that if he would only come out of the bathroom immediately I would cease to be so snipey and unpleasant to him, that I would take down my Orangemen wall calendar, that I would memorize all of Cuchulain, or at least the first act. It was a tidal wave of certainty, I can't describe it any other way, I can only say that its disorienting effects made me slow on my feet as I heard a silence, and then a crash, and then muffled and embarrassed laughter from both of them, and Bella's voice saying, "That was very forward of me, I'm sorry, but I consider it my birthday imperative to make an ass of myself at least once," and Declan's voice saying, "Come on now, no need to apologize, you're fine. You're grand. Should we go back out, then, do you think?"

And then my legs unlocked and I was out of that bedroom fast, faster than you can say Mary Robinson. And because the world suddenly seemed like it had new corners and edges for my mind to trace, I put on my coat and left the party. Flakes of snow were sticking to the pavement when I got outside, enough of them to cling to the toes of my shoes. Oh, discovery! The familiar landscape made strange and new! The city was quiet; it glowed.

Dear Annie,

Boys don't notice me. I am 5'2" and I weigh 123 pounds and I have nice hair, brown but fine. No boys ever talk to me. All of my friends have regular boyfriends and I have never kissed anyone or even talked much on the phone. It is getting pretty lonely out here. I would like to have some experiences but they never seem to come my way. What can I do about this?

—Not Popular in Montana

Dear Not Popular,

Let me begin by pointing out a few great things about not having a boyfriend. Instead of wasting time talking on the phone every night, you get to read great books, watch great movies, do an ace job on your homework, and generally invest in your future as a well-educated and serious-minded person, all of which will matter more someday than who you did or didn't kiss at the junior prom. Did I kiss anyone at the junior prom? See, I can't even remember. I can, however, remember reading *Great Expectations*, watching *Psycho* for the first time, and scoring a 5 on the Spanish AP.

I don't mean to be flip about this. Getting your first kiss is a very important event, and of course it's something to be impatient about.

But it *will* happen—it happens to everyone—and while you're waiting for it to happen to you, make hay by enjoying all the wonderful aspects of a boy-free existence. No burps to smell (except your own). No boring stories to listen to about band practice. No sharing your french fries. The list of perks is actually quite long, and I predict that someday, when you are sitting across from a smelly person in a restaurant who is eating your french fries and telling you about his band, you will look back on this time with great fondness.

As for what you can do to speed the process up: you can be brave about talking to boys yourself. Some of them are shyer than you might think, and might be very flattered to have you approach them. You can also ask your girlfriends and their boyfriends to keep an eye out, just in case they meet anyone who they think you should be introduced to. But otherwise, I wouldn't worry too much about it: you sound like a lovely person. And good things come to those who wait.

> Trust me. I've lived through it.
> Annie

Chapter Eleven

One thinks of New York as a vast, overpopulated grid of streets and skyscrapers, and of New Yorkers as private, anonymous rat racers, united only in their outrage over smoking bans and curbside recycling cutbacks. But as in the rest of America, New York has its neighborhoods and its neighborhood associations, even its informal consortiums of people organized to fight their grassroot fights, such as the lack of flame-retardant playground equipment in Hamilton Fish Park. The block my building sits on is represented by a group called the Tompkins Square Committee, whose citizen-members make their views known to City Council on issues ranging from pest control to street lighting. I don't attend their meetings, which they advertise, ironically enough, by stapling fliers to construction zones that specifically prohibit sign posting. But I do add my name to their petitions whenever someone with a clipboard catches me on my way out of the house, and I make an effort to skim the xeroxed newsletter that appears in the foyer of my building every other month.

Thus it was with some pride that I received the news from Lou Saccovitch, my liaison at Adele Goldberg, that the Tompkins Square Committee had named me Neighborhood Volunteer of the Month, for my efforts with the AGSC reading circle. Strictly speaking this was no big deal, a monthly award in a small neighborhood goes to every do-gooder sooner or later; Mrs. Lybynchek told me her own granddaughter had won it twice for teaching Tumbling for Beginners at the Head Start on Avenue B. Still, I was proud to be recognized for the little project I'd started, proud to be an engine of the cultural life blossoming at AGSC. The residents had even founded a homegrown lecture series on their former professional callings, called "A Day in the Life."

The ceremony in my honor, which took place in the atrium of the Senior Center, consisted of selected readings from my letters of nomination, none of which I'd known about until that afternoon. Mrs. Grossman had described me as a mensch, a term she went on to define in the body of the letter, since "the neighborhood loses so many yids every year." Pearl Coleman, my hardest-won ally, complimented my "enjoyable interpretations of some decent books." At the end of the presentation Lou set out some low-sodium goldfish and a tray of buffalo wings, and I got a hand-printed certificate and a week-long free subway pass. Mr. Frantal, who had photographed Dust Bowl families for the WPA, used a disposable camera to take pictures for my mom and dad.

If the events of July to December had been set in motion by my breaking an expensive piece of crystal, then the next half year was surely off to a more auspicious start. I don't have any great love for New Year's Eve, with its pressure to schlep around town in skimpy clothing even as the temperature dips below zero, but I like the promise of a new year, and I framed my Volunteer of the Month certificate and hung it over my bureau, to remind myself of at least one good reason for getting dressed smartly in the morning, rather than scrounging in the dry-cleaning pile for a shirt without stains.

Last Winter in Dame Street went into rehearsals in early December, which made Cam and Evan busier than ever. Declan, who had finished his final revisions of the script, was increasingly free. It had become clear to me in the weeks after Bella's party that he and she were not destined for anything like a romance, notwithstanding the Great Lavatory Caper. They were awkward and formal around each other at the Christmas parties we'd all been invited to, and Bella had completely lost interest in *Dame Street,* a telling turnaround from the young-Shakespeare riff she'd done behind the bathroom door. My relief at this near miss hadn't worn off with my hangover; in fact it had grown. I had conceived of Declan as an intelligent, charismatic figure before Bella threw herself at him, but as is often the case, his essential attractiveness had to be pointed out by someone else before I could see it myself. Those of us who've lived our lives on the pretty/plain cusp always fall for the vanilla good looks of guys like Cam; it takes confidence to see handsomeness in its less conventional forms, the same way it takes confidence to wear ethnic jewelry or vintage clothes. Anyway what I felt for Declan, or what I thought I felt, was a kind of territorialism: he'd taken an interest in me, I'd taken an interest in him, and we'd confided in one another, put in enough time together at bakeries and pizzerias and train sta-tions around Manhattan for us to be friends on a higher plane than he could possibly be with Bella, or with anyone else. She didn't even know about his girlfriend, and it was on Fiona's behalf that I pegged my outrage over Bella's advances, at least in the beginning. Oh, the heart is a stubborn organ, and goes to great lengths to mask its true desires; for the truer they are, the more trapped you will be as soon as you have named them.

Declan didn't mention Bella's proposition to me, not even in the weeks afterwards when we hung out a lot, drawn together like orphans during the holiday season to see the lighting of the Rockefeller Center tree and the free nativity pageant at Saint John the Divine. He was, had always been, brazenly direct about my private life, but when it came to his own he was all "go on, then" and "cop off," even when I dug around for news of Fiona. He never talked about her, though, so that our conversations often sounded like this:

"I've seen your old bank man at a producer's meeting this afternoon, and he looks as shifty as ever. You're better off without him, Rosalie. You're not missing anything there."

"You know I don't even think about him so much anymore, unless he's in the newspaper or something. I saw a picture of him in *New York Magazine* the other day and at first I just flipped by it, assumed it was another generic businessman in another generic gray suit. That's how far away he feels now. But this time of year can be awfully gloomy when you're by yourself, don't you think? It's easy to feel lonely in all this cold."

"Here" (passing me a crushed, greasy bag of Fritos), "They've come out with a new shape for these things, have a taste."

One night, after a screening of *Miracle on 34th Street* at Lincoln Square, Declan invited me up to his apartment for a cup of tea. I'd never seen his rooms before, and they looked as I'd imagined they would, sparsely furnished with basic tables and chairs he must have rented somewhere, and a hand-me-down couch too covered with books and papers to sit down on. He must have earned a decent amount of money for *Dame Street* to be able to afford an apartment on the Upper West Side, though nothing about the place suggested luxury or much of an interest in home décor. I nosed around the living room while he boiled water in an aluminum pot, searching out the revealing details that even the most haphazard living spaces offer up. Mixed in among the requisite writerly trappings were a few books of piano music (Motown and gospel, go figure), a nearly completed jigsaw puzzle of the Taj Mahal, and two small watercolors tacked to the wall with pushpins, dated from the year before and inscribed to him.

"I'd apologize for the house being a wreck, but it always looks this way," he said, standing over the stove. "The lady across the hall from me has a bonsai garden and a golden retriever. I feel like a criminal whenever I meet her, for keeping the apartment next door to hers such a mess."

The tea he handed me was blacker than pitch. "You just need to get yourself a plant or something. This place is nice, I think."

"I don't have the temperament for gardening. That's why I liked the glass flowers so much. There's some sugar on the table, if you want it. And I've got these, too." He lifted down a tin of chocolate biscuits from the top of the refrigerator. "Would you care for milk?"

I shook my head. It was easy sitting in Declan's kitchen with him, though the table legs were off balance and the fluorescent lights made everything slightly green. The room was homey, and out the window behind him it had begun to snow. The radiator sizzled, as if the woman with the bonsai garden were frying something next door. "This is a great night for tea. Thank you."

"We used to drink it on the hottest days of the year when I was growing up. My ma thought the sweating would cool us off and keep us quiet, but it would have taken something stronger than tea to do that."

"How many brothers and sisters do you have?"

"Five brothers, two sisters. We were a holy terror, the pack of us, especially in the summers."

I thought of my parents' quiet, orderly house, the central air-conditioning, the permanent supply of Popsicles in the Deep-freeze. All the Freon in the world couldn't make up for the holy terrordom of a gang of eight. "Do you keep in touch with them?"

"Oh, in my own way I suppose I do. I keep up with the ones I'm close to over the computer, and the news always makes it back and forth some way. We're an awful bunch for gossip, all of us." Declan stood up from the table and moved back to the stove, where he studied the pot of water as if something valuable had fallen into it. "I've got someone coming from there, now that you mention it."

"From Ireland?"

"That's right."

My mind was stuck on siblings. "Which one?"

"It's Fiona. She's coming to stay for a bit while the play's on, she wants to see the previews. Aer Lingus, that's who she works for, they're giving her some time off to come to New York." He put the pot back down on the burner and looked right at me. "She's coming in tomorrow week. You'll like her, I hope."

If my shock registered, one would have had to observe it in the unfinished half of a chocolate biscuit I had quietly crushed in my left hand. He hadn't mentioned the girl in months, and suddenly she was checking her bags and browsing through the Duty Free? "I'm sure I will," I said. "I mean, of course, of course I will. You'll have to let me show her around. I'd love to show her around town and the movies and restaurants and everything. It's such a big city, with the landmarks, and restaurants, and she should see it, of course. Of course I will."

"They're giving her a whole month off, which is a bit of a surprise. At least to me it is, anyway. I suppose I've gotten used to being alone here in my little flat."

And I supposed I'd gotten used to having him alone. "Are those her pictures in the living room?"

"They are, yeah." Declan sounded embarrassed, so I told him I thought the watercolors were lovely, which I did. "She likes to paint. She used to do a lot of it when we were in school together. I thought she should be a painter, she even studied it some at university. Now she's quite the businesswoman. I drive her bats, being so desperate with money, but you know, if you had the same interests as everyone around you, what would be the point of that?"

I nodded mutely, an inadequate response. But truly, truly, how does one make sense of a scene like that? There we were, just the two of us, sitting across from each other in the closeness of his kitchen at midnight, and now there was Fiona, the painterly airline executive, descending on New York in a mere eight days to claim her moody genius of a boyfriend and take him away from—from what? From me? I finished my tea and let the mug clatter to rest on the tabletop. My heart was beating wildly. "You'll have to let me know as soon as Fiona gets here and you're in the mood to make plans," I said, and it sounded eerily convincing, like one of those robots in a sci-fi movie that has all the mannerisms and gestures of a human being, but doesn't have a heart. "I'm so looking forward to meeting her. I can't wait."

What happened next was a strange stroke of fortune, good in some ways, bad in others, unexpected all in all. Grace called on Sunday afternoon and told me to get myself to her apartment as quickly as possible, that she'd pay for my cab. I had the whole ride across the Williamsburg Bridge to work myself into a state of panic, and when I got to her door, Grace's expression told me I hadn't been wrong. She pulled me into the bathroom and produced a white stick, sort of like an emery board only smooth and plastic. I knew instantly what it was, not that I personally have ever had to use a home pregnancy test, but all feminine health products have roughly the same design, clinical yet unthreatening, medical yet pink. I assumed from Grace's face that the two lines showing on her stick meant Jackpot, Congratulations, You're Going to Be a Mom.

"But we've used condoms every single time," she said in a wavering voice. "I don't understand how this possibly could have happened."

What they say about adrenaline is true: in an extreme moment, even the grotesque image of two people you know having sexual intercourse can be overcome for the situation at hand. "Condoms aren't foolproof, Grace. With perfect use they only work something like ninety-two out of a hundred times. And that doesn't even include human error."

"Okay, I don't need a goddamn lecture from the *GirlTalk* health department, thank you very much."

This was unfair, I'd only been trying to address how it might have happened, but obviously Grace was beyond wanting to know. "Have you told Jake about this yet?"

"Jake and Cam are at a Knicks game. No I haven't told him. My God, are you kidding? Jake's wearing a Patrick Ewing jersey and carrying a foam finger right now. You think he's ready for fatherhood? This thing can't be right. I should get another kit, and if this one's wrong I'm going to sue EPT for thirty million dollars' worth of psychological damage. I can't be pregnant, Rose. I can't be. I don't want to be."

She slumped down on the bathroom floor and started weeping. Grace is one of those people who only looks sweeter and more angelic when she cries. I slid the test stick out of her hand and rested it on the sink's edge, then settled down next to her on the tiled floor. In my mind I was thinking that maybe this wasn't the biggest catastrophe in the world—she was engaged already, after all. It's not like having a baby would doom her to a life of single-motherhood or even to a shotgun wedding, if that's what they're still called today.

"Listen, Grace, these things aren't always accurate; what you have to do is go to the doctor. I'll go with you tomorrow, how about that? I'll take a personal day from work and we can go together."

"Oh, forget it, forget it." She was crying harder now, and I had trouble understanding her because she was taking shallow little breaths and speaking through a tissue. "I'm never going to get any acting work anyway, so why don't I forget the whole stupid thing and start popping out the kids, right? I mean really, really, what would I be giving up? My temp job. My temp job that doesn't even cover my health insurance and that's it. Why don't I just change my name to Mrs. Jacob Weiner and move to New Jersey and start selling Mary Kay?"

"Gracie, Grace," I said, brushing the hair out of her face. "Come on, you're not going to do that. You're going to be an actress, a beautiful actress, if that's what you want to be, and you're not going to move to the suburbs because I won't let you. Right now you're exhausted and freaked out" (and hormonal, I thought but didn't say), "and you're getting way, way ahead of yourself. First of all, we don't even know if you're pregnant yet, and second of all, if you are pregnant you have plenty of options to consider, and time to think about all of them."

"I do not have options!" she hissed, in a voice so fierce I pulled away from her. "I am not twelve years old! I'm twenty-seven, and I'm educated and self-sufficient and engaged to be married, if I'm pregnant then that's what I am. We aren't kids anymore, Rosalie. That's the problem with you. We aren't kids."

The problem with me? The problem with *me*? Was I the one having sex without a backup birth control method? Before I could think, I had to get poor hysterical Grace off the bathroom floor and into bed, which was where she said she wanted to go. I gave her a glass of water and three Tylenol P.M., hoping the chemicals wouldn't hurt whatever tiny creature she might have been sharing them with. I got her into a T-shirt and pulled down the bedroom shades, and promised to stay with her until Jake came home. I passed the early evening on their couch, zoned out in front of reality TV shows of contests and daring feats whose nail-biting outcomes weren't anything close to the nail-biting mysteries of real life. I tried not to feel angry with Grace for calling me a child; she had good reason for being irrational, given what she'd just found out, and even good reason for being jealous. But was that all it was? Once, I went into the bedroom to check on her, and when I leaned down next to her she opened her eyes dreamily and whispered "Oh Rose, how free it must be to be you. You don't ever worry about anyone but yourself, you lucky, lucky . . ." Then she was out again.

My part in this drama ended when Jake got home from Madison Square Garden and I told him he needed to talk to his wife-to-be. He was pale as a ghost when he came out of the bedroom, and I offered to stick around and make dinner with him while Grace slept, but he said he was fine, he'd just as soon have some time to himself. That was the moment when I finally believed in their coupledom, that they weren't just putting the rest of us on, but were actually each other's closest allies, with only a recreational need for anyone else. They went to the doctor together that week, and sure enough Grace was pregnant, and sure enough they decided to play the hand they'd been given and hold on to Baby, though what private struggles and anguish their decision cost them I'll never know. Grace was a picture of good-natured accommodation and prenatal nerves almost immediately, in a victory of surfaces that had everyone convinced she'd gotten what she wanted. But I knew she felt more conflicted than she was pretending to be. I knew, even if she never said another word about it, that she was making a sacrifice, and that those of us whose stomachs were flat and whose breasts weren't swollen burned her like a reminder of all she'd given up.

Friends; immigrants; the first trimester. Against the backdrop of unplanned pregnancy nothing in my own life seemed very high-stakes, as Grace herself had so bluntly pointed out. Fiona's arrival was the next event on my horizon, and that barely even counted, since I would only be playing the role of tour guide and restaurant consultant. Each time I thought of meeting Declan's beloved I felt a pang of dread, but I knew this to be a selfish reaction, and Grace had made me so aware of my selfishness that I'd become obsessed with squashing it at every turn, offering my doggie bags to homeless people, helping Cam write his program bio, staying late at AGSC to be a fourth for euchre after the reading circle on Wednesday nights. When Fiona arrived, I would meet her and I would like her. Declan had been a friend to me in my hour of jilted need, and I would be a friend to him in his hour of blissful reunion. I would be the picture of feminine selflessness; I would give this flight attendant, or whatever she was, the warmest welcome of her lifetime. Even if part of me wished she didn't exist.

In the absence of any engrossing theater projects *GirlTalk* had become my main event every day, and perhaps because of this my apathy about work was at an all-time high. One can tolerate almost any form of drudgery with a proper amount of ironic distance, but without any immediate plans in the hopper I was, well, a teenage advice columnist, pure and simple, and this made my days in the office long and dull. One morning I came in to work to find the following note posted on my door: "RP: PLS COME BY ASAP, NOW NOT LATER. YRS, GK." It was rare for Ginger to beat any of us to the office, and rarer still for her to use pencil and paper, so I hustled over to the editor's suite with my Styrofoam coffee cup still in hand. Wendy, Ginger's assistant, shrugged at me like she'd seen the note but didn't know what it meant, which wasn't a good sign. I knocked lightly on Ginger's door.

"Come in, Rosalie, won't you have a seat while I finish up this call," Ginger said, waving me in. She seemed to be on the phone with someone whose job it was to oversee her garden, because she kept repeating orders like, "I understand, Mr. Rankin, but we put in an entire greenhouse for that purpose, didn't we, so if you have to use fertilizer then do it, just do it." Once she hung up, she sighed a weary sigh and located a piece of paper on her desk, which made her sigh another weary sigh and look at me.

"I suppose you know what this is about," she said, flashing the paper in my direction so that I could make out blue cursive handwriting and nothing else.

"I don't think I do," I said brightly, trying to sit up as straight as possible, Ginger being a posture maven.

"I expect you'll find some of the content familiar, though you may have to cast back in your memory, since it apparently took the girls in the reader mail department half a year to get this letter routed to my office." Her eye skimmed down the page. "'*The writer whose office is across the hall from mine thinks Ginger got artificially inseminated so she wouldn't ever have to sleep with her husband.'"* She flicked her eyes up at me. I met them, and sat straighter. "'*You can catch an STD from oral sex, so make sure to always use condoms. The polyurethane ones taste better than the latex ones.*'"

"I apologize," I said, before she could read any more. "I know what this is about. I was out of line that morning, and I had no business speaking publicly as a representative of the magazine."

"Yes, well Mrs. George T. Cardworthy seems to have taken understandably profound offense at your performance, and she wrote in September to alert me that she was canceling her daughter Mariah's subscription. God knows how it can take six months for mail of this gravity to cross my desk. It's hardly rocket science, opening the letters and getting them where they need to go."

I sat in my chair and waited for Ginger to fire me. I hoped it would not take long or be any more painful than it had to be. She sighed another weary sigh and opened a desk drawer and took out her PalmPilot.

"I have no idea how to use this gizmo, and Wendy refuses to teach me." She punched at the keypad a few times and buzzed Wendy, who came in and carried the PalmPilot off. I continued to wait to be fired.

"Look, Rosalie, I'd like to know what could possibly have been going through your mind to make you behave so disrespectfully, both to me and to this institution, which as far as I can see has treated you quite handsomely over the past several years."

"Nothing sensible was going through my mind, it was an act of complete immaturity." I meant that, I really did, plus my only angle was to play for the Strict Mom treatment; I would have to tell her about BS. "I don't mean this as an excuse, but I had just been through a very rough patch in my personal life, a bad breakup, and I was venting my frustration in highly inappropriate ways."

"I should say so. A breakup is hardly grounds for insulting your superiors and sullying the name of this magazine, as I would hope you'd know. Nor are you entitled to go around hosting impromptu question-and-answer sessions without my direct permission."

"I won't defend my behavior, Ginger, I can't; I can only tell you how sorry I am that it happened. Sometimes I feel like *I* could use some advice, and here I am, writing our advice column. I really do wish I'd been more in control of my emotions, I'm trying to learn how to do that."

"Have you thought about yoga?"

"I take yoga at my gym sometimes." The thing to do with Ginger is just to go with her, and hope for the best.

"I mean Bikram yoga, not your *gym* yoga. The heat is extremely purgative. You might think about it." She looked at the letter again. "The point is, Rosalie, there's no extra money in the budget for you girls to go around poisoning our subscription base. If someone had said these sorts of things in front of my daughters I would have sued, absolutely sued. This is a place of business, you do realize. I sometimes think a stricter dress code would help you girls understand that, all this collarless bagginess contributes to an air of lassitude I find editorially unproductive."

"I don't know how I can express the amount of regret I feel. I can only promise that it will never happen again."

"Indeed." Ginger had on her stern disciplinarian face. She was going to ground me, not fire me. "I'm taking you off all out-of-office assignments for the next six months."

I took the news with appropriate sobriety, without mentioning that I'd never once been on an out-of-office assignment in the past three years.

"And I'd like to see a weekly task report, please. If you feel anything less than thrilled with the lovely job you've got here, I can see absolutely no reason for you to stay in it."

I could see a few reasons, for example health insurance, but I didn't stay to share them with her. Instead I went back to my desk, turned on my computer, and got to work.

We've all read about people, perfectly enlightened modern adults, who are going about their life's business, drafting human resource policy, serving divorce papers, picking up the kids from Little League, when wham, a bus comes from nowhere and flattens them on the pavement, or a piece of mercury-laced fish gets brought to them on a bed of vermicelli, and suddenly there's the white light, the blinding tunnel, and then miracle of miracles, they wake up in their backless hospital gowns, safe, alive, plucked from the virtual cliffs of their own mortality, and changed forever for having been spared. Their life's work is now their opportunity to say thank you, to prove that they're worthy of the second chance they've been given. The janitors are pleasantly surprised by the generosity of their retirement packages, the annulment is canceled, the kids get taken out to dinner at the all-you-can-eat country buffet even after striking out and talking back to their coaches. It's *A Christmas Carol,* it's the happy old story of being born again, minus the religious fanaticism.

Ginger hadn't fired me. I had led a life of relative carnal adventure, and had never once wound up in a Planned Parenthood clinic. My friends were all still speaking to me, in spite of my ill-considered dalliance with one of their fathers. I had been, in my own small way, spared. And if I could begin to play out my gratitude by being a welcoming hostess to a friend's out-of-town guest, then that's exactly what I had to do.

Fiona Martin was curvy and redheaded, with a smattering of freckles that ran from the bridge of her nose to the lowest point of her décolletage. She chain-smoked, and had a deep gravelly voice that mesmerized the men she spoke to with its consumptive vixenishness. She favored platform heels and Lycra ensembles that got stingy around her hips. Declan organized a group-drinks outing for her second night in town, and when he introduced the two of us she leapt up, embraced me, and told me that she wanted to go shopping, that she'd heard New York was like Paris only tartier, and was that true? Cam and Jake, their eyes glued to the strip of flesh between the bottom of her shirt and the top of her pants, practically fell off their banquettes.

One hears about these yin-and-yang relationships, where duck hunters and vegans are moved to set aside their politics in the name of love, but the Declan-Fiona matchup was even more mysterious than that. I had imagined her as friendly, pretty, sweet—these being the qualities one ascribes to girls who work in marketing and stay true to their childhood flames. I had not imagined an extroverted knockout, and in the first hour at the bar my brain tried to sort through the million new pieces of tangible evidence in front of me, like some crazed slot machine whose icons wouldn't line up. She had an undeniable physical electricity about her, and Cam and Jake spent the evening looking as if they'd stuck their fingers in the socket; they couldn't keep their mouths shut, for drooling. Normally I don't find myself thinking about women as sensual beings, particularly, heterosexuality having been drilled into me by the conservative forces of my kindergarten, Sunday school, etc. But Fiona had sex dripping off her; it was almost impossible *not* to picture her rolling around on the floor of Declan's kitchen, covered in honey, the brain being very stubborn in its visual associations that way.

Still, for all her va-va-va-voom, there was something curiously platonic in her dealings with Declan, as they lit each other's cigarettes and passed the ashtray back and forth. They were extremely solicitous of one another, easy and familiar, but not exactly passionate in the way you'd expect of a couple that had been separated by an ocean for almost a year. Animal lust is bound to fade after decades, one never sees married couples pawing at each other the way the newly attached do. But shouldn't the occasion of a transatlantic reunion trump the ennui of familiar flesh, at least for a day or two? Or was their physical life so private in its intimacies as to be invisible to the naked eye? And how perverted was it that I was actually thinking about this?

Anyway, Fiona wanted to go shopping, and I offered to take her over the weekend so that Declan could sit in on rehearsals. Turns out this business of crass consumption and material acquisition is not an exclusively American phenomenon, as Europeans try to pretend. Though it does seem to be a female thing, by and large. The boys at rehearsal, the girls chasing around department stores opening charge accounts to save 15%

on the day's purchases. Funny, which patterns obtain from culture to culture.

I left the bar on the early side. Cam and Jake hardly noticed, that's how engrossed they were in Fiona's every eyelash-bat, but Declan stood up to say goodnight and thank me for joining them. He was a gentleman, in his own rough way, and that wasn't just showing off for his ladylove's benefit, either. It had been true since the first night we met.

Babysitting Fiona was an athletic proposition. She could shop for hours without breaking for nourishment or a toilet, and everywhere we went she made friends with the salesgirls, the elevator attendants, the customers in the dressing rooms next door. She was extravagantly outgoing—a stop in a deli for a pack of gum could run us a half hour while she schmoozed with the dark-skinned guy behind the counter about her cousin's summer experience backpacking around Irbid. She called everyone "Love" and "Gorgeous" before she'd been introduced. She wrote down her address for the girls on the perfume floor at Macy's, who said they would be passing through Dublin on a trip. An old man in the tie department, where we'd stopped to find a present for Declan, asked her to marry him. "Aren't you the sweetest thing," she said, knocking the brim of his hat. "I'm spoken for myself, but I've got a sister in Limerick you might fancy."

Liking Fiona had been a point of honor for me even before her plane touched down, and luckily it was easy to like her, in the way it's easy to like a twister that blows through town and levels Main Street, simply because the force of its energy is so complete.

She was a bombshell, and yet she was as friendly and unaffected as anyone I'd ever met. I helped her carry her shopping bags from store to store on our whirlwind tour of acquirable New York, and when we finally sat down for coffee in the restaurant on the top floor of Bloomingdale's, I asked her how she and Declan had met.

"We grew up together on the Northside of Dublin," she said, trying to light a cigarette underneath the table. "It was tough where we came from, a gammy part of town. We both wanted to get out, and that was enough to keep us together. Would you believe I was always the serious one in school, like I did my business courses by the time I was twenty-one and I've been working ever since. Deco had all sorts of jobs with useless pay, and he'd get sacked from them more often than not for his temper, but I knew he'd be famous for writing someday. I believed in his brains from first we met, and now everybody else is finding out about them."

"I can't believe you guys have known each other for such a long time. That's amazing."

"Well I didn't like him for the first ten years or so, so I don't know how amazing it is. He was a pestilential child, with an awful, sullen temper. But I always knew he had a brain in his head, even then."

"How old were you when you fell in love?"

"We were a couple of spotty teenagers. I don't know if we even understood what we were falling into, we were just kids. Now we're family, like, I've seen him go from a lad to a famous author. I don't know how I would have grown up in that place without Deco, or how I would have gotten out of it. He'd say the same of me. And now we're both on our way in the world, and here we are in New York City, would you believe. I think Deco likes it here. I think he's happy."

"He's doing really well," I said, not sure whether she wanted him to be happy in New York or not.

"He should be, he's had it in him for ages. He's a bit of a pain at first, but he's a grower, isn't he, our Deco?"

I had forgotten about that word, grower. I hadn't heard it since I'd lived in Dublin. It describes someone whose looks and temperament take a while to grow on you, someone you're surprised to find yourself liking so much. "He is," I said, handing Fiona an empty cup to ash in under the table. "He absolutely is."

I can hardly, at this stage in the game, pretend to have expertise in science and biology that I don't actually have. But an image stays with me, maybe from a children's book I once owned, or a homework assignment I copied off one of my more zoologically inclined friends. It is of snakes, outgrowing their scales, molting into bigger, more powerful snakes, having to literally shed their own skin in order to reach full maturity. Of course I am afraid of snakes, and suspicious of broadly drawn metaphors from the natural world, but it does seem to me that we can none of us move forward without letting go of some piece of ourselves, be it scales or feathers or fur or skin. Declan and Fiona were each other's childhoods—I began to understand this that afternoon in Bloomingdale's. And the way they treated each other as I watched them over the next week, with kindness and affection but without any palpable charge, spoke to their history and all the years they had in common, but not to their present selves. Some people choose for history—my own parents, for example, and maybe even Jake and Grace, in their own way. But the more I thought about *Last Winter in Dame Street,* and that character, Paul, risking his whole world for a chance at the life he belonged in, the more I understood what Declan's play was about. I was an English major at Harvard; I graduated Phi Beta Kappa and magna cum laude. I understand that literature is never plain autobiography, and that only the fool reads it as such. But then, I had never had a friend write something serious before. And it is only the pedant who fails to see the man in the work.

I was in the dentist's office waiting for a tooth-cleaning when I came by this next piece of news, after I'd read *People* from cover to cover and turned, under duress, to the *Wall Street Journal.* An item in the real estate section on trends in property divestment noted that Berglan Starker and his wife were selling their estate in the Adirondacks and donating the non-essential acreage to the National Forest Trust. The piece quoted downsizing socialites from all over greater New York, including Mrs. Starker, who said that the erosion problems on Fort Sassquam Lake prevented her family from doing necessary renovations and additions to their house. "She has also confirmed that she and her husband have bid on five hundred acres of ranchland in western Montana," the reporter noted, with some asperity. "Mrs. Starker, a lobbyist who represents cattle and agriculture interests with the firm of Browland Dickey, describes the move as purely personal."

I know there is a danger in imbuing events with too much symbolic weight, but it meant something to me that Fort

Sassquam was up for sale. All of us from First Born had been going there together for seven-odd years; a history of our emergence into adulthood was written into that house's floors and walls, from the trapdoor in the kitchen Grace had once fallen through to the planks on the deck Cam had shot up with an air rifle, drunk. It wasn't our property to keep or to sell, and maybe that was for the best, since how can you ever decide when something you're a part of should be over? This coming summer Grace would be swollen and expanding, and probably in no mood to strip down to a bathing suit or sit in the backseat of a car for seven hours, if what I've heard about pregnancy is true. Cam would be city-bound every night of the week except for Mondays, if the *Dame Street* reviews were good. And even me, even my dependable enthusiasm for the lake and the woods had dampened a little, at the prospect of sleeping one room over from Berglan Starker's marriage bed. It would be empty, of course, but I would still have to walk by it on my way to the bathroom if I had to wake up to pee in the night, which I inevitably do.

I felt worst for Bella, of course, who had been summering at Fort Sassquam for her entire life, careening around the lake on her speedboat, fishing for endangered species off the dock. She wasn't especially eager to talk about it when I called to ask her how she was feeling; there were the family compounds in Tahoe and Key West that she could always go to instead. "I don't want to complain about it," she said, almost sweetly. "The Fort was my favorite, but I'm lucky to have what I have. That's what I'm trying to remember, anyway." She seemed embarrassed that her dad could be pushed around so easily by his wife, who had hated the Fort since her first trip up there, and who hadn't been appeased by any amount of interior redecoration. The wife had won, and the Fort was gone. Bella's sadness made sense to me, but her surprise struck me as weird; she'd always raised such hell about being disappointed by her dad in the past, I wouldn't have imagined there was anything left about him that could disappoint her. But there always is, isn't there. There's always one more thing.

Dear Annie,

I will start by saying that my boyfriend is great and I really love him no matter what. But he has a couple of habits that I can't stand. For one thing, whenever I ask him a question he repeats it before he answers it. Like I'll say, "What time is the movie?" and he'll say, "What time is the movie? It's at seven o'clock." For another thing, he hums when we kiss. There are lots of examples like this. All of them are pretty small, but they really can add up and drive me crazy. Should I tell him, or how can I ignore them?

—Nitpicking in Alabama

Dear Nitpicking,

How's this for a no-fail solution: next time your boyfriend parrots your question back to you, try parroting his answer back to him. "The movie is at seven o'clock! The movie is at seven o'clock!" Imitation can be a useful way to highlight what drives you crazy and why: try humming a little bit of the *Titanic* theme song when he leans in for his next goodnight kiss, and see if that doesn't quiet him down.

Unfortunately, the fact of the matter is that every single person comes with a few weird habits, and the key to romantic happiness is finding the person whose weird habits irritate you least. The next guy you date may not be a part-time backup singer, but he may walk around with his thumbs stuck in his belt loops, or he may chew too loudly for your tastes. The best thing to do—if you can bear it—is to tune out his minor eccentricities, instead of calling him on all of them. Because as soon as you start calling him on his, he gets to call you on yours, and next thing you know you'll have a boyfriend who's telling you how to hold your fork.

If keeping your opinions to yourself turns out to be too hard, you can either break up or pick his most annoying habit—only one, please—and launch a polite, discreet campaign to reform it. But remember, not all causes are worth a war. Who knows? A little light music during your next makeout session might even be nice.

Trust me. I've lived through it.

Annie

Chapter Twelve

Though I have been a theatergoer since my arrival in New York, I had never, before *Last Winter in Dame Street,* been on the guest list for a black-tie opening, which is the way they do things on Broadway. Evan has attended these events for years, usually lugging Manny Flax's coffee thermos and baby carrots in the pockets of his tux, and when I asked him what to expect from the night, whether there would be anything specially ceremonial on the docket, he puffed out his cheeks in exasperation. "It's just a show, Rose, like any other. It's not like you get free dinner, if that's what you're wondering about."

I had jitters about the theater community's reaction to *Dame Street,* which was strange since, when you came right down to it, I had nothing to do with the play's success. What had started out as jealousy had morphed into a kind of proximate pride-by-association, mostly because I wanted to be around when Evan and Declan got the recognition they deserved. I can remember this feeling from other times in my life: right after graduation, for example, when one of my roommates sold a screenplay about a group of drug runners posing as undergraduates at Yale; my envy then had been mollified by being close enough to feel like an insider on the whole deal ("No, they're not going to make it right away, in Hollywood they basically never do that."). With *Dame Street* my best friends were at the helm, which gave me the illusion, at least, of being somewhere on the ship. When industry items got printed about the play in newspapers, rumors of infighting among the production designers etc., I could do nothing but glow.

As previews got closer Evan invited me to come by and watch a couple of rehearsals, and whenever I showed up I found Fiona sitting in the back of the house doing crossword puzzles, looking pissy and bored out of her mind. Listening to people rehearse the same material over and over again can get old fast, so I went outside with her for smoke breaks whenever she looked dangerously close to hurling her pen or newspaper at the stage.

"I don't understand how you can watch this shite so many times," she'd say, blowing smoke. "It's driving me mad. It's like being made to sit through Mass for six weeks in a row. I know it's an important time for Deco, but he could have the decency to take me to lunch every few days, couldn't he? The only time we see each other is after rehearsals, and then his brain's a fog, he's ratting on about line change this and cue change that. The damn thing's written, isn't it? And aren't I here to see him, not the inside of this blasted theater?"

Fiona had a point; this couldn't have been the visit she had bargained for. "Why don't you let me take you to lunch? I don't think I could stand watching as much of this as you have, and I'm supposed to be a professional. You've got to keep your distance from this place if you don't want to go bonkers."

"Let's go then, Rosalie, if you want to. I can't take another day of those crap sandwiches from the market across the street."

I took her to a diner on Fifty-fourth and Broadway, just

around the corner from the theater. She picked at a plate of chicken salad and drank three diet Cokes. We talked about the grayness of New York in late February, how it was just like Dublin only colder, with worse wind. Her mood brightened as she told me about a trip to Majorca she'd taken with some of her girlfriends from work; they'd gotten discounted airfares and spent two weeks at Club Med, snorkeling and sailing and working on their tans. I pictured Fiona, a Venus on the half shell dressed in a wetsuit, splashing in the surf and drinking sangria in a cabana on the beach. Her idea of a vacation wasn't sitting in the back of a rehearsal room in Midtown Manhattan; I could see her thinking it, but I didn't know her well enough to ask what that meant, whether it signaled anything about the way she and Declan were doing. I was afraid of my own reasons for wanting to know. For all her easy friendliness I'd only known Fiona for a couple of weeks; the gap between sociability and intimacy can't be bridged that quickly, after a certain age. Too, there are ways in which you ought not to come between a couple, some information is better kept close. Declan and Fiona might have been getting along like a house afire in the privacy of his apartment; physical chemistry can erase whole days of boring rehearsals and deli sandwiches, if it's strong enough. Maybe sex was sustaining them—though from the leaky look in Fiona's eye as she pushed her food around her plate, I wouldn't have bet her plane ticket on it.

I feel almost silly including this here, but during the late weeks of *Dame Street* tech I got a callback for a summer Shakespeare festival in Virginia, in some town on the vacation-thick shores of the Potomac the casting people showed me a brochure of after my audition. They were considering me for an ensemble role, which meant lots of rotating pageboy/messenger action, but it also meant understudying two of the season's major parts, including Katharine, the French princess in *Henry V.* The famous anatomy lesson was the scene I'd been told to prepare for my second callback, which presented me with the not-insignificant challenge of learning, in the three days before my audition, how to speak French. I rented the movies—both versions, Olivier and Branagh—and I checked out a stack of language tapes from the public library, but by the end of the second day my audition sides looked as daunting as ever, with all the gratuitous *g*'s and *z*'s that make French people sound so nasal and fey. I had two choices, and since skipping the callback was not what I wanted to do, I took my life in my hands and called Bella for help.

"*Repetez* after *moi,*" she said, and then strung together a bunch of foreign words that must have been obscene, from how hard they made her laugh. "I told you, Rose, I hate French people, and I hate the French language, and I'm not going to be responsible for its dissemination across the New World. Anyway the edgy stuff is all Spanish right now, they're doing *Fefu and Her Friends* at Circle Rep, that's what you should be auditioning for."

"I'm auditioning for everything, Bella. I'm auditioning for every stupid part anyone will see me for, and this ensemble gig is the callback I've gotten, and I'd rather play a lot of roles than Lady-in-Waiting Number Two, but I'd rather play Lady-in-Waiting Number Two than nothing, and I would really, really appreciate it if you could come over here and help me figure out how to say this stuff. I wouldn't ask unless it mattered, you know that."

There was a long pause on the other end of the line. I could imagine all the lip-sucking that must have been going on. "For the most part, the letters on the ends of words are silent, so try to imagine that they aren't there. It's a spoken tongue that thrives on eliding consonants until words bear no recognition to how they look on the page, a kind of linguistic xenophobia. Think about that until I get over. Then we'll do *r*'s."

She can be counted on, Bella, in her own way. Perhaps these desperate moments are when friendships should be judged.

O Seigneur Dieu! ils sont les mots de son mauvais, corruptible, gros, et impudique, et non pour les dames de honneur d'user. Je ne voudrais prononcer ces mots devant les seigneurs de France pour tout le monde.

I got the part.

June 1–August 22 in coastal Virginia, seven hundred bucks a week. I could have my own room on the top floor of the actors' dorm, Equity-qualifying credit, and free meals. Twenty-six lines spread across three plays, and a minimum of four guaranteed performances as either the French Princess or Boyet in *Love's Labour's Lost* (which is technically a man's part, but a good one, and anyway Shakespeare is all about drag). I imagined the darkened black box theater (400 seats), the glistening view of the Potomac from my attic window, the blue crabs my cast-mates and I would go out for after the show, and I felt, I can honestly say this, like an actor. Imagine: a whole company of cast-mates. Some of them would be pretentious, of course, humming scales in local coffee shops and complaining about the prohibition against nude sunbathing, but some of them would turn out to be friends. And what about the director, would he want to rehearse me for the leading parts, or would I sit in the house and take notes while he rehearsed the principals? Would I get any accent coaching? Costumes? These are the things professional actors think about. What a sweet, sweet thrill it was, to count myself among their ranks. If First Born was to be docked for the run of *Dame Street,* I could keep working, keep acting, even without my friends.

My parents sent a bouquet of pink roses with a card addressed to "Our Princess." (Did they understand that I would just be an understudy? Should I have explained what that meant?) Jake and Grace and Bella took me out to dinner at a real French restaurant in Brooklyn and made me do all the ordering, which was sweet and mortifying, even the waiters seemed amused. Grace, in particular, was excited about the idea of multiple courses, and ordered herself a cheese plate before dessert. *Frrromaagggge.* Cam and Evan, who were by now trapped at the theater twenty-four hours a day, sent espressos to the table, and a bottle of champagne.

A couple of days later, still revved up on the high of having some news of my own to spread, I stopped by Declan's apartment to tell Fiona I'd gotten the part. To my surprise Declan answered the door in his pajamas. It was midafternoon; I'd expected him to be at the theater as he usually was, and for a frightening second I had the thought that I'd interrupted a conjugal visit, so I started speaking quickly and loudly to cover my embarrassment, and also any sounds that might issue forth from the bedroom, excruciating to imagine the three of us trying to hold a conversation under such circumstances.

"I came by to tell you guys I got a part in a summer stock thing, Shakespeare in Virginia. Fiona knew I had the callback last week," I said, noticing Declan's pajamas, blue with old-fashioned white piping which suited him quite well, shocking to make those observations about a man whose girlfriend was waiting for him in bed.

"Fiona's not here," Declan said, pulling out a chair for me at the kitchen table and sitting down on one himself. "She's gone to see a film around the corner. She'll be back at half three; if you'd like a cup of tea, you can wait."

"Oh, okay," I said, suddenly able to feel the apartment's stillness. "I don't want to bother you, though, if you're working."

"Not on anything to speak of." He didn't make a move to put the kettle on, so we sat there at the table, me still in my coat. "Shakespeare in Virginia, is it?"

"That's right. The bard goes down South. Awwll the worrld's a staige," I said, in a lame attempt at a drawl. "Looks like I'll be there from June to August."

"That's a good bit of time."

"Ten weeks, I guess." I picked up a saltshaker, ran my thumb over the white porcelain top. "So what movie is Fiona seeing?"

"Ehm, something about life on other planets in the future, I think it was. She likes the scary films. She sees them in the daytime so they don't frighten her so much."

"I can't bear suspense. I'm afraid of *Lassie.*"

He nodded abstractedly. I'd never known Declan to be so quiet.

"Are you okay?" I asked, noticing now that his pajama top was buttoned one off, so that it hung against his chest at a cockeyed angle.

"I am, I think. I've been away from the theater for a few days now. Evan says it's the right thing but it's driving me mad. Have you been by, yourself?"

"Not lately I haven't. But I'm sure if Evan thinks you don't need to be there he's right. He has a good sense for that—at a certain point you probably have to let go a little, let the script speak for itself."

The look Declan gave me then was anguished, he seemed acutely pained, almost like Lear in those crazy pajamas, though I suppose I just had Shakespeare on the brain. "Hey," I said, not sure what I even meant by the question, but compelled to ask it again, "is something wrong?"

The struggle to put his thoughts in order was plain on his face. I waited, remembering the feeling of our last night at that table, when he told me Fiona would be coming to visit. We hadn't spent ten minutes alone since then, and now I understood why that had been the right choice. A man in his pajamas begs questions: what has driven him into them in the middle of the day, what kind of sadness or confusion in the face of the world's demands? (And of course what is beneath their cottony thinness, you'd have to be a nun not to wonder that.) I had the ugly sense of digging around for confirmation of what I suspected: that things were going badly with Fiona, that she was at the movies by herself because they'd fought, that her love of sci-fi bespoke a fatal incompatibility between them that could no longer be ignored. I didn't want to hope these things—I wanted to be selfless and good, a friend to both of them. But why else was I sticking around to find out what was wrong?

Declan kept his eyes on the table as he spoke. "I'm fine, Rosalie. You're grand for asking. I've just been thinking that it's no easy job, not for any man or woman it isn't, to know how to risk your life so that you might save it."

Hyperbolic stuff, this Irish compulsion to discuss one's perfectly normal life as if it might be in actual jeopardy. But that was what I loved in Declan—he took himself seriously. He thought hard. It made me feel small, venal, to have hoped he would say something dismissive about Fiona. He was more honorable than that.

His play was going to be beautiful. I told him that, since it was the last concrete thing we'd talked about. And then I said goodbye.

And now we arrive at the John Loeb Cavendish Theater, on the rainy evening of March 21, for opening night of *Last Winter in Dame Street*. To set the scene: at seven o'clock it's just barely light out, the clouds a low blanket in the sky. Cars have started pulling up outside the theater—not limousines, as you might expect to find at a movie premiere in gas-guzzling Los Angeles, but Scandinavian compacts with the passengers in back. Gingerly they emerge, the white-haired gentlemen in tuxedos and their frightfully thin wives, a cliché but uniformly true, to be escorted by porters with umbrellas for the four-second walk between car and marquee overhang. There are no flashbulbs or celebrity-stalking crowds at an event like this one, no red carpet in the true Hollywood sense, but the tourists walking towards Seventh Avenue, cameras poised for the neon assault of Times Square, still stop for a few moments to watch. The people pouring into the theater are not famous exactly, not household names, but they command attention in their dignified, patrician, businesslike way. It's worth standing in the rain for, a glimpse of an invitation-only spectacle like this. It's what you come to New York to see.

Now back to the wings of the theater, where the stage manager is calling one hour into her headset and sound cues are being triple-checked, props inventoried on the prop tables. Manny Flax wanders the maze of dressing rooms and points his cane into each one, telling his stars a final ancient dirty joke to keep them fresh on their feet. Evan straightens his bow tie in a bathroom mirror, feels for a checklist in his pocket, straightens his tie again. Declan paces the garbagey alley behind the stage door, smoking like a man condemned, unaware that he's mucking up his tux in the rain, or at least unconcerned. William Howlitt Smith lies on his back on his dressing room floor and visualizes an empty ocean beach, a focal point of energy off on the horizon. He waits for his soothing cucumber eye mask to set. Cam gargles with hot tea and honey, then swigs salt water from a plastic bottle, too nervous to notice that he's got his regimen backwards, too dizzy even to taste. Fifty minutes now. He hears it piped in from the tinny speaker above the full-length mirror. Ladies and gentlemen, cast and crew: your call is fifty minutes.

The show will go smoothly, of course. Professional operations like this one always do. But the buzz of nervous energy backstage would be impossible to quell, if anyone even wanted to; it's the charge the actors live for, the moment they feel themselves most alive, balanced on the top step of the ladder after the climb, before the plunge. The prayer hour, a director once called it, when he heard his actors whispering their lines over and over before going on. The ancient Greeks worshiped and performed in the same outdoor spaces, on the very same stage. Theaters have always had a touch of the sacred about them, the red velvet curtains, the costumes, the stage.

Grace, Jake, Bella and I got to the Cavendish at 7:25. Evan had set aside a block of four tickets for us in the seventh row, and Jake picked them up at the will-call window while the rest of us shook the rain off our clothing under an awning across the street. A word on dress: normally I am restrained, even conservative, when it comes to formalwear, scarred as I was by the Michelin Man pink satin prom dresses of my youth. But since Evan had gotten us such high-visibility seats, and since I was going to be sitting next to a woman clad in the billowy size 10 of early pregnancy, I'd been emboldened to buy a new dress, of cerise silk, with spaghetti straps and a form-fitting cut more revealing than my usual attire. Underneath it I had to wear that uncomfortable boob-support tape, which suggests to me that women who are in the habit of spending money on expensive dresses usually splurge on the plastic surgery that makes them wearable. But I was determined to look my best in an audience full of important people (Berglan Starker), and I am not even going to say how much money I spent on the outfit since a sense of confidence, as the advertisement goes, is priceless.

The lobby of the Cavendish Theater is baroque but small, disappointingly so, which meant that all pre-show schmoozing was confined to the aisles of the theater and the small bar nestled between the restrooms in the basement. Bella, who switches into producer mode at the sight of a ticket stub, had it in mind to get backstage to tell our friends to break legs. I had written out three good-luck notes from an old box of cards I'd brought home from Dublin, photographs of Saint Stephen's Green (Evan), the Shelbourne Hotel (Cam), and the River Liffey, looking onto the Northside quays (Declan). Each note said how proud I was, and how I'd be the first person on her feet when the final curtain fell. On Declan's note I included a P.S. telling him that I probably would have fallen in love with Dublin, if I'd known the city as he made it live onstage. I gave Bella the notes and watched as she bossed her way past the human chain of ushers and house managers. Once she disappeared, Grace and Jake and I squeezed through the crowded lobby to the bar downstairs.

There is something pleasingly old-fashioned about a bar in a theater, or even the idea of such a thing, harkening back to the time of martini lunches and train station lounges, before people got so health-crazed and puritanical about booze. Men in tuxedos crowded around the mahogany bar, and if it hadn't been for Grace's grubbing about the dangers of secondhand smoke, the era might have been anyone's guess. Guinness and Jameson's were on the house, somebody's cute idea of an Irish pub theme, and while Grace and Jake settled down at a table I went to get us drinks. Wedging my way up to the bar, conscious, I suppose, of the plunging redness of my dress against the parting sea of black ties, as in that old Madonna video, I saw Berglan Starker, coming out of the men's room towards the bar.

Of course I had assumed Berglan Starker and his wife would be at this event, had counted on a sighting at least, but had not, for some reason, counted on having it in plain view of Jake and

Grace. I knew he and I would have to say something to each other, and had anticipated the vagaries of the conversation with each Merry Widow getup I tried on in the week before the show. But I had not pre-planned a single thing to say, not even what sort of attitude I might cop, for it had seemed (at a distance) like such preventative fussing was more brainpower than the situation deserved. If you spend your work week poring over the neurotic calculations of girls whose lives are ruled by the quest for love, it becomes a point of female honor to take these sorts of encounters coolly. But now, as BS raised his eyebrows and began to move in my direction, I felt the full force of my bad planning come crashing down on me, as I would now have to wing it completely, and with an audience of spectators not twenty feet away. Berglan carved out a space for himself next to me at the bar. He looked as handsome and commanding as ever, not at all fazed by the prospect of chatting with his former lover while his wife looked on from across the room, though formalwear is no doubt a mask behind which the skilled chief executive can hide any anxiety, large or small.

"What a long time since we've had the chance to see one another, Rosalie. How have you been? You look smashing in that dress, by the way."

"Hi. My friends Jake and Grace are right over there behind me," I said, with a horrible lack of smoothness.

"So they are." He bowed a little in their direction, but I couldn't see whether they waved back. "Tell me what you've been up to this winter. I've thought of you so often and now here you are, looking wonderful."

"Auditioning and working, mostly. I just got a part in a Shakespeare season for June." Without the fine print it sounded almost glamorous.

"Shakespeare! Congratulations! Someplace beautiful, I hope?"

"Virginia. It should be nice enough."

"Sublime, sublime."

What would we have been saying to each other had we not been surrounded by watchful eyes? Encounters with ex-lovers are supposed to be harrowing, recidivistic trials that throw you back into the emotional wilderness of grief and loss. But considering BS now, it was hard to imagine an emotional wilderness in which he might play a part. He looked so polished, so impenetrable, it was almost hard to remember I'd ever seen him in anything less than a tuxedo. Metaphorically speaking, I sort of hadn't: he'd never really revealed himself to me in the way that true lovers do, people who are interested in intimacy beyond the hidden secrets of the flesh. I felt my old question rising up again, of why he'd chosen me in the first place. But that wasn't an answer I'd gotten out of him before, and it seemed unlikely that I would now, in this crowded lobby, fifteen minutes before the curtain went up. Anyway asking now would sound too operatic, as if I'd been thinking of nothing else since our last morning in Starbucks all those months ago, and I didn't want to give him that impression, because it wasn't true.

"I was sorry to hear about Fort Sassquam's being sold. I have such fond memories of my time on that lake."

"Yes, so do I." He put his hand on top of mine and gave me a squeeze. To Jake and Grace's unsuspecting eyes it would have looked avuncular enough. "No shortage of fond memories tonight, is there?"

"Um, I guess not," I said, stupidly, stupidly, every word clunking out of my mouth a reminder of my youth and inexperience.

"I think of you with great fondness, Pink. I hope you know that. And I hope you'll come out to Montana with Bella sometime; you're always welcome there. We'll all of us miss the Fort, but I really do believe in the forest trust, and I'm determined not to second-guess this decision. It pleases me to think of that land becoming part of the larger Park, we couldn't have held out forever. Anyway the place in Montana is beautiful, you can come for fly-fishing season."

I'm sure he was right; I'm sure Montana is beautiful. And I'm sure second-guessing is anathema to anyone with his amount of money and power. Berglan Starker's past must have been littered with the debris of his split-second decisions, the casualties of gut instincts he'd acted on without looking back. I knew this from experience, after all. And now I was glad for it, glad that he'd known what to do about me and just done it. How lucky I was, to be young and spry, able to fall and stand up again. I felt almost indomitable, looking at Berglan Starker, and it wasn't a feeling of revenge or victory or even pride. It wasn't really about him at all. I would never go fly-fishing in Montana. I hate fishing, and I hate eating trout, and I would never have to bother to pretend otherwise.

"I have some friends who live on the coast in Virginia. My brother, Bella's uncle Newland, built himself a house there. It's quite something to see. If you call me at my office I'll get you his addresses and phone numbers and such."

"Okay, that'd be great," I said, smiling back. Over his shoulder

I saw his wife advancing on us. Her hair was blonder than I remembered its being, and she wore a suit, powder blue with gold buttons, that was tailored within an inch of its life. She looked firm and pointy, like an anchorwoman, or maybe a judge, someone you'd rather get a fax from than sleep next to, though of course my opinion would be biased. "It was good to see you," I said, picking up the glass of lemonade I'd ordered for Grace. It was even true: there was nothing to be frightened of in Berglan Starker, nothing in particular to regret, though I don't imagine I'll be having more affairs with married men in the future, they have structural limitations that aren't worth the perks, if you are truly interested in love. "I'm looking forward to meeting your brother. And now, if you'll excuse me, I should get back to my friends."

My friends, when I rejoined them, appeared to have overcome the thirst that had sent me to the bar on their behalf. Grace didn't take her eyes off me as I set her drink down on the table. Her face was pale, and her mouth hung open so wide it would have been easy to pitch peanuts into it. Pregnancy, even in its earliest months, seems to be a period of total capitulation to the impulses of the body.

"What?" I asked, after she refused to shut her mouth and stop staring at me. "Do you want me to put something in there?"

"I can't believe you," was what she said. It hung in the air for a second, a single, quivering arrow, and then she really let loose: "I can't *believe* you! Cam guessed it was Mr. Starker, but I kept telling him it had to be someone at the magazine, that controller you used to go on about with the All America trophy. I defended you! I said there was no possible way! We all figured it had to be a married man, but Bella's *father?* I can't believe this. I'm speechless."

"He's so old, Rose. He's, like, Viagra-old. I mean, my dad has hair in his ears and he's ten years younger than that guy. Isn't it kind of gross?"

"We don't want to know whether it's gross! We don't want to know anything about it! Watching him paw at you was quite enough!" Grace's face was red and splotchy. She looked like she might explode. "When Cam said you'd been sleeping with some-body I honestly didn't believe him. Then he found that stuff in your apartment, and he said you told him it was true. But I *still* thought he was crazy, I really thought he was out of line and jeal-ous, riffling through your notes and papers like that while you weren't home as if he had some kind of droit du seigneur right to spy on you. I defended you! You would have told me, I said to him. I was so sure, I was really positive. I would have told you."

But what had Cam found that made him suspect Berglan Starker? The tie? The scotch? What notes and papers had I been foolish enough to leave lying around? Not that it mattered, I wasn't going to deny anything, though one's natural impulse in such a circumstance is to try to claw holes in the evidence, as if by undo-ing the proof you can undo the thing itself. But now all that mat-tered was who knew what, i.e., Bella, and how to make sure the story stopped before it got to her. I also wanted Grace to know that it was all over between me and Berglan Starker, though that seemed not to matter to her much because when I told her all she said was: "Oh, please. You can sleep with whoever you want to sleep with. I just hadn't realized how little you trusted me. But now I guess I know."

People's emotions are a mystery, even to themselves. Grace was furious, truly outraged, but I don't think it was the affair that made her so mad. No—what she truly couldn't brook was the secret, the fact that I'd been up to something she hadn't known about. It was the same way I'd felt at her engagement party: shut out, cast to the margins in her adult life. That was the betrayal I would be punished for, I understood. My affair with Berglan Starker had revealed not just my streak of licentious selfishness— in a way everybody already knew about that—but graver by far, my disloyalty. Of the two crimes, only the second was impossible to forgive.

The electronic bell chimed three times. People started looking for places to leave their drinks. Grace hoisted herself out of her chair and stalked off towards the stairs without waiting for either of us. Jake gave me a look that was half apologetic, half embarrassed, like he was stuck on the image of me in bed with Bella's dad. We walked upstairs together. The show hadn't even begun.

Grace; Jake; Bella; me. That was how we filed into the seventh row, silent, all of us, except for Bella. She had seen the guys backstage, had gone with Evan to find thread for a button that had come loose on his shirt. Things were running about eight minutes late, she said, the usual. I buried my face in my playbill and wished I could melt into my seat. From the corner of my eye it looked like Grace was doing the same thing. Bella chattered on, oblivious. It seemed clear enough that she didn't know anything about her dad and me. I had that conspiracy to be grateful for, at least.

. . .

If someone had asked me, I would have said that no single night could have possibly been worse for the revelation of my betrayal, packed in together as we all were. But luckily, it is not the sinner's place to choose the time her punishment is meted out. Who will believe me when I say that once the curtain rose on Declan's play, all of this sordid confessional business no longer mattered? Or who knows, maybe it was the sordid confessional business that made the play fly and sing as it did, from the overstuffed living room of William Howlitt Smith's ex-wife to his arrival on the Dublin scene with his pretty American boy (Cam) in tow, to their heartbreaking romantic dissolution, to Howlitt Smith's speech at the end of the first act on the futility of trying to return to a place that has ceased to exist. It was both beautiful and impossibly sad, that play, everything about it, and it worked on me like a slow simmer as I sat there in the dark, reminding me of all the places in my own life that had ceased to exist, both literally (Fort Sassquam) and metaphorically (Fort Sassquam), reminding me that a lie, undiscovered, may just be a bit of dubious convenience, but a lie discovered is a fissure that can never be erased. For some people, it is music that speaks this way, echoing straight from the recital hall into the listener's heart. Others are moved beyond reason by landscape, the mountains, a view of the sea. For me it is only the theater, which takes me out of myself and melts me, then folds me back in. I leaned my head down and closed my eyes and tears slid down my cheeks. The hand that squeezed my elbow was Bella's.

. . .

The *Dame Street* afterglow was at an Italian restaurant three blocks from the theater. Grace begged off, claiming she didn't feel well enough to go, so she and Jake got into a cab and Bella and I walked north together. Bella couldn't stop talking about how weird it had been to watch Cam do a gay sex scene with William Howlitt Smith. "He looked so *normal,* kissing a guy," she said. "Where do you think he got all of those moves?"

I raised my eyebrows to suggest that some of his techniques might have been borrowed from my repertoire, and Bella gave me a mock shove.

"Slut," she said, laughing. "I hope he gave you credit in his bio."

In the early stages of the party, everyone milling about seemed devastated by the play's conclusion, of Paul alone in his mother's flat, cleaning out her apartment after her death. I'd never really thought about it before, but the play could be seen to have slightly homophobic overtones, as in leave your wife for a man and watch your own mother die of grief. When I ran this past Bella she didn't seem worried. "She dies of a stroke, Rose. The gods stopped punishing characters for their misdeeds sometime around Aeschylus."

The arrival of the euphoric cast and crew, who looked as if they'd been doused in a case of champagne, turned the mood at the party around. Early word, as we overheard while placing our drink orders, was that the reviews were going to be brilliant: someone had seen Hal Cormeer from the *Times* weeping during the last scene, and the woman from *Variety* had jumped to her feet for a standing ovation at the end of the first act. It's amazing how quickly the echoes of a performance are drowned out by speculation on ticket sales and Tony nominations. But business is business, even in art, and it's green of me to be amazed. Speaking of business, Berglan Starker was nowhere in sight, which felt like a small turf victory for me.

Since our friends were swarmed by admirers, Bella and I got cocktail plates and went to the antipasto bar. I didn't have any appetite, but the free-food reflex is impossible to suppress. When we sat down, Bella poured out a dish of olive oil and fixed me in her gaze. My cheeks started burning before she even opened her mouth.

"I have two confessions to make to you, Rosalie. I don't want you to say anything until they're over, okay?"

There are only so many confrontations a girl can take in a single night. I opened my mouth to protest.

"I'm serious: no interruptions or I quit talking, and you have to hear what I have to say. The first part is that I made a totally drunken and louche pass at l'auteur at my birthday party, by whom I mean Declan. The whole thing was morbidly humiliating; I'll spare you the play-by-play, but believe me when I say sincere mortification would be the overarching theme. For a few days I even thought about trying to get Dad to withdraw his investment in *Dame Street* just because I was so embarrassed about getting shot down. But thank God I didn't, since this play is going to be pure gold at the box office."

I already knew this, or at least I knew the first part of it. I put down my glass at the mention of her dad.

"The second part is, hmm, shall we say, more directly relevant to you. When you asked me to give Declan your card before the show tonight, I of course did. No complaints on my end, as you'll remember, though truthfully I was less than thrilled about the whole errand, apparently I look like a U.S. postal carrier in this dress. Anyway, when I stopped by Declan's dressing room he wasn't in it, and as I went to leave your letter in front of his mirror I noticed that he had written a letter to you, coincidence of coincidences, who would ever expect a *writer* to *write a letter* when the girl he wants to talk to is in the same building. But the point is that I sort of read his letter to you, and I now feel that it would be appropriate to summarize its contents. Ready?"

"You read it, Bella?"

"Correct, though I am gearing up to rectify that misstep now, by fulfilling the author's original intention, that you should have the following information. Point A: Fiona of the Perpetual Midriff Top has returned to Dublin, having correctly ascertained that her Deco won't be coming home anytime soon, or at least anytime soon enough to suit her. An amicable parting on both sides, he claims, each of them having come to terms with the fact that their relationship has more to do with their pasts than with their futures, though when have you ever heard of anything so convenient as that. The girl can smell a rat, if you ask me. Point B: As Mr. Pearse is no longer attached, he wonders whether you might be receptive to the following information: that he is in love with you, that he has been in love with you since he met you last July, that he would like you to convert to Catholicism and bear him sixteen children and take up arms for the Troubles. That last part I made up."

I was—who wouldn't have been?—stunned. My mouth had turned to cotton. This is what people mean when they use the term dumbstruck, which doesn't have the word dumb in it for nothing, it could have been mutestruck, after all. "I . . . Jesus, Bella, I . . . is that it?"

"Yes. I mean no, I also slept with Clive Nagsby while you two were going out junior year, but I've given you enough material for one night, I think."

"You slept with Clive Nagsby?"

"Oh, get over it, Rosalie. You aren't so lily-white yourself. Let she who is without sin cast the first stone."

Here are three things I learned in the space of that night: in times of interpersonal crisis, you can count on people to be themselves, maybe even a more perfectly distilled version thereof. Of the three friends who'd found out about me and Berglan Starker, Grace was shocked and wounded, Jake wanted to see a videotape, and Cam, when I caught up with him at the party, had already forgotten about the whole thing. Or maybe he was just too pleased with himself to care, because after planting a big wet kiss on my neck he introduced me to a tall blonde named Cheri, who looked like she'd been on the cover of the last issue of *Cosmo*. "Relax, Rose," was all he said to me, when I tried to suggest we had some issues to discuss. "The past is behind us, I don't need to go there if you don't." Then he dropped his voice and said: "Cheri has a twin sister, can you believe that? She just told me about her like ten seconds ago, they live in the same apartment and share a bedroom. I'm like, *whoa*."

Thing #2: The truth is not an ideal to be pursued with blind unilateralism, for though in some cases it may set you free, in other cases it may handcuff you to the past, which is, in Cam's penetrating analysis, behind us. If I had told Bella about my eye-blink of an affair with her father, which was really and truly over and done with, on both sides, she would have been doomed to live and relive those two months in her imagination over and over and over again, until her very ability to exist in the present would be frozen by bitterness and rancor. Think of Miss Havisham in *Great Expectations*. I mean, even the comparatively insignificant Clive Nagsby revelation still had some bite to it, Bella was my fucking roommate that year.

Thing #3: People are compelled by an instinct more powerful than moral will to read other people's private notes, diaries, letters, and cards. Do not leave envelopes unsealed. Invest in a paper shredder. Nothing you write down is ever truly safe.

In spite of the brimming fullness of my heart, I had to wait in a receiving line to get to Declan, the entire artistic team was so swamped. However much I would like to be the kind of woman who cuts to the front of a line to leap into the arms of her newly declared beloved, we are all constrained by who our mothers raised us to be, which is, in my case, someone who waits her turn. Manny didn't recognize me when I inched by him, but I heard him telling a group of reporters that he was through bowing to mammon and directing musical theater, a life in art was too precious to waste. Evan, when I got to him, was more lit up than I'd ever seen him before. He'd already been asked to interview for three projects in development, including one at Lincoln Center. Lincoln Center! I know I promised I wouldn't skip ahead, but I was sure he would get it, even then.

When the line finally brought me face to face with Declan, the din of the party was so loud I could barely gather my thoughts. We usually think of secret notes and their interception as a relic of a bygone time, e-mail and cell phones having obliterated such Romeo and Juliet–esque liaisons dangereuses. Was it this air of sixteenth-century courtliness that accounted for my reserve? Or is it always just queerly formal, seeing someone for the first time after such momentous feelings have been expressed, especially when the expresser doesn't know that you're privy to them yet?

"Your play was beautiful, Declan. You should be tremendously proud of everything that happened tonight." My heart was singing; I couldn't smile enough.

"I have something for you," he said, reaching into his breast pocket. His voice was hoarse, practically gone.

"I already got it. In a way." This to start us off in the habit of honesty, which I mean to adopt as a general principle, even though it necessitated some awkward explanation about Bella's being a snoop, not really the ideal conversation under the circumstances. When I got through it Declan did something that was even more surprising than what he'd declared in the letter, if anything could be more surprising than that. He put his arms around my waist and lifted me up, clear up off of the floor.

"Do you have any idea how many questions I've sent you at that bloody magazine you write for?"

I am sure I looked shocked; I am sure I had looked shocked for the past five hours and I am sure I went on looking shocked for the next week at least. Also, my boob tape was coming unstuck. "At *GirlTalk*? What do you mean?"

"I've tried to give myself up to you a hundred different ways, and I get a form letter back each time. I'm a bleedin' professional playwright. Who do you have to be to get a letter printed in that column of yours? John Keats?"

His kiss was so silvery that every inch of my body melted and my shoes slipped right off me onto the floor. When he finally set me down I had a serious case of goose bumps and two bare feet. One could either interpret that as the perennial risk associated with wearing backless heels, or as a metaphor for the carefree openness and unadorned perfection of new love.

I am a freshly hatched romantic. But freshly hatched romantics can be quite gratingly sweet, and I will keep my opinions to myself.

To the Person Who Writes Annie Answers:

I am in a bit of a bind, as the person I'm in love with does not seem to care, particularly, whether I am in love with her or not. I have not yet screwed up the courage to come out and tell her just what I am thinking, as the situation at hand is complicated by the existence of another woman, and I fear being made to look unscrupulous, which I am not. I cannot tell if this person, the one I am in love with, is even very fond of me. I certainly am not a perfect specimen by any means, though the imperfections in my character may not be as fatal as they perhaps appear to the critical eye. I am, for example, honest and straightforward. I can be quite doting and affectionate, given the opportunity. I suppose what I am saying is that I should like to be given this opportunity, and I think there is a way, even a very specific way, in which you could help me with my troubles.

> *Thank you for your time in this matter.*
> *New York City*

Chapter Thirteen

Having become something of a hotel aficionado, I am not speaking lightly when I say that one of the loveliest inns in the country, which shall have to remain nameless so that I can continue to afford to stay there, can be found on College Hill in Providence, Rhode Island. Each of the guest rooms is charmingly appointed with old New England antiques, highboys and brass beds and handmade quilts, etc., but there are no musty-smelling closets or over-zealous proprietors to make conversation with during breakfast, no creepy shelves of bric-a-brac gathering dust in the corners. Views on one side of the inn are of the beautiful brick campuses of RISD and Brown; on the other side you can see Rhode Island's stately capital building, only partly obscured by the new cineplex and mega-mall they've put up downtown, which, all things considered, could have turned out worse.

For here is what I've come to understand: there is a coldness, a Big Brother unnaturalness, to the finest luxury hotels. The twenty-four-hour availability of a four-star chef, the commodious bathrooms with Jacuzzi jets in the shower stalls, the turndown service that somehow coincides with the exact five minutes you've stepped out for a newspaper, your every need answered before you even knew you had it: it's all a little *Brave New World*.

Yes, there are advantages to corporate uniformity, there are even service features you might yearn for as you and the 210-pound man sleeping next to you struggle to find peace in a colonial bed built for colonial midgets. But inns have history, or as the brochures always say, character, and these qualities seem to me to be assets with which no amount of La Prairie bath and shower freebees can compete.

I do not speak hypothetically, by the way. Declan weighs 210 pounds, and takes up a great deal of room in bed. This seriously mannish weight, or at least my delight in it, suggests to me that I am overcoming my weakness for insubstantiality in favor of something more solid, more significant. It's weirdly sexy, actually, to be going out with somebody nearly twice my size. It makes me feel very delicate and feminine and protected, which is probably a turn-on just because it's so improper to want to feel that way, as if I could be picked up and carried over a threshold, bride of Frankenstein style, or conversely, I could be a bird-like Red Cross nurse in 1916, tending to a burly soldier temporarily bedridden by a piece of shrapnel in the knee. The intimate imagination thrives on contrast. Also, I like it that Declan has a bit of a stomach on him, it makes me less self-conscious about my own.

A tableau: the dining room of — Inn, Monday morning, Memorial Day weekend in Providence, RI. Declan is eating an Irish Breakfast, which he has ordered only so that he can complain about the items that are not authentic enough in his view, for example the rashers, which are mere Oscar Meyer bacon strips, and therefore not up to task. I am having half a grapefruit and an apple turnover. We are both having coffee. Declan is reading the newspaper and I am consulting the schedule for shuttles between the downtown hotels and College Hill, since my maniac desire to protect my little inn (coupled with Bella's genetic preference for the razzle of room service and glass elevators) has landed Cam, Cheri, Evan, and Bella in a Courtyard Marriott over by the mall. We are here, all of us, for Grace and Jake's engagement party, which will be held this late afternoon at Grace's parents' huge old house on Benefit Street. The day is perfect, two-thirds spring and one-third summer, with every tree, bush, and shrub in sight bursting with sweet-smelling blossoms. Declan knows the names of these flowering plants, a writerly pretension to be sure (the wind tickled through the box elder, blah blah blah). But he has so few pretensions that I can let one slide.

Declan has discovered the way to hold a newspaper so that it bleeds as much black ink as possible onto every fabric and surface in a room: flesh, tablecloth, toast crusts. Under his supervision a single newspaper, even a seemingly slim holiday edition, can expand to more than ten times its folded size. He is a scientist in such matters. His furrowed eyebrows behind the Circuits section make my heart buckle and bend with love.

"I'm going to go up to the room and get ready," I tell him. "We're meeting everybody to walk over at two." I pantomime shaving, which I'd like him to do before we go out.

"Right," he says, looking up from his paper. "Don't worry about me. I've got my tie right here in my pocket."

"Your pocket," I repeat, my insistence on appropriately pressed neckwear compromised by my awesome affection for the slob in front of me. "If you would please give me the tie, I'll hang it in the bathroom while I shower."

Declan stands up and takes a last swig of coffee, the white and blue porcelain cup tiny in his hands. "If you think my tie is going to get that kind of show while I sit down here reading the paper, you're a lunatic. Come on, then. Up we go."

The other guests in the dining room—parents of Brown students, visiting scholars with their campus maps—smile at us as we leave, remembering, perhaps, what it is to be young, full of breakfast pastry, full of love.

The blanks between the opening night of *Dame Street* and Memorial Day weekend are easy enough to fill in. The buzz at the *Dame Street* afterglow had been spot on: most of the reviews were raves, and ticket sales shot through the roof. Some highlights Evan chose for the newspaper ad: "a haunting contrivance from an original new voice, sure to be among us for a long time to come"; "as breathtakingly real as contemporary theater gets, and not likely to be forgotten anytime soon"; "a tour-de-force in the passion of a life fully lived, Howlitt Smith's best performance to date"; "an unblinking triumph from veterans and newcomers alike." Is it the Hopi Indians who deliberately weave a mistake into their rugs, so that the gods won't think them prideful? Well, the *Dame Street* cast got a couple of slams, too, which kept certain people's (Evan's) feet on the ground and reminded them of their fallibility. It seems unkind to repeat the pans word for word, but a certain air of overwrought lugubriousness in the production values was noted more than once.

Declan and Evan got a lot of professional attention out of all of this, but it was Cam whose face started popping up in magazines, Cam who got recognized walking down the street. He even got invited to do a guest spot on *Saturday Night Live*—not host-ing, but some walk-on joke about Broadway, how not every male stage actor is gay. We all gathered to watch it air at Jake and Grace's apartment. It was weird to see our Cam on TV, he looked relaxed and confident, a little heavy in the jowl but the camera supposedly does that to everyone. Some girls screamed and cheered as he stepped out onto the stage. I felt a little shiver of the future, like maybe we would all be sitting on the living room floor watching Cam on TV for a long time to come, but when I said that to Evan he smiled and patted me on the knee. "I wouldn't be too sure about that. It's not easy, reading those cue cards so quickly, you know."

Other news is that I'm jobless. This came about swiftly, as soon as I mentioned to Ginger that I'd gotten some acting work, which makes me think she'd been looking for an excuse to replace me ever since she busted me for the Hanson church basement incident. She was weighing out a cup of couscous on a little scale when I went to see her, but she stopped her measurements when I told her about the play.

"Three months in Virginia, you lucky girl! I hope you ride horses. But what a loss for all of us. Your column is one of the finest parts of this magazine, always so sensible. I hate to think of your leaving, though the theater-sur-mer arrangement sounds like a dream. I myself have never acted, per se, but when I was a girl I did some hand modeling and found it quite addictive."

"Actually, I was wondering if I could talk to you about the pos-sibility of my staying on, maybe taking a leave of absence for the summer. I'll be earning a stipend at the theater, so I could afford to take those months unpaid. I could write my columns from

Virginia and e-mail them in, like a freelancer, then come back full-time at the end of August. I'd really like to keep my spot on the staff."

"Oh, my dear," Ginger said, and I knew immediately that she wasn't going to go for it. "You know how I feel about freelancers. I think of our lovely staff as such a team, and I'm afraid team players have to come in every day for practice. It's probably just how your director feels about his play—you couldn't very well stay here in New York and be in it at the same time, could you? I wouldn't think so, no."

I didn't argue with her. I had written Annie Answers for three years; that's about as long as any one person should give advice on any subject, no offense to Abigail Van Buren, who should also take some time off to refill the well, or at least to get a new haircut. Quitting *GirlTalk* would mean coming home at the end of the summer to a different New York, a New York where I was an actress, first and foremost, and not a team player. And oh my God, about that. If you're going to have to put up with that kind of corporate philosophy nonsense, why not go to business school and get yourself a real salary?

The one thing I did before I left *GirlTalk,* other than the ritual desk-cleaning and poster-dismantling, was to spend a day in the Reader Mail office, trying to scare up the anonymous letters Declan had sent in. According to the RM assistants, the magazine gets an average of 80 pieces of correspondence per day, which then gets sorted and grouped by department. I had always chosen my own Annie question from the stack of advice column mail every month, then routed the rejects back to RM to be dealt with (i.e., form-lettered and shredded) by the girls there. Declan's notes must have made it to my desk as they arrived, but they were gone by now, recycled into oblivion along with the rest of teenage America's heartbreak and torment. By nature I am not sentimental, not given to saving ticket stubs or pressing roses, but I would have liked to lay eyes on those letters once more, to see what I had missed the first time. The beginning of love is one of life's great mysteries; imagine having written evidence of what your beloved felt and thought in those earliest moments. I made Declan reconstruct the letters from memory as best he could. Of course he hadn't saved them on his computer, he is far too full of Celtic superstition for technological practicalities like that.

Ah, the slippery, golden days of falling in love. On the night of our first kiss, Declan and I had raced home to my place and done the one thing you are never supposed to do hastily with someone about whom you feel seriously. But honestly, once one is no longer a virgin, the whole take-it-slow approach to the bedroom strikes me as a pretty pointless charade. The thought actually occurred to me, as Declan and I climbed the stairs to my apartment, that maybe *he* was a virgin, the proscriptions of Irish Catholicism having such a powerful hold over his artistic imagination. But my anxieties were soon put to rest. As this was the first time I had ever gone to bed with a writer, I couldn't help but think of the two sex scenes in *Dame Street*, the gay one (weird) and the honey one in the kitchen (hot). Not that I would make any blanket assumptions about the relationship between autobiography or even firsthand experience and art, but these questions do, perforce, arise.

Going to bed with such a large person was another first for me, and I had some qualms about it, based on those playground aphorisms you hear about the size of a man's shoes corresponding to the size of his et cetera. This turns out to be true, at least in the one case I have now experienced, though not on the frighteningly grotesque scale suggested by the reading materials that used to be scattered around Cam and Jake's old apartment. It also turns out not to be a scary or painful thing, unless you are allergic to over-the-counter lubricants, in which case you can get a prescription.

But even if the love act is not scary or painful, falling in love, I have found, is both. I don't know how to explain this exactly, but in my first weeks with Declan, I was more disastrously emotional than I have ever been before, bursting into tears at the sight of a pigeon hobbling around on only one leg, flying into a rage at the produce stock boy for being out of strawberries when I needed them for a tart (I bake now, it's repulsive), getting nervous to the point of nausea about an interview for a temp agency on Wall Street. It's as if whatever moored me, whatever used to make me cool and impassive and blasé, has completely vaporized, and I have been reduced to a heap of exposed nerve endings. Love is supposed to make you happy, why else would whole holidays be devoted to it, it is supposed to bolster you and thrill you and make you feel complete. But for me the first stages of love were agonizing, like walking out of a darkened movie theater into an extraordinarily bright noontime sun and waiting, blinded, aching, for my eyes to adjust to the light.

Was it because I had come so close to missing what had been right under my nose? Because I wasn't falling for someone easy and familiar, like Cam, someone who might as well have been my brother for all the ways in which we were alike? Because I was used to being alone, and people who are used to their aloneness may yearn for love but have organized their lives very nicely without it, thank you very much? I don't know why the experience was so disconcerting. All I know is that whatever control I'd once had seemed to slip away from me, and when you hear about this phenomenon in greeting cards and country music songs it sounds pleasant and enjoyable, but it isn't, not if you have to live through it. It robs you of your ability to concentrate. For days you eat nothing, then for days you binge eat like someone with bulimia, only you don't have bulimia. In my case, falling in love made me tremendously nervous, naked, you could say, before the smallest signifiers. Declan's last-minute unavailability for dinner. Rain on what was forecast as a sunny day. Traffic jams, newspaper headlines, overcharges at the dry cleaner—there was code in all of it, I felt it all too dearly, the tiny pinpricks of the world pierced me like knives. Whoever enjoys being in such a state must also enjoy roller coasters, hang gliding, and craps. I was painfully alert to everything around me, all the time.

Leaving home is never easy, and leaving home in the early stages of a love affair goes against every decent speck of instinct we are born with. But young women who have had the advantages of a costly education do not skip out on acting gigs to scrub around town with their boyfriends, however much they might secretly yearn to. I had lined up a subletter for my apartment, one Sophie Rubenstein, a law school roommate of Jake's younger sister who had a summer internship at a cosmetics company. Bella agreed to fill in for me at Adele Goldberg for the months I'd be gone. "I like being around old people, with their crazy stories about

D-Day and Black Tuesday and going to Europe on ocean liners and stuff," she had said. The other arrangements were pretty simple, actually. I cleared out my drawers for Sophie Rubenstein, packed two suitcases, had my mail forwarded, stocked up on shampoo and tampons and Woolite (just in case there were no drugstores in the Commonwealth of Virginia), and that was that. Leaving for three months felt like it should have been a bigger deal. I spent the whole train ride to Providence, where I was going for the engagement party before heading south, convinced that I'd forgotten to lock the front door or turn off the oven. "Relax, Rose," Cam said, on the train up. "You would have to have turned it on once in your life to forget to turn it off."

In Providence, Declan and I spent the early afternoon before the party walking around the Brown campus. Adding to our general new-love nervousness was the nervousness of an imminent parting, and we held hands and bumped against each other often, we walked so close. Kids mad with spring were out on the sunny quads, reading and throwing Frisbees and ashing their cigarettes in the tulip beds. You can practically smell the hormones in the air at college campuses in the months of April and May, and the electricity of spring fever was contagious and irresistible, even though Declan and I must have looked ancient, midlife-crisis-aged, to the undergrads lying on the grass. We squeezed each other's shoulders and arms and all available parts, as we paused in front of the historic markers on the buildings and listened to the reggae blaring out of the dorm windows. Public displays of affection are not much the style in frenetic New York, but in the lazy, sloppy mode of the tank-top-clad kids all around us, I yearned to tackle Declan to the lawn and wrestle him out of his suit, which he had sweetly put on for the engagement party, wrinkled tie and all.

"That's how I imagine you and your friends looking, back in the day," he said, nodding towards a group of students sitting on the library steps.

"Not quite. We never wore hemp or Birkenstocks."

"Berets and Chinese slippers, then."

"And black wool turtlenecks. Even on the hottest days."

He stopped walking and looked at me. We were under a stone arch, in the shade. "Do you know, Rosalie, I sometimes feel as if you and the others have known each other for such a long time that I'm only a temporary interloper, and that's as much as I'll ever amount to? I often think of all the school years you shared, the brick buildings at Harvard and the perfect lawns and the gorgeous-looking young people lying on them, and it makes me jealous, isn't that awful? Jealous that you had this without me. Jealous that you even got to have it at all. I had the most piss-poor excuse for an education, which you already know so there's no use in me going on about it."

"You can go on about it if you want to."

"It just seems hard to me. I'd like to have shared everything with you, I'd like to have been a part of all this brilliant life, and obviously I wasn't. It couldn't be more obvious if I was walking around here in my city bus uniform right now."

"You're walking around here in a suit and any one of these kids who reads the *New York Times* has heard of you. It's not as black and white as you make it seem."

"Forget the suit, forget that part of it. What I'm saying is that I wish I had known you during your school years. I'm hungry to be a part of your life, part of your past the way the rest of them are, Cam and Evan and them, and I don't want you to go away from me now."

This is what I mean about the painful strangeness of falling in love. Stand beside your lover on the most beautiful spring day of the year, clean and well fed and dressed in brand-new clothes, and you will likely feel too wracked and nervous to enjoy any ounce of it. "I don't want to go away from you, either. Come to Virginia with me. You can write there, and live in my bed, and I'll bring you meals from the cafeteria in Ziploc baggies and sneak you into the shower under my towel. I don't want to leave now, not without you."

"When is it that I'm coming to see you, then? June fifteenth? That's only two weeks Friday, isn't it." This is how it is with Declan: the clouds blow in, the rain pounds down for a minute or two, the clouds blow out. "This is grand summer work. I'm proud of you for getting it. You're going to be lovely down there."

"It seems like such dumb timing. I want to go, I just wish it didn't have to be now."

We didn't talk anymore about our separate pasts that afternoon, since there's nothing to be done about them. It's funny—I think of myself as a young person, as being barely old enough to claim a proper past. What happened last year or three or five years ago seems too recent to belong to anything so grandiose as that. I like to imagine that maybe Declan and I walked by each other in Dublin once, maybe even in Dame Street; maybe we sat in the same tea shop or bought newspapers one morning at the same store. Maybe there's a speck of shared past out there waiting to be discovered, and we just haven't found it yet.

The front of the Lerners' house on Benefit Street was awash in so many white balloons that it looked like it might lift off. Mrs. Lerner let us in and gave us all hugs, even Cheri and Declan, whom she'd never met before. "It was so lovely of you to come up to Providence on your day off, look how beautiful you all are, such grown-ups. You seem to have become taller, somehow," she said, jingling the ice cubes in her highball glass. "The guests of honor are outside in the back, arguing over how to arrange the food trays." Tan men in navy blazers and coiffed women in floral dresses were crowded all over the house, looking very cocktail-hour at the country club. In the backyard, where the Classical High School jazz band was playing "Night in Tunisia," Grace stood talking to a cousin I recognized, looking radiant in a yellow dress. Pregnancy hormones should be bottled and added to all facial cleansers and shampoos. Jake came over to greet us, carrying a plate of chicken kabobs.

"Are you working this event?" Evan asked.

"Passing a tray of finger foods turns out to be the fastest escape route from gin-soaked future in-laws. I recommend arming yourselves immediately."

"Shall we skip the finger foods and go straight for the gin?" Declan asked, counting heads. "I'll go fetch us some."

Cheri giggled, which is one of two sounds I've heard her make since she started turning up on Cam's arm after opening night. Her other trick is a sort of guttural purr that makes her sound like she's got hot peppercorns caught in the back of her throat. I kind of like her. Her legs come up to my shoulder blades, and she doesn't talk. It's nice for Cam to get to be with someone like that.

"I can't believe you're getting married, you idiot," Bella said. "You realize that after parenthood, the only major events left to look forward to will be divorce and death. I bought you that juicer on your registry but I wasn't about to carry it up on the train, so it'll be waiting for you when you get home."

"You'll be the first person we make juice for, Bella. That was very sweet of you."

"Don't mention it. I'm full of admiration for you health nuts, anyone who can drink a glass of parsley deserves to live forever."

When Declan came back with a tray of cocktails and a ginger ale, I took the can and the glass of ice and brought it over to Grace.

"You saved me," she said, once her cousin moved off. "There are more members of my family here than I even knew I had."

"Are you really not allowed to have a single drop of alcohol until the baby's born? Because I'd be happy to pour one-third of this gin and tonic into your glass while no one's looking."

"One-tenth. Hurry up before somebody comes over here to give me another set of nonstick tongs."

Grace and I were on decent terms these days; we could joke about Jake's crazy mother and the various physical indignities of pregnancy, which apparently wreak havoc on the whole female plumbing system, you have to wonder why more people don't adopt. Mostly we stuck to safe, generic topics, because when it came right down to it she hadn't really forgiven me for my affair with Berglan Starker, as we both knew. She pretended she had, pretended that what was over for me was over for her, but she behaved in my presence rather like Mary Magdalene behaved around Martha, scooping up my empty soda cans when I came over before giving me a decent chance to clean up after myself, asking politely about the most banal topics in my life and then apologizing for prying, remarking admiringly on the sleeveless shirts and dresses of my spring wardrobe while she went around wearing straw-colored linen tents. I would like to believe, am hopeful, that part of our troubles have to do with bad timing, and are therefore only temporary: my affair with Bella's father came to light just at the moment when Grace's own sexual attractiveness and availability withdrew into shadow, and maybe the wrongness of what I'd done with Mr. Starker was compounded in her mind by resentment, since she could no longer even entertain such fantasies, was too busy reading Dr. Spock and researching breast pumps in *Consumer Reports*. There is an unforgiving martyrdom to Grace, just as there is a willful selfishness to me; maybe this is why we have been best friends all these years, so that I can feel dangerous and complicated and she can look on with self-righteous piety. My attempts to broach this subject hadn't gotten very far, which was why we were often left talking about nonstick tongs and other stuff so non-controversial as to be meaningless. But now that I was leaving town for the summer it seemed dumb to keep on mincing words; I would almost rather have no friend than a friend who harbors resentments but won't speak them out loud. So after we stood around sipping on our gin and tonics for a minute and staring at our friends across the yard, I marshaled up my courage and asked what I'd been wondering for a while.

"Do you ever think that by being such good friends, you and I have locked each other into certain roles?"

Grace didn't miss a beat; that's how well she knows me, she can sense when I start to dig around before I've even lifted the proverbial spade. "Only to the extent that all friendships do, I wouldn't say any more. I think it's mostly romantic relationships that are really in danger of doing that, trapping people into habits and cycles that become hard to break. Did you feel that way, before? Or do you feel that way with Declan, now?"

This was her standard move, pretending she wanted to know something about BS and me, then taking it back. She did a lot of edging up to the subject, but she never had mentioned it directly after that first night. "I don't know what you mean by 'before.'"

"I meant to ask about Declan, that's who I'm really thinking about. He looks great in that suit, by the way, he cleans up nicely."

"He and I have only been seeing each other for two months. We don't have habits or cycles yet."

"Wow, was it really only two months ago that Fiona left town? Well you guys will if you stay together, it's inevitable. Jake and I do. But you know, those roles arise for a reason, and the flip side is being so familiar and comfortable with each other that you know what to expect. I guess that probably sounds dull and middle-aged of me. The early stages of a relationship are much more exciting, but I've never had the nerve for it, like you do."

"Right. Me and my famous nerve." I meant this to sound facetious, but she just looked at me beatifically, the sacred vessel at peace. Something will have to change between the two of us, now that Baby is on the way. People say that a baby's arrival divides all of life into Before and After, and I am hoping that against the grand and awesome backdrop of parenthood, my affair with Berglan Starker will fade into the annals of foolish entanglements we got mixed up in when we were young. I am hoping to be forgiven, for having done it and for having kept it a secret, and for going on to be an actress and for doing all the things Grace will never get to do. But really, this is such an odd consequence for my transgression to have brought about. All that worrying about Bella, all those nightmares that she'd impale my head on a stake and mount it on the gates of Gramercy Park, and now Grace is the one who can't let the whole thing go. Fallout comes from wherever you least expect it, I guess.

"Do you realize that by the time you get back from Virginia, I'm going to be eight months pregnant? Have you ever even seen anyone that pregnant before? They show you pictures at the doctor. It's like a horror movie." This as a signal that serious conversation was closed, although I suppose pregnancy is serious, too, in a nothing-to-be-done-but-might-as-well-gripe-about-it-anyway fashion.

"You guys have to get better air-conditioning. It's going to be hot in July and August."

"It's already hot. I have to take a cold shower before bed every night. I've considered carrying a paper fan in my handbag and I'm only five months in. It's scary. What am I even doing with a handbag in the first place? When did I get so old?"

"A handbag doesn't make you old," I said, swallowing the last of my drink, thinking that she had a point, in a way, those teeny mini-purses so in vogue for summer really aren't designed for women our age, even the shoulder straps are too short to be comfortable.

"I haven't said hello to everybody yet," Grace said, walking over to the patch of lawn where our friends were sitting, Cheri on Cam's lap, Evan on a folding chair, Jake and Declan on wooden benches.

"Cheers, let's hear it for the woman of the hour," Evan said, and everybody whistled and raised their glasses. "I brought cigars for the gentlemen, we can have them now."

"Cigars are for people who wear suspenders and drink port," I said. "You shouldn't smoke them unless you aspire to hedge fund management."

Evan passed cigars to Declan, Cam, and Jake. They took turns with the trimmer and the lighter.

"Where's Bella?" Grace asked. "Did she jump the fence?"

"She's in the house talking to some friend of your dad's whose first name is Captain," Jake said. "They have an Adirondack connection. They were looking pretty cozy on the couch when I went inside a minute ago."

Grace raised her eyebrows but let it go. I sat down next to Declan on his little bench and put my arm around his neck, which was sticky and, unlike his face, closely shaved from the haircut he'd gotten the day before.

"Do you want to try a puff of this?" he asked, holding his cigar out to me.

"No, thank you. I just started a long-term regimen to increase my chances of living forever. But it smells pretty good on your suit."

The band came back from their break carrying Cokes and ice-cream sandwiches. They opened their next set with "My Funny Valentine," my all-time favorite standard, a song that captures the inscrutability of romantic attraction. I like the Chet Baker recording of it best. He sounds so forgiving and amorous, there's no sneer to his version at all, which is just right, in my opinion. Singers can sneer about a whole lot of things, but nobody likes a sneering love song.

Engagement parties are warm-up acts, practice runs for the real event. And in a sense, the goodbyes I would be saying to my friends tonight were much the same thing. First Born was shelved for the time being, parenthood and Broadway had seen to that. I was terrified by this development, terrified by what it meant for all of our friendships and the parts we would continue to play in each other's lives. But I had also gotten myself to Virginia, and there would be good things about spending the summer there, for sure. Proximity to water. New actor friends. A serious role to work on and perform at least four times, maybe more, if the real princess came down with, say, poison oak.

Some guests on the lawn started to dance, family friends and the Lerners Senior and even the few little kids whose party clothes were stained with dirt and cake frosting. The late afternoon breeze was warm and it carried on it the scent of freshly mown grass, a smell I miss in New York as much as I miss the sight of stars in the night sky. I come from a town of freshly mown lawns and starry night skies, and a lifetime in New York, if that's really where I'm going to spend mine, won't ever make me stop yearning for such elemental things.

. . .

In the shower, back at the inn, Declan asked me about my parents, who were coming to Providence for breakfast the next morning before we all went our separate ways in the afternoon.

"I'm not going to open my mouth, you realize that. There weren't any such things as dentists where I grew up."

"You're going to have to open your mouth because they're going to ask you at least one hundred and thirty-six questions about Ireland. They're obsessed with trying to figure out why I had such a bad time there, and they're going to try to change my mind over breakfast by getting you to say lots of nice genial things about the place. They feel guilty about my not liking it. As if my going had been their idea."

"I'll submit my answers on a notepad. Between the three of us we'll bring you 'round."

"Never. I'm intransigent on this point and you may as well know it. I'm very protective of my miserable year in Dublin. It was character-building."

"I do know it. You've made it perfectly clear every time we've been in the same room together. Now stand over here and let me soap your back. Sweet Jesus, you have the loveliest back in all the world. How will you ever get it soaped properly without me?"

"I won't, I won't." We hugged until the water in my nose and ears made me pull away from him. "I know I'm being a horrible ungrateful baby, but I don't want to go away. Or I wish they would let me bring you, and I wish you were free to come."

"I'm going to be waiting for you when you get back, so if that's any part of what you're worried about, you can leave off with it.

This is only an adventure. Nothing's going to disappear while you're gone."

Nervousness works on me like a drug, it has all my life, so I sat up in bed reading *Love's Labour's Lost* after Declan fell asleep. What a weird title for a play, when you think about it, especially a play that ends happily. And how annoying that I was going to have to wear tights and a tunic, maybe even a spirit-gum beard. Such are the occupational hazards of my chosen career. After three acts I tiptoed out of bed and went over to the desk by the window, where I opened the packet of materials that the stage manager had sent me and reread all the chamber of commerce brochures about the region, including *Colonial Williamsburg Beckons* and *Richmond: Would-Be Capital of the Glorious South*. Maybe Declan and I could visit one or two of those places when he came down to see me. Or maybe I would even take a field trip by myself, on my first day off. Think of all the brave people, thousands of them throughout history, who set sail for Virginia without knowing what to expect. The promise of freedom and independence was enough to make them turn their backs on home and embrace what amounted to an uncharted wilderness. If they could do it, and on those fragile storm-tossed ships, I could do it, too.

Acknowledgments

For indispensable advice and support, I would like to thank the following people: my editor, Carol Houck Smith; my agent, Timothy Seldes; Richard and Kristina Ford; Larry Kirshbaum; Joseph Regal; my teachers Charles Baxter and Eileen Pollack; and my MFA classmates at the University of Michigan. I am especially grateful to my sister, Andrea, the rest of my family, and most of all, to Scott Matthew Hutchins.